THE FINAL RECKONING

BOOK THREE OF
THE DEPTFORD MICE TRILOGY

ROBIN JARVIS

A PETER GLASSMAN BOOK
SeaStar Books
New York

THANKS TO SUE HOOK FOR

HAVING FAITH IN THE DEPTFORD MICE

AND TO DAVID RILEY FOR HIS UNFLAGGING

ENTHUSIASM THROUGHOUT.

Text and illustrations © 1990, 2002 by Robin Jarvis
Afterword © 2000 by Peter Glassman
Jacket illustration © 2002 by Leonid Gore

First published in Great Britain in 1990. Reprinted under license
from Hodder Children's Books, a division of Hodder Headline Limited.

SEASTAR BOOKS
A division of NORTH-SOUTH BOOKS INC.

First published in the United States in 2002 by SeaStar Books, a division
of North-South Books Inc., New York. Published simultaneously in Canada by
North-South Books, an imprint of Nord-Süd Verlag AG, Gossau Zürich, Switzerland.

Library of Congress Cataloging-in-Publication Data is available.

The text for this book is set in 11-point Walbaum Book.

ISBN 1-58717-192-9 (reinforced trade edition)
1 3 5 7 9 RTE 10 8 6 4 2

Printed in U.S.A.

For more information about our books, and the authors and artists who create them,
visit our web site: www.northsouth.com

CONTENTS

THE MICE

Arthur Brown
Enjoys his food and tries to look on the bright side of things.

Gwen Brown
Widowed mother of Arthur and Audrey, she is also very fond of
Thomas Triton.

Arabel Chitter
Silly old gossip who gets on the nerves of everyone in the Skirtings.

Oswald Chitter
Arabel's son is an albino runt. Recently cured of a terrible illness by the
power of the Starwife, he is made to wrap up well at all times.

The Holeborners
They live in the city and are governed by the Thane, a kindly wise mouse.
Under him are the ministers, who advise on all matters of everyday life.

Kempe
A traveling peddler who enjoys lewd songs. He helped Audrey and Arthur
when they journeyed to Fennywolde.

Marty
A young foraging cadet of the city, he wants to be as brave as his
hero, Piccadilly.

Piccadilly
A cheeky young mouse from the city,
Piccadilly has no parents and is very independent.

Audrey Scuttle
Now the wife of Twit, the fieldmouse, she still thinks of Piccadilly
and regrets her treatment of him.

Thomas Triton
A retired midshipmouse who lives on the *Cutty Sark*, he is always
ready to confront his enemies, sword in paw.

THE OTHER CHARACTERS

Barker
A crazy old rat whom Piccadilly befriends. There is more to
Barker than meets the eye.

The Bat Elders
These are four wise old bats: Ashmere, wisest of councillors; Ingeld,
Consort of the Lady; Heardred, Keeper of the Hidden Ways; and
Ohthere, Lord of Twilight.

The Green Mouse
The mystical spirit of spring and new life whose power wanes
in the autumn and dies when winter sets in.

Jupiter
The evil spirit of the hideous sewer cat has returned. He
has cheated death and now wants revenge.

Kelly
A fat rat with sharp fangs, he only opens his mouth when there
is something to put in it.

Old Stumpy
A newcomer to the underground regions of the city. No one knows
where he has come from, but he is stirring the harmless rats to war.

Orfeo and Eldritch
Bat brothers who can see into the future, they live in the attic
and give confusing advice to the curious.

Smiff
A snotty-nosed follower of Old Stumpy and a nasty bully, only
he and his mate Kelly know where Old Stumpy has come from.

The Starwife
An ancient old squirrel who lives under the Greenwich
observatory, she possesses the magical Starglass.

THE STORY SO FAR

The Final Reckoning *is the third book in the story of the Deptford Mice. The first book,* The Dark Portal, *tells how Audrey and Arthur Brown venture into the sewers looking for Audrey's mousebrass, a magical charm given to her by the mystical Green Mouse. In the dark tunnels they meet Madame Akkikuyu, a fortune-telling rat, and are later pursued by a terrifying rat army commanded by Morgan, the lieutenant of the mighty, yet unseen, Jupiter. With the aid of their friends Oswald, Twit, Piccadilly, and Thomas Triton, Audrey and Arthur are able to foil Jupiter's evil plans to swamp London with the Black Death. The Rat God emerges from his lair and to everyone's horror is revealed as a monstrous cat. Audrey flings her mousebrass into his face and it explodes, sending him plunging to his death in the deep sewer.*

In The Crystal Prison, *the Starwife, an ancient and wise squirrel, forces Audrey to take the now mad Madame Akkikuyu to the country. With her brother and Twit they journey to Fennywolde–the fieldmouse's home. But soon several young fieldmice are found murdered, and Madame Akkikuyu is tormented by a voice that only she can hear. The country folk at first blame Audrey, and she is about to be burned as a witch when Twit saves the girl by marrying her. Horrified, Madame Akkikuyu learns that the voice belongs to the unquiet spirit of Jupiter, and she is made to perform a ceremony that will free him from the other side. In a bid to prevent his return she throws herself onto a fire, which engulfs the whole of Fennywolde. The mice escape to safety, and Audrey and Arthur return to Deptford unaware that the vengeful spirit of Jupiter is free and more powerful than ever.*

THE PEDDLER

The hedgerows were spotted with berries red as blood, and black, ragged-winged crows flapped over the empty fields shrieking in ugly voices.

Autumn's full glory was nearly spent: the bright copper of the beeches was now a dull brown and the number of muddy pools grew daily.

A breeze suddenly stirred some of the dry leaves and for a moment they danced on the air like living things. A hedgehog poked his snout out from under one of the russet mounds and sniffed the air cautiously. His small, beadlike eyes peered out at the world and blinked wearily. The wet nose snuffled around inquisitively: something was approaching. The air was different and now the breeze brought a strange jangling sound. The hedgehog began to shuffle backward uncertainly, but kept his eyes fixed on the bank path. The noise grew nearer, and with it came a voice raised in song.

"When leaves do fall and the sun goes shy
I reach for my bowl and the hours roll by
For the juice of the berry do make me so merry
With my legs in the air, my head 'neath a chair,
I'll burp till the spring comes 'round again"

The hedgehog stayed to hear the chorus, which was made up of various tuneful belches, before turning away in feigned disgust. These traders really were a disgrace! He waddled off to find some slugs to eat.

Kempe sauntered happily along. He was in high spirits. It had been a good week for business and his packs bulged as never before. He was looking forward to the Traders' Fair in a fortnight's time. All the traveling mice would be there to exchange news, sell their wares, look for bargains, and meet old friends and rivals. It was the only time in the year when everyone could meet up and see how the others were doing. Kempe loved it all and there was a jaunty bounce in his step and an excited twitch in his tail to prove it.

He ran through in his mind all the things he would have to do: of course he would have to stock up on certain goods, it was nearly his busiest period—Yule was fast approaching. Kempe chuckled to himself and made a mental note to find larger packs to hold his wares.

Kempe thought of the feasting that took place during the midwinter festival and thought about where he was going to spend it himself. There had been numerous invitations made and he had nodded to those kind mice who had offered, but privately he knew all along where he would be at Yule: at Milly Poopwick's place. She was a hearty, round mouse. Widowed three times, she was now on the lookout for husband number four, and there was always a grand welcome for Kempe there. He grinned to himself as he thought of her. Life with Milly would not be so bad after all; things were never dull while she was around. The traveler pulled himself up sharply and tutted. The idea of settling down had never occurred to him before and a startled look crossed his face. He was a traveler through and through, and hated staying in one place for too long.

"Reckon you're gettin' old, Kempe me boy," he told himself. "Try a day or two at me darlin' Milly's and see how it goes; after that there's other deals to be struck. Once Yule's over, folks' thoughts'll turn to spring and the makin' of mousebrasses."

He sighed contentedly. It looked as though he would be kept very busy indeed, and the lovely Mrs. Poopwick would just have to wait if she wanted to catch him. Kempe kicked away the leaves that had drifted over the path and chortled to himself.

The pale sun hung low in the colorless autumn sky and sparkled over the surface of the rippling river. Kempe looked at the lengthening shadows of the trees and decided it was time to bed down for the night. Not far off, he knew the perfect place.

It was an old stone wall close to the riverbank. It was very thick, and parts of it were hollow, making wonderful shelters inside. Kempe swaggered up to the wall and found the opening he usually used. It was near the ground and partially hidden by moss. The traveler cleared the moss away from the entrance and tried to enter.

A look of surprise registered on his furry face as his pack became thoroughly wedged in the gap; he had forgotten that it was fuller than normal. With a groan and a curse he tried to heave it in.

"Drat and blast! Bother and blow!" he ranted and puffed as he strained at the bag straps.

All his pots, buckles, pans, spoons, and beads clattered and rattled. The opening was just too narrow for the fat, bulging bag. And as he was strapped to it he could not turn around or do anything useful to relieve the situation. He squirmed and struggled and cursed out loud.

"Plague take it!" he snarled. The pack was wedged firmly and refused to budge. The traveler went red to the ears and looked ready to burst. "'Tis a cruel joke to play on an honest trader!" he fumed to himself. Then with one final effort he pulled and heaved. Dust fell from the stones all around and the inevitable happened: there was an ominous tearing sound and the pack split open.

"Bless me!" wailed Kempe as he fell headlong into the hollow wall. His wares flew everywhere, jangling raucously as he crashed to the floor. The contents of his pack spilled out and buried the alarmed mouse.

Kempe groaned and raised his head. A pink ribbon hung over one eye and he blew it away impatiently. When he saw the mess all around he gave a weary sigh. There was more clanging as he fumbled with the straps and buckles that bound him to the forlorn-looking pack, which hung empty from his shoulders.

"To be sure, Kempe laddy," he muttered to himself sadly, "there's a tidy bit of work for you to do here before you sleep tonight." He began to gather up all the ribbons, silks, beads, trinkets, and tassels that lay scattered in the dust.

Inside the wall it was dry and safe from the wind, but it was also dark. Kempe delved into a smaller bag and fished out a candle stub. He lit it and gazed about for any treasure he might have missed. There, in the corner, something glinted and threw back the flickering light.

"Hello," Kempe said thoughtfully. "And what may you be then?" He stopped and picked up the object with nimble fingers. Before him was a small, delicate silver bell, which tinkled sweetly as it rolled into his palm. He held the candle closer and examined the bell with interest, talking to it as though it were a lost child.

"Not one of my little darlings are you?" he addressed the tiny thing. Kempe narrowed his shrewd, gleaming eyes. "But I get the feeling as how we've met before, little one." He shook the bell and listened to it in satisfaction. There was no doubt. It had once belonged to the young mouse from Deptford he had met not so long ago. It was one of two bells she had worn on her tail. Kempe wondered about that mouse and her friends. They had been going to a place called Fennywolde when he had known

4

them—they must have returned to Deptford and mislaid the bell on the journey.

"I shall be passing by Deptford soon," Kempe told the bell. "That Oldnose will want stocking up on stuff, I expect. I'll drop you off with your mistress. Stick with Kempe—he'll see you safe home."

The traveler shivered. It had grown very cold all of a sudden. A deadly silence descended on the world outside. He could no longer hear the sounds of birds or the wind high in the trees.

"Storm must be comin'," he said, and stepped through the opening once more to take a look at the weather. Everything seemed normal enough. There were no heavy clouds in the sky, yet there was a strange, charged feeling in the air, as if the world was holding its breath, waiting for something to happen. Kempe hummed a tune to himself as he walked down to the river's edge.

"Don't pick your nose laddy or wipe it on your paw
I'm not being faddy, 'twill make your nostrils raw."

It was terribly cold outside, and an icy blast seemed to be blowing down the river. Kempe shrugged at the unpredictability of the weather and made to return to the relative comfort of the wall, where he could warm his paws over the candle.

His movement caused the silver bell to jingle in his fist, and as if that were a signal, the storm broke.

A vicious, icy wind bore down on him, and a strange, thick fog rose up out of the river. Before Kempe had reached the wall the fog had rolled up the bank and surged around him. The traveler was uneasy—this was no ordinary mist. The fur on the back of his neck tingled as an awful sense of horror and fear swept over him.

The fog was impenetrable and it now completely surrounded him. It bit into his flesh with cold, clammy fingers. He stamped his feet desperately as he groped for the safety of the wall opening, but it was no use.

A deep, rumbling purr began, menacingly soft at first, then slowly growing deeper and more fearsome. Kempe's legs trembled and he could feel his heart beating wildly in his chest. There was a monster hiding in that mist—some mind-numbing terror from the deep, cold regions had come to claim him. Scarcely conscious of his own actions, only of the overwhelming horror, Kempe waved his arms about in despair as he felt the monster's freezing breath fall on him. In his paw the little bell tinkled, an incongruously delicate and beautiful sound.

There came a savage roar and Kempe cried out as the bell was torn from his clenched fist by an invisible power, and he wept with fright to see it float up into the fog, where an immense, dark shadow was gathering.

"No!" screamed the traveler, stumbling backward. "Leave me, please . . . I have done no harm . . . I . . ."

From the evil shape that was mounting before him there came a sneering, mocking laugh. It ended in a cruel snarl, and Kempe gasped when he saw what form the shape began to take.

Then high in the smothering fog a bitter blue light flashed, and a great spear of ice hurtled downward. That was the last thing Kempe ever saw, for he felt a sharp pain in his chest before he fell to his knees and collapsed lifeless on the ground. The terrible ice spear had pierced his body and the blood that trickled out froze quickly. The shadow in the fog purred to itself, and somewhere in that blanketing grayness a small, sweet bell tinkled softly.

YULE

The old, empty house in Deptford looked blankly out at the wet, wintry world. The neglected building was the home of many mice, but only at special times of the year would they all come together to celebrate the various mouse festivals. There was the Great Spring Ceremony, where mousebrasses were given out to those young mice who had come of age, there was Midsummer's Eve–a particularly magical time–and finally there was the Festival of Yule.

Yule occurs in the midst of winter, when cold storms batter and rage outside. It is a time of hardship for most creatures and all the more frightening because food is scarce. This is the time when the midwinter death kills the old and the very young. For many long years mice have gathered together during Yule and lit fires to keep the ravening spirits of cold and ice away.

They feel themselves to be particularly vulnerable during this season because the Green Mouse, their protector and symbol of life, is dead. Every autumn, when the harvest has been taken in and the last fruit falls from the trees, the great Green

Mouse dwindles and dies. Throughout the long, dark winter months his spirit is neither felt nor seen as death binds him close, and only when the first sign of spring appears is he reborn once more. It is through these bleak, dangerous months that mice have to survive, and those who dwell out of doors dread it.

In the Skirtings, however, Yule was much looked forward to. The mice had a plentiful supply of food from the larder of the blind old lady who lived next door, and so the threat of winter was never felt as harshly by them. They would light fires to roast their store of chestnuts and mull their berrybrews. For them all the seriousness and the danger of the season had been forgotten, and Yule had become a time of feasting and telling ghost stories.

This year the Hall had been decked out with sprigs of evergreen and bright streamers, which some of the children had made. They took a long time preparing the food, and many an impatient husband received a sharp smack from an anxious wife as he tasted the mixtures when he thought she wasn't looking. Those children not involved in making streamers mooned about, sniffing the different smells that wafted through the house. There was Mrs. Coltfoot's tangerine jelly and Mrs. Chitter's spiced fruit buns, Miss Poot's almond tart and Mr. Cockle's own berrybrew. All these wonderful smells to savor! The children smacked their lips and longed for the days to pass quickly.

A large roof slate specially kept for the occasion had been hauled out of the cupboard where the Chambers of Spring and Summer had also been stored. This they put down in the center of the Hall and built a fire over it. That night all the mice from both the Skirtings and the Landings were gathered around the crackling flames, warming their paws and listening to tales. Some were cleaning their whiskers, wondering if they ought to make another attack on the feast nearby, while others were dozing contentedly, musing on things past and long ago. Most of them, however, wanted to hear ghost stories, and the younger ones turned to the stout, retired midshipmouse Thomas Triton to entertain them.

"Take the hat, Mr. Triton, please!" they begged. "Tell us a scary moment from your days at sea. Give him the hat, someone."

The hat in question was an old, battered thing of burgundy velvet stitched around with gold thread and beads of red glass. It had somehow become the traditional hat of the storyteller in the house, and only he who wore it could command everyone's attention. Thomas Triton stepped reluctantly into the circle of yellow firelight and placed the hat on his head. He knelt down and began his tale. All eyes turned to him and they were reminded of the fact that outside all was dark by the story he told them.

"'Twere a night such as this," he said in a deep, resonant tone, "not long before I went off to sea. I was staying in an old farmhouse. There weren't no moon and it was bitter cold. I was much younger then—and rash—an' all evenin' I'd been listenin' to stories like you are now. I was fair put out that I had no tale of me own to tell, so I persuaded the best friend I ever had to come with me an' visit the haunted barn."

An appreciative murmur ran through his hushed audience.

"Well, the loft of that there barn had a sinister reputation among us mice—nobody ever went there if they could help it. 'Twas said that the frightful ghost of a murdered mouse haunted the place, and we were all mighty skeered of it." Thomas paused and gazed solemnly around at the young faces gaping up at him, their whiskers gleaming in the firelight.

"So," he resumed, "me an' my friend, we leaves the safety of the farmhouse an' makes our way to the barn. Our hearts were beatin' fast an' we held tight to each other's paws. We was both shiverin' with fright, but on we went. Now, as I said before,

9

'twere a dark night, but the shape of that barn reared up in front of us blacker than the night itself. 'Twas an ominous place, and one of the bravest things we did was walk across that lonely yard to that big, black shape. Anyway, when we gets there I goes in first. That barn hadn't been used in years an' it smelled all damp and musty. I wondered if rats lived there, but my friend had a sniff around and said there weren't none. Ah, he could smell an east wind comin' he could—what a good nose he had! Well we look up to the hayloft where we mean to go. All is quiet an' the only thing we can hear is ourselves breathing. I makes my way to the loft ladder and begins to climb.

"'Don't go, Tom!' hisses my friend suddenly, 'Let's go back!'

"'No way,' I answered. 'Come on Woodget, lad! Don't stand there frettin'! Ain't no such thing as ghosties.'

"I climbed up to the loft and looked about me. The wind was gettin' in somewhere an' rustlin' the old rotten heaps of hay. It was black as tar up there, an' I was glad when Woodget put his paw in mine. 'Come on,' I said, 'let's scout around a bit.' Through the smelly old straw we went, a-fearin' what was around the next corner or what might pop out at us. But apart from the rustlin', all you could hear were two mice breathin'— him an' me. We walked all around that loft, an' not one ghost did we see. I didn't know if I was relieved or disappointed, so we returned to the loft entrance an' I let go of Woodget's paw to climb down the ladder.

"'What a waste of time,' I said, exasperated. 'I told you there were no such thing as ghosties, Woodget!'"

Here Thomas stopped his tale and his eyes bulged as he raised his eyebrows. "Then," he continued in a wavering voice, "to my horror I hear my little friend a callin' up to me from the barn floor, shoutin', 'You comin' down now Tom? I'm gettin' scared down here on my own.' My fur stood on end and for a moment I was frozen to the spot. I dare not look to right or left, and the silence—you could have cut it with a knife. I don't know

how long I was frozen there, maybe only a second, but it felt like a lifetime. Then Woodget twitched his tail and rustled the straw below, breaking the ghostly spell."

The audience gasped and cooed, "But whose paw were you holding, Mr. Triton?" piped up one of the youngsters.

"That I don't know lad," Thomas replied, "an' I didn't stay to find out. Woodget an' me were out of that barn faster than anything."

A shiver of excitement rippled through the assembled mice. They liked Thomas's stories–he had been to so many places, and they loved to hear of his adventures.

"Tell us another," they pleaded.

The midshipmouse laughed but shook his head. "No," he refused gently, "I've worn the hat too long and you know your rules. One yarn per wear–let someone else have a turn." He removed the faded velvet hat from his head and passed it on to Master Oldnose, who had been waiting close by for some time. He used to be the main storyteller, and he spent many evenings making up new stories especially for the Yule Festival. He did not like Thomas's popularity, and he took the hat from him stiffly. Several young mice groaned rudely and wandered away from the fire as Master Oldnose began "The Story of Bohart and the Friendly Moon Spirits."

Thomas stretched himself and left the circle, winking at his admirers. A young albino mouse came running up to him excitedly.

"Oh Mr. Triton," he said, twisting the ends of a green scarf together in his paws with enthusiasm, "that was smashing! How on earth did you manage to sleep after that?"

"None too well, young Oswald," the midshipmouse replied with an amused twinkle.

The albino blinked his bright pink eyes and nodded. "It was the best ghost story we've had here for years, and it was true as well–it actually happened to you–gosh!"

"That's right lad, but don't you start goin' off again on dangerous journeys like the last one. You know how terrible they can be and what they can lead to."

Oswald nodded. Earlier in the year he had ventured down into the sewers. He returned suffering from such a dreadful cold that nobody thought he would survive. Now he hugged himself and sucked his teeth. "What happened to your friend Woodget, Mr. Triton?" he asked. "Did he go to sea with you, or did he stay at the farmhouse?"

The change in Thomas's mood was startling. His expression altered dramatically and pain registered in his face. "By Neptune I wish he had stayed there," he said thickly before excusing himself and walking briskly away.

"Oh dear," stammered Oswald, staring after the midshipmouse. "I do hope I didn't say anything wrong."

A plump mouse stole silently up behind the albino with a huge grin on his face. "BOO!" he yelled suddenly.

Poor Oswald jumped in the air and wailed. When he saw who it was he said crossly, "Oh Arthur, you frightened the life out of me—especially after all those ghost stories." Arthur began nibbling a chestnut that he had been carrying and beamed wickedly. "Yeth," he mumbled with his mouth full, "old Triton's tales are good, aren't they? He comes to visit us quite often and we nearly always get a story from him."

"You are lucky." Oswald sighed enviously. "You get to go to cousin Twit's home and have adventures there. And to top it all, Mr. Triton comes and visits you."

Arthur licked his lips thoughtfully. He did not like to say that in his opinion the midshipmouse's visits were not just for him and his sister. He had come to the conclusion that it was really their mother whom Thomas came to see.

Arthur and his sister Audrey had been back in the Skirtings for two months now, after their adventures in the country. On their return home Arthur and Audrey found that Thomas had been looking after their mother while they had been away and had taken to calling her Gwen—an unsettling thing for them to hear. She had been obviously embarrassed when he said it in front of the children. Gwen Brown still addressed the midshipmouse as Mr. Triton but she said it with a growing warmth that Arthur and Audrey had not heard since their father had died.

"Where is Audrey?" Oswald was staring at everyone gathered around the fire and looking beyond at the groups of husbands sipping the mulled berrybrew. Their jolly wives were fussing and gossiping in a corner and his own mother, Mrs. Chitter, was there, leading the tittle-tattle, but there was no sign of Audrey.

Arthur shrugged. "In her room, I suppose. She said she'd come, but you know what she's like. Since we've been back she's gotten worse—won't join in anything and hardly eats. Mother worries about her."

"Do you think she misses Twit?" ventured Oswald.

Arthur shook his head. "No, I told you it wasn't like that. Twit only married Audrey to save her from getting hanged—there was nothing else in it."

"Oh," murmured Oswald. "You know, I still haven't gotten used to calling her Mrs. Scuttle—it doesn't fit somehow."

Arthur agreed and turned to watch the group around the fire. Master Oldnose had finished his tale—much to the relief of everybody except the Raddle sisters, who clapped very loudly and praised him no end. The hat was held up for the next mouse ready to tell a story and up stepped Algy Coltfoot.

"This should be good," said Arthur. "Algy's stories are always funny." The two friends wandered over and sat down in the dancing firelight.

*   *   *

14

Alone in her room, Audrey fiddled with the ribbon in her paws. She had not yet tied it in her hair and was staring down at it dumbly. After the terrors of Fennywolde she had found life in the Skirtings very dull, and the nosiness of several mice had irritated her no end. They all wanted to know just why Twit had married her. Mrs. Chitter even inquired if she ought to start knitting little bonnets and booties. Audrey made it very clear then that nothing of that kind would be necessary—indeed she had put quite a few noses out of joint, and at the moment she was not the most popular mouse in the house.

The sound of a whisker fiddle filtered into the room and gradually brought Audrey around. She decided it was time to join the festivities, so she tied the ribbon in her hair, slipped her last remaining bell onto her tail, then jumped off the bed.

In the Hall the fire was still crackling merrily, and Audrey emerged to find a crowd of mice still laughing over Algy's story. The hat had been passed on to Arthur, and Algy had wandered into a corner to practice on his fiddle with Mr. Cockle accompanying him on the bark drum. On the far side of the Hall she saw her mother talking to Thomas Triton. Audrey made her way over, passing chattering wives whose gossip suddenly ceased as she drew close enough to hear them. Some of them nudged their friends and whispered to each other once she had gone by, then the chatter began again.

"There you are Audrey." Gwen Brown smiled. "Have you had anything to eat yet?" The girl shook her head and moved close to her mother's side. Gwen put her arms around her daughter. "Audrey love, you haven't eaten properly since you came back from Fennywolde—do have something. There's a big bowl of lovely soup over there."

Audrey took a biscuit and nibbled it as she watched everyone enjoying themselves. Her mind went back to earlier in the year when Oswald was healed by the magic of the Starwife. There had been celebrations then too. At that time the young gray mouse from the city—Piccadilly—had been staying with the Browns; Audrey missed him.

Algy and Mr. Cockle struck up a dancing jig, and as nobody had taken the hat after Arthur, there were many eager to join in. The mice formed a great ring and began to dance around the fire. Thomas dragged Gwen and Audrey into the dance, and soon everyone was out of breath. Nearby, the Raddle sisters watched and tittered behind fluttering paws—it was too cold for them to sit in their usual place on the stairs. Arthur did not like dancing and it looked too boisterous for Oswald, so both of them stood to one side, forming some plan.

"But Arthur," protested Oswald, "Mother's sure to hear if I get up in the middle of the night."

"Not if you're careful," Arthur said, "but if you're too scared . . ."

"Oh, it's not that," Oswald put in hastily. "It's just that I don't see why we have to go there! Why don't we just take some of the food here?"

"Because that would be too easy. Look Oswald, do you want a secret feast tonight or don't you?"

The albino fidgeted with his scarf, then nodded. "So long as you don't jump out at me again."

"Promise. Just meet me in the great kitchen when every-one's asleep."

"Very well," agreed Oswald meekly.

Audrey abandoned the dancing. It was surprising how nimble Thomas Triton was. His white, wispy hair glowed like fine gold before the fire and those same flames picked out the vibrant chestnut glint in the hair of her mother. Audrey was astonished to find herself admiring them as a couple. She wondered if her mother would marry the midshipmouse: both were lonely, and Audrey felt that her late father would approve.

The night continued, the fire burned lower, and some young rascals decided to put whole chestnuts into the heart of the flames. After some minutes there was a series of loud cracks and explosions as the chestnuts flew apart. Mice ran squeaking in all directions amid the confusion, but when they discovered what had happened, the culprits were packed off to bed with smarting bottoms.

The music gradually slowed and the fire became a mound of glowing embers. Mr. Cockle swayed unsteadily on his feet and his wife looked sternly at the empty bowl of berrybrew at his side.

"Get you home, you silly old mouse," she hissed at him. "Every time, you do it, don't you? Oh the shame of it."

"Ah, but you're beautiful darlin'," he slurred while puckering his lips. Biddy Cockle shooed her husband out of the Hall, and the other mice decided to go to bed as well.

"I'll be off to my ship," said Thomas as he took leave of Gwen. He pulled on his blue woolen hat and went down into the cellar, where he passed through the Grill and took the shortcut to Greenwich via the sewers.

Gwen smiled and went into the Skirtings. She popped her head into Audrey's room, but her daughter was already sleeping soundly. Arthur was busy making up his bed in their small kitchen. He used to share the room with Audrey, but now that she was married it did not seem right somehow.

"Good night Arthur," Gwen said affectionately. "Good night Mum," he replied pulling the blankets up under his chin. She extinguished the kitchen candle and went to her own room.

Arthur stayed awake for an hour until he was certain that his mother had fallen asleep, then he got out of bed and tiptoed out of the Skirtings.

The Hall was lit with the ruddy light of the fire's dying embers, and eerie shadows flitted over the walls. Arthur swallowed nervously. Ghost stories were all very well if you went straight to bed afterward. There you could pull the bedclothes over your head if the dark frightened you, but to embark on a midnight quest for food was—well, alarming, especially as his imagination was beginning to make sinister shapes in those shadows. Grim demons seemed to be hiding in the darkness, ready to pounce on him with sharp fangs. Arthur took a deep breath and ventured down the gloomy Hall.

In the kitchen it was very dark. Arthur jumped down the single step and felt the smooth linoleum beneath his feet. A chilly draft ruffled his fur. It came from the passage that led to the outside—it had been unblocked that morning to bring in the evergreen sprigs that decorated the Hall. Obviously someone had forgotten to seal it up again. The draft made him shiver and he began to wonder if a secret feast was really worth all this.

"Psst! Arthur!" A tall shadowy form beckoned to him from the deep darkness ahead. Oswald had been there for ten minutes and he did not like it one bit. "Where've you been?"

"All right, I'm here now, aren't I?" Arthur replied. "You ready then?"

Oswald nodded quickly. "Let's hurry, Arthur. I'm freezing."

Arthur felt his way to the far wall, jumped onto an old wooden box and scrambled up a pipe. "You should have put on those things your mum made for you," he called down to the albino.

"I have," said Oswald awkwardly. Recently Mrs. Chitter had knitted her son a woolen hat and a pair of mittens to match his scarf, but up till now he had been too embarrassed to wear them. "I don't want to catch another cold," he wheezed as he labored clumsily onto the box and heaved himself up the pipe.

Arthur put a finger to his lips. "Ssshh—whispers only, from now on," he warned. "Come on."

Through crumbling plaster and dry, flaking timber they went, then they hopped along the wall cavity.

"Here it is," Arthur said, coming to a break in the brickwork. The two mice squeezed through and, emerging from the wall, they found themselves in a large, echoing space.

"This is the Larder," Arthur whispered, greatly pleased with himself. He rubbed his tummy expectantly. "This is the vegetable shelf. We don't want to bother with anything here. There's another one above with all sorts of gorgeous things on it. We can climb onto it just over here." Arthur moved over to the wall, where a vertical row of half hammered-in nails acted as a ladder.

Oswald looked puzzled and put a mittened paw to his mouth. "But Arthur," he began slowly, "there are no vegetables on this shelf. There's nothing here at all."

A loud disappointed groan came down from above. "Oh Oswald," moaned Arthur glumly, "this shelf's empty too, not a crumb or a blob of cream—not anything."

"Oh dear," sighed Oswald. "No secret feast for us then."

"But it's far more serious than that," said Arthur fearfully. "Don't you see? The Larder has never ever been empty! There was always something here for us—oh Lord, what are we all going to do? We rely on this place for our food! We must go back and tell the others. We shall have to save what's left of the Yule feast and live off that till we find more food."

Oswald began to sniffle. He wept all the way back through the wall cavity and when they were in the kitchen once more he could contain himself no longer and burst into tears. "We'll all die," he sobbed.

"Quiet!" hushed Arthur. "Listen, there's a commotion in the Hall. I wonder what's going on."

He and Oswald ran to the kitchen door, leaped up the step and raced into the Hall. There they stopped and took in the scene before them.

All the mice from the Skirtings were in the Hall and making for the stairs. Some were still half asleep and blinking drowsily, covering long, cavernous yawns with their paws. Others were fussing around looking worried but eager to get to the Landings. The Raddle sisters appeared with their hair done up in curling papers and Master Oldnose was chasing everyone along and trying to keep some sort of order in the proceedings. Some of the mice were saying things like, "Oooh isn't it marvelous, I've never heard of this happening before, have you?" while others grumbled sourly, "'Tis the first sign of doom— mark my words."

At last Arthur caught sight of his sister and pushed through the crowd to talk to her. Audrey turned around when he called her name and a look of relief came over her face. "Where've you been?" she questioned him. "Mother thought you might have been responsible for this."

"What do you mean?" asked Arthur, puzzled. "What's been going on here?"

"It was about half an hour ago," she explained. "There was a terrible noise coming from the attics—I even heard it in my room, it woke me up. Well, all the folk on the Landings rushed about to see what the matter was, and then one of them came down and called us all upstairs to see what was happening. We're just going up now."

"But what *is* happening?" Arthur demanded impatiently.

"Come and see for yourself. We're on our way to look out of one of the upstairs windows."

"But that'll take ages, look how slowly the Raddle sisters are going."

Oswald's voice called out to them suddenly. "Over here," he shouted from the kitchen, "through the passage that leads to the outside."

"Brilliant," answered Arthur. "That'll be much quicker." So he and Audrey ran into the kitchen, and with Oswald they went through the short tunnel that led to the small garden.

It was a bitter, frosty night and there was a halo around the bright, waning moon. The night air was so cold that it bit into the nostrils of the three mice, and Oswald hurriedly buried his nose in his scarf. "There," said Audrey pointing to the sky. They

20

looked up into the black winter sky. Out of the rooftops of every house all around, hundreds of bats were emerging. From the Victorian terraces, out of the tall estate buildings, from the old church at Deptford Green, even from the tower blocks, the winged creatures of the night were flying. They swarmed about the chimney pots and swooped down over fences. They skimmed the tips of trees in Deptford Park, then rose high into the air, where they joined a seething, dark mass already gathered there.

"There must be thousands of them up there!" exclaimed a bewildered Arthur.

"I've never heard of them doing this before," said Oswald wondrously. "I didn't realize there were so many of them around here."

The sky was thick with the movement of the bats, and their high voices filled the night as they called to one another in their secret language, which they taught to no one. For a while they remained above Deptford, waiting until all their brethren had joined them, then all of a sudden they departed. They left in a fast, wailing rush, and down on the ground Audrey felt the draft from their wings brush faintly upon her face.

Then they were gone and the sky was empty once more, save for the moon and the frosty blue stars. Silence fell over Deptford.

Audrey, Arthur, and Oswald craned their necks back to try and look for any stragglers, but there were none. Oswald, who had the keenest eyes in the Skirtings, just managed to spot the vast, dark bulk of the bat hoard as it flew toward the city, and then that too merged into the surrounding night and was lost. Arthur was the first to speak.

"Well," he gasped, "what do you make of that then?"

Neither Audrey nor Oswald could answer him. This had never happened before in their lifetime. They both glanced warily back up to the sky.

"I suppose the bats from our attic, Orfeo and Eldritch, are with that lot," mused Arthur.

"I don't like it," said Oswald. "Bats know things–they see into the future. If they've all left it doesn't look too good, does it?"

"I agree," admitted Audrey. "I wish I knew what was going on. I hope it doesn't mean that something awful is going to happen."

It was only then that Arthur remembered what he had discovered. With a worried face he turned to his sister and said, "Sis, I forgot to tell you. Oswald and I went to the Larder just before, and it's totally empty."

Oswald put his mittens over his cold, tingling ears. "This is the end," he said. "We have no food to survive the midwinter death, and the bats have left us to face something worse. We're all going to die!"

MAD AND BAD

Piccadilly swept the hair out of his eyes and looked across to his friend. "Anything yet, Marty?" he called.

Marty held up a half-eaten piece of nougat with bits of fluff stuck to it.

"Yuck!" Piccadilly grimaced. "Leave that for the slime suckers. We don't have to eat that muck."

The gray mouse had settled down again in the city. He was a useful forager and knew the best places to find "good grub."

The city mice were highly organized. They lived in a rambling system of tunnels that were collectively known as Holeborn. It was an ancient civilization with strict customs and rules to obey.

Those who dwelt in Holeborn were governed by the Great Thane. He was a venerable mouse whose family had ruled for centuries. Beneath him in importance were the ministers—these were mice who excelled at organization, and all had their own different guilds to run. The minister of dwellings super-

vised the digging of new tunnels when the need arose and allot-
ted empty homes to the needy who would join the Holeborners
from time to time. There was the minister of craft, who taught
the children in a large, spacious chamber. There they learned
everything they could in order to survive life in the harsh city.
The minister of supplies was concerned with the gathering of
food and other useful items, all of which were distributed so
that everyone had their fair share—there were no "privileged" in
Holeborn. The quick-witted, nimble mice were allocated to him
to go into the foraging parties.

It was one of the most perfect mouse societies to have existed in the whole country. Everyone enjoyed their work and
nobody thought themselves superior to anyone else—even the
Great Thane was known to all as 'Enry despite his noble line-
age. The Holeborners knew that the smooth running of the
community depended on each and every one of them.
Hundreds of generations of mice had happily lived this life, and
they were, above all, content.

Piccadilly walked down the subway platform, swinging his
sack in one paw. All that week he had been assigned a group of
cadets. These were young, brassless mice, new to the work, and
he was enjoying their company. One of them, Marty, was a sensitive youngster—he had large, brown eyes and a fine, long nose
with constantly twitching whiskers, and down his back there
was an unusual dark mark in his fur like a flash of lightning.
Although Marty was gray like all the other city mice, he strong-
ly reminded Piccadilly of Oswald, and more than once this
week he had absentmindedly called him Whitey. Now Marty
was getting the hang of foraging and his sack was almost as full
as Piccadilly's when the shift ended.

Piccadilly sent the others back. When they had all gone he
stood alone on the subway platform. It was late at night, and all
the trains had stopped running long ago. Only the service lights

24

were on, and they made it a forbidding place. The tunnels were much larger then the sewers in which he had been lost, but the curved walls always reminded Piccadilly of them. He would often let the others go on ahead and stay behind to think of those times in Deptford and the good friends he had left there.

He sighed sadly. If only Audrey had liked him! Oh well, that part of his life was over now, and he just had to forget it. He hoped that one day he would be able to remember without it hurting anymore.

As he stood there, Piccadilly gradually became aware of two small points of light shining down in the darkness where the subway tracks lay, and it was only when the lights blinked that he realized they were eyes. It gave him quite a shock, but when he recovered he shouted sternly.

"'Ere, who's that down there? Come out now."

The eyes vanished as whoever it was turned tail and darted away.

"Oh no, you don't!" yelled Piccadilly, leaping off the platform. He landed between the tracks and set off in pursuit.

Whoever he was chasing was quick on his feet and scampered swiftly into the extreme blackness of the subway tunnel. Piccadilly charged along as fast as he could, trying to see the figure he was chasing. All he could make out was a hunched, furry shape dodging to and fro, with a thin, knobbly tail slithering over the never-ending silvery rails.

Piccadilly lengthened his strides, leaping over the blocks that supported the rails, and ignoring the pain of the sharp gravel under his feet. Slowly he began to gain on his quarry. With outstretched paws he caught hold of the clammy tail that lashed about before him.

"Aiee!" squealed a croaky voice as Piccadilly gave the tail a sharp yank.

There was a loud *clang!* as the unseen creature lost its

balance and fell heavily against one of the rails.

"Oh me 'ead!" whined the voice morosely. "Oh it 'urts, ooch, ah—ee!"

Piccadilly strained his eyes in the darkness to see what he had caught. An old brown rat lay on the ground before him. His thin, chiseled face was crossed by many wrinkles, and the fur around his temples was gray. The rat was nursing his head and uttering indignant cries through gummy lips—there was only one tooth in his head.

"What the blazes d'you do that fer?" he squawked woefully. "I didn't do nothin'."

Piccadilly looked at him distastefully—he did not like rats. There had been a time when he would cheerfully have kicked any rat's backside and blown a raspberry after it, but ever since his experiences in Jupiter's domain, rats made him nervous. This specimen looked harmless enough, however—it was too old to be anything else. Still, Piccadilly eyed him carefully. There had been some unpleasant rumors going around Holeborn lately about the city rats. Piccadilly thought this might be a good time to find the answers to a few questions.

"What were you spyin' on me for?" he asked sharply.

The rat mumbled to itself and folded its arms sulkily. "Got sore 'ead now," it said stubbornly. "Get a lump there, Barker will. Hates lumps, he does. Lump, lump, lump. Barker always gets 'em, he gets 'em from *them*—he gets 'em from you. Barker might as well punch hisself to save you an' *them* the bother." The rat pouted moodily and repeated, "Lump, lump, lump," once more.

Piccadilly groaned—he could not stand whiners, but he offered the rat a paw to help him up. "You're called Barker then?" he asked. There was no reply. "Is your name Barker?"

The rat had looked away rudely and remained obstinately where he was. "Lump, lump, lump," he grumbled peevishly.

26

"Get up or I'll give you some more lumps to worry about," warned Piccadilly, losing his temper.

Immediately the rat sprang to his feet but ignored the offered paw. "Barker go now?" he grunted.

"Not so fast, mate." Piccadilly caught hold of the rat's fur. "You haven't said why you were spyin' on me."

"Jus' watchin', that's all, weren't doin' no harm. Barker's all right, he is, ain't got nothin' to do with the new blood."

At this, Piccadilly raised his eyebrows and decided he would learn more from this old rat. "You hungry?" he asked.

Barker's tiny eyes lit up and he nodded hurriedly while rubbing his stomach. "Yes," he wailed sorrowfully. "Barker not eated fer days, an' that were only a mangy bit of orange peel. He saw mousey boy's sack of nosh—that's why he was starin', see."

"Come on then." Piccadilly began to walk down the tunnel once more. "I'll see what I can spare."

Barker smacked his gums together and followed warily. His bright little eyes flicked this way and that but always returned to the gray mouse in front of him, watching for any sudden movement or sign of danger.

When they were out of the tunnel Piccadilly climbed onto the platform and searched in his sack for something suitable. He felt it was all too good to be wasted on a rat, but he hoped he might learn something from Barker. Eventually he fished out two whole biscuits and passed them over.

Barker snatched them greedily and devoured them in the most disgusting display of bad manners Piccadilly had ever seen. When the biscuits had disappeared the rat nosed around for any stray crumbs and sucked his claws loudly. When he had finished he squinted down at the sack hopefully.

"That's enough for now," said Piccadilly, following the rat's gaze. It was time to get down to business. "Tell me," he began, "why are you so hungry? There's plenty of food for all you ratfolk to guzzle down here." He was puzzled by Barker's scrawny appearance—animals rarely went hungry in the city.

Barker pulled a face. "Bah!" he spat. "Not no more there ain't."

Piccadilly was startled by the ferocity of his outburst, and he recalled something that the rat had said earlier. "Barker," he began carefully, "what did you mean before when you spoke of 'new blood'?"

The rat clapped a claw over his wizened mouth as though frightened by what he had let slip and refused to say anything more. Piccadilly casually tapped the sack with his paw, and the meaning was not lost on his companion.

The rat lowered his head and swiveled his beady eyes nervously. In a rasping whisper he said to Piccadilly, "*Them* is the new blood. They make Barker's life a misery 'cause he won't join in. Pinch his dinner, they do—the scumbags! When he complains, they give Barker 'ead lumps. They not nice ratfolk, dangerous they are. Barker fears them. They sharpen their claws an' fangs! You stay away from them, mousey boy."

Piccadilly listened to the old rat's words and considered them carefully. There had to be a reason for this unwelcome change in the attitude of the city rats. Where were they getting this newfound bravery from? He asked this of Barker, and the old rat was in no doubt.

"Old Stumpy, it is," he whispered, shivering. "He not like us— he stirs up the rat lads and makes 'em bad. Tells 'em wicked stuff and mixes things up good an' proper. He don't like Barker. He laughs when he gives 'im 'ead lumps—'t'ain't fair, it's not."

Piccadilly repeated what the rat had said, "Old Stumpy . . ." he murmured, and something stirred in his memory—an unpleasant, ugly thought. His forehead creased as he leaned forward urgently. "Tell me," he insisted. "Tell me about Old Stumpy. Where did he come from?"

Barker quivered all over, and his scraggy ears drooped with fear. "Can't," he refused, shaking his head violently. "Barker tell nothin'! Them's big secrets, none must tell."

Once more Piccadilly tapped the sack, but the rat remained tight-lipped until another biscuit was brought out.

Eagerly he reached out and said hastily, "Him come some months back, he said 'e come from—"

"What's this then?" a strange voice called out from the darkness of the tracks. Barker leaped in the air, and his face was stricken with terror. He dropped the unfinished biscuit and covered his face. Piccadilly watched as four claws came over the edge of the platform. Then two great ugly rat heads appeared and glared at the whimpering Barker.

One of the rats was brown in color with matted, slimy fur from which a terrible smell issued. He had low, prominent brows and a slightly piggish snout from which two snotty rivers ran. The other rat was very fat, and his black fur was dusty. He was chewing the piece of fluff-covered nougat and so did not speak for some time.

The brown, smelly one scowled threateningly at Barker and gave a sneering grin to Piccadilly. "Evenin' Grayboots," he said, pausing to snort the two green lines back up his nostrils. "Has barmy Barker been botherin' ya?"

Piccadilly did not like the look of these rats—they were far too sure of themselves. Still, he was not prepared to let them frighten him.

"What's it to you, Stinky?" he asked cheekily. The rat blinked his red-rimmed eyes and chose to ignore the insult. Instead he turned back to Barker. "Now then, you old poxbag, what've you been sayin' to your young friend 'ere?"

Barker backed away and yowled, "I ain't said nothin'—'onest lads. Barker, he never says nothin' to nobody."

The brown rat snarled and Barker yelped with fright.

"Now then, pretty boy," sneered the rat, turning his attention back to Piccadilly, "whatever that old sot has been sayin', you'd best forget it pronto."

Piccadilly was not intimidated, and replied airily, "Why should I, Pongo?"

The rat growled, and his claws scraped along the platform, making an unpleasant screeching sound on the concrete. "The name's Smiff, boy,–you'd do well to remember that."

"Who's the lardy stuffin' his face?" inquired Piccadilly, smiling.

"He's known as Kelly. He don't talk much, only opens his gob when there's somethin' tasty to eat." At this point Kelly opened his mouth and proudly showed his sharpened teeth. He looked at Piccadilly in a most disturbing, hungry way.

The city mouse began to feel uncomfortable, but he knew that he must not show it. "A fine pair you are," he laughed rudely, "Smelly and Belly."

Smiff gnashed his teeth, and a murderous light shone in his eyes, but he controlled himself. "You should be more polite, laddy," he spat. "Not only that, you shouldn't go believing what Barker tells you."

"Why not, Bog-features?"

"'Cause he ain't all there, are you, Barker old chum?"

Barker looked across at Smiff with tearful eyes.

"Tell this nice young mousey why we call you Barker," continued the brown rat nastily.

Barker hesitated, not knowing what to do.

"Tell him!" snapped Smiff. "We calls you Barker because–"

"Because . . ." Barker's nose dribbled with his tears as he wept–"because . . . I'm barking mad."

Both Kelly and Smiff guffawed. Kelly showed his teeth once more, and all his nougat-colored saliva oozed down his chin.

Piccadilly watched them with a face like stone. "I don't

think that was very funny," he said sternly. "Tormenting some-one weaker than yourself–why, it's downright cowardly."

Smiff drew his breath sharply and wrinkled his pug nose in anger. Through gritted teeth he said, "Well, you are a nasty, rude little mouse, ain'tcha? I think we oughta teach you a few manners. Like to take me on would ya, freckle face?" He pulled himself up on the platform and licked his teeth in anticipation.

Piccadilly sprang to his feet and his paw flew to the small knife around his waist. "Just try it," he replied in deadly earnest.

Smiff edged closer but just then Kelly spoke for the first time. "Leave the toe-rag, Smiff. You know our orders–none of that stuff till He says so."

Smiff whirled around. "I'm not letting this cursed kid go, after what he's been sayin' to me."

Kelly hauled himself up next to the brown rat and shook his flabby jowls. "Leave it! Orders is orders. You know what He said: wait, there's time enough for this later."

"But I want 'im now!"

"Ya can't!"

For a moment it looked as if the two rats would fight each other, but in the end Smiff calmed down and spun sullenly on his heel.

Kelly turned to Piccadilly, "You'd best tail it kid, while you've got the chance."

Piccadilly picked up his sack and replied, "I weren't afraid of 'im, nor you, Fatty."

Kelly held Smiff back and shouted, "Just clear off or you will be afraid. You don't know what fear is yet, lad."

Piccadilly thought it was time to leave. He slung the sack over his shoulder and walked as casually as he could up the platform. His mind was racing. There was so much here to think about. He knew he had to tell the ministers what he had learned. The rats were becoming dangerous. When he was out of sight he set off at a run and made for Holeborn.

On the platform the two rats turned on Barker. The old rat retreated as far as he could against the tiled wall. He looked around desperately. The two faces before him were grim and menacing.

"Been telling tales, have you Barker?" asked Smiff. "You know what He'll do, don'tcha?"

"No, no," howled the old rat. "Barker said nothin'. Trust Barker."

"You'd best not have spilled the beans," said Smiff, raising his clenched claw.

"Don't hit Barker—spare him the lumps," he pleaded.

"I'm gonna teach you to keep yer mouth shut."

"Give 'im ten of the best." Kelly smirked.

The old rat's cries filled the tunnels until they were drowned by the sound of laughter—two hideous voices raised in mockery.

*   *   *

"Declare yourself!" said the mouse.

"Piccadilly—foraging party."

"Pass, friend." The mouse stepped aside and Piccadilly knocked on the old, wooden door behind him. "Forager," he shouted to whoever was on the other side. There came a muffled sound of iron bolts dragging over wood, and the great door opened a chink. A friendly young mouse popped his head out and ushered Piccadilly inside.

As he stepped through the doorway, Piccadilly glanced back at the single sentry and looked troubled. The sentry only carried an old spear, a blunt, ancient weapon handed down from his great-great grandfather, and on his head he wore a battered tin hat. Any determined enemy could get past him easily. The

great door itself was antique, put there when Holeborn was first established centuries before. It would not take much to break through. Piccadilly was very concerned. He hurried along the dimly lit entrance hall to the gathering point. This was an area set in the tunnel wall where all the foragers deposited their sacks. There three cheerful mousewives collected the goods and sorted through the supplies.

"Hello Piccadilly," said Agnes Trumper. "Had a good day?" She smiled at him as he handed his finds over.

"Not really," he replied. "Where's Flo and Edna tonight?"

Mrs. Trumper threw up her arms and scurried back over to him. "Oh darlin'," she cried, "I didn't tell you. There's a great meeting in the big hall. It's been going on for a while now. Flo an' Edna have gone to it. I would've too, but I knew you hadn't come back yet, so I waited."

"What's this meeting about then?" he asked.

"Rats, luv–an' what we can do about them. You won't have heard what happened to Charlie Coppit."

Piccadilly shook his head. "He's on the central shift, isn't he? What happened to him then?"

Agnes folded her arms. "You go find out, my duck. I'll sort out your lot, then pop up after."

Piccadilly waved farewell and pattered away. Through the maze of familiar passages he went. The tunnel system at Holeborn was exceedingly intricate and complex. It had been added to over countless generations in a haphazard manner, and only the minister of dwellings really knew the whole lay-out. Even he was not totally sure, having to consult various maps and plans.

Piccadilly jogged along. He gave a quick glance at the chapel when he passed it–there was no one there, not even the green minister, whose job it was to organize the celebrations of all things connected with the Green Mouse. There should have been a Yule gathering in there tonight–things must be serious

indeed for pious Percy to miss that. At last he came to the main
hall, parted the tapestry curtain, and went inside.

This was the largest single space in Holeborn. It was used
only rarely, for meetings like this hardly ever took place. It was
a great, long room with a high ceiling crossed by thick oak
beams from which hung many lamps. There was a raised dais
in the center of the hall, and on this sat the Thane. He was a
wise-looking mouse with small ears and a well-groomed
whiskery beard. He was nodding sagely to all that was being
said around him. On all sides of the dais stood the seven ministers, and each one of them was trying to be heard.

Around the dais was a sea of mice, filling the hall.
Practically every mouse in Holeborn was there. Piccadilly had
never realized there were so many. All were looking to the
Thane for an answer to their problems.

A paw tugged Piccadilly's arm. It was his young friend
Marty. He was sitting cross-legged on the floor, so Piccadilly sat
next to him.

"What've I missed?" he whispered.

Marty shrugged, "Not much. It took ages for everyone to get
in and settle down. We're just about to hear what happened to
Mr. Coppit."

"Good," Piccadilly said, and sat back to listen. The minister
of supplies, a short, well-built mouse, fiddled with his brass and
cleared his throat. "Mr. Charles Coppit," he called.

A figure came from behind the dais, clutching the side of his
face. "'Ere I am," he said.

"Now Mr. Coppit, would you like to tell everyone, in your
own words, what happened to you this evening?"

"Too right I would," came the reply, "an' I want to know
what we're gonna do about it."

"Ahem, just in your own words—when you're ready."

Charlie Coppit stood before the assembly and took the paw
away from his face. It was badly bruised and his eye was

bloody. A ripple of surprise ran through those mice who had not yet heard the news.

"I was on me shift with me cadets," Mr. Coppit began, "an' we were just ready to call it a day when we stumble across a pack of ugly rats, the foul rogues. Well one of 'em, a ruddy great brute, steps up an' starts messin' with our sacks. 'Leave that be,' I says to him, but this mangy good-for-nothing goes an' opens the flippin' thing and takes one of me finds out and eats it."

"What did you do then, Charlie?" continued the minister.

"I tells 'im to watch it or I'd crack 'im one. Well this rat goes and laughs in my face and swipes the sack away, and 'is mates take the others. Well I wasn't going to stand for that, so I tells 'em to give 'em back. The big rat calls me somethin' I don't wanna mention here in front of the ladies and socks me with 'is claw."

"And you returned here with your frightened cadets. How is your face now?"

"Throbbin'."

The minister turned to the assembly. "You have heard what has happened today. The rats are becoming aggressive and it is no longer safe to forage."

The Thane looked at his subjects gravely. "We are in a crisis," he said. "Those once-cringing, dull-witted creatures are rising against us."

The sound of thousands of mice exclaiming in horror filled the hall. The noise rose as they considered this news and the implications that it brought. Husbands held their wives tightly, and some children began to cry. Others muttered darkly to their neighbors, and some even began to pray.

Piccadilly could not hear himself think. The noise grew and grew, until every conversation was shouted. Piccadilly looked over the heads of the agitated mice to the dais where the Thane sat. It was like a lonely island set in a turbulent ocean of distraught faces. Suddenly the noble figure rose and held up his arms for silence. Five thousand snakes seemed to hiss, and then all was still and quiet.

"My friends," began the Thane mildly, "what we have heard is no doubt alarming, but surely we must think about what we can do." He turned to the minister of supplies. "Tell me, Bert," he said, sitting down again, "how long can we last if we shut our door tonight and not leave Holeborn to forage?"

The minister consulted a tally scroll and examined it closely. "What perishable food we have would only serve us for three days," he announced grimly. "After that, with the preserves we have made, about . . . two weeks, and that is stretching it."

The hall buzzed once more.

The Thane stroked his whiskers thoughtfully. "If the rats are indeed deadlier than before, what will be their course of action? Will they be content to harrass our foragers and leave it at that or are they even now preparing for war?"

The minister of dwellings spoke up. "'Enry," he cried, "why all this talk of menace and doom? One incident in a subway tunnel does not make it a dangerous place. I do not believe that the rats have turned vicious. How do we know they were local rats—they might have been traveling ruffians passing through. You know what it's like in winter—all sorts of folk tramp through the city. I say we must wait for more positive proof of malice before we close our door and starve—that would make the rats laugh, be they wicked or no."

"I can see your point, Ned," mused the Thane, "but for some time now, I have been growing uneasy. We must not be idle."

"Then tell the foragers to work harder so we can start stocking up."

"Don't you say anything against my foragers, Ned Fidjit," warned the minister of supplies.

"Gentlemen please!" interrupted the Thane kindly. "I do believe someone has something to say on this matter." He pointed to the back of the room, where an arm had been raised, waiting to be seen. "You there, what is it you have to say?"

The mouse in question rose. "Good heavens," said the minister of supplies, "that's one of my lads–Piccadilly. Good worker he is."

The Thane bent down and asked softly, "Isn't that the one who disappeared some months ago and came back with a fantastical tale?"

"That's the one."

The Thane straightened himself and muttered, "Well he might have something worth listening to then." He drummed his fingers on the sides of his chair and called out, "Speak, boy."

Piccadilly had been listening to the debate with growing impatience. He wanted to tell them what had happened to him. All this talk of closing the door and keeping the rats out was ludicrous. Bursting with frustration, he had stuck his paw into the air, much to the surprise of Marty.

"Put it down," his young friend had hissed at him. Then the Thane had noticed him and it was too late. Marty buried his face. "You've done it now," he said as Piccadilly got to his feet.

Now Piccadilly was standing, and every mouse in the hall was staring straight at him. He coughed nervously but lost his fear as soon as he began to speak.

"'Scuse me 'Enry," he said, "but I think you ought to know what happened to me tonight."

The Thane chuckled at the young mouse's forthright manner and waved him to continue.

"Well, it were like this," Piccadilly began and he told them about his meeting with Barker, what he had learned from him about the "new blood" in the rat population and how he felt that it was all down to "Old Stumpy"–whoever that was.

When Piccadilly had finished the Thane thanked him and turned to the minister of dwellings. "Well Ned, do you still doubt the ferocity of the rats?" The minister shook his head glumly. "No," resumed the Thane, "now we must really consider the possibility of war." He pointed to the minister of craft and said, "You must start making weapons, Sid. The old heirlooms we have won't be enough. Make spears, knives, and anything else you can think of that will give a rat the bashing of his life. We must also begin training ourselves in the devilish art of warfare. Rationing of supplies must start tomorrow, but the foragers will continue to go out until it is too dangerous." He sighed wearily. "What else can we do? I'm afraid I am not well versed in this—perhaps I should consult the chronicles of my celebrated forebear—he loved a skirmish, he did."

"'Scuse me," a voice called out.

The Thane looked up. "What's this, you again?" Piccadilly was waving his arm in the air once more. "Tell us what it is you have to say this time. Do you have something to add?"

"Quite frankly, I do," said Piccadilly standing up again. "I can't believe that's all you can think of doing!"

Everyone in the hall raised their eyebrows at this rude outburst, but the Thane took it with good humor. "And what would you have us do?" he asked.

"Well, you could put extra sentries on our borders for starters and then begin makin' a better door. That one's so old a determined worm could bash its way in."

The Thane leaned forward. "What else?" he asked, and all the humor had left his voice. He spoke as though it were one of his ministers he was addressing and not a cheeky young mouse.

Piccadilly continued. "If I were you I'd get Ned Fidjit to start extending the East Way beyond our boundary."

The minister of dwellings spluttered with indignation at the suggestion. "The East Way!" he exclaimed. "What has that old tunnel got to do with anything? The lad's potty."

"Let him finish," said the Thane.

"Look," explained Piccadilly, "in Holeborn we have lots of little entry points and secret exits, but only one main door. The rats know where that is and if they come charging through it we don't stand a chance, they'll have us cornered. We can't all squeeze through those small openings in time."

"I see what you mean," said the Thane. "If the East Way is extended and opened, we would have what amounts to a large back door that the rats know nothing about."

"Now you're catchin' on."

The Thane chuckled. "What an extraordinary young chap you are. Is there anything else you can suggest?"

"Actually 'Enry, there is. What we could do is discover the rats' plans and stay one jump ahead of them."

"How do you propose we do that?"

"Simple. We spy on 'em."

The Thane looked at all his ministers and came to a conclusion. "Young mouse," he said, "come here." Piccadilly weaved through umpteen rows of mice and stood before the dais. The Thane rose and clapped his paw on the mouse's shoulder. "Piccadilly," he announced grandly, "I name you the official minister of war."

A rush of whispers and shocked looks ran through the assembly. The seven other ministers began to protest in the strongest possible terms, but the Thane silenced them.

"You have been appointed because you excelled at organizing one thing or another," he said. "This youngster has more than proved that he is capable of the post. He has imagination and courage. We are too old and settled in our comfortable ways to give thought to battles and strategies—let the young take over where they can." He stared Piccadilly squarely in the eye and asked if he would accept the office.

"Sure thing, 'Enry."

The Thane held up his paw and declared to the thousands of gathered mice, "Here is your new minister of war!" A young cadet at the back of the hall led the cheers and applause.

40

"Well, what will your first act be as a minister?" asked the Thane.

Piccadilly clicked his tongue, mulling over the various options. Finally he said, "The most important thing is to discover who Old Stumpy is and see how strong the rats are."

"It will be a brave mouse who goes into the rats' lair," observed the Thane.

"Or a foolish one," added Ned Fidjit. "Tell me, Minister, who did you have in mind for this perilous mission?"

"Me," answered Piccadilly soberly.

From the back a tiny voice shouted, "And me."

CHAPTER THREE

OLD STUMPY

The last subway train closed its doors and pulled out of the station. The cold white light shining from the carriage windows receded down the dark tunnel. Somewhere, far above, the station gates rattled shut and an eerie quiet descended.

The platform was empty. Only discarded sweet wrappers moved on it, rolled by the draft that swept down the escalators. One of the papers fell off the edge and gently spiraled downward toward the shining rails.

Out of the darkness a claw flashed and seized the wrapper eagerly. An unpleasant sucking and licking sound followed, then the scrunch of paper being chewed.

Ting! a small, soggy pellet was spat out and smartly hit a rail.

"Garr!" snarled a voice. "Nothin' on that."

Smiff's ugly head reared over the side of the platform. The two snotty lines once again ran from his piggish nose. In one quick movement he was standing on the platform with his tail thrashing and eyes hungrily glaring around.

42

A second head appeared, and Kelly hauled his fat body slowly over the edge. His long, red tongue dangled from his mouth between yellow, sharpened fangs and licked the fur around his jowls.

The other rat sniffed the air cautiously, then darted to the far side, where an overflowing litter bin was fastened to the wall. With an eager yell, Smiff hurled himself against the side and clawed his way to the top. There he shoved his snout down into the mass of old newspapers, orange peel, chocolate wrappers, and used tissues.

His croaky voice echoed strangely inside the bin as he cried, "Aha! There we has it, my lovely!" and his brown, furry body fell headfirst into the rubbish.

Kelly waited impatiently below. Smiff had found something tasty and wasn't sharing it. Kelly growled and looked about for something to bang the bin with. He picked up a gray, oval stone and smashed it against the side. "What you got in there Smiff, you stink bag? Bring it out 'ere."

Kelly gave the bin another mighty *thwack*. It boomed like a gong and a startled yelp issued from inside. Smiff peered down at Kelly with a look of injured innocence on his dreadful face. "Kelly mate, what were that fer?"

"Bring it out 'ere, Smiff!" the fat rat demanded. "Don't bother to deny it, there's chips all around yer mush."

Smiff grumbled to himself and reluctantly fished out a greasy bundle of white paper. He threw it down and jumped after it.

Kelly was already on his knees, tearing it apart. Inside was a cold, clammy clump of chips and a half-eaten sausage. When he saw this, Kelly crowed with delight and crammed it into his mouth.

Smiff scuttled over and guzzled with him. Soon they were licking the papers clean and searching for more. The two rats belched contentedly. Their whiskers were matted down with grease and their claws glistened slimily. Kelly picked his fangs and stared into the darkness of the tunnel. Seeing something move he elbowed Smiff, who stiffened immediately.

"Who's there?" he snapped. "Come 'ere! Or shall I come an' get yer?" As he said this he raised his claws and their savage points shone menacingly.

"No, no," wailed a pitiful voice. "I'm a comin'!" Barker, the old scrawny rat, trotted dutifully into the light. There were terrible bruises on his head and several painful-looking lumps about his temples. Kelly sneered when he saw who it was and coughed up a blob of spit.

Smiff grinned and beckoned to the old rat. As Barker clambered onto the platform, Smiff winked at Kelly and quickly wrapped something up in the chip papers.

"What you doin', lads?" Barker asked as he eyed the bundle curiously. He could smell the delicious aroma of cold, vinegary fat. Barker drooled and rubbed his groaning belly.

"We been 'avin' a feast, Barker mate, but there's only a fish-cake left–ain't there, Kelly?"

The fat rat chuckled and nodded his great head. Barker swallowed and gazed longingly down. Tears welled up in the old rat's eyes. "I've 'ad no food since yesterday, an' that weren't much. Me belly's flappin' like an old sock. I'm real weak." He wrung his claws together and said softly, "I'm right partial to fishcake an' all."

Smiff snorted, "We ain't gonna give you our luvverly grub, you old fool–not unless you got somethin' to swap."

"I got nothin'," Barker admitted unhappily.

"Then clear off!" snarled Kelly.

Barker threw one last glance at the tantalizing bundle and shuffled miserably down the platform. The other two rats watched him go with smirks on their faces.

The unhappy, retreating figure paused near an untidy pile of rubbish and bent down. Smiff and Kelly frowned and strained their eyes to see what was happening.

"He's found somethin'," muttered Kelly sourly.

Barker was overjoyed. He clapped his claws together and rubbed his eyes in disbelief. There at his feet, amongst the colorful wrappers, was nearly a whole bar of chocolate, the kind with raisins and hazelnuts. Barker could not believe his luck and he cooed excitedly. He picked it up and Smiff's voice roared next to him.

"What you got there, Barker mate?"

The old rat jumped and held the chocolate tightly to his chest. "Nothin', Smiffy," he replied timidly. "Ain't nothin', honest."

"Looks like chocklett to me," Smiff observed, slobbering.

"S'only a grotty bit, trod on an' spat at prob'ly," Barker whimpered glumly.

Smiff's eyes gleamed lustily, and Barker could see the chocolate bar reflected in them. "Don't look too bad to me, Barker, not bad at all."

The old rat puffed and protested. "You can't 'ave it, it's mine, belongs to Barker, gimme as many 'ead lumps as you like, but it's mine."

Smiff raised his claws to silence him. "Don't worry, I'm not gonna thieve it. What do you think I am? I wouldn't rob an old mate like you." He smiled and put his arm around Barker's shoulders. "Us are pals aren't we?"

Barker looked doubtful. "Are we?" he asked.

"'Course we are, 'course, and as a pal I don't want to see you lose yer last toof—you'd get a shockin' toofache if you ate all that chocklett."

Barker's bottom lip trembled. "But Barker's starvin'."

"'Course you are, that's why I thought we could do that trade I mentioned before. Wouldn't you rather have a nice fish-cake than all that sickly chockie?"

"Fishcake?" the old rat repeated uncertainly.

Smiff waved his claw before his face, "Yeah, a scrumschiss, sucklent fishcake. Imagine, Barker–the crispy batter on the outside, all crunchy an' greasy, an' inside the soft mush of fish. Oh, I can't bear it," and he wiped invisible tears from his eyes.

A great bellow thundered from Barker's stomach. "Ow," he moaned miserably.

Kelly appeared at a signal from Smiff, carrying the bundle of chip papers. The fat rat ogled the chocolate with undisguised greed.

The smell of the vinegary paper was too much for Barker and he yielded at once. "Take it, take it," he cried, thrusting the bar into Smiff's paws.

"There's 'andsome." Smiff grinned. "Now, give our pal the fishcake, Kelly." The bundle was handed over, but before Barker could open it Smiff held his claws and said, "Don't forget, Barker, Old Stumpy's speakin' to all of us later. You'd best be there if you value your head." With their mouths full of chocolate the two rats leaped off the platform and ran into the tunnel, laughing.

Barker tore open the greasy paper then blinked. The slow realization that he had been tricked dawned on him. For there was no fishcake within–only an oval, gray stone. The old rat collapsed in a woeful heap. He thought of the chocolate that had been his and threw back his head, letting out a tremendous bitter howl of anguish and despair.

*   *   *

"What's that?" Marty clutched Piccadilly's arm in fright as the terrible wail rang through the deserted subway tunnel like a pronouncement of doom.

Piccadilly shivered. It was a sound of misery and hopelessness. The pain and resentment in the tortured voice cut into his

46

heart and left him breathless. "I don't know what it is, Marty," he admitted, "but we're going to find out."

The two mice followed the sound of the dreadful wailing. Piccadilly went first, with his little knife clutched tightly in his paw, ready for anything. Marty pattered behind him, his eyes wide with fear and excitement. He had never done anything like this before, and all his senses were alive with tingling thrills. He wondered what lay ahead. Would he see great dangers and have fierce battles? Marty hoped that he would be brave, whatever happened–he did not want to disgrace himself in front of his hero, Piccadilly.

They came to a turning; the source of the noise was just around this corner. Piccadilly tightened the grip on his knife and peered around. Marty held his breath anxiously, but was surprised to see his friend relax and chuckle.

"What is it?" he hissed.

"Nothing to worry about," replied Piccadilly, disappearing around the corner.

Barker's tears had dried up, and now his wailing had deteriorated into a rasping whine. His body was slumped over the torn chip papers, he was exhausted, and his bony chest ached from sobbing. Through sore, red eyes he stared at the oval stone and mournfully licked his solitary tooth.

"Poor Barker," he croaked hoarsely, "he never gets nothin'– only lumps. Lumps on 'is 'ead an' lumps o' stone to eat. Poor Barker." Slowly his knobbly tail began to tap the platform as a thought came to him. "But one day, one day Barker'll show 'em, won't he? He'll learn 'em, an' they'll all be sorry. If only they knew . . . ," he sniggered harshly, in a voice that was not quite his own. He did not notice Piccadilly creeping up behind him.

"Wotcha Barker, old chum!" shouted the mouse.

The rat squealed and buried himself under the chip papers, where he trembled and cowered.

"It's all right, it's only me!" Piccadilly tried to reassure him. A bleary eye peered cautiously out from the greasy bundle.

"Mousey boy," said the rat. "That you? You on yer lonesome?"

"No, I've brought a friend of mine to see you. Come out, Marty."

With a rustle, the papers shuffled backward apprehensively as the small figure of Marty came onto the platform. The young cadet eyed the shaking pile nervously.

"This is Marty," announced Piccadilly.

Barker's head rose above the chip papers and his whiskers quivered. The rat scrutinized Marty with suspicion and frowned as he smacked his gums. He stepped from his cover and walked slowly over to the cadet. Marty looked helplessly at Piccadilly but the older mouse made a sign telling him to stay still.

Barker sniffed the air about Marty and paced all around him.

"He's a friend," said Piccadilly.

The rat scratched his ears. "So you says, mousey boy, so you says, but Barker don't like him. This whelp has a freak mark branded on his spine." He pointed to the lightning pattern on Marty's back. "He'll let you down one day, mousey boy, Barker knows. Don't trust him with anything important–he'll go his own way and bring ruin on all, especially himself."

Marty opened his mouth in protest, but Piccadilly was smiling. He told Barker to be quiet. "I've come here to see you," he said.

The rat blinked and forgot his concern about Marty. "You come to see Barker, mousey boy? What fer–he ain't done anythin' wrong?"

"I want to have a chat, that's all."

Barker shook his head touchily. "No chat, we ain't got time

to waste with chat," but then he remembered his hunger and looked at Piccadilly hopefully, "unless nice mousey boy has present for Barker–biscuit perhaps, yes, no?"

Piccadilly could have kicked himself for not anticipating this. "Sorry Barker," he said, "I haven't got anything with me." The rat pulled a disappointed face and snorted. "But if you tell me what I want to know," Piccadilly continued hurriedly, "I'll give you enough biscuits to last a lifetime."

But Barker was not impressed. "Barker want grub now, not next time or tomorrow–he say nothin'!" He folded his arms and shut his mouth resolutely.

"Tell me about Old Stumpy, you barmy old snot gobbler," said Piccadilly sharply. "What are his plans?"

Barker fell back, dismayed. "No, Barker not spill beans–he want no more 'ead lumps, you keep away from Barker, mousey boy. He knows nothin'!"

Piccadilly rushed forward and caught hold of the rat's shoulders. Barker flapped his arms wildly, trying to escape.

"Last time you were going to tell me who Old Stumpy was," cried Piccadilly angrily. "Why can't you tell me now?"

Barker gasped and yammered, wriggling and twisting like a worm on a hook in his desperate efforts to escape. "We been told to say nothin' till He tells us to. There's big secrets in dark places–Barker not like them. Let him go, mousey boy, Barker got to go now, mustn't be late."

"You're staying put until you tell me what I want to know."

The rat was horrified and in a panic he screamed, "No, no! Barker must go, all must be there for the meet. He says all have to go or we get our throats cut." And with a tremendous burst of strength he broke free of the mouse's grasp and leaped off the platform into the tunnel.

Marty ran over to Piccadilly, who was tapping his feet in annoyance.

"What was that all about?" he asked, staring after the crazy rat running along the rails. "What did he mean about meetings? I've never heard of them doing that before. He really is barmy."

Piccadilly spun around and took hold of his friend's paw urgently, "This is it!" he exclaimed. "This is our chance to discover what is going on. If we follow Barker to this meeting, we could learn who Old Stumpy is and listen to his plans."

"Oh," murmured Marty in surprise, "but isn't that terribly dangerous?"

"You don't have to come if you don't want to, Marty," said Piccadilly as he jumped off the platform.

Marty wished he was at home with his three sisters. Now that it came to it, he didn't feel like being brave and fearless at all. He hesitated nervously on the edge of the platform, not knowing what to do, when suddenly he found that he had stepped off it and was standing between the shining subway rails.

"Knew you'd make it," said Piccadilly, by his side. "Now, let's go."

*   *   *

Smiff held a flaming torch high above his head and peered into the chamber. Everything was ready. A platform of bricks and boxes had been made in the center for the speaker to address them. Torches had been placed all around, and their brazen light licked over the grimy walls with lurid, dancing tongues. Everyone would be able to see their glorious leader.

The chamber was a forgotten service passage lined with thick, heavy-duty pipes and cables which ran from floor to ceiling. A ragged, foul-smelling cloth had been hung over the entrance, and Smiff found himself clucking with anticipation. Soon Old Stumpy would divulge his plans.

He sniffed violently and the two green trails of snot that had been dangling from his nose shot back up his nostrils. There came the sound of many feet dragging on the ground, accompanied by the swish of half as many strong, thick tails trailing behind. Smiff yanked the curtain aside, and the entire rat population of the city poured in like a colossal flood of fur.

Even Smiff was amazed at the number of rats. He had never seen so many of his own kind gathered in one place before. There were young rats and old, strong ones, bony ones, and wizened, hatchet-faced old sinners who cursed and swore. Numerous shady characters shifted uneasily, on their guard in case of treachery. Nobody knew everyone there, and no one was sure of the purpose of the meeting. A small group at the back began a gambling game and foul words filled the already polluted air. The atmosphere was tense but expectant.

Eventually every single one of the vile creatures squeezed into the foul den. Some had climbed up the wall and perched themselves on the cables for a better view of the platform. There were several thousand evil, gleaming eyes in the chamber, and all of them reflected the flickering torchlight like a treasury of hellish jewels. The stench of all their filthy, sweating bodies was atrocious.

Smiff leaned against the wall, glad to have pushed the stragglers into the packed chamber. He put his claws into his mouth and blew a loud whistle to tell Kelly to escort in their leader.

A frantic pattering caught Smiff's attention, and he looked crossly down the passage, wondering who would dare arrive so late.

"You poxy slug!" he bawled when he recognized Barker puffing up to him. "Where you been? We told you not to be late," and he dealt the old rat a cruel blow with his claws. Barker yelled and ran through the curtain, cowering and yelping.

Piccadilly and Marty had followed Barker at a safe distance–he had no idea they were following. They pursued him down pitch-black passages and tunnels, splashed through ice-cold puddles of stinking water, and squelched through ghastly stretches of thick mud. They knew that they were deep in the heart of rat territory; bad smells hung about like mists, and slithery slime dripped from the walls and oozed over the ground.

"I think we're nearly there," whispered Piccadilly. "There's a faint light up ahead."

They were viewing the entrance to the meeting chamber at some distance. They heard Barker's rough treatment at the claws of Smiff and saw a brighter chink of light as the old rat dodged inside. "What was that whistle?" asked Marty.

Piccadilly was not certain. "Sounded like a kind of signal–I wonder what for? We must find out what's going on in there."

"But we can't march right up and listen: there's someone on guard."

Their discussion was brought to an end when they heard a noise that froze their blood. Heavy rat footsteps were coming up the tunnel behind them.

Marty closed his eyes, waiting to be grabbed by rough claws, but Piccadilly caught hold of his paw and tugged him to one side. The rats behind them drew closer, and the mice heard Kelly's voice speaking.

"Everyone should be in there now, Boss. They're all dying to know what you've got to tell 'em."

Marty scuttled fearfully along the wall, away from the approaching rats. He and Piccadilly were trapped, with no chance of escape. Suddenly the wall against his back seemed to crumble and fall away.

Piccadilly wondered where his friend had gone. One minute he was at his side, the next he seemed to have vanished. He dared not call out, for Kelly and Old Stumpy had nearly reached him and would be bound to hear his voice. Something yanked Piccadilly's tail and he went sprawling backward into a hole in the wall.

Kelly and Old Stumpy passed by without noticing. Piccadilly had landed on top of Marty, and the two mice rubbed their bruises. Piccadilly looked about him.

"I think it's some sort of pipe," Marty breathed, when the rats were out of earshot. "What a piece of luck."

Piccadilly wished that he had been able to see Old Stumpy, but Kelly's large bulk had screened him. Now he ran his paws over the inner surface of the pipe thoughtfully. "I wonder where this goes?" he mumbled to himself.

"Never mind about that, let's go home," Marty pleaded.

"No, we still haven't discovered anything useful. I'm going to see where this pipe comes out. I think I can see a light up there." He was able to get to only his knees, for it was a very narrow pipe, and began to wriggle along. Marty heaved a sigh of resignation and followed.

Piccadilly crawled over heaps of debris until he made it to the end of the pipe, and his face was lit from underneath by lurid torchlight.

The meeting chamber was below him: he was looking out from high up in one of its walls. He was partially hidden from view by the thick cables that disappeared into the lofty ceiling. Piccadilly gazed down at the rat assembly in wonder and dread. He had never dreamed that there could be so many rats in all of London. He shuddered and edged back into the pipe a little.

"What is it?" asked Marty, catching up with him and craning his neck to peer over his shoulder. "Oh my!" he exclaimed on seeing the chamber and its occupants. He felt his knees turn to water and he looked fearfully at Piccadilly.

"Don't worry," said his friend calmly, "they won't see us up here, they'll all be too busy looking at Old Stumpy."

A commotion below made the mice look down again. The sea of rats near the curtain was parted as Smiff led their leader in.

"Make way, make way," he yelled, plowing through the throng.

Smiff stepped onto the platform and wiped his runny nose on his arm. "Brother rats," he called out proudly. "I 'as the 'onor to introduce to you our great leader, known to some of us lads as Old Stumpy!" There was a tremendous roar as the rats cheered and banged their tails with approval.

Old Stumpy came onto the stage; somewhere in the crowd Barker cringed and high above, watching from the pipe, Piccadilly choked back a cry of shock.

Old Stumpy was an ugly piebald rat. He had a ring through one ear and something glittery hung around his neck. His tail was just a stump, hence his nickname. Piccadilly recognized him at once.

"Morgan!" he spat the name contemptuously. Here was Jupiter's old lieutenant–that master of slyness whom everyone had presumed had perished when his foul master's tail had swept him into the sewer water. Piccadilly's face hardened; he remembered that it was Morgan who had handed over his friend Albert Brown to Jupiter.

"Do you know him?" asked Marty in surprise.

"I once swore I'd kill him," said Piccadilly. "I thought fate had cheated me of that but now ... who knows?" Marty saw the grim look on his friend's face and was alarmed. He had never seen Piccadilly like this before and it frightened him.

Down on the platform, Morgan greeted his subjects. He waddled across the stage, rubbing his claws together.

"Lads," he shouted, "how pleased I be to see all yer pug-ugly faces." The rats cheered and warmed to him immediately. Morgan stretched his arms open wide and began his speech.

"You be here because of blood," he screamed. "You have

none! Where be the hot, burning blood of the ravenous rat? It don't run in your veins–I should know, I comes from Deptford." The crowd murmured admiringly. Everyone had heard of the rats of Deptford and how vicious they were. "When I come 'ere," Morgan continued, "I couldn't believe me eyes. There you were, you miserable vermin, fawning and scraping–afraid of mice and yer own shadders! It made me honk, I were so disgusted."

He pointed to Smiff and Kelly and a few other fierce-looking brutes. "See what can be done if'n you forget yer lily-livered ways and follow me. Turn to the path of Tooth an' Claw. Let blood flow in the subways."

The crowd began to buzz. Some of the rats nodded eagerly and opened their slavering jaws. Morgan danced around the platform, whipping his audience into a frenzy.

"Why should us stay away from the puny mouse halls? What right have they got to the best pickin's? Rats are strong– we are mighty. Our teeth bite an' tear, we 'ave claws to slash and split open. Hear me you rats, have yer never 'ad the blood craze? Have yer eyeballs never burned with hate for everything save yerselves? Have yer never slaughtered and gorged on blood?"

The rats became possessed as Morgan's hate and hunger consumed them like a raging fire. They waved their claws in the air, slashing furiously like tigers. Those near the platform banged their fists on it passionately.

Morgan grinned. It was all going according to his plans. Now he would rule an army of rats–just what he had always wanted. His beady red eyes flicked over his followers and he nodded with satisfaction. Suddenly a voice shouted from the far corner and all turned to see who it was.

A scabby-faced black rat was trying to make himself heard above the din. "Hang on, hang on," he cried. "What do we wanna listen to 'im fer? We're 'appy enough, ain't we? So what

if the mousies call us names an' 'ave first claim to all the grub—
I prefer the stuff they don't want. We ain't no killers. You should
go back to Deptford where you belong, instead of stirrin' up
trouble 'ere."

The crowd looked at Morgan expectantly, but he merely
smiled. "Come forward, friend," he said disarmingly. "Come up
here where I can see you proper. I should like to talk with you."
His stubby tail thumped impatiently on the platform.

The scabby rat pushed through the crowd and was lifted up
next to Morgan.

"Tell me," said the piebald rat smarmily, "what be it about
me that offends you so?"

The rat shrugged, "'Tain't personal—it's just that I don't
think we should go around murderin' anythin' just for the sake
of it. Why can't we just go on as we always 'ave?"

Morgan whirled around and grabbed him by the scruff of
the neck. "This is what makes me sick!" he cried to the audience. "Cowardly weakling scum, he be no rat, he don't deserve
to live!" He threw the astonished rodent down, leaped into the
air, and lunged at him. With one swift slash of his powerful
claws he tore out the other's throat.

Piccadilly and Marty covered their eyes and felt sick.

The assembly was in confusion, not knowing whether to be
angry or afraid.

"That is what happens to the weak and spineless!" boomed
Morgan, kicking his victim off the platform. "Follow me and
you shall drink sweeter blood—mouse is better by far. A mouse's
flesh is tender and juicy, and when fried his ears are good
enough to die for."

The rats went wild. They tore the dead rat apart and tasted
what they could get their claws on.

"We go to war!" screamed Morgan triumphantly. "Death to
all mice."

"Death, death, death!" echoed the assembly, licking their lips and feeling the hatred burn behind their eyeballs. Morgan had done his work well.

Piccadilly and Marty held on to each other in shock. Marty was pale, and he shook all over.

"What are we to do?" he wept. "They're going to eat us all."

"We must warn them in Holeborn, Marty," said Piccadilly.

They began to ease back out of the narrow pipe, but in doing so, Marty dislodged some loose rubble. It fell into the chamber and the torches spluttered. Every bloodthirsty rat looked upward and saw Piccadilly's startled face.

"MOUSE!" they screeched at the top of their evil voices.

"Get him," commanded Morgan. "He'll warn the others."

The rats began to scramble up the wall toward the broken pipe. Piccadilly ducked out of sight but knew it was too late. He could hear their curses and their claws scrabbling against the bricks. Wildly he turned to Marty. "They haven't seen you yet, you've got to get out and warn everyone at Holeborn. I'll keep them busy here."

"I won't leave you, Piccadilly," squealed Marty.

"You must, but promise me you'll take the longer route to the East Way. The rats are sure to be watching the main entrance to Holeborn."

"I promise," said Marty, and he gave his hero a final hug. "Green save us," he prayed.

Piccadilly pushed him away. "Hurry up!" Marty slithered down the pipe and was gone. "Green save us indeed." Piccadilly shook his head. "I don't believe in no Green Mouse. Trust in yourself, lad—that's how you've managed before. I'll give those rats a run for their supper."

He took hold of his little knife and stuck his head out of the pipe once more. The walls were smothered in heaving bodies, each trying to be the first to catch him.

"Oi, dung for brains!" Piccadilly yelled to them, "Here I am—what are you waiting for?"

On the platform Morgan recognized the city mouse, and his temper flared. "Kill, kill, kill!" he stormed.

Piccadilly hurled rocks down at the oncoming rats. He hit one right between the eyes and it dropped to the ground, stone dead. But there were too many of them, and Piccadilly was running out of missiles. When they were within range, he lashed out with his knife. Claws splintered and flew, but the mouse could not keep it up; his arm ached and he decided it was time to leave.

"Marty should be clear of the ratlands by now," he thought, so with one final chop that lopped off a huge spotty ear, he darted down the pipe and into the tunnel.

"Where's 'e gone?" wailed the rats in dismay.

"He's escaping down the tunnel, you fools," screamed Morgan impatiently. The curtain was torn down and the rat army trampled over it.

"There he is," they cried. "Get 'im!"

Piccadilly ran as fast as he could. He raced down the tunnel like a bullet. The stones cut his feet, but he did not care—the rats were directly behind, and that was all that mattered. He shot through the slimy passages and out into the subway, leaping over the tracks and not daring to look back.

The harsh cries of the rats rang in his burning ears as they hunted him. Piccadilly saw an arch of light ahead; he was coming to a station. He could lose them there if only he could make it. With his heart pounding desperately, he raced nearer. Then he made his mistake.

He glanced over his shoulder and saw thousands of flaming eyes pursuing him—he was doomed. There was no way he could escape them. But he could not stop running. A sharp stab of pain seared through his foot as it struck the rail and twisted

awkwardly. Piccadilly howled, lost his balance, and fell headlong onto one of the blocks that supported the rails. His head
struck the corner with a mighty *crack!* and he rolled, uncon-
scious, beneath the tracks. A suffocating blackness engulfed
him and he knew no more.

MURDER IN THE PARK

Thomas Triton stirred in his sleep and dreamed deeply. Silver-armored fish flashed over his bed and splashed into the wooden wall while his forehead rippled and rolled. Green waving weeds spilled over the blankets and salty bubbles blew up through the pillows. Seagulls cried down to him as he drifted through the night on his raft of bedclothes. They wheeled and circled high above, their voices becoming faint and mournful.

Out onto the ocean of the dark the midshipmouse sailed, his white whiskers spread out into foamy waves, frothing and curling in the bed-raft's wake. Shadowy faces shimmered out of the black water, faces from the eddies of Triton's past when he was young and the spray was still fresh on his cheeks.

"Woodget," he called out in his slumber, grasping the empty air with tormented paws.

Like the Sirens of old, the haunting faces lured the sleeping Thomas to them. The sea tilted, swelling and churning as the rain battered down from the ceiling sky. Amid the wood-grain clouds another face loomed over him, a squint-eyed, evil phantom, riding on a serpent's scaly back and laughing with the tempest's fury.

"No, no!" beseeched the midshipmouse, grappling with the bedsheet sails that flapped in tatters and ripped out of his fingers.

The storm ravaged down and the bed spun. Drenched by the thundering waves, Thomas clung to the pillows wretchedly. Pale, spiny fish with luminous eyes rose from the depths to snap at his tail as the gale trumpeted in his ears. A huge, white-crested wave smashed down on him, and the bed foundered.

"Help, help," he spluttered, struggling to keep afloat. He gulped the air as the sea dragged him under and closed over his head. The mouse plunged into the cold dark from where no one returns.

Thomas fell from his bunk and hit the floor. With a grunt of alarm, he woke up. The blankets were on top of him, and for a moment he thought he was still dreaming. He rubbed his head dopily and blinked.

"You daft old fool, Tom." He sighed, shaking himself. But the terror of his nightmare was still with him, and there were salty tears in his eyes. The midshipmouse got slowly to his feet, but decided not to get back into bed. He crossed his small room and lit a candle. The inside of his figurehead glowed warmly, but Thomas was troubled. He sat down and filled his pipe with a pinch of tobacco.

A low rumble vibrated through the *Cutty Sark*, and Thomas scowled; there was a real storm passing outside. He drew on his pipe and reflected. The thunder rolled outside and then faded away.

"Bad night." Thomas shivered, blowing blue smoke from the corner of his mouth. "Glad I'm battened under the hatches safe an' sound." Yet he felt as if he wasn't safe. Trouble was brewing somewhere—his whiskers were twitching, and that was always a bad sign.

"'Tain't no use," he muttered, putting his pipe down. "You're no good to anyone like this, Tom. If you can't sleep you might as well take a look at the weather." He pulled on his hat and tied a red kerchief around his neck. He did not admit to himself that he did not want to go back to sleep again, and was just finding an excuse for not doing so.

In its dry dock, the *Cutty Sark* rested uneasily on her steel skewers. Thomas Triton stepped onto the deck and walked over to the rail, from where he surveyed the wintry world.

The night was cold and the stars shone brightly in the clear sky. The river was calm and its voice whispered softly against the jetties. Far to the left the old power station at Deptford Green was wreathed in a gray mist. The mist hung about the old, empty building curiously, shrouding the blank windows and melting away at the water's edge. The one, tall chimney stuck out of the mysterious cloud like a long, white periscope. It held Thomas's attention.

"First there was thunder," he observed slowly, "when the sky's as clear as day, an' now there's a fog lingerin' yonder. Somethin's afoot, I'll wager . . ." and he chewed his bottom lip thoughtfully.

The air grew cold and a bitter blast blew from upriver. The icy wind hurt Thomas's lungs as he breathed. It was unnatural. He shivered and decided to return below decks, where he could consider the problem in comfort.

"A tot o' rum's what you need, matey," he told himself as he descended the steps to the hold. He made his way to his figurehead, a white-painted girl wearing a turban of gold.

"Hello Princess," he said, patting the wooden folds of her dress, "did you miss me?" Thomas passed through the hole into his quarters.

The small candle was still burning merrily. Thomas poured some rum from a flask into a bowl and sat on his bunk. He took a sip and swilled it around his tongue. The liquid warmed him all the way down to the tip of his tail, and he wiggled his toes with pleasure. The sight of the power station wrapped in mist puzzled him; he could not remember seeing anything quite like it in all the years he had been at sea. Still, he had forgotten his nightmare, and before he could take another drink the midshipmouse yawned loudly. He took off his hat and kerchief, extinguished the candle, then clambered into bed. The delicious tendrils of sleep crept up and closed his eyes. Thomas nodded and began to snore.

TAP!

The midshipmouse rolled over and ignored the sharp sound.

TAP!

He pulled the pillow over his ears.

TAP!

Thomas sat up crossly. There it was again, an annoying knocking on the hull of the ship.

"What in thunderation is going on?" he fumed. "Can't a mouse get any sleep?" He threw off the bedclothes, pulled on his woolen hat, and stormed out of the figurehead.

"I'll teach whoever it is not to go wakin' a fellow up in the middle of the night like this. For mercy's sake, will they never cease that racket?" He strode onto the deck once more, only this time his face was angry and his bushy brows bristled sternly.

TAP!

Thomas flew in the direction of the sound. He stared over the side of the ship and peered at the concrete floor below. What he saw made him stutter with a mixture of confusion, anger, and wonder. For there, cowering in the shadows, was a timid squirrel meekly throwing stones against the ship.

"What in Davey Jones are you doin', lad?" barked Thomas.

The squirrel squealed in surprise and with a flash of his tail disappeared behind a railing and into some bushes. The midshipmouse sighed and drummed his fingers impatiently—squir-

64

rels were always jittery. He wondered why one would come from the park to get him out of bed.

A frightened face appeared through the leaves. "Mr. Triton," it ventured in a low whimper, "is that you?"

Thomas muttered under his breath, "'Course it's me, you stupid Nelly!" but he called out, "Aye, it's Triton. Come out of them bushes—you're in no danger here."

The squirrel stole into the light and crept over the concrete. He looked up at the towering black shape of the *Cutty Sark* and fluttered his paws. Shaking fearfully all over he said, "You must come . . . I . . . She wants . . . We, oh dear, this has never . . . It's so dreadful—oh, oh . . ." He began to cry dismally.

Thomas ground his teeth. The last thing he wanted was to deal with a sniveling squirrel. "Just tell me what the matter is," he called down.

The squirrel wrung his paws together. "The matter? Oh dear me, it's all so ghastly and hideous. With them dead and me here—oh, why me?" he wailed self-pityingly.

Thomas slapped the deck loudly and shouted, "For the last time, lad, tell me squarely what has happened or I'm off to bed again!"

The squirrel blinked—really, this mouse was stupid, hadn't he made it perfectly clear? Wasn't he listening? He cleared his throat and cried, "Murder! There has been murder in the park."

Thomas leaned further forward. "Murder?" he repeated softly. "Here's a pretty business."

"I've been sent to fetch you, Mr. Triton," explained the squirrel. "*She* wants to talk with you."

"Stay right there, I'll be down in a trice," said Thomas. He ran down to the hold, where he slipped behind the tall, forbidding figure of Neptune. As he went through the pitch-smelling, narrow passage beyond he was thinking hard. Murder—he wondered who had been killed and by whom. He did not need to ask who *she* was; Thomas knew that only the Starwife could

65

have forced one of her subjects out when he was in such a state. Grimly he brooded over the possible reasons she could have for wanting to see him, but he could think of none.

He emerged into the outside world and climbed down the ship's rudder. Once on the ground, Thomas began climbing the steps out of the large trough that enclosed the ship. He ran over to the squirrel.

"Tell me," he asked, "what's all this about murder, and why does the Starwife want to see me?"

The squirrel scurried under the bush and did not come from behind the railings. "No time, no time," he chirruped excitedly, "follow me," and he scampered away along a hedge.

Thomas did not like this–he wanted answers. He saw the squirrel dart and dodge in and out of cover all along the road that led to the park. With a resigned shake of the head he set off after him.

The squirrel nipped under parked cars, threaded its way through rails, slipped beneath buzzing sodium street lamps, and bounded under the locked park gates. Thomas puffed up behind. He ducked under the iron gateway, and the squirrel's voice called out from the lofty safety of a tree, "Hurry up, hurry up!" The midshipmouse saw a small, long-tailed shape flit from branch to branch overhead.

He looked over to the observatory hill and breathed in sharply. There was chaos up there and he could hear faint voices crying. The hill was a wreck; trees had been smashed down and great fissures made in the earth. Anxiously he wondered how it could have happened.

Squirrels were running everywhere, oblivious to the astonished midshipmouse climbing the steep hill path. Uprooted rhododendron bushes were scattered over the grassy slopes and clods of earth littered the pathway, and over all was a glittering layer of frost.

The night was filled with frantic cries and voices raised in misery. Thomas passed a group of squirrels huddled together weeping. At their feet lay the body of one of their comrades—he had been impaled by a slender spear made of ice. The body was frozen solid and white with frost. The unseeing eyes stood out like globes of black glass, and the stricken face was a twisted picture of terror.

As Thomas removed his hat, he noticed other groups racked with sorrow. In all, twenty-three young squirrels had been killed with ice spears wedged between their ribs. The sad little bodies littered the frosted grass. Thomas moved slowly through the crowds of bitter grief, his face pale and bewildered.

"Triton," came a cracked voice.

He looked up from the devastation, and there was the Starwife, leaning on her stick and trembling with the cold. The age-old mistress of the squirrel colony appeared more tired and careworn than Thomas had ever known her. She bleakly surveyed the wreck of her realm and whatever vitality she had was quenched.

"Ma'am?" he said in a distressed tone. "What has happened here?"

The Starwife turned her half-blind, milky eyes from the ruin around her and said hollowly, "We have been attacked." She was dejected and frail, and Thomas's heart went out to her. This once proud and imperious squirrel who had terrified many, including Thomas, was now shrunk to a shambling, pathetic creature whose grief and care were too much to bear.

She prodded the frozen ground with her stick and shuddered with the cold. "Triton?" she asked softly, "Would you take me away from this? Help me to my chambers please." He took her arm and led her through the destruction.

A hollow oak lay splintered and broken on the frost-covered grass, and under the tangled mass of its upturned roots a great hole was revealed. This had been the entrance to the squirrels' underground dwellings, where they stored all their winter food and their volumes of history, lore, and astrological formulae. Thomas and a few other squirrels eased the Starwife down the entrance. She could weep no tears, for all hers had been spent. She merely stared bitterly about her. Along the tunnels they went, and the Starwife began telling Thomas of the night's terrible events.

"I was not easy," she began. "The evening was drawing on, and a disquiet had settled heavily on my heart. There was something very wrong, and I was in a foul temper because I did not know what it was." She put her gnarled paw to her head and made a gesture signifying stupidity. "I examined the charts to try and foresee what might happen, but they were useless, as if something outside nature was influencing events. I threw the scrolls away and got down from my throne. I felt helpless—me, the Starwife, she who is supposed to know all things. I was mad with myself." Here she managed an ironic smile as she remarked, "I am such an old boot these days." Thomas nodded, remembering that he had once called her by that name.

The Starwife continued, "I thought I was overlooking something. Well, when I get forgetful and downright senile, I usually take a stroll and check on the stores—I find it helps, you know. I hobbled there on my own, telling my attendant, Piers, to get out of my way. Do you remember him, Triton?"

Thomas replied that he did. "Where is he anyway?" he asked.

The Starwife looked at the ground and limped along purposefully, "Piers is in my chamber—you will see him soon enough." She remained silent for a time and then resumed her account. "I was in one of the storerooms, confirming the tally list, when all of a sudden the temperature dropped and a freezing cold flooded through the tunnels. I did not know where it came from—it was not a natural thing. I made my way to a lookout hatch and peered into the night. Even my feeble eyes could not mistake what I saw. There was a great, dark cloud in the sky shot through with purple lightnings flying directly overhead. Suddenly a fog appeared; a thick fog that began to seep in. I heard some of my sentries cry out, and then there came a deafening rending and crashing. I don't mind telling you Triton, I was very afraid–still am. My stomach turned over with fright as I realized–well, here we are."

They had come to a tapestry banner hung across the tunnel. It was the entrance to her chamber. The Starwife motioned to Thomas to pass through. With some trepidation the midshipmouse did as he was bid. The Starwife waited for a moment before she followed him.

The room of the Starwife was smashed to pieces; the carved oak throne was split in two and the roof had been torn off. Everything was covered in deep frost and ice–more so than anywhere else. Thomas's feet sank deep into the biting whiteness, and he uttered little gasps as he felt them painfully tingle and turn almost blue.

He gazed fearfully about the destroyed chamber. Rubble from the roof had fallen in and filled the corners, and the shiny objects that had once dangled like the constellations were strewn about in heaps. He could hardly believe it was the same place. The violent destruction had been wanton–wrecking just for the sake of it. Thomas groaned in disbelief. But his attention was caught by a snow-covered mound at the foot of the throne. He ran over to it and knelt down. There was an ice spear stuck through its heart.

"Poor Piers," mumbled the Starwife gently, "you were loyal to the end. Forgive me." Her words caught in her throat and she stared fixedly ahead with dry, empty eyes.

Thomas turned to her, "I'm mighty sorry, ma'am," he said awkwardly, "I don't know what I can do for you, but if I can help in any way then . . ."

69

"Sorry!" she exclaimed with some of her old fire. "Sorry! Triton, you were not brought here to feel sorry for me and my folk. Look about you, you stupid seafarer–can't you see?"

Thomas was taken aback. He glanced around. Yes, there did seem to be something missing from the chamber, but he could not put his finger on what it could be. The Starwife slammed her stick down in agitation. "My Starglass, you fool!" she cried. "My Starglass has been stolen."

Sure enough, the ancient power of the Starwives was not to be found anywhere. Thomas knew that this was a great calamity, for the Starglass possessed tremendous magical forces.

The Starwife's shoulders drooped and she became tired once more. "I did not finish my tale," she said quietly. "Let me do so now." With her stick she scraped the frost from the cracked seat of her throne and lowered herself down. Sitting there, gazing at Piers's body, she took up her story.

"I realized that whatever was hiding in the mist had broken into my chamber. I heard Piers scream and then there came a deep rumbling, like a contented purr booming through the fog. The mist began to rise, and as it did so I saw something that stopped my heart beating." She raised her stick and pounded the floor in despair.

"What was it?" breathed Thomas.

With a quivering lip the Starwife shook her head and said, "There, in the dense midst of the fog, I saw the outline of a huge cat. It was as tall as a tree, and through its vast shape I could see the stars."

"I don't understand," stammered the midshipmouse. "You mean it was transparent?"

"Yes, it was not a thing of flesh and blood." She gripped her stick tightly till her crippled, swollen knuckles turned white. "I believe," she said in a quaking voice, "that it was the spirit of Jupiter."

"Green save us!"

"Let us hope that he can, Triton, for if Jupiter has indeed escaped the bonds of death and entered the living world once more, his power is beyond measure."

"And now he has your Starglass."

She hung her head. "Just so," she admitted sadly. "What he will do with it cannot be certain. He is now an Unbeast—an unquiet spirit not governed by the rules of the living. His presence in our world has thrown into confusion all the old prophecies. He has so changed the natural order of things that I do not know and cannot foresee what he may do. He is a fiend, and doubtless intends to use the Starglass for evil."

The wintry place fell into silence as Thomas digested what she had told him. It was so cold that steam curled from his nostrils and he puffed out clouds of vapor from his lips. If Jupiter had indeed returned, then he would no doubt seek out those who were responsible for his downfall. With a worried expression on his face, the midshipmouse thought of the Brown family and everyone else in the Skirtings.

He clapped his hands together in a vain attempt to warm them and said, "Ma'am, I must go and warn my friends. They should be told. If indeed that foul devil has risen from the dead, he will want revenge."

The Starwife did not appear to have heard him. Her wrinkled chin was resting on the smooth, worn handle of her walking stick. Thomas touched her gingerly on the shoulder.

"I heard you, Triton," she said gruffly. "I agree, the girl Audrey needs to be told—but not yet, stay awhile. I have duties to perform and I do not relish the thought of them." She hauled herself to her feet and all her old bones cracked in protest. "Curse this cold," she muttered, "and curse this old body of mine—it should have perished long ago. Take me back outside, Triton, if you would." Thomas took hold of her arm and led her slowly out of the freezing chamber and back through the tunnels.

The night was still grim and chill. The bright heavens shone down on the observatory hill, and the pale moon bathed everything in a stark, silver light. Since Thomas and the Starwife had left, the dead squirrels had been laid in a large ring on the icy ground. The ice spears were still stuck firmly in the bodies, as attempts to remove them had proved impossible, and the paws that touched these deadly, frozen weapons ached long after.

Many squirrels were busily carrying sacks of stores out of the tunnels and placing them some distance away in a large pile. The Starwife leaned heavily on her stick and let go of Thomas's arm as they came out into the still night air. She moved haltingly into the center of the circle of bodies and gazed at all the dead, anguished faces. From there she began to bark her instructions.

"You!" she cried, pointing to a squirrel hurrying by with an armful of parchment scrolls. "What are you doing? Leave all the histories and rubbish like that where they are. Yes, even the charts, take them all back to where you found them. None of that will be needed anymore–not by me anyway." The squirrel scurried away but she called him back crossly. "Don't go yet, lad, I have not finished. Now, when you have done that, I want you to fetch poor Piers and place him in the middle here. The Green knows he deserves that honor, worth the lot of you he was, though that isn't saying much. What are you waiting for? Get on with you."

The Starwife then turned to a group of mourners wailing hopelessly. She tottered over to them and waved her stick impatiently. "Make yourselves useful, you dozy lot," she snapped. "Go find the fuel and help with the packing. There'll be time enough for tears later."

Thomas watched her with a wry smile on his lips. He had to admire the old thing–she never spared herself. The way she doggedly went on whatever happened was an inspiration. Not long ago he had thought she had come to the end of her strength, yet here she was, bossing and ordering once more, doing what was best for her subjects whether they liked it or not.

The little he knew about squirrel ways was enough to know that they always burned their dead on funeral pyres. That now was the reason for their labors: one great bonfire to cremate all their murdered folk. No outsider had ever witnessed the ceremony before, and Thomas felt honored to be allowed to see this much.

Dry twigs and branches were brought and reverently placed between the bodies by young squirrel maidens who wore bands of silver around their brows. Then old leaves and pieces of oil-soaked cloth were put into the wood and all the squirrels began to gather round.

From the tunnel entrance came a solemn group, bearing the frozen body of Piers. They lifted him into the center of the pyre, and a hush descended.

Thomas wondered whether he ought to leave, but the Starwife caught his eye and signaled for him to remain. She hobbled around the great circle with her head lifted to the sky, and the ceremony began.

"Under the stars we are as one," she called out. "Theirs is the power of countless years. They see our grief and know our pain, yet still they shine and their light gives us hope." The Starwife paused and beckoned to the maidens, who came forward carrying small lamps. There was one for each of the dead, and each burned with a small tongue of silver flame. The maidens bowed their heads and held the lamps in outstretched paws.

The Starwife removed the amulet from around her neck. It was the symbol of her authority–a silver acorn. She held it up and the starlight flashed and gleamed over it. "From acorn to oak," she intoned gravely, "but even the mightiest of oaks shall fall. Thus do we recognize the great wheel of life and death and life once more. We surrender our departed souls under the stars and may the Green gather them to him." She kissed the amulet and at once the maidens began a soft, sad song. And as they sang they knelt by the pyre and pushed the lamps into the leaves and oil-soaked cloths.

Everyone took a step back and waited for the flames to spread. The maidens' song became louder, and all the other squirrels joined in. With his head bowed, Thomas listened respectfully; there did not seem to be any words, just a mournful tune that haunted him ever after.

The twigs and branches began to crackle and snap as the fire took hold and the whole ring was ablaze, but the flames were silver white and leaped high into the air, until a tall cone of cold light shone out on the hillside. All the squirrels took hold of each other's paws and moved slowly around the pyre. One of the maidens brought a small bag to the Starwife. It was of dark blue velvet with a solitary star design stitched onto it.

"Speed to the Green," she said, delving into the bag and bringing out a pawful of leaves and herbs. She cast them into the fire, and the flames burned a brilliant emerald and roared in Triton's ears.

Thomas was astonished. The years seemed to melt away from the ancient squirrel. He felt as though her spirit was standing before the fire, not her bent old body, and it was a proud, noble force. She appeared more regal and beautiful than anything Thomas had ever seen—an almost divine majesty with a silver acorn burning fiercely at her breast.

And then, it was over. With a final burst, the green flames dazzled the eyes and died down. The fire turned to embers and black ash flew upward. The bodies of the dead were gone, and the world seemed gray and dull. The maidens left in a graceful line, and all the other squirrels turned away. Thomas fidgeted with his hat and waited for the Starwife to join him.

She was old once more and staggered over, muttering to herself, "Never had to do that many before—we had less deaths

in the uprising." The velvet bag was still clutched in her paw as she dismissed those who tried to help her. She came before Thomas and jabbed him in the stomach with the handle of her stick. "Swear on your life you'll make sure I get a send-off like that one," she said.

Thomas frowned. "Me?" he asked. "What about your folk– they'll see to it, surely?"

The Starwife snorted. "Don't be a fool, Triton. Why do you think I let you watch? My 'folk,' as you put it, are leaving. Haven't you seen them packing and getting ready?"

"Leaving?" gasped the midshipmouse. "But why?"

"Because I've commanded it. I am sending them all away, this place is not safe anymore–nowhere is, really, but it will keep them busy while I do what I can."

Thomas began to suspect what the Starwife was up to. "You, you're not going with them then?"

The old squirrel prodded him in the ribs. "Don't be an idiot! Why do you think I brought you here in the first place? You are going to take me to the Skirtings."

Thomas spluttered in protest. "But, but . . . whatever for?"

"I have business there," she snapped. "You need to warn the Brown family, and as I cannot see what will happen in the days to come I must see the bats and ask their advice."

Thomas groaned.

CHAPTER FIVE

THE BEACON FIRE

The morning was chill and dismal. Large colorless clouds were fixed in the bleak sky, and a ghostly frost touched everything. The grass in Deptford Park was white, and the branches of the trees seemed to shiver miserably. The sun was hidden by the thick, blanketing clouds, and the light that fell on the land was dull and lifeless.

Audrey ate a small breakfast. The news about the food supply had dismayed all the mice in the house, and the elders were trying to think of possible new sources. She left the breakfast table, where Arthur was staring morosely at his empty bowl, and went out into the Hall.

A heated discussion about the food situation was taking place there. Master Oldnose vainly called for order, but everyone ignored him and thumped their tails on the floor, shouting at the tops of their voices.

"We won't last long with no grub," cried Tom Cockle.

"I don't fancy living off cabbage water for weeks on end," moaned a despondent Algy Coltfoot.

Audrey passed them by. They would find a solution without any help from her. Besides, she wanted to see the outside world and have a look at the weather. When she had returned from Fennywolde she discovered that she missed sleeping outdoors, and the atmosphere of the house now seemed oppressive and suffocating to her.

Into the kitchen she went, and quickly ran over to the little passage that led to the yard. It was still unblocked, just in case the mice were forced to go foraging should the crisis grow worse. A terrible, icy draft blew through it, and Audrey rubbed her arms as she pattered outside.

The yard looked naked and ugly; the concrete ground was covered by a thin layer of rasping ice, and the hawthorn bushes were a dangerous tangle of spiky branches and needlelike twigs. The fine strands of spider's web linking the sharp thorns were picked out by the frost and looked like shreds of phantom rags torn from a specter's robe. Beneath the hawthorns a wren pecked hungrily at the frozen earth, chipping away at the stone-hard soil for all she was worth. Audrey watched it hop here and there, trying to find softer ground.

"The poor thing," said a voice behind her. Audrey turned, startled, but it was only Oswald. He looked very comical in his scarf with the matching hat and mittens.

"It's going to be a hard winter," predicted Oswald grimly.

Audrey agreed. She usually looked forward to the long winter nights with the rushing wind howling around the house and layers of beautiful, soft snow covering the rooftops, transforming them into fairy-tale mountains. It was nice to hear the bitter weather beating against the walls while she was cozy in her bed or sitting in front of a fire listening to tales with a bowl of hot milk steaming in her paws. She fondly remembered other winters when her father was alive and how he would put his comforting arm around her as she snuggled next to him and dozed dreamily. In those days she thought that nothing in the world could harm her, because he was there, to protect and look after the family.

Oswald huddled in his scarf and blew through his chattering teeth. Audrey shook herself out of her thoughts and considered the present weather. It was not like previous winters; there was no beauty in it—even the frost was unlovely. Gone were the delicate lace patterns on the windows. Only a phantom grayness lay over the yard, and the world looked dead and smothered.

"Let's go back inside," she suggested, and Oswald readily agreed.

When they were in the kitchen once more, a confused babbling reached their ears. It came from the Hall, and many voices were raised in curious exclamations.

"What can be going on?" asked Oswald, scurrying over the linoleum to find out. Audrey ran after him and they helped each other up the step into the Hall. There the discussion had broken up, and all the mice were gathered around the cellar door.

Oswald glanced at Audrey with a puzzled expression on his white face. Few in the Skirtings ever ventured near the cellar; the Grill was down there, and beyond were the sewers, which had once been Jupiter's terrifying realm. All the mice feared the cellar. Nervously, Oswald approached the crowd and fiddled with his scarf.

A hearty voice boomed from behind the cellar door. "Budge up mates, make room for us there!" It was Thomas Triton.

Oswald sighed thankfully, but his relief turned to surprise when a different voice added sternly, "Out of my way, you stupid mice!"

Audrey clutched her paws and stepped back in fear—she knew who that was and she hated her. "What's going on?" Oswald asked Algy.

"It's Mr. Triton," the mouse replied with round, excited eyes. "He's brought the queen of the squirrels to visit us."

Thomas edged past the cellar door and led the old squirrel after him. It had taken a long time to bring her through the sewers from Greenwich. It was the first time in many long years that the Starwife had left the observatory, and her old legs were not used to it. She had limped along, cursing her crippled body and continually stopping to rest. When they had come to the Grill she had run her arthritic fingers over the ornate metal and shuddered. "The spells on this were strong," she had said, wiping her paw disgustedly. "The iron remembers its Lord, and now that he has returned, perhaps the dark magic will awake."

Now she blinked in the light of the Hall and peered around at all the expectant, curious faces trained on her.

"What are you staring at?" she said haughtily. "Haven't you ever seen a squirrel before?"

Actually, the mice hadn't, and all wanted a good look. They elbowed each other for a better view and stared quite rudely with their mouths open.

The Starwife slammed her stick down. "Have you nothing better to do, you idiots?" she cried. "Out of my way there," and she swung her stick before her. The mice fell back in surprise and cleared a path. Tom Cockle was not fast enough, and the old squirrel's walking stick caught him sharply on the shin. He hopped away, howling.

The Starwife made her way through the crowd and looked at the stairs vexedly. "More of them," she muttered, rubbing her aching back.

Just then Master Oldnose came forward to welcome her. "Greetings," he said, beaming from ear to ear, "what an honor, to have the great Starwife herself in our midst."

She squinted at him and sniffed. "You must be Oldnose, I've heard about you." He bowed, greatly flattered, and smiled even wider until she added, "It's true—you are a daft, pompous old nibbler whose opinion of himself is greater than his brain." The

Starwife left him opening and closing his mouth like a goldfish and walked over to Audrey, whom she had just noticed slowly backing away and heading for home.

"Stay there, girl," the old squirrel snapped, "don't pout, it spoils your looks." She stood in front of Audrey and tapped her stick thoughtfully. "I've heard about Fennywolde," she said. "You must tell me what happened in detail later." Audrey nodded respectfully, but the Starwife had turned away and was looking for Thomas. "Where's that old fool of a sailor got to?" she grumbled irritably.

The midshipmouse had slipped in to see Audrey's mother, and the two of them now came out of the Browns' home. Gwen looked at the squirrel steadily–she had not forgiven her for sending Audrey away. "Hello," she said politely but without her usual warmth, "can we do anything for you?"

"Don't worry," the Starwife reassured her, "I'm not going to steal your daughter, but you can help me–could I have a seat, please? I think my legs will give way if I don't sit down soon."

Gwen Brown called for Arthur to bring out a stool. By this time every mouse in the house had gathered in the Hall to see the unusual visitor. Those snobs from the Landings crept down the stairs and gawked unashamedly. The Raddle sisters took their usual place on the second step and peered around the banister rails, nudging each other and tittering to themselves. Oswald's mother came out but could not get through the throng to talk to Mrs. Brown and introduce herself to the Starwife–it really was most infuriating, and she scolded her husband for not calling her out sooner. Arthur came out carrying a stool and took it to the Starwife. She thanked him and eased herself down. A hush fell. Apart from the sound of Mrs. Chitter's gossiping, everyone grew silent; evidently the squirrel was going to address them. The Starwife surveyed the mice and pounded the floor with her stick. Mrs. Chitter jumped and stopped prattling.

"Mice of Deptford," the squirrel began, "I bring grave news. I believe that your greatest enemy, Jupiter, has returned from the other side."

For a second there was a stunned silence, then uproar, with everyone talking at once. "Pooh!" said Mrs. Chitter. "Rubbish," said Tom Cockle, laughing. Audrey said nothing. A shadow fell over her and over everyone who had been in the altar chamber when the Lord of the Sewers fell to his doom. Audrey, Arthur, Mrs. Brown, Thomas, and Oswald remained silent and waited for the Starwife to continue.

"Enough!" she shouted angrily. "Stop this at once. Dare you doubt my words? Listen, the world is weeping, nature is plagued by a dark spirit, unleashed from the darkness of beyond. In life he was called Jupiter–now he is a phantom, an Unbeast more powerful than anything this troubled world has ever known. You pathetic, weedling, idiotic creatures cannot imagine the forces this abomination controls, now that he has my Starglass."

Audrey gasped, and the rest of the mice sensed the urgency and fear in the squirrel's voice. Slowly they began to believe her and they murmured to each other in worried whispers.

"What are we to do?" wailed Biddy Cockle hysterically.

"I do not know," the Starwife replied, shaking her head. "Without my Starglass I cannot see how we may rid the world of this black fiend. How does one destroy that which has already been destroyed? Jupiter is dead, yet still he torments us. That is the problem. We cannot kill what is no longer alive."

"But then we are lost," stammered Master Oldnose. "It is hopeless."

The Starwife raised her stick to quell the rising panic. "Perhaps not," she said. "My powers are gone, yet I am not the only one so gifted–others have the ability to see into the future and know the secrets it jealously guards."

"You mean the bats?" asked Arthur suddenly.

"I do indeed," she announced. "I have come from Greenwich to have an audience with the bats who live in the attic here. They will be able to tell me all I need to know, and together we may come up with a solution." She paused. Everyone was groaning with despair. The Starwife pounded her stick impatiently. "What is wrong?" she demanded.

"The bats have gone," Gwen replied. "They abandoned us two nights ago! I do not think there is a single one left in Deptford."

The Starwife stared at her as though she were mad, "Then we *are* lost," she murmured. "Without their aid all shall perish." Her last hope was crushed, and she bowed her head in defeat.

The Raddle sisters began to weep, and several others joined them. Audrey wondered what would happen. Jupiter would surely seek her out and get his revenge. To her astonishment she did not feel afraid, and she found herself scowling rather than crying. It was a strange mood, which she did not understand. She felt that her fate was bound up with that of Jupiter and curiously enough with that of the Starwife also. She looked at the squirrel seated before her and felt very sorry for her. Whatever hatred she once had for the creature was swept away by a need to ease her cares.

Audrey knelt down and took hold of the Starwife's paws. "Don't worry," she said, "something will happen. Trust in the Green Mouse–that's what my father always used to say."

The Starwife looked at her with those milky eyes and stroked her hair. "Child," she said, "it is winter and the Green Mouse sleeps. Only when spring comes will he awake." She shook her head sorrowfully. "And I do not think spring will ever come again."

"You don't know that," Audrey insisted. "Only the bats know now what will happen. If only we could get a message to them, I'm sure they'd help."

At her words the squirrel's ears quivered and she sat bolt

upright on the stool. "Of course," she cried, clapping her paws together excitedly, "you excellent child. Where were my wits? I am too old for this, my time is truly over if I cannot remember squirrel history. Triton, help me to my feet at once. There is little time."

"What are you going to do?" asked Audrey.

"I shall summon the bats," declared the Starwife exultantly. "I am forgetting much. A beacon fire was used to call them very long ago when our colony at Greenwich was in its direst need. The bats came then—let us pray it works a second time." She glared around at all the confused mice and barked out her orders. "You over there, stop standing like a dummy and fetch some wood—you, go find some rope—you, just get out of my sight. I don't like your face."

The rest of the morning was spent constructing the beacon fire. This was not as easy as it sounded, because the Starwife ordered that it be built on the roof. Arthur and Thomas Triton climbed up inside the wall cavity and hopped along the rafters to where Arthur had once spoken with Orfeo and Eldritch—the place seemed empty without them. The two mice clambered up the fallen beams and crawled out of the hole in the roof. It was terribly cold and windy up there, but somehow they managed to build a small platform out of broken slates and blocks of wood.

They lowered a rope down the wall cavity to where Algy Coltfoot was waiting with bundles of collected twigs. He tied them to the end and gave it two sharp tugs. The rope and the twigs jerked upward and disappeared into the darkness. When several of these bundles had been hauled up, Thomas and Arthur sat with their backs against the chimneys, puffing and rubbing their chapped paws.

From out of the cavity hole, the face of Master Oldnose appeared. He cleared his throat and told them that the Starwife was getting impatient in the Hall and wanted to come up.

Thomas was amused. There was no way the old squirrel could climb up to the attic, and he thought Master Oldnose was pulling his leg until a faint voice called his name from below.

At the bottom of the long drop to the Skirtings the Starwife shouted crossly up at the midshipmouse and told him to make a cradle at the end of the rope. Then she sent several mice up to help him. Algy, Mr. Cockle, and Reggie and Bart from the Landings scrambled up as fast as they could.

After a while a strange triangle descended from above. The end of the rope had been tied to a piece of wood just big enough to sit on and then knotted a little way above that to form a kind of swing. It was lowered gently to the ground, where the Starwife struggled into it. Sitting on the wooden seat and still clutching her stick, she grasped the rope with her paws and called to be pulled up.

In the attic the mice took the strain and heaved on the rope. Slowly the Starwife was raised, ascending through the wall space, using her stick to stop herself bumping into the bricks. She seemed to be quite enjoying herself and hummed an ancient squirrel tune in the dark. Eventually she reached the attic and was helped out onto the roof.

The afternoon came and wore on, and the leaden sky began to turn black. Not content with waiting below, all the other mice wanted to know what was happening, so the remaining husbands climbed up, and their wives took turns in the Starwife's cradle. In the end, everyone was up in the attic or standing precariously on the roof, where the Starwife began to tie the twigs into a pyramid shape.

When the framework had been made, the squirrel searched in the velvet bag she had brought from Greenwich. "Good," she muttered, "I have all I need." Clutching the bag close to her, the Starwife raised her head and told everyone, "We shall not light the beacon till night falls; it will not be long."

Audrey was sitting next to her mother. She closed her eyes

against the blustering wind and huddled closer to Gwen. Oswald was nearby and Mrs. Chitter was fussing with his scarf, "Don't you get a chill like that last one," she clucked.

Arthur gazed at the world in astonishment. When he had been in Fennywolde he had climbed the cornstalks and enjoyed the feeling of being high above the ground, but that was nothing compared to this. He did not feel the cold as he was too absorbed in the panoramic views. In the distance he could see the vague blur of the city, and not too far away the tower of St. Nicholas's church rose between the buildings. Beyond that . . . Arthur put a paw over his eyes. The tall chimney of Deptford Power Station loomed out of a strange white mist. He frowned, scratched his head, and shivered, but not because of the weather; there was something uncanny about that place. Arthur fancied that he was being watched–he did not like it and tried to look away, but the power station fascinated him. It seemed to have a presence–he could almost hear it breathing and waiting. Arthur shivered a second time.

The short winter day was drawing to a close. Deep shadows gathered under the surrounding houses, and street lamps clicked and buzzed as they blinked on. The dusk fell, and the mice on the roof had to strain their eyes to see each other.

"It is time," said the dim shape of the Starwife. For an instant Thomas's face was illuminated as he struck a light from his tinderbox. He passed it to the squirrel and she bent over the beacon and waited patiently for it to catch.

The twigs kindled and a warm yellow glow lit the circle of mice, who drew instinctively closer to the welcome flames.

The Starwife pulled from her bag a glass vial containing a dark red syrup, the juice of special berries. She sprinkled it over the fire and at once it spat and sparks flew out. The mice gasped and fell back in alarm. The flames then turned a rich, deep purple and tapered high over the rooftops.

"Now, we wait," said the Starwife, crouching down.

The beacon blazed furiously, yet the flames did not seem to be burning the wood. They remained in its fierce heart, untouched by the heat. It was the tallest fire the mice had ever seen, a slender, violet beam reaching up into the heavens.

The beacon was seen by many; far away, resting for the night beneath a hedge, the Starwife's subjects looked up and wondered, pigeons ruffled in their roosts, a fox slinking up to a dustbin paused and raised his brows. From Deptford Power Station there came a deep rumbling purr.

On the roof, everyone waited anxiously. All eyes were trained on the sky, searching for the flutter of bat wings. The Starwife did not move. Her paws rested on her knees, and before the flames her silvery fur shone like a brilliant amethyst. She stared silently into the fire.

The hours dragged slowly by. The mice rubbed their sore eyes and warmed their paws. The slates of the roof were cold and terribly uncomfortable. Some mice gave up looking for the bats and mumbled in disappointment.

Audrey lay on her back gazing upward. She could see only the black sky with the livid finger of flame stretching above her.

Arthur had stopped looking for the bats long ago and now concentrated his attention on the mist around the power station. Now and then he thought he saw a faint blue flickering glow in there—perhaps it was his imagination, but he continued to watch the distant building suspiciously.

Thomas Triton thought of the rum he had left unfinished in his quarters. He stroked his whiskers slowly, and his mind wandered down the sea lanes of his youth—he coughed and hid his face quickly.

The beacon spluttered and the tall fire shrank and grew yellow. The flames crackled and consumed the twigs greedily. The Starwife sighed and a tear fell from her eyes. "They do not come," she whispered hoarsely. "We are alone and must die."

The mice got to their feet and began to file along to the hole in the roof.

Oswald was the only one still watching the blank, dark sky. His mittened paws swept over his cold, pink nose. "If only the bats had come." He sighed longingly.

"Oswald, Oswald," called his mother, "the show's over now dear, come inside at once."

Reluctantly the albino had to look away from the sky as he cautiously got to his feet and followed his mother. Then, just as he lowered himself down into the attic, he lifted his face one last time and held his breath incredulously. There, in the faint distance were two dark shapes flying toward the house.

"Look, look!" yelled Oswald, jumping up and down. "The bats are coming, the bats are coming!"

The few mice who were left outside peered into the sky. Gradually, their eyes being less sensitive than Oswald's, they discerned the flitting shapes high in the air.

"He's right," shouted Audrey joyously, "they really are coming."

A chorus of approval broke out spontaneously as the mice cheered the bats and applauded the cleverness of the Starwife. The old squirrel merely nodded and lightly touched her silver amulet in gratitude.

Those who had disappeared into the attic now popped their heads out and hoisted themselves onto the roof once more.

"Triton," chirped the Starwife, "help me to my feet, I think my bones have set. I cannot greet our cousins in such a manner. That's better, aahh." Her back creaked as she stood with the midshipmouse's help.

By now the bats were well in view. The orange light of the street lamps lit them from beneath, and it was Arthur who recognized them. "It's Orfeo and Eldritch," he piped up, as he waved to the newcomers.

"Welcome, you voyagers of the twilight," called the Starwife solemnly.

The two creatures alighted daintily on the roof tiles and wrapped their leathery wings about themselves as though they were cloaks. Orfeo raised his foxy face and looked down his long nose at the Starwife. "By what right does the Handmaiden of Orion summon us?" he demanded haughtily. "Was the debt our ancestors once owed to her forebears not paid long ago?" He waited for an answer.

The Starwife shook her stick at him bad temperedly. "Don't you start any of that malarky with me, young lad, this has nothing to do with what happened then, and well you know it. I asked you here because of Jupiter."

Orfeo snorted and spread his wings. "Beware the ear that whispers, did we not tell the fat one?" he pointed accusingly at Arthur and allowed his brother to continue.

Eldritch moved his noble head and shifted his position. "Old dame of the night," he said to the Starwife, "you did not 'ask' us here, you sought to summon, and by an old trick of one of your venerable predecessors. She was wilier than you and her power greater—for do I not see the truth here? You have lost your trinket, that secret you kept hidden under oak has been stolen."

"Hah," scoffed Orfeo joining in, "what a merry jest this is, the queenly one bereft of her magic devices—what misfortune!" And he laughed out loud. "No more tricks from her, no longer does she sit enthroned, her realm is ended."

The Starwife endured their jibes and hateful comments without saying anything, but Audrey could not. This was the first time she had heard the bats speak, and she found them just as intolerably rude as she had once found the Starwife.

She pushed forward and interrupted their mocking voices. "Oh, very funny," she said. "Just stop it, it isn't fair to pick on her—why are you so cruel? She hasn't done anything to you."

The bats glared at the mouse who had dared to speak up.

Orfeo hid his mouth behind his wings and murmured, "She has a champion."

"Enough," said the Starwife at last. "You have had your fun. By all means laugh at me—I am nothing, just an old squirrel who grew too proud and thought she was invincible. I am still paying for my mistakes. Do not make any of your own to regret."

The bats calmed down and became serious. "Did you think we were ignorant of the Unbeast?" asked Eldritch. "We knew He had returned in spectral form, which is why all our brethren are gathered together at this very moment in the greatest council ever held in our long history."

"The road is dark, Starwife," warned Orfeo somberly. "There are paths we cannot see; the future is closed to us also, yet a solution must be found. The fiend must be dispatched, and soon."

The Starwife listened to them and a determined expression crept over her wrinkled face. "Very well," she said, when they had finished. "I had hoped you could advise me, but it would seem you are as powerless as I." She could not resist letting slip a quick, smug smile. "It would seem we must join forces properly."

The bats looked at each other. "She cannot mean . . . " spluttered Orfeo.

"I fear she does." His brother laughed raucously. "She really expects us to carry her to our meeting." He prodded the squirrel with his wings. "You do, don't you?"

"I see nothing amusing in the suggestion," she replied acidly. "Surely it is the only thing we can do—with my knowledge added to yours we might stand a chance."

Eldritch wiped the tears from his eyes and shook his head, "Apologies, dear, whimsical madam, but no, we are not going to take you to our council, that is not what we had in mind—unless . . ." The Starwife raised her eyebrows expectantly.

"Unless . . . you were the one who saw our coming before all others."

"What nonsense is this?" she asked. "The albino marked you first, but what does that signify?"

"My dear lady," they cried together, "it means that Master Pink Eyes is to be our honored guest at the council." The bats turned their attention on Oswald, who gulped and bit his mittens.

"Do you think it was the beacon that drew us hither?" Orfeo asked. "We knew who was behind it: your tricks do not work on us any more, ancient crone, but you did enough to bring the white one up to the roof. *He* is the one we sought, he is the last link. We need him at our council, not you."

Oswald stammered and the Starwife fumed. She cursed the bats and their prophecies, incensed that a dithering albino runt should be chosen to attend the great meeting instead of her. "You idiots!" she stormed furiously.

But they were not listening. The bats sidled up to Oswald and wrapped their wings about him. "This is the one," they crooned. "Come, fly with us, into the night air, Master Pink Eyes, soar up and forget your feet have ever touched the soil."

"I . . . I," Oswald gabbled idiotically in disbelief, "I don't know . . ."

Mrs. Chitter had been listening to the proceedings with mounting concern. Now she could bear it no longer and tried to pull her son away. "Just you leave my boy alone, you nasty creatures," she told them. "Come here Oswald, leave them be, they'll go away and leave you alone."

Oswald was yanked by the scarf as his mother tried to drag him from the bats. With his head in a whirl he found himself shouting, "Yes, yes I'll go with you." Mrs. Chitter squealed and collapsed into her husband's arms.

"Don't worry, Mother," Oswald cried, as the bats flew up and lowered their feet for him to take hold of. He stretched out his arms and tried to catch one of the dangling legs, but it was no good in his mittens, so he pulled them off with his teeth and tried once more.

"Oh my," he breathed as his feet left the tiles. "Goodness me," was all he could find to say as the roof receded below him.

"Good-bye, son," called his father.

"Aaagghh!" wailed his mother.

"See you soon." Arthur waved cheerfully.

The rooftops sailed by as Oswald and the bats soared higher and higher into the black night. The albino held onto their feet tightly and wondered if he had done the right thing, but it was too late to turn back, and the glittering sight of the city sprawled ahead of him.

"This is it," he said to himself, "a real adventure all my own." Oswald stared down; they were very high now, and the houses looked like matchboxes. He suddenly felt terribly sick. "Oh dear," he thought, "what have I got myself into?"

CHAPTER SIX

THE BOOK OF HRETHEL

The biting wind cut right through Oswald's fur, and his scarf thrashed and flapped wildly about. A sudden icy gust snatched and tore the woolen hat from his head. He cried out as he saw it sail far away into the night.

"My hat," he moaned as he felt his large, naked ears throb with the cold.

The bats showed no sign that they had noticed. They were talking to each other in their secret tongue which, to the albino, sounded like a mixed-up jumble of high-pitched squeaks. He was beginning to feel quite alone, and thoroughly regretted his rashness.

The world was much larger than he had ever imagined. It twinkled and glittered below—a vast sprawl of tiny lights stretching in every direction, as far as his sensitive eyes could see. The great River Thames wound darkly around the renovated wharves and disappeared beneath slender bridges like a path of glass. The glow of the city danced brightly over its still surface, and the brilliant white stars reflected there shone like gleaming diamonds set in the riverbed.

"What think you of the night, Master Pink Eyes?" asked Orfeo out of the blue.

"It's beautiful," replied Oswald, gazing around breathlessly.

"He does not hear the music," said Eldritch to his brother. "Unlike his cousin the witch husband, the night speaks not to him."

"Nor shall it speak to any of us if the Unbeast remains in the world," added Orfeo. "Let us hurry to the council."

They flew over the river and made for a grand, domed building, and Oswald saw that the sky around it was crowded with dark winged shapes. The air was thick with bats all fluttering about the great dome.

"What is that place?" asked Oswald curiously.

"Yonder is the divine hall of the many bat guilds," replied Eldritch importantly. "For ages uncounted have we met there in times of peril, though never has the danger been greater than now."

They circled the huge dome three times and called in their own language to the thousands of other bats. Dangling below, Oswald could not help feeling that they were talking about him. Several black shapes drew near, and bright, alarming eyes stared for a moment at the albino and then were gone. Their faces were incredibly ugly and as different from Orfeo and Eldritch as it was possible to be. The strange bats weaved around the gold cross on the top of the building, then came back and spoke to each other in harsh voices. A wide, nostriled snout jabbed the mouse's stomach and snuffled up to his face. Oswald closed his eyes in disgust and his skin crawled at the touch of that horrible wet nose, but he knew he was being inspected and so endured it. These were the bat guards, a fierce squadron who patroled the air space, making sure no intruders or spies could get into the council.

"Stay very still, White One," whispered Orfeo hastily. "If you move suddenly they will cast you down."

Oswald bit his lip and tried not to move as the brute sniffed his head. But the slimy bat slobber ran down into his ears and the mouse was tormented with a desperate urge to wipe it off and shoo the ugly thing away.

He must have passed the test, for at that moment the guard plummeted down and Orfeo and Eldritch followed. Oswald rubbed his ear on his arm and grimaced. He hoped there would be no more guards like that.

They spiraled down, past mighty pillars and figures carved in stone. Oswald saw the guard in front swoop sharply up and then alight on a wide balcony that ran all the way around the base of the dome.

"Prepare yourself, Master Pink Eyes," cried Orfeo, "your lofty journey is at an end." With their wings outstretched they glided onto the balcony and dropped the mouse gently down.

The guard gave Oswald a black look and with hunched wings marched over to a fissure in the stonework. He grunted and motioned for the mouse to crawl through. Eldritch, however, stepped in and said softly, "Do not fear, White One, I shall pass through first and my brother after you. We are safe now." He disappeared into the gap and Oswald followed him.

Through a narrow space they squeezed, and Oswald heard Orfeo say something to the guard before he joined them. The way was difficult, and once or twice the mouse thought he had gotten stuck, but the thought of staying in that dark place forever forced him on grimly.

Eventually the passage gave way to the inside of the dome. It was the most magnificent sight Oswald had ever witnessed; the place was cavernous. Below the gallery on which he stood were eight immense arches richly decorated with mosaics of angels, bordered with blazing gold. In the niches between the high windows there were enormous sculptures of saints with their fingers raised in blessing, and overhead were rich paintings. Yet all around, clinging to the gilded carvings, huddled in the shadows of the great, hanging from the rails and sitting beneath the statues were thousands upon thousands of bats. They were everywhere: the beautiful walls were absolutely covered in furry bodies, and hushed whispers echoed around like an angry sea crashing against cliffs, rising and falling like the sound of the tide.

Oswald was amazed. The bats filled the building, clustered on every available foothold and ledge. Orfeo raised his voice and called solemnly, "He is here, the pale one has arrived."

The clamor rose immediately as the assembled bats all squeaked shrilly. Oswald had to put his fingers in his ears because the noise threatened to pierce the drums. Some of the bats began to cry out in the common tongue, "He is here, he is here," and others cried, "Show him to us, where is he?"

"Master Pink Eyes," said Eldritch, "we must show you to our brethen. All wish to see you, come." The bat flew up and Oswald reached for his feet once more. Slowly they ascended and Eldritch circled inside the dome so that everyone could get a good look at the mouse. Keen, curious eyes gleamed steadily at Oswald, who did his share of staring. Somber voices whispered, and proud heads nodded as the mouse flew by.

Eldritch flew higher and he bowed his head reverently. Before him was a line of four ancient, white-haired bats. Their wings were tattered with age and their tall ears drooped; their brows were crossed by a hundred wrinkles, yet their eyes were as sharp and as disconcertingly bright as ever they had been.

Eldritch hovered in front of them and greeted each one, "Hail to thee Ohthere, Lord of the Twilight; hail Heardred, Keeper of the Hidden Ways; hail Ingeld, Consort of the Lady; and hail Ashmere, Wisest of all Councillors."

The venerable bats welcomed him, "Salutations Eldritch," said the one called Heardred. "You have done well." His voice was like the rustle of leaves, and he extended a flimsy, papery wing to Oswald. "So this is the pink-eyed one whose coming was foreseen long ago."

Another of the old bats coughed and peered at the albino with a sneer on his face. "He is too sickly a specimen," said Ohthere. "He will never do—I agree with Ingeld and fear Ashmere is mistaken in this."

Oswald scowled—he did not like to be called sickly. He decided it was time to say something. "Excuse me," he piped up, but the ancient bats ignored this and continued discussing him as if he were not there.

"I say he will not succeed," remarked the one called Ingeld. "We cannot rely on those outside our brotherhood. Folly I have called it and folly it remains."

"Peace," said Heardred. "The runt has been chosen—there is nothing we can do."

Oswald scowled again, and this time positively shouted, "Excuse me!"

The row of bats looked up in surprise and all around, thousands of voices were raised in scorn, "Did he say that?" they asked, scandalized. "The cheeky whelp!" They beat their wings together demonstratively. "Be still, peasant," they hissed.

Ashmere, the only councillor who had not yet spoken, studied the mouse carefully and the shadow of a smile crept over his bearded face. "Master White Skin," he said gently, "forgive my brothers. It is their way to talk thus and no ill was intended. You must remember, it is a long time since we have spoken to an outsider." He opened his wings and made a space beside him. "Come," he said, "sit here and listen to our council—for you are important in our designs." Eldritch heaved a sigh of relief as he deposited Oswald next to Ashmere, but before he flew back to Orfeo he gave the mouse a reassuring wink.

Oswald was terribly nervous. Here he was at the most important meeting ever held, to discuss the worst foe the world had ever known, with the greatest number of bats anyone had ever seen. He felt extremely small and alone. What use would he be? He looked at the four proud elders and his heart quailed. What an experience this was! If only Arthur were here or his friend Piccadilly–they wouldn't be afraid like he was.

"Master runt," said Ingeld abruptly, and Oswald quickly gathered his wits, "you know the reason for this meeting?"

"I think so," the mouse replied shyly. "It's because of *him*, isn't it? You're going to think of a way to get rid of him."

The elders chuckled to each other and shook their heads. "Get rid, you say," began Heardred, amused, "if that were only possible–but you of all creatures should know that that is impossible. Were you not present at Jupiter's death? Did you not think then that he was gone forever? His spirit is far too great for us in this age to deal with. Long ago our ancestors had the cunning, but we do not. Many skills have been forgotten and neglected, and the crafts we practiced in the dark years have no place in the world of today." He hung his grizzled head sadly.

"Yet Jupiter was a creature of the old times," said Ashmere. "He lengthened his life through secret arts and endured long centuries hidden in the blackness under Deptford. Only by the old ways can his spirit be quashed and banished forever to the furthest reaches of the Pit."

"That is only your belief," interrupted Ingeld. "We cannot be certain. Heardred has said that the Hidden Ways are closed to us, we cannot know how this unholy spirit may be dispatched."

Ashmere turned to Oswald and explained, "The dilemma is this, White One: we have tried to glimpse the future to see what will befall us, yet we cannot."

"That is why we summoned all our kin to this council," said Ohthere. "For two nights we have joined our powers and attempted to project our souls beyond these desperate hours, but it has proved futile."

"But why can't you see what will happen?" asked Oswald.

99

"Because there is no future to see," replied Heardred darkly. "Jupiter is trapping the world in an eternal winter. There will be no more seasons, no spring or summer to count the days by and break down the years; he is freezing everything and locking us into eternal blackness. There will be no future for anything: fish, flesh, feathers, or fur–all will end."

"And soon," nodded Ohthere, "for the tally of remaining days is short–we have foreseen that much."

"But this is dreadful," cried Oswald miserably. "If this is the end of everything I want to be with my friends and family–why have you brought me here?"

"Because of the hope of Ashmere," answered Ingeld, stretching himself and sniffing affectedly. "Personally, I wish it to be known that I do not agree with his theory."

"We are all aware of that," said Heardred reproachfully, and a strange look passed between them as though this was a sore subject that had been fiercely debated.

Ashmere put his wing around Oswald and scratched his beard thoughtfully. "It is difficult to describe to the uninitiated, but I shall try to explain." He cleared his throat and began, "When I was young a vision came unbidden to me. It is usual amongst our kind to send our spirits forward through time to see the future, but this did not happen then. I was flying through the velvet night and the song was sad and mournful, when I saw before me a snow-covered land and heard the Lady's voice tell me that a mouse with pink eyes would save all. It was the only time I have heard her, and never have I forgotten it. Then news came of Jupiter's downfall and we saw him rise again and grow mighty. I think you are the one who can stop him."

Oswald felt faint. He did not like the direction things were taking. "But I'm not brave," he protested. "I can't fight or anything like that."

"It will not be anything like that," assured Ingeld sourly.

Heardred shuffled forward, rubbing his wings together. "Whatever happens," he said, "it must be soon–there is little time left to us. It will not be long before Jupiter tries to use the squirrel queen's Starglass and comes into his full power. Our blow must be before then."

"But what am I to do?" asked Oswald. He was terrified at the thought of confronting Jupiter.

"Let Ashmere tell him," sniped Ingeld. "It is his foolish hope."

Ashmere lowered his voice and spoke kindly to Oswald. "I have said that the old ways are needed to deal with the foul spirit, and that none here have the skill or learning to exorcise him. Listen White One. Beneath this building there is a chamber where our forefathers kept their ancient writings in a book of lore. There you will find spells and prophecies from long ago; bring it to us and . . . "

"Just a minute," broke in Oswald, "what do you mean I will find?"

"Simple runt!" cried Ingeld impatiently. "Your first task is to venture down through the narrow, blackened ways; we are not made for such crawling and groping–that is the rodents' lot."

"Please," implored Ashmere, "we cannot make you, but for the sake of all creation you must find the spells that will banish Jupiter forever."

Oswald looked into Ashmere's eyes. They were anxious and pleading, and he took courage from the confidence this ancient bat had in him. "Very well," he said meekly, "I shall go and find your book."

Ashmere turned to the thousands of other bats and called out, "He will go! The pink-eyed one has accepted." Their cheers were tumultuous and roared around the dome. Oswald blushed and looked at his feet with embarrassment.

"It will fail," muttered Ingeld, shaking his head bitterly. "The Consort of the Lady knows this folly will end in disaster— we cannot escape our doom." But no one heard him, and he pulled his head into his wings.

"Go now," said Ashmere quickly, "for all time is precious— we dare not waste any more." He turned to face the gallery and gave three sharp whistling squeaks. "The ones who brought you hither shall take you down into the crypt of this place, but you must find the Book of Hrethel on your own. Take care, and may the grace of the Lady go with you."

Two figures rose from the dark mass of bats and fluttered over to them. It was Orfeo and Eldritch. They approached the ledge of the elders and flew above the mouse.

"Take him below and show him the entrance to the chamber," Heardred instructed them.

"Come, Master Pink Eyes." Orfeo laughed. "Fly with us once more."

Oswald took hold of their feet and they lifted him from the ledge. The elders grimly watched them flit around the dome and descend to the floor hundreds of yards below.

Down they went, past the gilded keystones of the arches and the carved wooden cherubs frolicking around the splendid organ case. Oswald felt he could spend a whole week there admiring everything, but they swooped between two mighty columns and landed on the cold marble floor.

"This way," said Eldritch, hopping over to a great wooden door and popping inside. Beyond was a steep stairway, leading down into complete darkness. The two bats waited for Oswald and said to him, "In yonder crypt there is no light, you will stumble and fall there."

"Master Pink Eyes," said Orfeo seriously, "my brother and I have decided to bestow upon you the gift of bat sight—for seven hours only you will see all as we do. You shall have the power to 'see in the dark' as your folk would put it—yet that will not be

102

the limit of the gift, for if you accept the vision of us moon riders then you must prepare yourself for anything that comes
unbidden to you."

"Not lightly is this granted," Eldritch added, "for rarely do
we allow the outsider into our secret, shaded world, and you
have seen so much already, White One."

"Yet the actions we take this night will shape the lives of
everyone," said Orfeo. "Let us begin if the mouse is willing–I
shall be the lender."

Oswald wondered excitedly what it would be like to be able
to see as a bat. The night would no longer hold any fear for him,
he would be able to pierce the shadows and lift the veil of darkness. "Yes, I'll accept," he said breathlessly.

"So be it," they replied.

The bats circled around him and raised their wings. Orfeo
lifted his head and began to chant strange words, and a crown
of moonlight seemed to settle on his brow. At first Oswald
thought it was a trick of the light falling through the great doorway, but then a golden gleam formed in the bat's eyes. It grew
larger and brighter, until they blazed and illuminated the entire
stairway with their brilliance.

"Oh my!" exclaimed Oswald wondrously. He was delighted
to see bat magic. Master Oldnose had often told old tales in
which the bats were far more magical than they are now.

"Take the gift," Eldritch's voice whispered in his ear.

The mouse put out a trembling paw and touched Orfeo's
glowing face. The light that poured from his eyes was suddenly sucked along Oswald's arm, bristling his fur as it went, then
up into his head. For a second his ears were ringed with fire
and sparks crackled beneath his eyebrows, then it was over,
and all light was extinguished as if nothing had happened.

"What do you see?" asked Eldritch softly.

Oswald blinked, his eyes watered and he rubbed them.
Slowly he looked around. What a difference there was. The

world was now a silvery gray, yet he could see everything quite clearly. There was Eldritch smiling at him and there was Orfeo. He appeared tired and worn; the granting of the gift had obviously taken a lot out of him. As Oswald peered around he discovered that nothing could escape his sight. He saw spiders spinning silken webs high above, teasing the sticky strands out of their bodies with their hairy legs. That was not all. To his amazement he found that if he concentrated hard enough the walls seemed to melt away and he could see into the next room, even outside. The mouse stared up, and the rafters, joists, stones, plaster, and lead dissolved, and he saw the bat guards patroling the sky. Oswald gazed to the south and the rooftops zoomed by. Over the river, through the houses, out to Deptford he bent his thoughts, and the old empty house swelled up before him. Then down into the Skirtings, where the Starwife was talking to Audrey, and his mother was scolding his father, and then out again, over the tower blocks, passing through the church, until the power station loomed ahead, cloaked in mist, and two enormous, evil eyes stared straight at him. . . .

"Enough!" cried Orfeo, gasping. "I shall perish." He had slumped to the floor, exhausted.

"What have I done?" asked Oswald, snapping his mind back beside the two bats.

Eldritch answered for his ailing brother. "You go too fast," he said. "The gift has been borrowed only. Orfeo has lent his sight to you and much of his strength also—you must be careful not to spend it wantonly and without purpose. Discipline the vision and use it like your own. Do not let it consume and rule you; keep it under control or it will run away with you and my brother will die."

"I'm sorry," said Oswald hurriedly. "I never realized, I thought it was magic and could do anything."

"This is . . . but . . . an exchange," Orfeo wheezed painfully, "a talent we . . . possess. The true magic lies in the old

104

chamber of Hrethel beneath the stones of this . . . building."

"Orfeo is right," Eldritch said briskly. "We waste time! My brother shall remain here—he will be no use to us down there. He will be as blind as a mouse. Come."

Oswald said farewell to Orfeo and thanked him for the gift, then he began the long climb down the steps. He tried very hard to keep his mind on the task set for him, and he had to use all his willpower to clamber down. How tempting it was to use his new, marvelous sight. He had only to think about it and he could see anything and look anywhere he desired. No secret would be hidden from him—"Oswald the sharp-sighted," everyone would call him; they would gasp and say, "However did you know that?" It would be so easy to surrender and let his mind flit from here to there—he could even see his cousin Twit all the way in Fennywolde if he wished. Nothing was too remote now. It was too much for him to bear, to be given this astounding vision and not be allowed to use it fully. Suddenly he remembered the drawn, haggard look on Orfeo's face, and all thoughts of wasting the sight trickled away—he did not want to make the bat suffer on his behalf. Oswald put his head down and got on with the job of getting down the stairs.

At the bottom Eldritch was waiting for him. "Hurry," he whispered, "this way," and half jumping, half flying, the bat raced off.

The crypt was a gloomy place, even though Oswald could see. The ceiling was vaulted, and frayed banners hung like chained ghosts. Before him Oswald saw huge figures couched on marble slabs, frozen in attitudes of peaceful sleep. For a moment he thought they were alive, but soon realized that they too were made of stone. There were many of these frightening effigies, and the mouse began to wonder if he would be better off without Orfeo's gift. The still, silent statues were creepy, and he did not like turning his back on them, just in case they came to life and sneaked up behind him.

Eldritch came bounding back impatiently, "Do not delay, we must press on," he said urgently.

"What is this?" Oswald asked. "Who are all those people there?"

"This is a place where the dead are laid. The great and glorious are here: warriors, philosophers, artists, and the vastly wealthy. All their efforts, hopes, conquests, labors, and dreams are meaningless now—they lie in their crumbling dust, dumb and powerless. Death is the grand master of all—no one escapes him."

"Except Jupiter," put in Oswald quietly.

"Just so. Now follow me," Eldritch set off again and the mouse went after him, not wanting to be left alone with the morbid marble portraits.

Over smooth tiles and brass nameplates smelling of metal polish the two figures leaped. The crypt was like a warren, with openings and avenues leading off, but Eldritch ran along the central area, past a high, black sarcophagus and over to the whitewashed wall.

"Somewhere, somewhere here," he muttered, patting the base of the wall with his wings. "The entrance was here, pray it has not been sealed over."

Oswald stood back and watched the bat grope and stroke the stone. "When was the last time you came down here?" he asked.

"It has been many years since any of my kin ventured into the chamber of Hrethel—we abandoned the old ways long ago but no bat may cross this threshold and survive."

"What do you mean?" asked Oswald growing nervous. "Is there something wrong with the chamber?" Eldritch did not reply and concentrated on searching for the entrance. Oswald repeated his question, greatly worried. The bat shrugged and did not turn around. There was something he was hiding.

"If I'm going down there I want to know," said Oswald

crossly, but as he frowned at the bat his new sight began to show him strange things. A hunched, wizened winged creature was revealed to him. It was huddled over a great book in a dark room and a cruel sneer was on its face. Oswald felt afraid: he did not know what was unfolding before his eyes, but a dreadful shudder ran through him. The evil-looking bat turned the pages of the book and threw back his head in wild, mad laughter.

Eldritch stiffened, sensing what the mouse was seeing. He whirled around and shook Oswald roughly. "Come back, White One," he cried, and the albino put his paw to his reeling head.

"What did I see?" he stammered, clutching the wall to support his wobbling legs.

"That was Hrethel," replied the bat with a quivering voice. "Long ago he was the Warden of the Great Book. It was the most powerful position in our order. Our forefathers were strong then and wielded the power of the book to maintain their position." Eldritch's eyes grew moist and he averted his gaze, almost from shame. "But Hrethel was not worthy—he was a tyrant and the book became his private tool. He neglected his lesser duties and no longer attended the councils, withdrawing to his underground chamber, weaving spells about the threshold, denying access to any other. It took all the knowledge my ancestors had to destroy him. Many were slain and their skill passed from this world. Hrethel perished but the charms on the threshold survived and no one could retrieve the Great Book. We took a different road then and left the old ways behind, believing that if they had spawned Hrethel then they may spawn another like him. It is better to live humbly than to rule with fear, that is the lesson my grand sires learned, and we have never regretted it. Hrethel was a crazed monster and we do not speak of him. Now you know all our secrets, White One." He sighed. "Is there nought you will not worm from us? Go, the entrance is found. Pass through and bring us the Great Book."

He had come across a small hole where the surrounding plaster was thin and brittle. Quickly he made the gap large enough for Oswald to crawl through, then he gave the mouse one last embrace. "I cannot help you once you have found the chamber, for my eyes cannot enter there. You will be on your own and have to face your fears."

"Wish me luck," whimpered the albino timidly. Eldritch nodded. Oswald knelt down, squeezed through the hole, and vanished from sight.

He dragged himself along the narrow way, the stone ceiling pressing down on him. Oswald wondered how far the chamber was; he did not like the thought of toiling through this cramped space for too long. Presently he came to a ledge and peered down. There was a steep drop, down into the foundation, which looked like the only possible route to take.

"Oh dear," groaned Oswald, wriggling around and dangling his feet over the edge, "this is where I break my neck."

He lowered himself as much as he could and hunted for a foothold, stubbing his toes many times before he found one. Gingerly he began climbing down, not even thinking how he could manage the return journey carrying a book. Suddenly he lost his footing, his toenails scraped down the smooth stone and Oswald fell back, wailing.

He plummeted down and landed heavily on his back, squeaking in surprise and pain. For some time he lay there, not wanting to move in case he discovered that he could not. He had fallen on hard soil. To one side the foundation wall of the huge building rose up above him, and on the other was a wall of earth. Oswald had fallen down a gap that had widened between the two. He groaned and slowly sat up. His back ached and he rubbed it.

Carefully the mouse struggled to his feet and looked around. The wall of earth had old bricks embedded in it, blackened and cracked from some great heat long ago with here and there the remains of charred timbers. But there was no time to wonder what had happened, he had to find the Book of Hrethel. Oswald searched for a clue as to where the chamber lay, and came across another passage.

It was broader than the other one and he did not have to crawl, though he was unable to stand up in it properly. He had to walk bent almost double, and crouching like that did his sprained back no good at all. Once, when he could stand it no longer, he lay down and stretched himself until his spine cracked gratefully and he sighed with relief.

In that curious way, Oswald descended deeper into the earth. The very soil began to turn black and the tunnel walls were soft and velvety with ancient soot. His paws were covered with ash and his feet trod on sharp cinders. Oswald began to cough, the smell was acrid and the disturbed soot tickled the back of his throat. The amount of ash began to grow—it lay against the walls in deep, soft heaps, and the albino was forced to wade through it. In some places the ash was so thick it came up to his chest. He did not like it at all. It was like being stroked lightly with feathery fingers, and it sent shivers through him.

The passage opened out and there was a low doorway set in the black wall. It was choked by old, dusty cobwebs, and mysterious symbols were scratched on the stone lintel. Oswald shook himself, unleashing clouds of billowing soot that made him gag and splutter.

When the soot had settled, Oswald ran his fingers over the doorway. He touched the thick webs and they clung to him horribly. The mouse steeled himself and pushed through the smothering curtain.

The chamber of Hrethel was covered in dust. After Oswald had wiped the clinging cobwebs from his face he held his breath and opened his eyes wide.

It was a large room with stone walls supporting many shelves. Upon these were all sorts of strange objects: jars containing thick, brown liquid in which unpleasant black things floated; curious instruments and bags of powders; small baskets holding dried leaves; countless terra-cotta pots and bowls; a bottle of blue glass; magical-looking designs on moldering charts and a pewter model of the crescent moon.

In the middle of the chamber was a long table of gray stone. More webs covered this and the wooden dish upon it. The floor was strewn with straw and fragments of broken pots. In one corner there was a great, upturned iron cauldron, and the rusted chain that had once suspended it from the large hook in the ceiling now snaked over the ground. But Oswald had yet to discover the horror of Hrethel's chamber. When he did he squawked and leaped back in fright. There, in a niche, beside one of the charts, was the dried-up figure of a mummified bat.

Nervously, Oswald edged forward toward the figure. The creature had been old when it had died. The fur was brindled with age, and the wispy, goatlike beard was white. It was a disgusting object: the head was propped up on the folded wings, and the neck was just bone and wasted flesh. The bat's eyes were like two brown raisins on stalks, which bulged out of the sockets and seemed to stare back at the albino. The skin around the lips had shrunk and withered, pulling back over the yellow teeth, forming an alarming sneer. It was this that Oswald recognized—he knew from his vision that this was Hrethel himself. He closed his eyes, but with Orfeo's gift he could still see the grotesque thing.

Oswald stepped back warily and looked away from the dead bat. He still had to find the book. Anxious to leave the eerie chamber Oswald began to search. He looked under the cauldron, cleared the webs off the table, and peered around the shelves, but it was nowhere to be found. He sat down on a pot and thought hard. Where would Hrethel have hidden the Great Book? An idea came to him and Oswald grubbed about on the floor, testing the flagstones for secret entrances. After an hour

he gave that up and started knocking on the walls to see if they sounded hollow. When his knuckles were red raw he put his paw under his chin and tapped his tail with irritation–he was totally confused. Maybe the book had been burned like every-thing outside.

The shriveled figure of Hrethel seemed to be laughing at him. Oswald glared at him with a mixture of anger and frus-tration. "Stop it!" he shouted. It may have been foolish, but the tension that had been mounting in him was released. He smiled at his idiotic notion–the bat was long dead and could not do him any harm. He had been avoiding that part of the chamber in his hunt for the book–then it dawned on him. Eldritch had said that he would have to face his fears. Where else would the book be but with its master?

Flushed with excitement, Oswald went over to the pre-served bat once more. Hrethel stared malevolently at him, but he was not afraid. He put out a tentative paw and touched one of the folded wings. It was drier than a dead leaf and twice as delicate. It crumbled to dust instantly. Hrethel's sneering head had nothing to support it and crashed to the ground in millions of parched pieces. Only the lower half of his body was left, sit-ting incongruously in the niche, surrounded by flaking parti-cles of itself, and beyond . . . was the Great Book.

Bravely Oswald cleared the dusty remains of the bat away and reached into the recess. His guess had been correct: even in death Hrethel had wanted to guard his treasure. The book was half as large as the mouse, bound in leather with silver hinges. The corners of the binding were gold, and a thick strap sealed the book tightly shut.

The mouse heaved it onto the table and breathlessly untied the strap. He hoped the pages were not as dry as Hrethel had been, or the book would never survive the journey upward. He threw the strap down and gazed at the cover. The leather was weathered and greatly stained, but it was still possible to see the tooled design. It was a crescent moon with a pointed star behind it, and in the grooves there were traces of gold leaf; it must have been a beautiful thing once. Oswald could easily imagine how powerful it must have been and the terrible spells it contained.

A tingling sensation thrilled his fingertips when he touched the binding–it was like holding an angry bee in a jar, with it banging and buzzing furiously against the glass. The Great Book seemed to have a life of its own, anything was possible, knowing what was written in it.

With a fluttering heart Oswald opened it. The first page was blank but seemed firm enough. At any rate it did not crumble to dust when he turned it over. The next page was blank also, and the next. Suspiciously Oswald flicked through the entire volume and slammed it shut. It was empty! By some black art, before he died, Hrethel had made all that was written disappear–making sure no one could ever read the spells after he had gone. In his mind Oswald heard a mocking laugh come down the centuries to him. The Great Book, though a magical thing in its own right, was useless.

CHAPTER SEVEN

THE DEMON THIEF

The grim evening closed around the old house and sealed it in darkness. The shades of winter gathered as the eternal cold ravaged down with unrelenting force. Deptford was tightly locked in the bleakest night it had ever known. The rooftops glistened with frosty ground glass, while icicles spiked and skewered down from the gutters, looking like the eyebrows of some stern, ancient creature. The pavements were smooth, treacherous traps for the unwary, and the roads were rivers of black ice. Not a soul stirred outside, doors were bolted, and curtained windows tried to shut out the wailing wind. Up above, the white, brilliant stars blazed with a fierce intensity not seen for many years as the hollow night swallowed the world whole.

In the Skirtings, Arthur dragged the blankets off his bed and made his way to the Hall. A great fire crackled there, dancing and leaping wildly, casting huge menacing shadows over the walls. It had been decided that everyone should sleep in the Hall as the previous night had been so dreadful. Everybody had shivered in their beds and pulled the clothes high over their

114

heads, but in the morning noses were frozen and ears numb. Nobody could remember the weather ever being so severe. Now families were putting their bedding around the fire and settling the younger ones down, hoping they could get some much-needed sleep.

Many were still hungry. The food situation had become worse, and meals were now prepared and eaten together in the Hall to make sure everyone had the same amount. Cupboards were emptied and resources pooled. Mrs. Coltfoot came up trumps with a dozen jars of homemade preserves, and Mr. Cockle passed around some warming berrybrew punch, but for supper all they had had was thin soup with no bread to dip in it. Master Oldnose had organized a foraging party that afternoon, but after some hours they returned with empty sacks and heavy hearts, chilled to the bone. There was no food to be found anywhere. Thomas Triton had made several journeys to and from Greenwich, bringing what meager stores he had. They helped, but they did not go far, and the mice's spirits sank very low.

Audrey held her paws near the flames and put her head on her mother's shoulder. The firelight flickered over her face, and tears sparkled in her moist eyes. She was thinking of another fire–last summer. Sadly she hung her head. Gwen stroked her daughter's glowing hair and untied the pink ribbon, then she looked across at Thomas Triton and smiled. He was telling the youngsters rambling tales of his voyaging youth and they listened intently, defying the yawns that crept up on them unexpectedly.

At the edge of the circle of orange firelight sat the Starwife. Two days had now passed since Oswald flew off with the bats. The old squirrel had stayed in the Skirtings, confident that sooner or later they would realize their mistake and come back for her, but the skies remained empty and no one came. When she finally realized that her advice was not wanted, the

Starwife seemed to wither and grow weary, her inner fires and indomitable strength quenched at last. Now she sat with her patchy tail curled around her knees. She had not eaten since her arrival, and there were dark circles around her eyes, suggesting that sleep too had abandoned her. She was as still and as silent as death. Occasionally her lips would move in time to some ancient prophecy or secret writing. The Starwife was deep in thought, lost in lonely memories, dredging up all the forgotten rhymes and words of lore she had ever learned. It was slow, painful work, exhuming the dusty, dead knowledge from the faded, dry corners and finding no clues there. Somewhere there had to be an answer–if the bats refused her help then she had to do it alone.

To the mice the Starwife was something of a one-day wonder. They had all become accustomed to seeing her rock gently to and fro, muttering strange-sounding words. She had not moved since they had all come down from the attic, and to them she was now almost a figure of fun, a loopy creature to be pitied. The majority of them did not associate the terrible cold with Jupiter and thought she had been talking gibberish. Without her imperious ways she was like any other sad, old lady, and the mice were making the mistake of underestimating her.

"Poor old dear," tutted Mrs. Chitter indulgently. Only Thomas and Audrey gave much thought to her crouched figure. In the midst of his enthralling tales the midshipmouse would chance to look up and catch his breath in concern at her shrunken, shriveled shape, but an infant's tug at his arm would bring him back, and the green seas would roll and the wind would blow once again.

Audrey was thinking more and more of the squirrel. She recalled her visit to Greenwich, when the Starwife had sat enthroned, ruling her subjects absolutely with her iron will.

116

She had been perilous and powerful then, and the mouse pitied her present condition—how frail and spent she appeared.

In the dim, half-light of the crowding shadows, almost as if she had heard Audrey's thoughts, the Starwife stirred out of her meditations. Her shoulders sagged and her bony back bent farther forward. She dragged her crippled paws over her eyes and stared desolately at the floor.

Gwen looked curiously after her daughter as the girl rose and made her way over to the Starwife. When she heard her coming, the squirrel turned her milky eyes to the mouse and arched her brows questioningly. "Come to see if I'm still alive, have you, girl?"

Audrey chewed her lip uncertainly. Actually she wasn't sure why she had come over. "Do you want anything to eat?" she ventured at last. "There's not much, but you'd be most welcome to it."

The squirrel shook her head. "Thank you all the same, child," she said kindly, "but no, I could not manage anything at the moment."

"But you haven't eaten anything since you came," insisted Audrey.

"Then I shall starve!" exclaimed the Starwife forcefully. For a moment she glared at the mouse then scolded herself. "No, no, this will never do. Forgive me, child. I'm a stupid, old creature who doesn't know any better. I've had it too easy all my life, you see. I'm too used to giving orders."

Audrey sat down next to her, hugging her knees. "Do you miss your people?" she asked.

The squirrel smiled. "My people," she muttered. "Yes, I miss them—but not those cowardly ditherers I had to control in Greenwich, they were never my people." It was plain from Audrey's face that she did not understand, so with a great sigh the Starwife explained.

"My fur is gray now, what's left of it, but I am not from the race of the grays; age has merely played that trick on me."

Audrey thought she understood. "Oh," she broke in, "then you were a red squirrel. I've never seen one of those, I thought they went away years ago."

The Starwife lowered her eyes sadly. "Yes, they went away," she echoed, "never to return. The red folk were a hearty lot, braver than those miserable wretches I've had to put up with all these years, but even there you are wrong, child." She raised her head proudly and in a grand, sorrowful tone said, "I am a black squirrel: the noblest race ever to have breathed the sweet acorn-scented air."

"I've never heard of those," admitted Audrey.

"No, and you never will again, I should imagine. I have not been able to trace any of my kin. We were scattered by war and envy many years ago–long before I took up the silver and became the Handmaiden of Orion." Her words were wistful and full of regret. "And now there is no one to take my place. I have searched and searched, but all traces of the black squirrels are gone. I think I am the last–our line shall end with me, and the dynasty of the Starwives also. I fear the silver acorn will not be worn by any when I have passed on." She fell into brooding silence and lost herself in the tangled threads of her thoughts again.

A child cried, shattering the crackling, chattering calm, and the Hall sank into a shuddering cold that not even the fire could thaw. The night seemed to creep and claw closer, suffocating any talk and oppressing everyone. The dismayed mice raised their worried faces in the pale flame glow–something unnatural was happening.

A bitter wind wailed outside and blasted through the keyhole. The fire spluttered smokily and all eyes smarted. The children whimpered and held onto each other in fear, and Thomas pulled the battered storyteller's hat from his head and listened breathlessly. The grim, grave dark pushed down, and the flames gave one last cough and went out. Someone screamed. The only light in the Hall was the ruddy glare of the spitting embers, which daubed those near to it a hellish red as though they were drenched in blood.

"What's happening?" whimpered Mrs. Cockle in panic. "Light the fire again, please!"

But the fire refused to be lit. It was as if the cold had seeped into the wood and frozen it beyond the reach of flames. Thomas struck frantically at his tinderbox, but nothing would catch.

"It is no good, Triton," came a croaky voice from the darkness. The midshipmouse paused and glanced around: there, staggering into the light, was the Starwife. She hobbled forward, leaning heavily on her stick and gritting her teeth against the grinding pain of her set bones. "This is not a natural cold," she said, trembling, "and well you know it! Put your box away—we might need it later, but it will not help now." The squirrel faced all the frightened mice and raised her stick. "Listen to me, mice of Deptford," she called urgently, "Jupiter is abroad. It is he who spreads the evil winter, his is the dark will behind all of this."

The mice mumbled and whispered. Mrs. Chitter pulled the blankets over her shoulders and scurried forward angrily. "I don't believe it," she cried, distraught. "None of this happened till you came, you're the evil one." She started to sob hysterically. The Starwife pounded her stick and gave Mrs. Chitter a sound slap across the face. The mouse gasped and fainted in surprise.

"Take her away," said the old squirrel, gazing around to see if anyone else protested. "I've no time for idiots! If you don't listen to me then you are all doomed–simple as that." The mice kept silent and the Starwife nodded in satisfaction. "Is there a

119

way we can get out of this place without climbing to the roof or going through the sewers?" she asked impatiently. "I must know Jupiter's strength."

"There's the yard," piped up Arthur from the gloom.

"Good," snapped the squirrel, "let us go there." Some of the mice decided to stay where they were. But others wrapped their blankets around themselves and trailed obediently into the kitchen, where, under orders, Master Oldnose began pulling out the scrunched-up papers that had been stuffed into the hole that afternoon when the unsuccessful foragers had returned.

The Starwife tapped her stick impatiently. "Hurry, you silly slug," she ranted scornfully.

"That's the lot," puffed Master Oldnose, discarding the final piece. She had already limped into the passage, and the other mice crowded after.

Outside it was unbelievably cold. The concrete ground glistened, and the branches of the hawthorns were bleached a deathly white. Fine fingers of mist skulked in the darkness, squeezing and throttling all they snatched at. The night poured into the yard like black tar in a bottomless pit. It was a midnight world, blacker than ink and full of icy snares. The old tin bucket near the fence clicked and cracked as the frozen rainwater it held strained and split the frosted rivets on its side.

The mice stepped out and clouds of breath gusted from teeth-chattering mouths. The old squirrel glanced around like a dog hunting for a scent. She held her stick out before her and tapped the tinkling grass. She grunted and ran her aching fingers over the rasping, frosted wall. "It is as I feared," she told Thomas darkly. "This is as it was in my chamber. The enemy swells in strength and puts forth his infernal powers. There cannot be any doubt: tonight he will use my Starglass." The Starwife hissed through her teeth, shook her fist at the darkness and struck the fence with the walking stick in her frustration. "I must know what is happening," she snapped furiously, then an idea seized her and she whipped around. "Can anyone climb this fence?" she demanded.

"I can do it," volunteered Arthur suddenly. He pushed forward, rushing and slipping over the ice. He had learned the skill of nimbly scampering up stalks in Fennywolde, and a fencepost wasn't that different.

"Excellent, child," said the squirrel, eagerly patting Arthur's back. "Up you go and tell us what you see."

Arthur stood at the bottom of one of the posts and blew on his chilled paws before gripping it. The sharp, needling frost clung and tore at the warm skin, and he stifled a squeal as he ripped his tender paw away. "It's too cold!" he exclaimed, shaking and blowing.

"Yes, it is cold," admitted the Starwife, "but it will get colder and colder until the very blood in your veins freezes, so climb, boy!"

Arthur grumbled under his breath, but tried once more. He clutched the post and pulled himself up. The touch of the icy wood scraping against his body made him want to drop to the ground and dash into the Hall, where he could throw himself onto the fire's embers. However, he managed to hold on and began to climb. Up he toiled, higher and higher. The frost stabbed and seared his shrinking palms and he had to close his eyes tightly, blocking the pain from his mind, ignoring the agony, focusing all his energies on his goal—he had to reach the top.

Below, the mice huddled together to keep warm as they watched his slow ascent. Gwen Brown put her paw to her mouth and her heartbeat quickened as she prayed for her son's safety. "Be careful, Arthur," she called up to him frantically.

The tubby mouse's nails ripped and split as he clawed his way to the top, feeling nothing but the ice cutting into him and the freezing air slicing up his steaming nose. And then he was there—he was gasping for breath, but he had made it. The

harsh, bullying wind plucked and flattened his ears as he struggled to balance on the topmost rail of the rickety old fence.

"What do you see?" the Starwife's voice floated up to him.

Arthur surveyed the land before him, over the garden next
door and beyond the empty street. The flats opposite reared into
the starlit sky but were partially hidden by the patches of pale
mist that flowed slowly across the blind windows and groped
hungrily at the latches. Arthur shivered. In the corner of his eye
something glimmered. He twisted around sharply. Past the
church there was the black shape of the power station, squat
and solid. It rose out of a sea of thick, billowing fog, and in its
tiny windows something blue flashed and sparked. He recalled
what he had seen while sitting on the roof waiting for the bats,
and with a shock realized that that was where Jupiter had
made his base. Arthur could have kicked himself. Why had he
forgotten all about it? If he had been more alert he would have
known, and they could have organized a group of the bravest
mice to go and spy on the wretched place.

"Well?" the Starwife's frail voice asked.

He looked down and saw the pinched, chilled faces of his
family and friends that were all turned to him. "He's in the
power station," he called down. "That's where . . . " but he did
not finish what he had started to say, for at that moment a terrific rumble shook the ground and the fence swayed alarmingly. Arthur held on grimly but did not move, for even as he raised
his eyes back to the old disused building, a great plume of
smoke belched out of the power station's chimney. It rose
steadily into the clear night sky and hung there purposefully,
gradually swelling into a vast, dense cloud through which bolts
of fierce lightning spat jaggedly. Deafening thunder cracked the
heavens as the last of the foggy column issued from the chimney and joined the waiting mountain of ghostly vapor. And in
the midst of the great cloud, Arthur could plainly see the faint,
shimmering outline of an enormous, demonic cat. Slowly the

terrifying bulk of the menacing, supernatural fog began to move. It drifted over the chimney and away from the mist-enshrouded building, out toward Greenwich. The thunder boomed through the echoing night, but amid its roar Arthur clearly heard a high, triumphant, screeching laugh.

Arthur half slid, half fell down the fencepost. Frozen splinters cut into his paws and feet like cruel little daggers, but he paid them no attention. The image of the awful black spirit transporting himself to Greenwich in the fog was engraved in his mind, and he could think of nothing else.

He landed on the ground with a bump and a thud, his bottom sizzling with the cold as he sat on the icy concrete, gazing stupidly up at the astonished crowd of mice who gathered around him.

"Arthur dear," cried his mother, "whatever's the matter?" She rushed forward, but the Starwife's stick flashed out and prevented her from reaching him.

"He has seen the Unbeast," said the squirrel in a quaking voice. "Tell me boy, what happened? Where is he now? Does he come this way?"

Arthur snapped out of his bewilderment quickly and scrambled to his feet. "No," he stammered, "he hasn't come for us yet, but I don't know what we'll do when he does. I never realized how immense his powers are—we haven't a chance against him."

"Where is he?" repeated the Starwife hurriedly. Arthur pointed south with his bleeding paws. "He went in the direction of Greenwich," he told her, shaking his head. "You should have seen him, it was dreadful. He rose out of the old power station like steam from a kettle. I saw his shape form in the mist, and you could see through him to the stars—it was horrible."

The Starwife took several steps back. A look of consternation crept over her wizened face, and her milky eyes were filled with dread. "Greenwich?" she muttered worriedly to herself.

"Why there? There is nothing of any use to him left in the chambers—the charts and histories hold no significance—unless . . . " A terrible gasp shrieked from her and she waved her arms in panic. "Quickly," she cried, turning to Thomas Triton, "hurry to the observatory—I must know what Jupiter intends there! My heart quails, something profoundly evil is afoot!" The stick clattered to the frosty ground as her legs gave way and she sank in despair to her knees, sobbing hopelessly.

Desperately frightened, the mice imagined all sorts of horrors taking place. "What's going to happen?" asked Algy Coltfoot with a wail. "Are we all going to die?"

"See to her," Thomas said gruffly to Gwen.

Mrs. Brown was already bending down and trying to calm the stricken Starwife. "Come now," she soothed, "let's get you up. It won't do your old bones any good soaking up all that cold, will it?"

The squirrel reached out to the midshipmouse and implored him to go to Greenwich for her. "You must, I can feel his presence. I believe I know what he is trying to do—on no account must he succeed."

Thomas took hold of her trembling paw and squeezed it reassuringly. "I'll go," he said, "though I don't know what I will be able to do."

"Just report back to me," she told him, taking her stick from Audrey, "only hurry."

Thomas nodded. "I'll go straight away," he said, pushing through the crowd and heading for the hole in the wall.

"Good luck," Gwen called after him. "Keep out of danger."

Audrey hugged her mother tightly. "I'm sure Mr. Triton will be all right," she said. "He knows how to look after himself."

"I hope so, dear," Gwen replied. "He is a silly old mouse sometimes, but I wouldn't like any harm to come to him."

Her daughter smiled knowingly up at her. "Let's go back

inside. There's nothing else we can do out here is there, Arthur?" There was no reply. Both Audrey and her mother turned around, but Arthur was not there. "Now where's he gotten to?" Audrey tutted.

The Starwife looked up at the twinkling sky and rubbed her arms. "The end has come," she whispered softly, "and I am not ready."

In the ruddy light of the Hall, Thomas Triton pulled on his woolen hat and tightened the red kerchief around his neck. "What happened out there?" asked Jacob Chitter.

"They'll tell you when they come in," Thomas replied, striding over bundles of bedclothes to get to the cellar door.

A panting figure came rushing toward him. Lit by the blood-red glare of the dying embers it resembled a demon, and Thomas had to blink before he recognized who it was. "Arthur?" he said. "That you, matey? What do you want? I haven't got time to chat, you know." He ruffled the mouse's hair and squeezed through the narrow doorway.

"Wait, Mr. Triton!" Arthur called after him. There was no reply, so he forced himself through the gap.

In the cellar it was nearly pitch black, and the cold flowed and pulsed from the hard stone walls and bare flagstone floor. Arthur squinted and strained his eyes. The midshipmouse had already jumped down the steps and was making for the Grill.

"Mr. Triton!" Arthur called again. "I'm coming with you!"

Thomas was amused and scratched his head. "If you think I'm going to let your mother bawl me out for takin' you with me, you need to have your head examined."

But Arthur was not to be fobbed off—he folded his arms resolutely. "If you send me back I'll only follow you, and think of all the time we're wasting now."

Thomas scowled and then his face brightened. "I'm not going to argue here, and I could do with the company. Come on, matey." He turned back to the Grill and with a swish of his tail was gone. Arthur grinned and followed through the once-feared entrance.

The sewers were dank and dripping, and the arched, red-brick passages had a fine layer of glittering, frosty, diamond dust. Below, the deep water carried along small, drifting islands of filthy, black ice. A bitter draft whistled through the tunnels, cutting straight through the two mice.

Thomas and Arthur hurried along as fast as they could, without saying a word to each other. It needed all their concentration to watch out for hidden slippery patches that lurked on the shadowy levels. Arthur trotted behind the midshipmouse, glad to be away from the Skirtings—at least his mind was not dwelling on food anymore. Silently they made their way along the narrow ledges and winding ways, avoiding the dangers as best as they could. Arthur did not venture down into the sewers very often. The last time had been on his way back from Fennywolde, and so his sense of direction in the tunnels was easily confounded. To him it seemed as if they were going entirely the wrong way, but for Thomas this was a journey he made every day, and what's more, his instinct for the points of the compass was so strong he could have navigated his way blindfolded out of the darkest, most difficult maze ever invented.

"Here we are, miladdo," the midshipmouse said eventually as they turned a corner and entered a passage that was filled with pale blue light. "This is where we get out."

They squirmed through a grating and Arthur looked around to discover the great locked gates of Greenwich Park nearby, rising high and stark against the midnight sky. The naked trees beyond were flecked with frost and their branches reared up menacingly, waving their sharp, savage twigs, shredding the eerie mist that dared to drift too close to their barbs.

The two mice ducked under the iron gates and pattered

stealthily up the path to where they could get a clear view of the observatory. There they caught their breaths and stared. The hill was shrouded in thick fog through which occasional flashes of cold light burst and crackled heavenward. "He's in there and no mistake," Thomas said sternly, "but what the devil is he up to?"

Arthur shivered. It was a weird sight: the fog seemed to be almost a solid thing with a life of its own. It clung tenaciously to the hillside, wrapping around and around, obliterating the hill and the observatory built there. Only when the strange internal lightning jabbed out could the dim outline of the onion-shaped dome be seen for the briefest of moments, before the fog snatched the sight away once more.

"We go up there," Thomas said, pointing into the heart of the unnatural cloud.

Arthur gulped and agreed. Somewhere in there lurked Jupiter. Up the slope they tramped, until they reached the edge of the swirling mist. As they approached, fine tendrils of vapor snaked out and writhed smokily around their ankles, trying to pull them in.

"I don't like this," said Thomas, disgusted at the clammy touch of those whispering caresses. The vapor rose above his knees, then covered his waist. "I never saw anythin' like this in all my years at sea," he muttered as the fog swelled up to his chest. He noticed with a shudder that the parts of his body that were covered began to tingle and prick uncomfortably, as though the mist were attacking them. "Give me your paw, lad," he called out quickly. "If we're separated in this, we'll be lost forever."

Arthur gladly grabbed hold of Thomas's extended paw. He hated the insidious cloud: it seemed to be devouring him, making him feel as though he were drowning in a phantom swamp. The urge to run away nearly overpowered him as, with horror in his large, round eyes, he saw the midshipmouse disappear completely. The frightening mist brimmed up to his own chin. Arthur tried to hold his breath–he didn't want any of that hateful stuff in his mouth–but by the time he had to exhale he too was engulfed.

Thomas swept his free paw over his forehead and coughed; the damp was already seeping into his lungs. He had thought it would be a simple task to walk uphill in any fog–after all, one only had to keep going up the slope and eventually the summit would be reached–but he was not finding it as easy as that. The soles of his feet were numb from the cold and any sensation that they did manage to feel was merely the tingle of the mist needling and pricking them. After a short while he decided that they should have reached the observatory and frowned in consternation. He knelt down, an action that Arthur found very alarming as he imagined the unseen mouse to have fallen down a hole.

"Don't worry, matey," Thomas's thin, flat voice reassured him. "I'm just getting my bearings. There, this isn't too removed from normal fog after all: there's always a clearer bit just above the ground. I've been leading you around in circles, my young friend–old grog swiller that I am. It's all right now though–I'll be bewildered no more." He groped back to his feet and strode smartly up the invisible slope.

A dark, vast shape reared out of the mist before them. Arthur tugged at Thomas's paw, but the midshipmouse laughed grimly. "'Tis only a bush, don't fret." The large, leathery leaves of the rhododendron swept over the mice's heads as they passed it by. Thomas was more confident now. He nodded and spoke quietly to himself as new landmarks sailed out of the vapor. Black railings flew into view, and when he saw these he patted them and sighed with relief, "Thank the Green for that," he said to Arthur. "Now we can follow these and get to the top in no time–I just hope we're not too late."

Keeping the railings on their right, the mice traveled on,

more quickly than before. Arthur could now see the blurred shape of the midshipmouse's hat bobbing in front of him and thought his eyes were growing accustomed to the dense fog. There! He could distinctly see Thomas's ears—the fog was getting thinner. "Mr. Triton," he uttered in surprise.

Thomas spun around and Arthur could see his face clearly. It was very grave. "Yes," said the midshipmouse quietly, "I've noticed, the cloud's not as thick now, and this is where things get real hairy for you an' me."

"But we can see now," said Arthur in a brighter voice.

"Maybe," returned the other soberly, "but by the same token, we can also *be* seen. The dangers are not yet over, they merely begin. We have crossed the barrier—the fog was just a shield to foil prying eyes. Now we shall see the demon hiding inside and maybe we shall wish to be blind once more."

The path came to an end and they found themselves on top of the hill. Wisps of mist flowed by, but it was not as dense as before. The grand structure of the observatory towered up behind the rails, disappearing into the shrouded night—Arthur could even see the stars when he looked up. He let go of Thomas's paw and rubbed his own together. He suddenly felt very vulnerable and exposed, as though there were countless eyes all around, trained fixedly on him, watching and waiting.

Thomas pattered along the bottom railing and darted over to the cover of a statue. He beckoned to Arthur to do the same. When they were both crouching at the foot of the sculpture, Arthur turned a curious face to the midshipmouse and asked, "What is it? Have you seen something?"

"No lad, not seen—listen."

Arthur cocked an ear toward the observatory and held his breath. Amid the clatter of the frozen oak branches nearby, an evil voice was speaking—no it was chanting. It was very faint, but the quality of that sound was unmistakable: it was totally fiendish.

"Jupiter!" exclaimed Arthur hoarsely. "But where is he, and who's he talking to?"

"He ain't talkin' to no one, lad," replied Thomas in a sour tone. "I've heard him speak like this afore, when me an' young Willum spied him and that hench-rat of his on the heath yonder. Jupiter is castin' a spell."

The world was lit suddenly by a brilliant flash of lightning. Thunder rolled and the earth trembled. At last the Lord of the Winter was revealed and the two mice covered their faces in fear.

The last traces of mist swept back like a curtain, and there he was, the Tyrant of the Dark. He stood astride the observatory dome and cackled. The unquiet spirit of Jupiter was immense, his huge, flickering outline reaching high into the night sky. It was still that of a cat, but one of nightmare proportions. Ice fell from his transparent fur, and where his gleaming, cruel feet touched, a bitter, arctic frost sparked and fizzled, freezing everything. The dome creaked and a long crack shivered around it. The ice that flowed over it was as strong as steel. It gleamed bitterly with the deep blue of the eternal void, and icicles larger than stalactites stretched down to the ground.

A howling gale tore around Jupiter's huge head. From his mouth his deadly breath hailed down, full of winter's hatred for the living. His savage teeth were like swords of polished, pale metal, forged by cruel, satanic fingers for a demon's armory. His nostrils dripped with tongues of cold flame, and his ears were pressed flat against his spectral skull. But the eyes of the Unbeast were the most terrifying of all: they shone out into the darkness, blazing fires of pure malice. They seared into anything their baleful glance fell upon, withering the trees and cracking the ground. This was where the lightning was born. As Jupiter recited his dread words his eyes dazzled and a stream of fatal energy burst forth, tearing the sky apart and searing into the blackness of space. His snarls were like thunder, and his anger a blizzard.

"Hear me servants of the dark void," his voice hissed upward. "I am the Lord of the World. While you cringe, trapped forever in your exile, know that I, Jupiter, have unlocked the gates of death, and trouble once more the unhappy land. I call you to witness now the tumult I bring." He raised his mighty arms over his head and laughed wildly. Between his cruel claws something small shimmered with a silver light.

"The Starglass," breathed Thomas fearfully. He and Arthur were very afraid; they could not believe what their eyes were seeing. Jupiter was indeed a creature of nightmares. They felt like two insects brought before a god, but they could not run to save themselves. Everything now seemed hopeless: there was nothing they could do against such a foe—all was lost.

In his huge, brutish claws the Starglass of the Starwife looked like a tiny toy, but it was the only way Jupiter could achieve his goal. If the old squirrel had been there she would have ordered Thomas to destroy it at once. But she was far away, and the mice had no idea what was about to take place. They thought that nothing worse could happen—they were never more wrong.

"Slave of the timeless stars," bellowed Jupiter, "obey your new master!" and he called out a sentence of harsh, powerful words from the far reaches of the abyss. "Remael sen Hoarmath eis Hagolceald!" he proclaimed defiantly, and he threw back his head with a mad, insane gurgle in his ghostly throat.

The world seemed to hold its breath. All noise ceased, and even the wind dropped as Jupiter completed his spell. The hush became deafening as the seconds stretched into minutes. In his claws the Starglass began to pulse with light. It throbbed and vibrated violently, until Jupiter himself shook. The dome split further and bricks tumbled to the frozen ground. But Jupiter laughed at the top of his voice, and his screeching cackles were heard all over the trembling world.

Down at the base of the statue, Arthur fell to the ground and hid his face. The noise was too much, and he thought he was going to faint at any moment. Thomas pressed his nails up into his hair, the woolen hat was pushed off his head, and he ground his teeth together in agony as the Unbeast's voice pierced his very soul. Arthur squealed and writhed around in his torment, then with one final groan of despair he fainted. For him the pain had come to an end. The midshipmouse looked at his young companion, but was unable to help. Shortly he too would pass out, but he summoned his reserves of strength and raised his head back to the black fiend on top of the observatory. The Starglass in Jupiter's iron grasp spilled out its power. The magic of centuries stored in its depths poured forth, and a high-pitched scream issued from its heart.

"No," gloated Jupiter coldly, "you must obey me, I know your secret name and have uttered the charm laid down long ago. The celestial pivots are loosened, and I command you to hold the heavens once more." The silver light from the Starglass suddenly soared upward. The Unbeast yelled in his triumph and danced on the dome like a maniac.

Thomas felt Jupiter's shrieks of joy boom around his head and he cried out in pain. It hurt so much that he started to hallucinate. It seemed as if the very stars swirled and boiled. Thomas shook his head, dragged the paws from his face, and stared intently at the heavens. He was not imagining it–the stars were indeed exploding and seething. That was the final horror. The midshipmouse felt all his strength trickle away, and he collapsed, senseless, next to Arthur.

The night sky quivered, the fierce starlight shook and waned. A host of wailing voices filled the air as one by one the stars were extinguished. Their light streamed to the earth, slivers of brilliant thread shooting out of the black chasm. The

slender beams were sucked down to the observatory, down to where Jupiter was waiting, flourishing the Starglass, down into its depths where the brilliance was impossible to look upon. As fiery rain they descended, and lamentations issued from all creation. The constellations were quenched, snuffed out by the tremendous powers of both Jupiter and the age-old Starglass, and all who witnessed it fell to their knees and prayed. The endless, eternal void came flooding in, and the world was plunged into darkness.

Not one single star was left in the pitch-black sky—all their precious, angry light was trapped in the glass, and Jupiter was its master.

CHAPTER EIGHT

RE-ENLISTING

Somewhere a gong was booming. Colored spots and flashes dazzled Piccadilly and his head throbbed, threatening to explode. He stirred and groaned in agony. His tongue was stuck to the roof of his mouth. The darkness was damp and his face was pressed against a grit floor that cut into his bruised cheek. The dots and blurs that danced before him subsided, and he tried to focus his eyes. He took in where he was. It seemed to be a shallow pit beneath one of the subway rails. The city mouse lifted his head and discovered that the booming gong was actually his brain.

"Oh," he grunted, putting a fragile paw to his forehead. He winced and screwed up his face as he felt a lump the size of an egg. Piccadilly raised himself slowly and checked his condition. Thankfully, no bones were broken. He decided to try and stand. "Gently does it," he told himself. His pounding head made him sway unsteadily and his legs felt like jelly. Resting against the side of the pit, he tried to remember what had happened to him. He had been running, tripped, hit his head, and fallen down.

Piccadilly suddenly felt very hungry. He must have been out cold for hours, perhaps even a whole day. He licked his dry lips and spat the horrible taste of stale blood and bitter oil from his mouth. It was then he remembered whom he had been running from.

"The rats," he cried, and glanced fearfully down the dark tunnel, but it was empty and quiet as the grave. "They can't have seen me trip," he concluded gratefully. "The twerps must have run right over me without realizing." The smile that had formed on his lips froze and he sucked the air in sharply.

"Holeborn!" he exclaimed, panic-stricken. "What has happened? Did the rats attack?" He hoped Marty had gotten back in time to warn everyone.

He hauled himself out of the pit and made for the station ahead. How still everything was, no foraging parties or lookout scouts anywhere. An uneasy feeling descended on his spirit and his steps quickened.

He hastily made for the main entrance to Holeborn, his mind racing and his heart missing every other beat–if only this could be some horrible nightmare. He was close to tears as he thought of all the harmless mice trembling with fright in their homes or fighting to the death against the rat army. He gripped his knife. If the war had begun, then he was ready; no rat would stand before him as long as he had the strength. He would make sure they never feasted on mouse suppers.

A noise round a blind corner brought him to an abrupt halt. There came the sound of shambling footsteps–it was unmistakably a rat. Piccadilly leaned against the grimy tunnel wall and wished he had been more cautious. What if there was a whole band of rats camped outside the main doors? He would have run straight into them! He held his breath and listened fearfully. How many could he handle at once? he wondered. A cold gleam flashed off his little knife as he drew it slowly from his belt and readied himself.

"'Tain't right, let's us run while we can an' leave 'em to it. We don't want none o' it do we? No, no more lumps on me 'ead."

Piccadilly relaxed and lowered his knife; it was only Barker, and he was sure to be alone. The mouse waited for the barmy creature to turn the corner, and before he knew what was happening, Piccadilly had grabbed and pinned him against the wall.

"Aiiee!" screamed the rat in surprise. He made such a terrible noise that Piccadilly had to put his paw over his mouth.

"Ssshh," he hissed. "If I hear you so much as breathe, I'll give you so many lumps you won't be able to count them. That's better. We don't want your mates comin' to see what all the fuss is, do we? Now, what happened?" he snapped through snarling teeth. "Where is everyone–did they get away or what?"

Barker stared at him with a mad, terrified look in his eyes and wildly shook his head. "'Tweren't Barker," he denied quickly, "he 'ad nothin' to do wiv it, 'tweren't him, no!"

Piccadilly felt sick. His eyes grew large and fearsome, so dreadful to look on that the rat cowered down and whimpered. "Tell me!" he exploded. "What happened to all the mice in there–they got away, didn't they? The place was empty when your lot arrived, wasn't it?"

Barker sniveled and opened his mouth to cry. He twisted his old, bony head on his scrawny neck and shivered miserably, "'Tweren't Barker," he insisted, "he wouldn't touch mousey meat."

Piccadilly stood back and choked. He stumbled and gaped, unable to believe his ears. The rat watched him warily and looked for an opportunity to escape. "You're lying," Piccadilly said at last, and his face hardened. He lunged forward and caught hold of Barker's throat. "Tell me you're lying!"

Barker's bottom lip quivered and he coughed and spluttered. The mouse was throttling him. The rat's eyes nearly popped out of his head and he wheezed and gasped as

Piccadilly's fingers squeezed the breath out of him.

Piccadilly suddenly realized what he was doing and pulled away sharply. He stared at his paws as though they belonged to some other creature. "I'm sorry," he said slowly. "I didn't know what I was doing. Please, tell me what happened."

Barker rubbed his neck and croaked like a frog. "The battle didn't last long," he admitted warily. "Barker stayed to one side—he don't like no fightin' an' rough stuff." He half closed his wrinkled eyes and an expression of pity crept over his weary face. "We thought you had reached the mouse halls, mousey boy," he continued. "Old Stumpy urged us on and we charged into them. The lads were mad wiv the blood craving, an' when Barker looked into their faces he were right scared. There was a bad, crazed light in their eyes, an' it made Barker wanna run right back where he came from—but if he had they would've tore 'im to bits, sure as muck is muck. It were like being swept along by one o' them movin' stepways; no way could he slip off an' hide till all was done." With his back against the side of the tunnel Barker sank down onto his haunches and took hold of his head. "Them mouses hadn't a clue what were happenin'," he said. "The lads burst in on 'em and pounced on all they could; they was took totally by surprise. Your folk should've got ready an' armed 'emselves, lad. It were sickenin', seein' how easy they was cut down—like straws they fell."

At this point Barker covered his ears, and a large tear fell from his snout. "I can still hear them," he wept to himself. "They were squeakin' and cryin' for help, but all that came runnin' were got like them. All them small, high voices still ring in me ears—make 'em stop, it weren't Barker, please mouses, I'se so sorry." For some minutes the rat sobbed and was unable to say any more.

Piccadilly felt cold. A dull wave of shock washed over him and his stomach lurched inside. He put out a paw and touched

Barker's tear-drenched claws. It did not occur to him how bizarre the situation was, that he should be comforting a rat who had been part of an army that had slaughtered all his friends. "Are they all dead?" he asked thickly.

The rat raised his head and gazed sorrowfully at the mouse. "The ground was scarlet! Old Stumpy made all of us check out all the halls and tiny rooms, and there were awful yells as families were dragged out and taken away to be peeled. Now Old Stumpy's callin' himself King of the City." The rat buried his face in his claws and cried his eyes raw.

A terrible look came over Piccadilly, his jaw tightened and the color of his eyes matched the steel of his knife's blade. He would not rest until he managed to fulfil the oath he had sworn long ago: Morgan had to die.

*   *   *

Kelly chuckled to Smiff as he draped a mouse skin over his shoulders and twirled around, "Ain't I luvverly?" he said, dribbling all down his front. "The belle o' the ball—that's me." And he swished down the hall, dragging the forlorn skin behind him.

Smiff hooted and threw another crispy mouse ear into his jaws. What a fight it had been! Never could he remember having such a marvelous time. And the feast! Mouse ears and juicy mouse meat—succulent and tender, not too well done, roasted ever so slightly until the outside was brown but the inside was still rare. He had never tasted such things before, but they seemed to stir some ancient, dormant spirit in him that lusted for more. Even though he was stuffed he still had the craving.

He thought longingly of the brown gravy they had made and his mouth fell open as he drooled at the memory. Old Stumpy had told them the best ways to eat mice, and how right he had been! What a marvelous general Old Stumpy was. Smiff picked up his bowl and drank a toast to his leader—mmm, warm fat—delicious.

Nearly all the rats were in the main hall, the one in which the mice had held their meeting just a few nights before. They caroused and slapped each other on their backs as only conquerors can. No one regretted joining up, and this, their first campaign, had been an outstanding success. Only five of their number had died, when a small group of elderly mice had leaped out of nowhere with sticks and swords in their paws, shouting war cries and charging defiantly into the rat horde. The stand had not lasted for very long, and the mice were soon skinned. The gray fur Kelly was sporting had been one of them. The rats told crude stories and cracked wicked jokes at their victims' expense. Three blackhearted vermin seized some skins and used them as grisly puppets, acting out parts of the battle, relishing the killing and torment. A crowd gathered about them, and raucous laughter shook the hall. Almost all of them took up mouse furs and placed them on their heads like ghastly hats. They peered through the blank eyeholes and poked their tongues out of the mouth spaces. They were a debauched, disgusting sight.

Morgan sat on the Thane's throne and sniggered to himself—what a day this had been! This was what he had always longed for: to lead and be in control of a vast army. His hatchet face smirked from ear to ear as he thought of it. If only some of his old lads could see him now. For a moment he thought back to his former days in Deptford; he was well out of that. He could still not understand how Jupiter had duped him all those years, pretending to be a rat god when all the time he was just some mangy old cat getting fat from his labors.

"Pah!" he spat on the floor and glanced again at his new lads. What a joy they were, and so enthusiastic. Morgan tried to

140

remember his first taste of mouse. He had probably reacted in much the same way. But the supply of those tempting scamperers had been meager in the Deptford sewers. His Lordship had seen to that–any that ventured down were sent straight to Him. Morgan scowled. Why was he dwelling on the past so much? He had been in the city for several months now, and not once had he bothered to think of those horrible times when he had fawned and scraped to those burning eyes.

"Cheers, Stumpy!" saluted a gorged rat waddling past the dais with a bowl of blood in his claws. Morgan returned the greeting and bent his piebald head to drink from his own bowl.

The slurp died in his throat as he stared down into the brimming bowl. His chisel-shaped snout was reflected in the swirling thick liquid, but only for a moment. Something strange began to happen. The blood became cloudy and ice spiked in from the edge into the center, until it was frozen solid. Morgan gasped but could not tear his eyes away. Somewhere, deep in the heart of the blood-red ice, two points of pale, frosty light appeared.

"No," murmured the rat in disbelief, "not again."

The glimmering, icy-cruel eyes filled the bowl until their ghostly radiance fell upon Morgan's face and flowed out over his shaking claws. The eyes were a fierce blue, the dead color of the terrible void, and their eternal cold burned into the rat's mind.

"Morgan," called a distant, familiar voice.

The color drained out of the rat's face as he recognized the speaker. "It cannot be . . ." he stammered, "you are gone–drowned deep."

"Morgan," repeated the voice in a whisper, and the eyes in the ice seemed to look into his very soul.

"My Lord?" the hackles rose on Morgan's back and a chill crept under his flesh. "Is that you?"

"Verily 'tis I, Jupiter, your Lord and Master." The voice spoke hollowly and with an edge to it as bleak as death. "I have come to claim my lieutenant."

Smiff looked up from his mess, wondering if he ought to be sick so as to fit in more grub. He smiled around at all the contented, mouse-hatted rats and raised his greasy claws to Old Stumpy. The salute was not acknowledged. What was he doing there? The general seemed to be staring into his bowl. Where was that queer blue light coming from? Smiff frowned and staggered to his feet–something odd was going on.

"Listen to me," lulled the voice of Jupiter softly, "I have returned from the far reaches of death and need my old, trusted friend by my side once more."

Morgan's will was slowly ebbing away. Every second he looked into those eyes and heard that dreadful voice, the less he was able to wrench himself free. "No," he struggled to say through the spells that were being wrapped around him, "I won't never work fer no damned cat–not no more! I got me own life away from yer now, an' there's no way I'll come back–not if you be Hobb hisself."

But it was not easy to escape from Jupiter. Gradually the icy whispers needled their way into Morgan's heart. The rat began to listen to Jupiter's melodious words, for they had the same heady effect as strong wine. His lids drooped over his beady eyes and he fell victim once more to Jupiter's powerful voice. He mourned when the words ceased–he wanted to hear them forever, he would die to hear them. A great passion swelled up in his breast; he would bind himself to this magnificent Lord and do whatever he wished. How could he have lived without him all this time?

"I need you, Morgan. Come back into my service," said Jupiter. "I see you have fashioned an army for yourself–excellent. Bring them to me, let them be my beloved subjects and worship my beautiful cold. The Genius of the Black Winter wishes to be adored as his body once was."

"Anything you desire, Majesty," Morgan answered with his old subservience, "I'll round up the lads and take 'em to yer, we'll kiss yer feet and never give you cause to doubt our love." Jupiter laughed softly, and Morgan was enchanted by the cruel sound.

"You all right, Boss?" asked Smiff by the side of the throne, as he eyed the bowl suspiciously. "You look a bit peaky like. What's that funny light?"

Morgan looked up sharply. He saw Smiff as though he was looking through a black veil that twisted and distorted everything. "Nothing wrong with me, lad," he replied mechanically. "Get yer things together an' tell the rest of the boys we got to move on."

"What you talking about, Boss?" cried Smiff in astonishment. "We don't 'ave to shift from 'ere yet. There's plenty o' nosh left, an' it's not as if there's anythin' to be afraid of. We're on a cushy number 'ere, why don't we stay?"

Morgan's claws flashed out and Smiff's right ear was torn in two. Smiff clapped hold of his head and jumped back in alarm. "Obey me!" snapped Morgan viciously, and he rose from the throne to address the astonished onlookers. "Prepare to depart," he told them. "We leave within the hour."

The rats looked at each other curiously. What was Old Stumpy up to now? they wondered. "I ain't finished me grub," grumbled one. "Shaddap!" hushed another. "He must know what he's up to. The Boss knows what's good fer us; we can trust 'im, don't you fret."

Smiff walked away from the throne greatly troubled. His ripped ear throbbed and the blood trickled between his claws. Something was wrong and he did not like it. Old Stumpy did not seem the same. He went off sourly, searching for Kelly.

"Most faithful servant," said Jupiter in Morgan's ear, "bring your rabble to me at Deptford. I have a use for them."

Morgan bowed, the eyes disappeared, and the ice melted in the bowl, then he turned to his waiting lads.

"What are yer hanging about fer?" he barked. "Get yer kit together—we go to Deptford."

"Deptford?" they repeated with dismay. "What we goin' there for?" Nearly everybody in the city had heard of that place and the horror that once ruled the sewers there. The rats shook their heads doubtfully. They didn't like the sound of this—all knew the rumors of the dreadful Jupiter, and nobody wanted to go anywhere near Deptford. "Ain't goin'," some grumbled defiantly.

Morgan snarled and shook his fists at them, "Ain't goin'?" he bellowed savagely. "How dare yer! Haven't I led you aright so far? Haven't I let yer taste mouse flesh?"

The rats mumbled with shameful faces, "But Deptford," implored one. "Why there?"

"Because it is the fairest of lands," replied Morgan with a yearning in his voice. "There the pickings are richer than anywhere else. The mouses are plump and just ripe fer peelin', an' there ain't no others to get in our way. All the ratfolk there upped an' died a while ago."

"We don't wanna pop our clogs."

"You won't, my fine boys. Those old stories were a pack o' lies put about by them selfish sewer louts who didn't wanna share the bounty wi' no one. Well, they're gone now, an' what's left is acres of tender squeakers with none to harvest 'em. What a waste." Morgan was winning them over. The greed was still fresh in their hearts, and they would do anything to get their claws on more mice. "Let's hurry," he cried impatiently. "Vinny—raise our standard, we go to war! Deptford shall be ours." He grinned to himself; they would make excellent subjects for his master—it would be like the good old days.

The rats' lust for more blood swept away any doubts, and they cheered at the images Old Stumpy was painting for them. "To Deptford," they cried, throwing their mouse-skin hats into the air.

In a silent corner Smiff and Kelly elbowed each other. Only they knew that their great leader came from Deptford; he had told them when he first arrived in the city. He had also said that it was the most terrible place he had ever been, and had trembled when he mentioned it. The two rats eyed the stump-tailed general warily. Perhaps he had outlived his usefulness and a new leader would have to be chosen. They decided to bide their time and wait for an opportunity to depose him. Kelly licked his claws and bared his sharpened fangs in anticipation.

*   *   *

In the gloom of the subway tunnel, Piccadilly rocked on his heels, cradling his face in folded arms while the heavy fringe of dark hair hid his downcast eyes. The future for him looked stark. With Holeborn destroyed and packed tight with rats, there was nothing he could do. At first he had considered barging straight in to kill as many of the brutes as he was able, but Barker had stopped him, and now that his anger had cooled, Piccadilly was numb inside. He could not believe that all those mice were gone forever. He thought bitterly of the Green Mouse—if he really existed he would not have let this happen. An ironic smile curled over his covered face. Perhaps he was cursed. That might account for all the misfortunes that had occurred in his life. His parents had been killed when he was very young, he had lost himself and ended up in the Deptford sewers, where his new friend Albert Brown perished; the only girl he had ever liked had not cared for him, and now this. Piccadilly's past unrolled itself before him and he hated what he saw.

145

Barker had remained with the city mouse. He looked troubled and twitched his ears cautiously. The rat was frightened. It was dangerous to stay so near to Holeborn; at any moment the marauders might spill out and pounce on them. With his one tooth he nibbled his lip worriedly and counted the lumps on his head. If only the mousey boy would go away somewhere, he could finish what he had been sent to do. At every strange sound Barker jumped and flung himself to the ground–his nerves were shot to pieces.

Piccadilly reared his head, his face set and grim. "I must know what happened to Marty," he said, turning to the rat. "Was he killed along with everyone else? Did you see him?"

Barker looked away and flicked a stone with his claws, "Barker never saw freak mouse," he replied eventually.

A faint hope entered Piccadilly's heart. "Then he could still be alive," he breathed. "He must have got lost around the East Way–that's why the attack was such a surprise; he never reached Holeborn."

The rat mumbled to himself, "Barker not see freak mouse or any other, he not like to see them cut down, he didn't wanna watch the peelin's."

But Piccadilly was not deterred. There was a chance that his young friend was still alive, and he meant to find him. He jumped up and was about to run toward the East Way when a dreadful sound reached his ears. There came a splintering creak as the great door was pulled open and horrible laughter issued into the tunnels–the rat army was leaving Holeborn. He heard the heavy tramp of their trudging feet come closer, and the hiss of their black, boiling breath whistled in the darkness, mingling with their foul oaths and filthy language. Barker yelped with alarm, twisting and turning this way and that, hesitating over where he should run. The unseen army poured from the gates, and the rustling slither of their blood-soaked, slimy bodies filled Piccadilly's jangling ears.

"Come on, lads," a harsh rat voice cried around the corner. "Where's that blasted Vinny with that poxy standard?"

Piccadilly looked at Barker desperately. This time there was nowhere for him to hide, there were no holes here, and the rats were too close for him to start running now. Barker looked blankly back at him, pouting miserably. If they found him with a live mouse they would kill him too.

There was no escape for them. Piccadilly whipped out his little knife and ground his teeth together, waiting for the first of the bloodthirsty monsters. He guessed that he would last for about thirty seconds—long enough, he thought, if Morgan was leading them.

A gnarled, yellow-clawed foot appeared, followed by a huge, black, furry body. The knife glinted in the gray mouse's paws as he braced himself for the onslaught that was to come. Suddenly a claw flashed out and slammed him against the wall. "Quiet, mousey boy," instructed Barker quickly, "stay in shadow." The old rat had grabbed Piccadilly, pushing him down as small as he would go, then stood in front of him, trying to obscure as much of the mouse as he could.

Piccadilly drew his tail in and flattened his ears. This was a crazy idea, and only Barker could have thought of it. Any second, hundreds of rats were going to flood by and one of them would surely spot him. He felt like pushing Barker aside and charging them anyway—at least he wouldn't be found cowering in a corner. But as he struggled to stand the barmy old rat sat down on his back and he could not budge.

The army trooped in, their eyes fiery and filled with murderous lust. First came the newly appointed standard bearer, Vinny—a short, squat, pigmy of a rat whose face was as wicked as sin and whose teeth were stained crimson. He carried the dreadful standard banner proudly before him and cackled at the top of his shrill voice. Barker glanced up and shivered when he realized what the army's standard was.

Piccadilly was unable to see anything. His face was pressed into his stomach, and although he squirmed beneath Barker for all he was worth, the rat had more strength than he had guessed. The evil creatures swarmed by with great, leering faces. Some still wore their grisly trophies on their ugly, slobbering heads and others chewed the remains of their feast. "'Ere, Barker," shouted one, "wot ya doin' there? Ain'tcha 'ad any grub yet?"

Barker coughed and shook his head, "I were waitin' fer you lot to finish before I started tuckin' in," he answered with feigned heartiness. "Can't wait to munch real mouseys."

"You daft old goat," they all hooted. "Only Barker would be mad enough to miss out–wot a loony." They were all so busy making fun of the old rat that none of them bothered to peer into the shadows and see what he was sitting on. "Well, 'urry up then," they told him, "we're not stoppin' around 'ere."

Morgan was in there snorting with them, but his high spirits were born of dark plans that his lads were ignorant of. He sneered and rubbed his claws excitedly. In his mind he saw the blazing magnificence of his master, and he was impatient to do His will once more.

The mass of seething rats continued to buzz through the tunnel; there seemed no end to them. All were gnashing and champing, licking their chops and smacking their lips at the thought of war. Some had found the few weapons the Holeborners had and brandished them over their heads, booming death cries and making up nasty skinning songs. They thrust on feverishly, whooping and brawling amongst each other, shouting obscene slogans at the top of their hideous voices till the tunnel seemed to quake.

Piccadilly stopped struggling; the ridiculous plan seemed to be working, and he was amazed at his luck. Soon the last of the ferocious army would pass by, but he wondered where they

were heading and felt sorry for anyone unfortunate enough to cross their path.

Smiff and Kelly brought up the rear. They were deep in secret discussion, glaring around shiftily to make sure no one could hear them. Smiff's ear was bandaged, and he covered his snotty nose to muffle his words as they plotted and schemed together. Suddenly he caught sight of Barker and spat. He felt like kicking someone.

"Oi!" he shrieked angrily. "Where did you sneak off to then? Come 'ere, ya barmpot."

Barker whimpered. If he moved they could not fail to see Piccadilly. "Shan't," he found himself saying.

Steam practically blew from Smiff's nostrils as he roared, "What! Don't you give me none o' yer lip, mate, get yerself over 'ere now, or I'll come an' get yer with a big stick." But Barker stood his ground defiantly. A horrible growl gurgled in Smiff's throat as he stalked toward him.

"Stop it," Kelly broke in. "Don't start a row an' draw attention to yerself, Smiff mate, there'll be time fer old sots like that later. Get back 'ere, we've got a job to do remember." He caught hold of Smiff's arm and yanked him back roughly.

Smiff relaxed and returned to his side, where he glowered and threw stabbing glances back at Barker. "I'll not ferget this, you old toe rag," he warned. "You'd better watch out, 'cause one day yer gonna wake up with yer throat slit."

When they had passed farther up the tunnel and out of earshot, Barker breathed a sigh of relief and released Piccadilly.

"Thanks," said the mouse, stretching himself. "That was a close one! I never want to be in such a tight spot again." But the rat was watching the army recede into the distance and seemed not to hear. Piccadilly rubbed life into his cramped legs, then folded his arms and frowned. "I wonder where they're going," he said curiously. "That's not the way back to their holes."

"It is war," said Barker, and he sounded almost gleeful. "There will be many battles, and the soil will be a blood marsh."

Piccadilly was unnerved. Sometimes the old rat really surprised him. "I can't worry about that now," he said, "I've still got to try and find Marty, and I suppose I ought to take a last look at Holeborn." With a heavy heart he walked around the corner and beheld the devastation of his home.

Barker stayed where he was, his mind ticking over with its own secret thoughts. When he looked up, Piccadilly had gone and he was alone. "No, mousey boy," he whispered softly, "you not find freak now. You must come with Barker." For a moment the rat straightened his back and was unrecognizable, tall and grim with a knowing gleam in his sharp eyes.

The great door hung sadly off its hinges and the wood was gouged with deep, fierce claw marks. The attack had been a mad frenzy—even if the mice had been warned, Piccadilly doubted if they could have escaped. He forced himself across the threshold and saw the first victim. It was the sentry, or rather the bits that were left of him. The ancient spear had been seized and taken victoriously away, but the battered tin hat had been too small to fit a rat. All that remained was a crushed lump of bent metal in a dark, grisly pool.

In a state of shock Piccadilly wandered into the entrance hall. The rations were strewn wantonly around, and with overwhelming grief he discovered Agnes Trumper's discarded apron. Small fires crackled here and there, over which little black pots had been hung. Piccadilly was not foolish enough to go and inspect the contents—the smell was enough. He staggered up the passage to the main hall. The rats had scrawled awful, crude pictures daubed in blood on the ancient tiled walkways. The carved pillars, had been defaced: all the marvelous wooden animals were now missing ears, legs, or heads, and here and there some beast had coarsely whittled shapes of his own and stuck them on with lumps of fat. Piccadilly looked into the Chapel of the Green Mouse. It was a wreck, and they had torn down the children's paintings from the walls. It was worse than he could ever have imagined. Here was a love of destruction and baseness he had not thought possible.

He stumbled on toward the hall. The tapestry curtain was torn to shreds. Piccadilly stepped over the rags and passed within. The large hall looked like a battlefield; the floor was strewn with well-sucked bones and a pile of skulls was heaped in one corner. Tatters and scraps of fur littered the place, and the huge brewing pans, which had been dragged from the kitchens, were now capsized, licked clean of mouse broth and ear crisps.

Piccadilly sank to his knees. Finally letting go of his emotions, he threw back his head, howling. He shook with violent sobs and his body was racked with weeping as the grief took possession of him. He tore at his hair and his cries were terrible to hear.

The minutes rolled on, and when he could cry no more, Piccadilly hung his haggard face, but he was empty and raw inside, almost as if he were dead too. His lips were dry and parched and his head pounded, but he did not notice. This had finally been too much. He had come to the edge of despair and stared into the devastating eyes of madness—just one blissful plunge and he would be gone forever, lost in the comforting maze of lunacy, never to return to the harsh, cruel world where his body suffered. His reason began to leave him, as a strange smile crossed his face.

"Mousey boy!" Barker's voice croaked at the entrance. "Mousey, snap out!" The rat scurried over to Piccadilly and slapped him sharply. "Not yet," he snarled, "Barker needs you a little longer." He crouched down and peered expertly into the city mouse's raving eyes, "Return from the dark shore,

Piccadilly," he commanded in a powerful voice that was not his own.

Piccadilly's body became limp and he fell into Barker's arms like a rag doll. The rat dragged him over to the tiny stream that ran along the side of the hall and splashed some water onto his face. Gradually Piccadilly came around, his eyes became sane, and he groaned.

"Drink, mousey boy," Barker pleaded in his normal, idiotic voice and he offered up a cupped claw to his cracked lips. Piccadilly spluttered and spat out the water in disgust–the rats had polluted the stream.

"Get off." He coughed, pushing Barker away. "I'm all right, let's get out of here." He stormed out of the hall, and Barker scampered closely behind. Piccadilly wanted to get as far away from Holeborn as possible, somewhere where there were no rats.

"Barker learn somethin', mousey boy," the old rat called after him. "Don't you want to know what it is?"

Piccadilly paused. "You haven't found Marty, have you?" he asked hopefully. Barker looked sheepishly at the floor. "No, he not found freak mouse, but he knows where Old Stumpy has gone."

"Back to his dingy little slime holes, I should think."

"No, he went to Deptford."

The gray mouse froze. "What did you say?"

Barker shrugged. "They've gone down to the river. Old Stumpy's takin' all the lads to Deptford, says there's lots o' fat mice down there."

The now familiar cold fear blistered down Piccadilly's spine. He stared at Barker and spoke quickly. "We've got to stop them, I have friends there." He raced down the passageway shouting, "Show me where Morgan is now!"

Barker chuckled.

153

*   *   *

The breeze was bitter. It nipped and pinched its way over the slate-gray river and carried in its sharp, invisible fingers light flurries of snow. The tiny flakes that were thrown into the icy water floated for some time before melting. It was a wintry dawn and not a soul stirred outside. The Thames moved turgidly around the rotten jetties, brooding and somber, bearing the refuse of mankind on its oily waves.

The steep river walls were riddled with small holes: behind the green, moss-covered stones, dark, dripping passages led off under the city. It was through one of these secret ways that Morgan led his army. He popped his piebald head out of a livid patch of damp moss and squinted in the dull light of the dismal daybreak.

He looked down and gauged the distance to the dark mud below. With a yell of determination he jumped and landed with a squelch. "Come on, boys," he called up. The rats rained out of the hole like water from an overflow pipe. They splattered in the soft, sucking sludge and covered each other from head to toe with it. When it came to Kelly's turn to jump he made a tremendous dent in the riverbank, throwing up huge, gloopy splodges. Some happily slung the slop at one another, enjoying messing about in the filthy muck.

"Calm down, calm down," ordered Morgan, pattering about in the oozing brown mud, his stumpy tail dragging patterns behind him. "This is the quickest way to Deptford, so you'll have to swim." The rats grumbled, but he glared at them and hobbled over to a large piece of driftwood, which he examined and carried to the water's scummy edge. He lowered it in and grunted satisfactorily; he, at least, would not have to get wet.

Morgan leaped onto his makeshift raft and called out, "Vinny, gimme the standard." The squat, smirking rat squelched forward and waded into the frosty river. The cold water wiped the smile from his lips, but he handed the banner over to his master. As he drifted gently away from the bank Morgan addressed his army.

"War and bloodshed!" he cried, flourishing the standard with one claw and clutching a glittering pendant to his breast with the other. "Follow me to Deptford, my fine soldiers." Then the current gripped the driftwood, and Morgan began to sail downriver.

The rats on the shore wasted no time. They yahooed and dived into the glacial water, shrieking and gasping in the ice-cold waves. But rats are very strong swimmers, and these were no exception. Their tails thrashed and whisked in the river, churning and convulsing the surface like a storm at sea. Smiff and Kelly waited till the last had gone before they too charged into the freezing water. With Morgan sailing before them, and the standard fluttering over his head, the rats began the long swim to Deptford.

For over half an hour the bank was still and quiet. The gray light grew brighter, but no sun shone through the dense white clouds. The snow began to stick on the silted shore, and a fine powdery layer formed over everything.

Piccadilly came slithering and sliding out of the hole in the stone wall and fell wriggling down. *Splat!* he plowed into the mire.

Gloosh! Barker was buried headfirst. He kicked and jerked his legs while his knobbly tail whipped about and sent up vast sprays of mud.

"Hang on," said Piccadilly, coming to the rescue. He grabbed hold of the rat's feet and yanked him out. Barker was a sorry, bedraggled sight. He glistened with thick, wet slime, and his startled, round eyes peeped out of the muck comically.

In spite of everything, Piccadilly could not help laughing. The rat looked so funny covered in mud from the top of his head all the way down to his navel. He clutched his sides and pointed at the bewildered Barker who merely blinked stupidly and blew dirty bubbles from the corner of his mouth. Piccadilly shook his head as the humor subsided and trudged to the river's edge, where he shaded his eyes with a paw and stared. In the distance, under a bridge, he saw a frothing, seething mass, and in front of that some kind of boat with a sail—no, it was a flag.

The ghastly mud squished coldly up between his toes, and the brown water welled in. The city mouse shivered at its icy touch; he realized he would not be able to swim in that. What he needed was a boat or something similar. He started to look around the shore.

"What is mousey boy looking fer?" inquired Barker, wiping the slime from his face and smearing it over the rest of his body.

"Something that will float," Piccadilly replied distractedly. "Lend us a paw, will you?"

The two of them hunted about in the rubbish, turning over bottles and tins, throwing them into the water to see if they floated. Barker liked this game and soon forgot what he was looking for, content with just throwing things into the river. "Splash splash, plop plop," he sang happily, doing a ludicrous dance in the mud.

Piccadilly ignored him and continued the search. Finally he found the perfect thing: a red plastic pudding bowl that was big enough for two. Eagerly he began to look for something he could use as paddles and came up with a broken wooden spoon and a large, strong gull's feather.

"Help me," he called to the prancing Barker, "I've got to pull this bowl into the water." He dragged his finds down toward the river's edge.

Barker wandered curiously over to him, studying the plastic bowl intently, "Mousey boy going to make breakfast?" he asked hopefully, rubbing his slime-spattered belly.

Piccadilly puffed and took a breather. "This, my dear chum," he declared proudly, "is going to be our trusty vessel— even old Triton would approve."

"Vessel?" queried the rat. "Our vessel? Barker not understand."

"Yes you do." The city mouse laughed. "I've got to get after Morgan, and you're coming with me."

Barker began to protest again, but Piccadilly marched right up to him, grabbed him by the scruff of the neck, and made him climb into their new little boat. Barker whimpered as he clambered in. The plastic flexed and wobbled alarmingly. He thought of what it would be like when they were actually sailing in it and screwed up his face in misery.

Piccadilly pushed and heaved the bowl and the rat into the water. It lurched and nearly turned over, and Barker wailed out loud and gripped the sides for dear life, but only succeeded in making matters worse. The boat bobbed about threateningly and the rat dropped down out of sight, cringing on the bottom with his arms over his head. Piccadilly splashed after and hauled himself inside.

"Now," he said, once the rocking and tilting had eased down, "take this, Barker lad," and he handed him the large feather, while he took up the wooden spoon.

Barker gazed at the feather stupidly, not sure what to do with it. Grinding his teeth in exasperation, Piccadilly showed him how to place it in the water and draw it back. After several minutes of frustrating coaching they began to paddle. At first the bowl spun around, getting nowhere, as Barker's efforts were pathetic—he was too busy staring fearfully at the cold, dark river all around them. Piccadilly smacked him on the back of his head and the rat cried out.

"Paddle!" shouted the mouse angrily. "We've got to catch up with them."

Barker put his head down and started to row properly. The little red bowl with its two unlikely mariners set off down the Thames as the snow began to fall thick and heavy. Soon they disappeared into the white, whirling curtain, and when Piccadilly looked back at the city it was a vague blur hidden by the wintry weather. "Sorry Marty," he said regretfully. "I'm sure you'll be able to take care of yourself. I've got to go now, but I'll be back, I promise."

The faint vision was cut off by the all-engulfing blizzard. The gray mouse would never set foot there again.

SHOWING THE WAY

The snow fell monotonously over everything; the roofs of Deptford were draped with thick, white folds, while the roads became choked and impassable. The park was obliterated under the ever-deepening layers of snow and ice, and the trees groaned as their branches creaked beneath the weight of the new, wintry foliage. Nowhere escaped the driving flakes. They drifted into doorways and piled up against windows, they clogged the ice-clad gutters and piled against walls in huge drifts. The blizzard was unrelenting. All morning it raged and continued steadily throughout the afternoon. The bitter weather seized the land and gripped it fiercely.

The shore of the river was a playground for the wind. It whipped up the falling snow and sent it dancing in flurries around the rotten wooden jetty that stretched down from the power station. The water's edge was frozen solid, and the ice radiated out across the Thames in sharp, narrow blades.

A faint noise floated over the water as a splashing, thrashing sight paddled into view. Morgan and his army had arrived at last.

The piebald rat tossed back his head and squinted at the power station. He beat his stumpy tail on the makeshift raft excitedly–his master was in there waiting for him.

"Hurry, you swabs!" he shouted over his hunched shoulder to the army, which struggled and spluttered in his wake. "Not long now, my worshipful Lord," he crooned dreamily to himself.

The rats had swum fast and hard, and the river had grown ever colder as they drew close to Deptford. Their chests were tight and nearly bursting with exhaustion, and the weaker ones flopped their arms about and floundered miserably. Some of their number had already surrendered to the aches that racked them and the cold that bit into their claws. They gasped their last and ceased all struggling–the river closed over their heads and they sank lifeless to the murky bottom. Their comrades made no attempt to save them–"good riddance" was their harsh attitude. The army would slow down for nothing.

As they neared the power station the rats had to fight against drifting blocks of ice that bobbed stubbornly in their way. Morgan chortled as he kicked the obstructions out of his path. With a *clonk* the raft hit the edge of the ice floe and shuddered to a halt. It bumped gently against the side and the water lapped over the plank, covering Morgan's toes. He spat and considered the problem. There was still a great distance between him and his master's base, but the raft would float no farther and he did not want to get wet. Using the end of the pole bearing the standard, he gave the ice a quick prod–the edges flaked away, but the rest seemed to be quite firm.

Licking his lips, Morgan stepped nervously from the plank and flopped onto his belly.

"Gar!" he snarled, spitting up a contemptuous green glob.

Cautiously the sour-faced rat wobbled to his feet and slid warily along the ice, using the standard for support. The army hauled themselves out of the water behind him and shook themselves. They puffed and cursed, clapping their claws and howling at the cramps that had set in. But there were too many of them, and the frozen platform could not support their weight. With an ominous splinter the section of ice they had clambered onto split, and they tumbled shrieking into the river once more.

Morgan, having slithered safely ashore, watched them and hooted at the top of his croaky voice. He thought it was hilarious and held his sides, pointing at his unfortunate followers and shouting rude insults at them.

Amid the churning, half-drowning mob, Smiff and Kelly glowered. "I've 'ad it wi' that lousy mongrel!" Smiff ranted and he swam ashore. His fur was matted with icicles and frost, but he paid it no heed—there were other things on his mind. Kelly waded up after him, shivering despite his bulk and whistling through his chattering teeth.

Morgan saw them approach and sniggered at the sight. "Look what the cat's dragged in," he cackled. Neither of the rats smiled. Their faces were grim and menacing.

Morgan eyed them with suspicion; they were planning something. "What's got into yer scurvy heads?" he barked, playing for time.

"You ain't no boss," hissed Smiff, "you're just some jumped-up little nasty what don't know when he's well off."

Morgan's eyes flicked sideways. The rest of his army were shaking themselves out of the water a second time and would soon be here. "What's this mutinous talk, Smiffy lad? Ain't I led you to good pickin's?"

"Maybe," replied Smiff grudgingly, "but we don't like what's goin' on now. Where's all these squeakers you said Deptford was full of? And why is it so perishin' cold around 'ere? You tryin' to get rid of us or wot? There's somethin' not right about you now, Stumpy. Yer not the same as before–you got a crazy look in yer gogglin' eyes. I don't trust yer no more."

"That's right, boy," growled Morgan. "I 'ave got somethin' up my sleeve, and rest assured you'll be the first one to get it when the time comes, and then all my gallant lads will know what it's like to serve a true master."

Smiff gaped as his low cunning grasped Morgan's words. "Then the stories were true, you pox sucker! You've brought us 'ere to grovel before *Him!*"

Morgan cackled triumphantly.

"Kill 'im," rumbled Kelly, sucking his fangs. Smiff leaped forward and pounced on top of Morgan, knocking him backward and clamping his hands around his throat.

"Rip 'is head off," urged Kelly, tittering into his claws.

The breath rattled in Morgan's throat as his teeth snapped at Smiff's arm and tore a chunk out. Smiff squeaked and released his stranglehold. Seizing his chance, Morgan kicked him off his chest. He glanced around. The other rats were coming ashore now, and he raised his voice for them to hear. "Like to see yerself as leader, would ya, Smiff?" he shouted, knocking the wind out of the other with a terrific thump to the stomach.

Smiff crumpled up and gagged. "I'd be a better one 'an you!" he coughed. The army gathered behind him, but he was unaware of them–all his consuming hatred was focused on Old Stumpy. The other rats looked at him and their leader curiously, wondering what was happening.

Morgan smirked. This would be easy. "Tell me again," he gurgled, "repeat what you just said, as how you an' Kelly there would kill me an' make the lads do as they was told, nicking the best pickin's fer yer own greedy guts an' makin 'em do yer dirty work."

Smiff straightened and stared at Morgan as though he had gone mad. "I never . . . " he began, but Kelly tapped him on the shoulder and he whipped around to see the hundreds of steaming rats champing furiously at him. "No," he protested innocently, "don't you see he's connin' yer? This is just . . ."

But they did not let him finish. Morgan had cleverly let them overhear Smiff's desire to be leader, and that was enough for them. With a mad yell they dived forward and fell on Smiff and Kelly. Morgan stepped back and let his loyal, misguided followers deal with the mutineers. A slow grin spread over his face as he listened gleefully to the racket.

Smiff screamed as the army clawed and hacked at him. Kelly put up a good fight, charging through them as far as he could until a knife flashed out and stuck in his neck. Screeching, he crashed to the snowy ground, squashing the life out of one who could not get out of the way. The skirmish did not last long; a spear was soon raised and brandished aloft to the wicked cheers of all. Mounted on it was Smiff's head.

"Well done, lads," cried Morgan, "well done. That's givin' those lousy scum their due. Now where's Vinny?" The small rat came scurrying out of the jubilant crowd and took up the standard. "To glory and war!" Morgan shouted. "Follow me!"

The army waved their claws in the air and cheered. The fight with Smiff and Kelly had gotten their circulation going again, and the taste of delicious, burning blood on their tongues made them forget the cold altogether. "War," they echoed in a frenzy.

Morgan scampered up the shore, trudging through the deep snow that lay along the sloping jetty. Behind him came his army–wild-eyed and gnashing, eager for murder with death dripping from their claws. Smiff's head waved above their ears and they trampled Kelly's blood into the snow till it was a mire of pink slush.

*   *   *

"Barker tired, his arms drop off," whined the unhappy rat.

Piccadilly sighed wearily. His companion had not stopped moaning since they had set off. Their little red boat sailed around the old docks, and the shores of Deptford came in sight. "At last," the city mouse said, relieved. "Look, Barker, we're nearly there now. That's Deptford, and I think that hill beyond is Greenwich–yes, that must be the observatory, do you see?" He was getting excited now that he was nearing the home of his friends. He wondered how Oswald was doing in this weather. He'd surely have another cold, and Arthur would probably be having snowball fights in the yard and coming off worse as usual. Piccadilly did not stop to think of Audrey. He had decided to let that situation take its own course.

Barker paddled miserably. He had lowered his face when Greenwich was mentioned. "Ain't goin' there," he muttered, "an' mousey boy can't make Barker."

Piccadilly laughed. "Don't worry, we don't have to go that far, anywhere around here will do."

Presently the plastic bowl nudged the edge of the ice where Old Stumpy's raft forlornly bobbed up and down. Piccadilly used his wooden spoon to keep his vessel steady. "We have to get out here," he told Barker. "Careful though, or we'll both be in the drink."

Barker shivered at the prospect. "Poor Barker," he whimpered, staring at the sloshing water and the smooth, brittle ice.

Piccadilly leaned out of the bowl and signaled for the rat to do the same. Gingerly they put paw and claw on the tingling ice and pulled themselves slowly out. Without their weight, the empty bowl popped up and tumbled over, quickly filling with freezing water and sinking without a trace.

Barker did not like the ice. He gave it a cautious lick to see what it tasted like and spat. "Yak yak yak!" he gargled disgustedly.

Piccadilly struggled to his feet and balanced precariously on the slippery surface. After a few tentative steps he grinned and started to slide about, as though he had done it all his life. "Get up," he said to the rat as he circled neatly around him.

"Pah!" sniveled Barker, watching the mouse show off. He flicked his knobbly tail and tried to stand. With a loud smack he fell down again and rubbed another lump that was rising on his head. The ice was as smooth as polished glass, and try as he might, the rat failed to stand up for long. Several attempts and countless bruises later he decided it would be best if he slid along on his belly, it was much safer that way. With a sweep of his claws he shoved off and the frozen river flashed under him. Piccadilly smiled as he skidded by the rat-sledge. Barker began to enjoy it and chuckled as he mastered the art. "Wheeeee!" he sang, zooming over the ice at breakneck speed. Unfortunately he had given no thought to how he would stop, and as the shore loomed up he realized his mistake. The rat shot off the river with a howl and plowed straight into a snowdrift.

Piccadilly skated to the shore. Barker was buried, and his mournful voice spoke desolately out of the snowdrift. "Wah, ohh," he cried self-pityingly. The gray mouse laughed and waited for him to emerge. "Poor Barker," mumbled the rat, shaking the snow out of his ears. "Poor old thing, always 'appens to 'im, don't it?" But Piccadilly was not looking at him now. He had seen two dark shapes on the bank and was walking over to them.

Barker stumbled out of the snow and followed him, curious. The bodies of Smiff and Kelly were sprawled on the ground before them.

"Ach!" Barker sniffed coldly. "Kelly got his after all." He looked at the other, headless body and twisted around, trying to see who it was. "Must be Smiffy," he decided, spitting on them. "No more lumps for Barker, he always reckoned he'd outlive 'em."

Piccadilly felt nothing. He had no pity for the dead rats, but he did not like Barker spitting on them. "Don't," he scowled. "They're gone now, let them rest in whatever peace is due to them. Wonder what they were fightin' about though?"

Barker giggled. "They ain't gonna find no peace where they've gone–Barker knows, hah hah." Piccadilly looked away and walked slowly to the jetty. When he was out of earshot Barker stooped down and whispered in Kelly's ear, "Now you'll pay. Your torment has only just begun! Tell Hobb I sent you." And he made a curious sign in the air over the body.

"There are tracks over here," Piccadilly called out. He was studying the footprints made by Morgan's army. The snow was already covering them and in another ten minutes they would have disappeared. "They went up there," he said, pointing up the jetty. "If I hurry I might be able to catch up with them and see what they're doing." The mouse took hold of Barker's claw and shook it vigorously. "Thanks for helpin' me get here chummy, but you don't have to come with me now."

The rat blinked and shook his head. "But what will Barker do without mousey boy? Don't send him away now, he don't know where he is–he'll freeze an' starve on his own. Let him come with nice mousey, please, yes?"

Piccadilly smiled. "Okay, you can come, just follow me and don't make a sound." He ran up the jetty and with a secret, sly grin the rat scurried after.

The jetty joined a narrow lane lined on one side by a block of flats and on the other by a high brick wall. This was pitted with curious craters and pockmarks as though blasted by some spiteful force. The damaged wall held a door barred by cruel-looking railings but Piccadilly and Barker ducked under these and gazed at the power station before them.

It was a solid, square building of old brick, surrounded on three sides by an overgrown dump, which the snow had transformed into a vast white plain. Behind it glistened the frozen river. It was a forbidding, lonely place, feeling the full brunt of the wintry gales, and Piccadilly had to shake his head to dispel the disquiet and fear that seemed to flow out from it.

Barker scrutinized the building keenly. He pulled a sneering face and muttered to his companion, "Look, mousey boy, 'tis the shape of a gigantic cat done in brick."

The city mouse half closed his eyes and agreed. There was something about the power station that resembled a crouching cat. The arches at the front were the teeth and claws, and the small windows its eyes, with the chimney as the tail. He put his paw to his mouth and pondered—something strange was going on here. Perhaps he ought to go straight to the Skirtings.

Barker saw his indecision and sucked his gums patiently. Then in a soft whisper he said, "Tracks lead that way, mousey boy, what we do?"

That seemed to make up Piccadilly's mind. His first priority had to be Morgan. "We go in there," he answered firmly. Barker bowed and chuckled to himself.

*   *   *

The gale ravaged down, driving the snow into Morgan's streaming eyes. An icicle hung from his earring and he held grimly on to the shining pendant around his neck. He leaned into the biting wind and waded through the heavy drift. Not far now, he told himself. He had led his army over the dump and around the back of the power station, where he knew there was an entrance.

His followers said little. It was enough to force their way through the howling blizzard without trying to make themselves heard. They bent low and pressed forward. The deep snow made their legs ache and they wished they had brought those mouse skins with them to wrap around their frozen ears. Vinny was blown to and fro as the storm snatched the standard and tried to tear it from his claws. Wailing and squealing, the short rat staggered backward, then sideward as the banner madly flapped and flailed above his ugly head. He, like everyone else, was trying to guess why the boss was taking them to this forsaken place—and where were all the promised mice? Some of them began to suspect that maybe Smiff and Kelly had been right all along. The one carrying Smiff's head glanced up at it apologetically. The beating snow that drove between them played tricks on him, and the dead, ghastly face appeared to wink in a "told you so" sort of way, then stared accusingly down, its nose still running. With a yell, the fearful rat threw the trophy away and nibbled his claws nervously, waiting for something awful to happen.

Morgan waddled over to a low, broken window and squeezed himself inside. As he stared about him, his ears were still ringing from the gale, and he shook the snow from his shoulders.

Inside the power station was an impossibly huge chamber. Morgan's panting breath was caught up and sent echoing around the wintry walls. Slanting shafts of light grubbed through the filthy upper windows but failed to illuminate the immense gloom. The derelict building was crusted in frost, and savage spears of blue ice were suspended from the lofty ceiling, transforming it into an immense cavern of crystals. Morgan grinned. Truly this was an appropriate palace for his lord—a frozen cathedral of inverted, glassy spires, a fortress of cold, withering death. He peered into the glimmering distance to see if he could catch sight of his god, but all was still and silent.

"Let us in!" bawled his army, stamping outside the window. "We're catchin' our deaths out 'ere."

Morgan tutted. That would never do—not after he had brought them all this way for his master's pleasure. He stepped aside and let his army surge past. In poured the ragtag, snowy bodies. They coughed and spluttered, shaking their claws and blowing clouds of steam from flaring nostrils—it seemed colder

169

inside than out. Vinny swore as he tried to worm his way in. He cursed the standard as it got itself stuck in the window, and as those behind him raised their voices impatiently, the air turned even bluer. With a heave and a shove the pigmy rat shot through and went scooting across the floor with a squeak.

"Welcome lads," cackled Morgan, herding them inside. "That's right, get you in 'ere."

When they had recovered from the gale outside, the shivering rats began to look about them. They whistled at the cruel beauty of the icicles and stared at the frost-blistered walls. "Wot's all this then?" they asked. "Where's 'em whisker twitchas?"

Morgan waved his claws for silence and led them to the middle of the empty building. "No doubt yer all dyin' to know what I brought yer here for," he addressed them smarmily.

"Too right, Stumpy!" they replied curtly, stomping their aching feet on the ice-rasping ground.

"Then know this," he told them. "There dwells here a power greater than the world has ever known, mightier than a mountain, wiser than the night and stronger than death."

The rats looked at one another. "He's flipped his lid," they mumbled in surprise.

"Idiots!" snapped Morgan. "Lice fodder! Listen, I speak the truth." He threw back his head and raised his arms in exultation. "Hear me Lord of the Deadly Dark," he cried, "witness the subjects I bring to you!"

The army's initial astonishment at Old Stumpy's sudden madness turned to anger as they smelled betrayal—they had been tricked! They thought of the long, dreadful swim and the murder of Smiff and Kelly, and growls snarled in their throats. They could have stayed in Holeborn after all. Yellow teeth were bared and ground together as eyes shone red and blazed furiously at the piebald rat. The army closed tightly around him with deadly intent and slavering jaws. Vinny dropped the standard and joined them, eager for the kill.

"Master?" Morgan called out as the first blow struck his head.

The rats pounced on him with hatred burning in them, but at that moment a terrific rumble shook the building and they paused in alarm. Vinny drew his flat head into his shoulders and looked up. "AAAIIEE!" he screamed.

His fellows stared at the icicled ceiling and uttered squeals of fright and dismay. There, forming amid the frost, were two large, cold eyes.

"It's *Him!*" they screeched, scrabbling over one another in panic. Morgan let loose a triumphant hooting laugh and backed away.

Jupiter purred. The walls trembled and the ground shuddered. The rats were thrown down and with howling, terrified faces they struck the floor. Morgan bowed reverently to his old master.

As the shape of the grotesquely huge cat spirit formed high above, the wailing rats fought each other to get to the broken window, but it was no use. Jupiter laughed at their puny efforts, and his voice cut into their hearts like a knife of ice.

"Come, my subjects," he boomed, "worship me and my beautiful cold."

The rats cried pitifully, cutting themselves on the broken glass in their struggle to get out, but it was too late. Jupiter roared and his breath hailed down on them. The icicles broke from the ceiling, raining bitter death on the rats below. Screams and squeals seared the air as the rats were impaled by the ice spears. Their aim was deadly, smashing through the chest of every one of them. In a moment it was over; not one rat was left alive, except Morgan. The power station was filled with death. The hundreds of fallen rats stared unseeing at the spears in their broken bodies. A faint frost was already spreading out from the evil spikes, and the countless eyes glazed over with rime.

Morgan staggered through the frozen corpses. At last the spell wore off, the scales fell from his eyes, and he was free of Jupiter's magic. With a sick stomach Morgan realized what he had done.

A wicked voice chuckled above. Jupiter had his old lieutenant back. It amused him to keep Morgan alive, despairing in the knowledge of how he had led his loyal followers to their deaths. The rat had finally achieved everything he had desired, and Jupiter had taken it from him. Morgan fell to his knees and wept for his lads. How could he have done this to them? In his corrupt heart he cursed Jupiter and wished he had died too—better that than cower in his shadow once more.

"Take your place at my side," Jupiter hissed at him. "Be my high priest and commander of my armies."

Morgan sobbed and hid his face. He was trapped and enslaved by this fiend forever. Bitterly he agreed. What else could he do? "Yes, my . . . Lord," he stammered sorrowfully.

A shadow flicked across the broken window. With a shocked, appalled face Piccadilly hurried away from the power station. He had seen it all, and his mind was reeling. Scurrying behind came Barker. He wore an odd expression—the barmy rat seemed to be impressed rather than frightened.

* * *

Thomas Triton swigged the rum, and his throat burned deliciously. He had never needed a drop so badly in his entire life—what a terrible night it had been. He passed the bowl to Arthur and the young mouse drank it down, spluttering afterward and grinning at the tingling sensation that tickled him down to his tail.

They were gradually thawing in the warm quarters of the midshipmouse. After Jupiter had stolen the stars he rose from the observatory like a terrible demon from the dark times and he passed overhead screeching with hellish laughter. Slowly the mice came to and discovered a stark, gray dawn breaking drably about them. Without uttering a word they staggered with frozen limbs down the hill. Wearily Thomas guided Arthur to the *Cutty Sark*, where, trembling, they crawled into the figurehead and lit every candle they could find.

Arthur's paws itched at his growing chilblains, and he rubbed them till they were red and blotchy. He had never seen this place before and he gazed with interest at the cheery maps and faded pictures of exotic places that adorned the old sailor's quarters. Thomas's sword glowed on the wooden wall, sparkling brightly in the orange light of the candle flame. Arthur liked the model ship Thomas had built, and he examined it carefully as the midshipmouse stuffed his pipe with tobacco and lit it. Both mice remained silent for some time, not wishing to disturb the other's peace.

Blue smoke rose from the pipe and gathered about Thomas's head. "Do you remember what happened last night?" he said at last.

Arthur looked at the smoke that puffed out of Thomas's mouth and nodded quickly.

"Yes," he replied. "Jupiter was there and he made such a dreadful noise that we passed out."

Thomas considered him through the curling smoke and grunted. "It's a good job we weren't out for long, we'd have perished in this weather for sure. The midwinter death would've netted us." He stared at a small lead anchor charm that lay near the model ship and like some ghostly oracle of the deep, briny waves, spoke gravely through the hanging pipe smoke. "There was something you did not see, matey. That black-hearted villain stole the stars last night." He held his paw up to silence

Arthur's ridicule. "I know it sounds daft but it's what I saw. And tell me, do you now doubt that his powers can do such a thing?"

Arthur had no answer to that. "What shall we do?" he asked meekly.

The midshipmouse shrugged and drew on his pipe. "I don't know, maybe nothing, but we must go back to the Skirtings and consult the Starwife. We can only be certain that this is not the end of Jupiter's schemes." He rolled off his bunk and tapped the pipe on the side. "Get yourself together mate, we're off again."

*　　*　　*

The Starwife was mourning for the stars. From the instant Jupiter began his incantation she sensed his dark purpose and knew she was powerless to prevent him. She had remained in the freezing yard to witness the destruction of the heavens, and when it was all over and the void came flooding in, she limped back into the old house a pathetic, broken figure.

The dawn had been bleak, and the snowstorm raged savagely outside. Audrey listened to the blizzard beating against the house, wondering what other catastrophes lay ahead. She could hardly believe that the stars had all disappeared, and she prayed that Arthur and Thomas were safe.

The mice of the Skirtings were gathered around the Hall fire, hungry and afraid. Master Oldnose recited a prayer, calling on the Green Mouse for deliverance. Everyone joined in, paws clasped beneath their chins and voices lifted in despair.

Audrey would not take part. She knew that it was no good. The Green Mouse was dead and could not hear them. His power was for the spring and summer only. She wandered away from the fireside, past the kneeling mice to where the Starwife rocked on her heels by the stairs. The old squirrel appeared worse than ever, her tear-stained cheeks had caved in and her fragile skull could plainly be seen. Her arms were nothing more than brittle sticks loosely wrapped with wasted flesh, and her rib cage protruded so much from her body that you could almost see her frail heart pitter-pattering behind the rattling ribs. Audrey guessed that she would not live much longer.

A milky eye fluttered open and focused smartly on the girl. "Don't you fret, child," said the Starwife hoarsely. "You haven't got a corpse in your Hall—not yet." She managed a faint smile and turned stiffly. "So, you are not praying with everyone else," she observed dryly. "I see your mother there, why do you not join her?"

"It won't be any use," Audrey replied. "He can't help us this time."

The Starwife nodded feebly. "True enough. While the Unbeast keeps spring at bay, the Green Mouse cannot answer, even if he does hear them. You are a sensible child—too much so, perhaps." She fingered her silver acorn, the pale lids slipped over the eyes once more, and her head fell drowsily onto her chest.

Audrey reluctantly left her and returned to the fire, where, the prayers having finished, Master Oldnose began singing songs from the spring celebration to lighten everyone's spirits. It did not succeed. The attempts were halfhearted and the sound dismal. He abandoned that and tried to think of something else. The hours ticked by and the snow continued to fall steadily.

The afternoon was just creeping up on them when Algy Coltfoot jumped to his feet and whispered, "Shush! Something's coming up the cellar steps."

The mice murmured worriedly and Mr. Cockle took a burning stick from the fire and held it before him, ready for any trouble. The cellar door creaked open and they all fell back.

"Arthur!" exclaimed Audrey, dashing forward to hug her astonished brother.

"Get off, sis," he protested, pushing her away and blushing as his mother ran forward to kiss him.

Thomas laughed as he came through the door, and Gwen had a kiss for him too. Mr. Cockle put the stick back in the fire and everyone sighed with relief.

"Here's a hearty welcome," said Thomas happily.

"I'm so glad you're both safe," beamed Gwen. "Arthur, don't you ever go off like that again, and how dare you take him with you, Mr. Triton, without telling me first."

Thomas swept the hat from his head and bowed. "Apologies, ma'am. I have no excuse, and beseech your forgiveness."

Audrey giggled, but whatever she was about to say was forgotten as the Starwife hobbled forward. "Triton!" she called bad-temperedly. "Where've you been, you lazy mariner? Report to me, I said, but I didn't mean some time next week!" She made her way painfully up to the midshipmouse and stood imperiously in front of him.

Thomas sighed and loosened the kerchief around his neck. He studied the squirrel closely. It was obvious that she knew precisely what had happened. "I'd be wasting my breath," he said gruffly. "You know well enough."

"Don't take that attitude with me, Triton!" the Starwife snapped. "I sensed what the Unbeast was doing, but you were there! Tell me exactly what you saw."

The midshipmouse glanced at Arthur and began. He walked over to the fire and related the terrible events of the previous night. The mice listened to him with fearful expressions, uttering sharp cries of dismay and covering their faces when he described Jupiter on the observatory.

Throughout his account the Starwife's face was solemn and grave. When he had finished she turned briskly away and resumed her position by the stairs. There she sat in brooding silence and closed her eyes.

Thomas fidgeted with the hat in his paws and looked at her

in consternation. What was she doing? This was not what he had expected from her at all. He went after the squirrel and waited. She did not move. He coughed—surely she hadn't nodded off. An eyelid opened slightly, showing a watery slice of clouded eye, "What do you want of me, Triton?" she asked in a flat voice. "Can you not leave me in peace?"

"No, I can't," he shouted in exasperation. "What are you sitting there like Neptune's mother for, you silly old devil? Here's that foul fiend taking the stars away an' all you can do is mope about!"

"What do you suggest I do?" she asked in a deceptively calm tone. "What do you think I am able to do?"

Thomas shrugged. "I don't know," he answered frankly, "but we must do somethin'. I don't reckon this is the end of Jupiter's tricks. There'll be more, I'm certain of it."

The Starwife stared at her gnarled paws. "But of course," she admitted, "he will not stop yet, not until he can be certain that spring will never come again."

"What do you mean?" asked the midshipmouse. "What else can he do? For pity's sake, you crafty old baggage, will you not tell us what's going on? You've got a pretty fair idea, haven't you? Everything's figured out in that crusty old brain box of yours, but you're not letting on." He threw his hat down in anger.

She turned her half-blind eyes full on him and he was prevented from saying anything more by the power that poured out of them. He had riled her and she proved that such an action was still dangerous. "So be it!" she raged. "You shall know and you shall tremble as I have!" The squirrel glared around at the astonished mice and harshly told them, "The Unbeast has destroyed the stars of the night. Next he shall destroy the day star—soon the same magic will be used on the sun."

All the mice in the Hall gasped and squeaked. Those who had sneaked down from the Landings scurried back up the stairs to tell everyone. The Starwife closed her eyes again and breathed deeply. Thomas fumbled for words, but was too stricken to say anything. Could it be true? Could Jupiter really blot out the sun? His legs wobbled and he sat himself down sharply in case he collapsed. All eyes stared at the old squirrel.

Audrey knelt beside her and tried to talk. "There must be something we can do," she said. "He must have a weakness, there has to be a way." The Starwife did not reply, so Audrey repeated herself. Still nothing. The squirrel was ignoring her. The mouse fumed and folded her arms crossly. "I'm glad you are the last of your kind," she blazed. "I think you're horrible!"

The milky eyes blinked and a desolate tear welled up and spilled down the hollow cheek. "There is nothing we can do, child," sobbed the Starwife hopelessly. "Jupiter has no weaknesses." The defeat in her voice was heartbreaking. Audrey immediately regretted her outburst and hugged the forlorn creature tightly.

The afternoon lengthened and the daylight began to fail. Some murmured fearfully, but the Starwife held up a paw and reassured them, "Do not fear, it is not him, not yet. Last night must have taken its toll, and the power will be spent for a while. Jupiter will not be able to use my Starglass today, but all too soon will it be ready again."

Thomas hated sitting about doing nothing, but what could they do? He wished he had brought his pipe along. The fire needed more wood, but there was hardly any left in the house. He was wondering if he ought to go out and find some more, when his thoughts were interrupted by a chirpy voice.

"This some sort of indoor picnic or what?"

The mice jumped with surprise and spun round. Arthur could not believe his eyes. "Piccadilly!" he shouted happily.

The city mouse grinned from ear to ear as his friend rushed forward and shook his paw. "Careful Art," he warned with a laugh, "it's so cold it might drop off." Everyone gathered around to welcome the cheeky young mouse back to the Skirtings.

"I can't believe you're here," cried Arthur, overjoyed. "What made you leave the city? Was life getting too dull?"

A shadow passed over Piccadilly's face and he looked away. "Wotcha Mr. Triton," he said, changing the subject.

Thomas eyed him strangely before returning the greeting, "Welcome back lad. If you don't mind me sayin' so—you look awful."

Piccadilly grunted and was about to say something to Master Oldnose, when Audrey pushed through the crowd and said sheepishly, "Hello Piccadilly, I'm glad you came back—I missed you."

He blinked and was at a loss for words. He had often wondered what her first words would be if they ever met again, but he never counted on "I missed you." The city mouse shook his head in disbelief; he always thought Audrey had disliked him, and now here she was, smiling coyly. "Hello," was all he managed to come up with. A light bloomed in her rich brown eyes and he stepped back in surprise. Somewhere, deep inside him, was born an urge to kiss her. It alarmed him and he coughed and turned hastily away.

"I never thought we'd clap eyes on you again after you went off like that," said Arthur. "Why are you here?"

Piccadilly collected his wits and spoke seriously, "That's a long story . . ." But before he could say any more, he put his paw to his mouth. "Oh, I nearly forgot, I've brought someone with me."

"Who is it?" asked Audrey. "Where is he?"

"He . . . I left him," Piccadilly stammered warily, unsure how to put it, "I left him in the cellar after we came through the Grill."

"Don't leave him down there, lad," ordered Thomas. "Bring him in."

"But . . . you don't understand," Piccadilly tried to explain.

179

"Oh well!" He cupped his mouth in his paws and yelled through the cellar door, "Barker! You can come in now."

"This one of your city friends?" Arthur inquired as they waited for him to appear. A strange slapping slither came up the steps, and the mice stared at one another curiously.

"Barker coming, mousey boy," cried a croaky voice. Audrey backed away, Arthur scratched his ear, and Thomas scowled. They recognized the sound of a rat when they heard one. In waddled Barker.

"A rat!" screamed Mrs. Chitter, leaping to her feet. "We'll be eaten alive!"

Most of the mice had never seen a rat before, but all knew how vicious they could be. They shrieked and scattered everywhere. Some tried to leap up the stairs, but tripped and fell over each other; others headed for the Skirtings, where they all tried to squeeze in at once and got jammed in the entrance. Cries and wails rang around the Hall as the mice charged about, demented with terror. Algy became tangled in the blankets and squealed as he smashed into a pile of unwashed soup bowls.

Barker laughed and jumped up and down. He thought it was a game and started to chase some of the mice, which only made matters worse. Piccadilly groaned. He was afraid something like this would happen. "Barker," he shouted, "stop it, you crazy old nit!" The rat took no notice as he had pinned Mrs. Chitter to the wall and was busily engaged in tickling her under the chin. She let out a howl and slid to the floor in a faint, while her curling papers popped out of her hair as it stood on end. Piccadilly ran over and tried to grab him, but Barker was enjoying this too much and dodged out of reach. With a bound he had leapfrogged over one of the Raddle sisters and blown a raspberry at the other. He chased Biddy Cockle and pulled a blanket over Master Oldnose's head. "Barker!" bawled Piccadilly, not knowing whether to laugh or be cross.

Barker pranced around the Hall until he skidded to an

abrupt standstill. He had nearly crashed into the Starwife, and now she was staring at him fearlessly, but her brow wrinkled and a curious look crossed her face. The rat caught his breath in surprise and hissed. For a moment the two seemed to strive mentally with each other as though they were locked in a secret duel. There was a strained, struggling silence between them, and their eyes smoldered with enmity.

Piccadilly ran up and took hold of the rat's tail, "Gotcha!" he cried. "Don't worry, folks," the city mouse called out to all the distressed mice, "he's with me. He's harmless, I promise—just a bit nutty, that's all." He dragged Barker away from the Starwife and led him back to his friends.

Throughout all the commotion, Thomas, Gwen, Audrey, and Arthur had remained calm. They realized that if Piccadilly had brought him, then Barker could not be dangerous. Even so, the midshipmouse did not like the look of the barmy old rat. Arthur, however, had split his sides laughing, and when Mrs. Chitter fainted he felt as if he was going to bust. Now he wiped the tears from his eyes and settled down, as the chuckles gave way to smirks.

"Sorry about that," Piccadilly apologized. "This is Barker—I had to bring him with me. Like I said, it's a long story, but first of all—Jupiter is back."

*   *   *

Piccadilly drank the soup and tried not to pull a face—it was as weak as dishwater. "Thanks," he said trying to sound as though he had enjoyed it, "that was—very, er . . ."

Gwen took the bowl from him and nodded with understanding. "Yes, I know." She smiled. "It isn't very nice, but that's all we have, I'm afraid."

The city mouse was sitting in front of the fire soaking up the warmth. It seemed like ages since he had last had time to relax and wiggle his toes. Barker sat next to him sniffing his bowl suspiciously. He lapped up some of the soup and swirled it around his mouth. It had taken quite a while for the panic to die down. Some mice were still hiding in the Skirtings under their beds, and no amount of persuasion would draw them out. A few brave ones hovered near the fire and studied the rat keenly. He didn't look as fierce as they had imagined.

Mrs. Chitter had to be taken away to her little room, where she whimpered in her sleep and had horrible tickling nightmares. Strangely enough, the Raddle sisters were among those who crept closest to the fire to see the strange newcomer; they had never had such an exciting time in all their lives and secretly hoped for more.

Piccadilly was listening attentively to Thomas as the midshipmouse brought him up to date with events. He was sorry that Oswald was not here; he had been looking forward to seeing "Whitey" again. Occasionally his eyes would rove sideways to where Audrey sat and she smiled back at him. When the tale had ended, Piccadilly sat up stiffly and bit his nails.

He then related his own story. As this was news to everyone, more mice crept around. They were all astonished and dismayed to learn that Morgan was still alive, and gasped at the point where Holeborn was attacked. Throughout all this, Barker shot furtive glances at the stairs where the Starwife had been, but she was not there now and he craned his neck to see where she had gone.

Thomas rubbed his whiskers, puzzled. "It don't make sense," he muttered. "Why would Jupiter call an army of bloodthirsty rats back here, only to kill them as soon as they arrive?"

"Maybe he's potty," suggested Piccadilly. "I can't see any other reason for it. Unless he just likes to kill things—that wouldn't surprise me."

But Thomas was not convinced. "No, there has to be a

sound reason. He never does anything just for the sake of it, but we'll find out soon enough."

"Is there really nothing we can do?" asked Arthur gloomily. "Why don't we all put our heads together and see if we can come up with something?"

"I suppose it's worth a try," agreed Thomas. He stood up and grabbed everyone's attention. "We're going to have a meeting," he declared. "Anyone who wants to join in is most welcome."

When most of the mice had sat down, some still looking dubiously at Barker, they began. "Right," said the midship-mouse, "let's go over what we know about Jupiter."

"He's dead," Mr. Cockle put in bluntly.

"So we can't kill him," added Algy, stating the obvious.

Audrey tried to think of something she could contribute. "Oh," she announced suddenly, "he doesn't like the heat."

"How do you work that out?" Arthur snorted. His sister rolled her eyes impatiently. "Because if he did he wouldn't be freezing us to death, would he? He'd blast us with fire or bake us–that would be much quicker than waiting for us all to freeze."

Thomas puckered his brow with concentration. "You might be right, but Jupiter could just be bringing in the cold to prevent the Green Mouse's return."

"So where does that leave us?" asked Piccadilly, dismissing the ridiculous Green Mouse. "Jupiter *might* be afraid of fire, though I don't see why, if he's dead–I mean, it couldn't hurt him could it?"

Audrey sighed. "If only I still had my mousebrass, perhaps that would have helped–it worked before."

For the first time since his manic escapade Barker spoke. "Barker like pretty mouse danglers," he chattered brightly. "Him always wanted one, but all he ever had was lump, lump, lump."

Master Oldnose bristled and could not help stating acidly: "Rats do not wear the brass, they are for mouse necks only—the very idea!"

Barker waggled his tongue at the pompous creature. "Not true," he retorted, "nyah nyah!"

"Keep quiet," warned Piccadilly, "this is serious, we haven't got time for your pranks again."

Barker folded his arms sulkily and mumbled, "Not fair, no one listens to Barker. Rats do 'ave danglers—he saw one."

"What about the Starglass?" began Arthur. "Do you think we could get close enough to break it before Jupiter tries to use it again?"

"Never get near it," Piccadilly replied, shaking his head. "You'd be speared before you got within . . . "

"Shush," said Thomas. He had been watching Barker intently and wanted to know what he had meant. "Who did you see with a mousebrass?" he asked the rat.

Barker shrugged. "Not remember," he replied with a sullen expression.

Thomas slapped the floor angrily. "Tell me!" he commanded.

The rat fell on his face. "Don't hit Barker, no more lumps for him—please, he'll tell. Old Stumpy it was, it was him that had shiny mouse metal, wore it often he did, said it were his good-luck charm."

Audrey leaned forward. "This mousebrass," she said breathlessly, "what did it look like?"

Barker raised his frightened eyes to her and narrowed them as he replied, "Looked like a cat it did—whiskers an' all." A murmur ran through the gathering. "Audrey's brass," they uttered with surprise.

"Morgan must've found it in the water before he swam to the city," breathed Piccadilly, "what luck!"

"Praise be to the Green," exulted Master Oldnose. "Even in the winter he shows the way."

Thomas grinned with excitement. "So Morgan holds the answer. If we can take the mousebrass from him and throw it at Jupiter we might get rid of the old devil once and for all."

In the shadows the Starwife listened to their confident plans and shook her head sadly. What fools they were! Then she saw them laugh and tutted at her own arrogance. Perhaps they were right. Maybe it would work—just because they were simple mice did not mean they were incapable of great deeds—Jupiter had after all been destroyed by them once before. Her gaze moved from face to face. How eager and keen they were for this plan to succeed. She did not have the heart to say they might be mistaken, but she had grave misgivings. Something told her that it would take more than a mousebrass to vanquish Jupiter this time. He had outgrown the earthly confines and his might was incalculable.

Then the squirrel choked back a cry. There, in the midst of the crowd, Barker was staring out at her with a malevolent gleam in his eyes. The Starwife backed away, greatly troubled. There was something about him that was familiar and yet—oh, what was it? He had deftly parried all her attempts to read his concealed thoughts, and that fact alone alarmed her. Barker was not who he pretended to be—but who was he? She pressed her paws into her forehead and racked her brain, but it was useless. The squirrel chided herself—perhaps it was not important after all; she really must not get distracted from the main problem. The Starwife melted back into the deep shadows, and the rat watched her with an evil smile on his lips.

CHAPTER TEN

DUEL IN THE STORM

Audrey threaded the remaining silver bell onto her tail and carefully smoothed the creases in her collar. While the plans were being discussed in the Hall she had slipped quietly away and entered her bedroom in the Skirtings. She untied the crumpled ribbon in her hair and put in its place a clean one of palest pink. She admired herself in the small mirror that she had fetched from her mother's room and practiced her most winning smile. Piccadilly's unexpected return was the sole reason for this strange behavior; her heart was beating rapidly and her mind was crowded with wild fancies and impossibilities. When everything looked right and Audrey was satisfied, she gave one last critical glance in the mirror and turned to leave.

"Mother!" she exclaimed in embarrassed surprise, "How long have you been there?"

"Long enough," Gwen replied, shaking her head at her preening daughter. "Oh Audrey," she sighed disappointedly. Audrey felt her ears burn as she blushed shamefully. She felt as guilty as a thief caught in the act. "I was only . . ." she lamely began, but her words failed and she did not know what to say.

Gwen nodded. "I understand," she said with a knowing look in her eye, "you wanted to look your best for Piccadilly, didn't you?"

The girl hung her head. "Yes," she admitted slowly.

Her mother came forward and embraced her. "My darling child," she said softly, "you must forget the feelings you have for him. Things have changed, and you must act responsibly. Like it or not, you are married–you are Mrs. Scuttle now, Twit's wife."

Audrey burst into tears and buried herself in her mother's arms. "But it isn't fair," she sobbed. "It's Piccadilly I love, I know that now. I want to tell him how sorry I am for making him leave last time." She gulped the air down her trembling throat and poured out her heart. "If only I had been kinder then, things might be different, he might have come to Fennywolde and I might be his wife instead. I wish Twit had let me hang." Her choking words became tangled in the weeping, and for a minute or more she clung to her mother as if at any moment the ground would open up and a great pit of bitter despair would suck her down into oblivion.

Gwen closed her eyes and felt her daughter's pain. "But you cannot change what has happened, love," she whispered gently. "There are many things in this unhappy world we cannot alter. We must learn to live with our lot and find peace with ourselves. Come, dry your eyes now. In the Hall they are deciding who should go and take your mousebrass from Morgan. You don't want to let Piccadilly see you've been crying now, do you?" Audrey shook her head in determination and smartly wiped away the tears.

*   *   *

187

In the light of the fire Thomas looked around at the raised paws. Mr. Cockle, Arthur, Algy, Master Oldnose, Piccadilly, and several others from the Landings were bravely volunteering to go and hunt down Morgan. Thomas scratched his whiskers. It would be a dangerous mission, and he was not sure he could count on most of the mice. It was all very well being valiant now, but, in the face of death, how would they react? The midshipmouse decided to choose the ones he could trust, those who had already proved their worth–he pointed at Arthur and Piccadilly.

"You'll do," he said. "Three of us should be enough for one scurvy rat as long as we can get him away from the power station."

"We'll have to be quick," said Piccadilly, getting to his feet. "We can't hang about for His Nibs to use that Starglass again."

Barker had been picking his scalp throughout the discussion as though he was not listening. Now he jerked upright and asked, "Where mousey boy goin'? He can't leave Barker now."

Piccadilly patted the old rat on his head, "You stay here, you old loon," he told him. "You'll be looked after, don't worry." But Barker jumped up and pleaded to be allowed to go with the group.

"Please, mousey boy!" he squealed. "Barker not like to be left out–he can help against Old Stumpy. You need to get him alone. He knows Barker–Barker can lure him out of ice fortress, yes?"

Thomas regarded the rat with astonishment. "He's right, you know," he said. "It had been worrying me, how we were going to get Morgan alone. I think your barmy old friend ain't so addled as he pretends to be."

As if to prove him wrong Barker tittered idiotically and hid his face in his claws, but through them he peered over at the Starwife, who was sitting near the stairs. The squirrel, however, had not been listening, and seemed to be fast asleep.

"Maybe you're right," said Piccadilly thoughtfully. The rat glanced up sharply, but the mouse was only talking in response to Thomas's first words. "He might be useful after all."

"Are we ready then?" asked Arthur, impatient to be gone.

"In a moment, matey," Thomas laughed. "We're not going anywhere without somethin' to give that Morgan a right good bashing. If I remember rightly your mother has a sword some-where, that'll do for me. You lads see what you can find."

"I'm all right," said Piccadilly patting the little knife in his belt. "This is all I need."

Arthur frowned and wondered what he ought to take. He did not want a sword or knife, so he went in search of a good, stout stick.

"What about you, Barker?" Piccadilly asked the rat. "Aren't you going to have something to protect yourself with?"

Barker shook his head vigorously. "No, no, no," he yam-mered. "Barker never use weapon—they nasty and not nice. Barker trust mousey boy to save 'im if Old Stumpy gets rough."

Piccadilly chuckled. "Yes," he replied, "I'll look after you. We're a team now, aren't we, you barm pot?"

As Audrey came out of the Skirtings, she patted her face and made certain there were no tears to betray her, then, as coolly as she could, she made her way to the city mouse.

"Mr. Triton tells me you're off again," she said in a matter-of-fact sort of way.

Piccadilly had not seen her approach. "Oh, hello," he mum-bled awkwardly. "Yes, we're off to get your mousebrass—seems I'm always doing that, doesn't it?"

Audrey laughed, rather too quickly for it to be natural. "Yes," she said, "it does." There was a strained pause as both mice struggled to find something to say. Audrey's bottom lip turned white as she bit it to prevent her true feelings from blurting out, but he did not notice as he flicked his long fringe out of his eyes and battled with his resentment.

Barker looked at the two of them and hid the smile that grew on his lips, but it was too difficult. He giggled and winked at Piccadilly. "Ho ho, mousey boy, this pretty maid your girlie friend—yes?" He could not have said anything worse. Audrey flushed and turned beet red, while Piccadilly groaned and wanted to disappear.

The rat blinked with confusion, "Barker say somethin' wrong?"

Piccadilly coughed into his paw. "I'm sorry, Audrey," he hastily apologized. "Barker's not all there, are you, chum?"

Audrey stared at the city mouse with anguish in her eyes. This was her chance, she should tell him now. "Piccadilly," she found herself saying, "Piccadilly!"

He looked at her in surprise. There was a strange and urgent plea in her voice. "Yes?"

"I have to tell you something—it's important."

Piccadilly frowned. Audrey was certainly troubled about something. "Is everything all right?" he asked.

She shook her head. "No," she cried. "Piccadilly, I don't care what Mother says, and Twit only did it to save me, it's not as if I wanted to, don't you see?"

The city mouse did not see at all. He opened his mouth to speak, but another voice called out behind him, "Come on, lad!"

Thomas flourished a rapier in his paws and jabbed the air with it. "A fine blade," he said. "Let's give it something to bite!" Arthur was by his side and in his fists he held a large stick. With a whoop he swung it over his head.

Piccadilly backed away from Audrey, glad that he had been given an excuse to escape; she would only have mocked him or said something nasty. "Sorry," he chirped, "got to nip off now. Wot you waitin' for, Barker?"

Audrey watched him walk over to the others, who were waiting at the cellar door. She cursed herself for not telling him. A gentle paw placed itself on her shoulder and her mother's voice whispered in her ear, "It's better he does not know. Let him think you do not like him, for there's nothing you can do."

The mice of the Skirtings and Landings cheered the four intrepid heroes and wished them well. With hearty waves they passed down into the cellar, and Master Oldnose said a quick prayer. Audrey wept as she felt her heart break.

*   *   *

The evening closed tightly about the power station, and charcoal shadows lengthened over the icy dump. The storm still raged, and black, snow-swollen clouds filled the sky. Nothing stirred out of doors that night, and all creatures shivered in fear.

Down by the jetty, at the frozen river's edge, a little fist punched out the snow that had clogged up a drainage pipe. Thomas popped his head out and jumped down. He was followed by Piccadilly and Arthur, then, squirming and wriggling, came Barker.

The midshipmouse looked gravely toward the power station. A ghostly light was shining behind the tiny windows. "We have to draw Morgan out," he said, "and let's hope he brings the mousebrass with him."

"You ready, Barker?" asked Piccadilly uncertainly.

The rat gazed at the forbidding building and shook his head. "No," he whimpered.

But it was too late to turn back now and they took no notice. The city mouse led the others up the jetty. Barker lingered behind morosely and kicked over an oil can. It rattled and glooped across the ground. Thinking it might contain something sumptuous and tasty the rat scrambled after it and slid his expectant tongue down into the greasy insides.

"Pah! Yak!" he spat and choked, and stuffed a clawful of clean snow into his mouth to numb the acrid bitterness. With smeared, black lips and an equally black scowl he threw the can away. Barker glanced up and hurried after the mice, who, by now, had disappeared around the corner. Piccadilly had taken them to the gate in the pockmarked wall, and they were just ducking under the rails as Barker came scurrying up, spitting inky saliva onto the snow as he went.

Now only the snowy dump lay between them and Jupiter's fortress. Arthur held his breath and clutched his stick grimly. "Do you think we can get close enough without being seen?" he asked.

Thomas shrugged. "Who knows, but I'm hoping that this blasted weather will shield us from His eyes—for a while at least."

So, very slowly, they began to cross the exposed stretch of ground. They went in single file, with Thomas leading and dragging his sturdy legs through the deep, muscle-numbing snow. In a silent, trudging line they toiled, and the storm of Jupiter was their only protection against the piercing blue light that stabbed all too frequently from the power station and sliced through the icy darkness. They drew nearer to the building, and its massive, hulking shape reared above them into the pitch black night. A deathly, pale mist flowed around the walls, and Arthur shuddered, remembering the previous evening in Greenwich.

Bringing up the rear, Barker squinted up through the gale. He was as desperate as the others for this plan to work, though for entirely different reasons.

Thomas grunted as he labored with increasing difficulty through the waist-high snow. When he reached the wall of the great building, he pressed himself against the frost-covered bricks and spoke in a whisper to Barker. "This is where you earn your supper," he said beckoning to the rat. "Remember, all you have to do is lead Morgan out here and we'll take over."

Barker came wobbling forward and gibbered nervously, but

protests were useless, and Thomas shoved him around the corner.

The rat skidded and slipped out over the ice and snow, and with a long, drawn-out wail he fell on his face.

In the shadows, Piccadilly started and leaned forward with concern, but the midshipmouse pulled him back. "He knows what he's up to lad," he hissed. "He ain't hurt."

Barker lifted his face and stared intently at the low window with the broken pane. There was a movement behind it; Morgan was there, lurking in the gloom, spying and snooping, keeping watch for his foul master. Barker licked his lips and began the performance of his life.

"Oh, ahh, me 'ead! Oh them lumps–ooch, ah, eeh," he cradled his head in his claws and staggered drunkenly to his feet.

Behind the broken window a dark shape flitted, and two beady red eyes gleamed in the cold dark. "Who's that?" croaked a thin voice. "Come out where I can see ya!"

"Oh, ahh," came Barker's painful response as he flailed and jiggled about like a nervous jelly.

A pinched, sharply chiseled snout appeared through the gap. Morgan glared out into the storm and his eyes darted to and fro. "I knows that miserable voice," he snarled. "It's that crazy old duffer. What 'e be doin' 'ere? 'E can't 'ave swam all this way." A vicious-looking dagger flashed in his teeth as he wormed his way out of the window and stood seething with wickedness in the snow. He rubbed his claws together as he thought how pleased his mighty lord would be to have another victim. Where was the wretch, he wondered. Damn this accursed weather!

Amid the swirling storm Barker howled, "Help me, I'se hurt an' can't walk proper–me poor lumpy 'ead. Oooh . . ."

Morgan cackled and his stumpy tail slapped the frost eagerly. He took the dagger from his mouth and bent forward to gaze through the thick curtain of churning, beating flakes. "Tell me where you are," he called out. "It's me, your beloved general. I'll help ya."

The crafty old rat was now lying flat against the ground, and could see Morgan quite clearly. He saw the dagger clasped firmly in the evil creature's claws, but most important, he noticed the brass pendant swinging from his neck. Barker grinned—everything was going according to plan. With one deft movement he cupped his mouth in his fist and by some cunning art threw his voice so that it seemed to come farther from the left. "Stumpy, that you? I'se in agony, an' so blinkin' cold. What's 'appenin' to the world?"

Morgan swiveled his head on hunched shoulders and sniffed the battering wind with his nose. "I can smell ya, you old crow bait. What ya doin' around 'ere? Come closer. I won't 'urt ya, you know I always takes good care o' my lads."

"I'se over 'ere," cried the faint, deceivingly distant voice. "Quick—ooh, aah."

With a growl Morgan leaped forward, brandishing the dagger, and ran right past Barker's prostrate form. In the glimmering dark he lashed out with the cruel blade, slashing the snow and cutting the wind in his madness to find the old rat. "Where are ya?" he shrieked, charging against the storm and ripping it with his eager, bloodthirsty dagger.

Barker pulled himself up and slunk over to the shadowy corner where the mice were hiding. "He's out and alone," he told them quickly, "an' he's got the dangler around his scrawny neck."

"Well done," Thomas congratulated him hurriedly. He turned to the others. "Ready?" Piccadilly and Arthur nodded grimly and with one bound they all shot out of the darkness and raced through the blizzard toward Morgan. Barker remained hidden in the shade and waited.

Morgan whipped around and saw the three mice charging

at him. He cried out and tried to dodge back to the window, but his escape was cut off by Thomas and a rapier was thrust menacingly before his face. Arthur swiftly swung his stick and caught the rat's claw. The dagger dropped to the ground and Morgan yelped. Piccadilly's paw was steady as he held his own little knife and approached purposefully. This disgusting creature had been the cause of all his miseries.

Morgan stared openmouthed at the city mouse. "I know you," he cried, "you're a Holeborner, and before that you were in the sewers—you're the dainty morsel that got away." Piccadilly said nothing but came fiercely on.

"Morgan," snapped Thomas suddenly, "we only want that brass around your neck. Give it to us or we'll take it and we'll not be gentle."

Considering that the rat was cornered and weaponless he seemed very sure of himself. "Ha ha," he laughed, holding his sides, "so that's what you're up to. You cretinous scum! Nothing can harm my Lord, certainly not some poxy bauble. He has grown too strong for that!" and he continued to hoot with mocking laughter.

"Give it to us!" ordered Piccadilly. He ran forward and grasped the rat by the throat. Morgan jumped backward and threw the mouse off balance. Piccadilly fell down in the snow and his knife spun in the air, only to be caught in cruel claws.

"Don't deal in death, lad," Morgan whispered harshly in his ear as he pressed the knife against Piccadilly's throat, "not when your victim is a master of the craft. I've murdered and butchered more flesh than you're ever likely to see." He glanced up at Thomas and Arthur and told them to back off. "That's right, my lovelies," Morgan cooed, "if you don't want to see your little gray friend skinned in front of you, just keep away." He twisted the knife so that the gleam from it flashed on their faces, then he lifted his gaze and an insane cackle gurgled from his mouth as he looked beyond them.

Piccadilly squirmed in alarm as he saw the dreadful horror gather behind his friends. He tried to warn them but his own knife cut threateningly into his skin and pricked out a trickle of blood. "Behind you!" he managed to cry defiantly. Morgan growled and punched the city mouse hard in the ribs. The breath streamed out of Piccadilly and he lay helpless and gasping in the snow. Thomas spun on his heel and beheld the terrible sight. "Hell's bells!" he uttered fearfully. Arthur squealed and nearly let go of his stick in dismay. He could scarcely believe his terror-stricken eyes.

Hideous forms had poured out of the power station and mustered silently behind them. The shapes were blurred and indistinct, a trick perhaps of the dark and the snow that beat furiously against his face—but no, for a moment the wintry veil was parted and Arthur cowered—whatever they were, he could see straight through them.

Before him was a host of hideous phantoms. All of Morgan's slaughtered rats had returned in spectral form. Their eye sockets were empty and they stared blankly out at the frozen world. The faces of the apparitions still held the tortured look of their hideous deaths and hollow wails echoed into the night from their gaping, dead mouths. In their haunted claws each held the spear that had killed him, and the icy spikes were stained black with their own blood. They were tightly bound to their new master. His will it was that drove them—for in each of their chests a spark of cold starfire blazed. It was Jupiter's new army—regiment upon grisly regiment of ghastly ghosts. It was a bloodcurdling sight, and Arthur's skin crawled.

"Blood an' thunder!" exclaimed Thomas. Morgan threw back his head and let loose a high-pitched screech of a laugh, "What do you think of my new army? You are most honored; your lives will be the first they shall take." He kicked the winded Piccadilly to one side and ran to be amongst his phantom lads.

196

"I'm not afeard o' spooks," said Thomas undaunted. "They may look scary but when all's said an' done, they're dead an' can't hurt the living."

Morgan sneered at him scornfully. "I wouldn't bet on it, sea squeaker. My army still has claws to tear with, and now the lads have the deadliest of spears." He took two paces backward and bowed. It was a signal, and with horrible, tormented shrieks the dead warriors surged forward.

Thomas sprang toward them with his rapier, plunging the sharp blade directly into the heart of one. The specter's transparent fur parted as the steel slashed straight through it. Thomas thrashed the rapier up and down, tattering the dreadful spirit into a thousand pieces, but the wispy fragments melted and merged together once more, and the awful, lolling head mocked him. In a final effort, the midshipmouse sliced through the crackling white starfire that pulsed and glowed in the breast of the hellish thing.

He cried out as a spitting, ravenous frost shot out and devoured the steel blade, turning it to brittle ice that splintered and smashed on the ground. Thomas's paw blistered and became a hoary white as the blood in his fingers froze.

"Run!" he shouted, diving at Piccadilly and sweeping him up with his other arm.

"I'm okay," the city mouse told him, rubbing the bruises on his ribs and wriggling out of Thomas's grasp onto his own feet. "Where's Barker?" he called, suddenly remembering their other companion.

"Leave him!" bellowed Thomas. "He'll find his own way out of this."

The three mice pelted back over the dump as fast as they could. Behind them in deadly pursuit flowed the legion of wraiths. They hurled their ice spears at them and the glinting missiles soared through the night and came crashing close on their heels.

"We'll never make it," Arthur panted in dismay. "There's too many of them. We're goners." He spluttered along as best he could, but his stride was failing, his weight was against him, and he felt his lungs ache in his chest.

"Run, lad!" barked Thomas in his ear, but it was no use—what with fright and the cold Arthur was nearly spent.

Then it happened. An ice spear whistled past his cheek and crashed into the snow directly in front of him. He was moving too quickly to avoid it and the world turned upside down as he tripped and cartwheeled over. With a great flurry of ice Arthur tumbled down.

"Blast!" yelled Thomas, and he ran back to help the dazed mouse.

Arthur had stars before his eyes and his vision was fuzzy. For a second he did not know where he was. Thomas shook him roughly and rubbed snow in his face to bring him back to his senses. "Arthur!" he called urgently. The mouse blinked. In a wild panic Thomas dragged him up and heaved him over his shoulder.

The phantom host was closing on them. The midshipmouse struggled under Arthur's weight, but they were moving too slowly now. Arthur bobbed up and down, and the jangling, blurred visions before him fused and came together. He screwed his eyes up and smacked himself. Now he really was seeing stars—hundreds of them flashed and shone in the dead chests of the wailing troops who were now barely a few yards away. Another spear gleamed cold and cruel as it left the macabre claws of one of the spirits. It hurtled toward the fleeing mice with horrible accuracy.

"Aaarrgghh!" screamed Thomas as the spear sliced through his leg. He toppled over, and both he and Arthur crashed to the ground.

The wound was deep and the blood oozed out over the

snow. But it was no ordinary gash. Almost immediately a festering frost stole over the exposed flesh. The midshipmouse
groaned with the pain. "Go!" he shouted at Arthur. "Leave me,
I'm done for."

"I won't," Arthur cried. "Give me your arm." He tried to pull
Thomas to his feet, but it was no use–the army was upon them.

Piccadilly turned around to see what was happening. He
had outdistanced his friends and was appalled to witness the
terrifying specters bearing down on them. With his fists
clenched he ran forward, bellowing for all he was worth.
"HOLEBORN!" he bawled. He did not think of the terrible danger he was flying into. The sight of Thomas and Arthur
swamped by Jupiter's nightmarish forces was all he thought of.

A claw snatched out of the darkness and caught his arm.
But it was flesh and blood. "Mousey!" called Barker breathlessly. "Use your head, you can't save them like that."

Piccadilly stared into the old rat's eyes, confused and bewildered by what he saw there. A commanding light gleamed in
those cunning, bottomless pools. "What can I do?" he found
himself asking dumbly. "They're my friends."

Barker dragged behind him the oil can he had sampled and
discarded previously. "Leave it to Barker," he said sternly. The
rat bounded toward the shadowy host and called out strange-
sounding words.

Arthur and Thomas held on to each other as a hundred
spears of ice were raised and aimed at their hearts. Suddenly
the phantoms faltered and looked away, their grisly attention
summoned elsewhere. Above the squall and clamor of the
storm a voice was shouting strange words. The ghosts suddenly lost their will, and the starfire dimmed in their hearts as they
moaned and put down the spears. To the mice's astonishment,
Barker came crashing through the uncertain spirits and flung
the oil can at Thomas's feet.

"Your tinderbox, Triton!" the rat instructed sharply. "Hurry, the confusion will not last long." Sure enough, the starfire was already beginning to throb and blaze again. The ghosts were raising their fatal spears and hissing through hollow mouths.

Thomas fumbled in the upturned brim of his hat, where he kept his tinderbox. Quickly he struck a spark, and the oil that had spilled out of the can burst into golden flames on the deep snow. The specters fell back, gasping and clawing the air, dismayed at the heat and light. They covered their blank eyes and edged farther away.

The midshipmouse tugged the kerchief from around his neck and wound it tightly about Arthur's stick. He soaked it in oil and thrust it into the fire. The torch burst into life and he limped painfully to his feet. The wraiths scattered before him as he waved the flames in their dismayed faces.

Arthur leaped up and let Thomas lean on him. He could see that the wound was hurting the midshipmouse and he was finding it difficult to stand. "Come on, Mr. Triton," he said urgently, "we must get away from here."

Piccadilly ran up, delighted to see the phantoms recoil and disperse. "Go an' haunt a house." He laughed, snapping his fingers at them. He clapped Barker on the back when he reached him and gave the rat a joyous hug. "Brilliant, chummy," he said. "You're not barmy after all."

Barker was not smiling as he eyed the retreating legion cautiously. "Hurry," he told the city mouse, "their fear will not last long. The flames came unexpected, but their dark master will pour more hate and malice into the starfire that controls them. They will attack again. Look to your friend."

Piccadilly did not seem to notice that the rat was now speaking in a totally different voice, for he saw Thomas come hobbling toward him, leaning heavily on Arthur. "Let me help," he cried, dashing under the midshipmouse's free arm. "Barker says the army won't be scared for long," he told them. "We have to get out of here quick."

Thomas gave the rat a curious stare and thanked him for saving them. Barker was himself again and he shrugged, tittering into his claws, but the midshipmouse was not deceived. If the rat wanted to play games and be mysterious then let him, he decided. "We must get back to the Skirtings," he said, wincing at the gnawing agony of his leg. He handed the burning torch over to Barker. "Set fire to the rest of the oil," he told him.

The rat scurried back to the can and poured the dregs over as wide an area as was possible, then he lowered the torch and ignited it all. Fierce flames roared up and belched into the storm-filled night, and the ghostly warriors who were overcoming their initial fears were cowed once more by this greater blaze of yellow fury.

Barker looked around at them. Yes, Jupiter was very mighty to have created this ghastly horde in so little time. Things were grim indeed—their mission was a complete and utter failure. He turned to the power station and shook his bony fist at it, cursing the demon inside. Barker wondered just how unassailable Jupiter was. If only they had managed to take Morgan's mousebrass, that might have worked, but it was no use now. The mice were returning to their old house, and nothing could persuade them to risk such an action again. Barker could see no other way of dealing with the terrible Unbeast, and he cursed his own frail body, which was too weak to attempt such a venture.

His attention returned to the hissing, groping forces nearby—already they were braving the heat and drawing nearer to the flames as the starfire urged them on. The old rat glanced up and a thin smile curled over his cracked lips as he spotted his chance. Quickly he ran after the three friends, burying himself in the role of the idiot once more.

"Fire lit, nice crackly, toasty flames." He giggled as he

approached them. "Wailing spookies not follow now, no frazzle their ghostly whiskers." The mice paid him little heed, as they were putting all their efforts into helping Thomas stagger to the gate.

Barker persisted. "Look, look," he sniggered, "see how they not come after, how they long to."

As Arthur ducked under the railings and waited for the midshipmouse to follow, Barker yanked Piccadilly's arm and spun him around. "Look, mousey boy!" he said triumphantly. "Do you see them now?"

Piccadilly frowned at the rat but his eyes fell on the hundreds of spirits wailing and swaying aimlessly in the firelight. The flames fell on their twisted faces and the city mouse turned pale as his stomach lurched. There was the shade of Vinny, the loathsome standard-bearer, and above his head the banner still fluttered. Piccadilly had not seen it before, and now his heart stopped and a desperate cry formed on his quivering lips.

The standard was made out of a mouse skin: the paws were tied around the pole; two small circles marked where the eyes had been, and the legs flapped madly behind in the wild wind. But over the main section, the area that was once a mouse's back, there ran a jagged bolt of darker fur that resembled a flash of lightning.

"MARTY!" screamed Piccadilly. There, waving forlornly in the storm, was all that remained of his young friend. He had not gone by the East Way after all, and had been one of the first to die in the attack on Holeborn. Piccadilly dropped to his knees and howled. Barker stepped back and hoped he had gauged this mouse correctly.

A thousand agonies battered through Piccadilly's mind as he comprehended what he saw hoisted above the spectral heads. "Marty," he whispered softly, "you should have listened to me." His eyes were empty and desolate as he gazed at the sad little banner fluttering pathetically over the fiendish host.

Thomas and Arthur were now both on the other side of the rails and they stared at Piccadilly in amazement. What on earth was he doing?

"Piccadilly," called Arthur, "we might not have much more time. Come quickly before Morgan forces the army through the flames."

At the sound of that name a raging tempest welled up inside the city mouse. "Morgan!" he spat furiously, "I've put this off long enough!" And he sprang back over the snowy dump toward the power station once more.

"He's gone mad," cried Arthur fearfully. "What's the matter with him? He'll be killed!"

Thomas glared at the rat; there was something suspicious here. "Get you after that lad, Barker," he ordered, "and make sure you bring him back."

"Yes, yes," squeaked Barker, "mousey boy must not run off, Barker go fetch him." He darted away and did not bother to wait until he was out of earshot before laughing at his cleverness.

"Should we wait?" Arthur asked nervously.

Thomas put his paw to his forehead and racked his brain. There was nothing they could do here, it would be better if they continued on. It went against all his instincts, but he knew the situation was hopeless. They had to go and warn the others before it was too late. Piccadilly would have to catch up with them afterward, if he could. "We go on," he told Arthur bitterly.

*   *   *

Piccadilly's anger scorched his brain. He was blind to everything else; he had forgotten about his friends—only Morgan filled his thoughts. The piebald rat loomed large in his mind, blotting out all reason. The blood of thousands stained the evil henchrat's jaws—Morgan had to die.

The city mouse charged through the wailing spirits, who

were now stalking fearlessly through the fire. Their unclean claws tore at his fur as he thundered past, and the savage spears hailed after him. Piccadilly did not feel the rents in his sides where the talons of the dead gouged into him, nor did he feel the ice and snow battering into his face as he drew close to the power station once more. Only Morgan's leering mouth and sneering laugh drove him on. They danced before his eyes, images of madness that had to be destroyed once and for all.

Morgan was standing near the pane of broken glass, braced against the gale and cackling wickedly. His new army was magnificent! Nothing could stand before it–the world would be his to govern under Jupiter's rule. He tossed back his ugly head and hooted with pleasure, but the laughter died in his throat as Piccadilly came out of the storm to confront him.

A terrible light was shining in the mouse's eyes, and the rat stiffened with surprise. He looked for his army, but they were pursuing Thomas and Arthur over the jetty. Morgan was on his own.

Piccadilly bared his teeth. "Time's up, Stumpy!" he snarled, prowling forward.

The rat glared at him and drew himself up haughtily. "Get out o' my sight," he growled threateningly. "I've 'ad bigger 'an you fer breakfast, lad." But still the mouse came on, and the burning hatred in his face caused the rat to step back momentarily. "Gah!" he rumbled, "yer only an uppity squeaker, let's see the color o' yer blood." The knife he had taken from Piccadilly glinted in his claw and he scythed the air with it.

The mouse showed no concern at the sharp little blade that flicked and jabbed before him; his determination could not be broken so easily.

Morgan's tongue slid out of his slavering jaws and dangled thirstily over his whiskered chin. The remains of his tail swished the snow into two heaps behind as he lowered his head and steeled himself to pounce.

204

"Raaah!" he screeched, hurling himself at the city mouse.

Piccadilly stepped neatly aside and the rat careered into a snowdrift. The mouse dashed over but Morgan had already recovered and lunged at him again. A cold slice of pain bit into Piccadilly's shoulder as his own knife nicked the skin.

Morgan chortled. He liked to play with his victims. He paced around and threw the knife from one claw to the other, teasing and tormenting Piccadilly.

"Hah!" he struck out suddenly and slashed at the city mouse's chest. Piccadilly gritted his teeth and clutched his breast. The blood welled up between his fingers, but he did not care. All his sorrows and fury volcanoed inside him, and with a mad yell he exploded into the piebald rat, bowling him over like a rag doll.

The mouse threw himself on top of Morgan and with a fist clenched harder than stone smote the side of his head. The rat shrieked as the blows fell one after another. A paw stronger than iron hammered into his belly and a bloody mixture of spit and broken teeth spurted from his mouth. Morgan wriggled and the knife flashed up across his attacker's arm.

Piccadilly caught his breath as the steel wove a net of cruel light about him. With one paw he tried to catch the claw that wielded it while the other closed around Morgan's throat.

The bitter blade cut into his fingers but he grasped the rat's claw and forced it back, squeezing like a vice. The knife fell from Morgan's clutches and he writhed violently. His stumpy tail thrashed like a headless serpent, beating against the mouse's back, and he craned his neck to bite anything he could reach.

Piccadilly heaved his knee up under Morgan's chin and the snapping jaws clacked shut as he stretched out for the knife. His dripping fingers closed round the handle and with a deadly grin he brought his face close to his enemy's.

"Now I've got you," hissed the mouse as the blade was

pushed against Morgan's ribs. "Just one shove and you're history, so you'd better lie still or there might be an accident."

Morgan's squirming and churning ceased. His frightened eyes stared down at the greedy blade that pressed dangerously close. "Don't gut me!" he begged piteously.

The knife dug perilously into his skin and Piccadilly laughed grimly. "That's right," he said, "I want you to know what it's like to be at another's mercy, for you to wonder when exactly am I going to plunge the steel in and take your life. What's it like Morgan? Are you excited?"

But a resigned calm had descended on the rat. He closed his beady eyes and when he opened them all traces of fear had gone. "Kill me, I'll not beg," he croaked. "Don't you see a swift end will be better than what He in there has in store for me? Go on lad, plunge the blade in–feel what it's like to kill. Already your eyes betray you, you're enjoying yourself, aren't you?"

Piccadilly wavered. It was true, breathless and injured though he was, the thrill of the slaughter was something he was looking forward to with relish. It did not matter about anything else–Marty, Jupiter, Audrey, he had forgotten them, now all he wanted was murder. He gazed at Morgan, aghast.

The rat cackled softly. "Well well, you squeakers have your worth after all," he admitted sourly. "There's little difference 'tween you an' me, lad. Right now there's more rat in you than mouse. What a fine captain o' my guard you would've made."

"I'm not like you," protested Piccadilly, struggling to stay sane. "I'm not!"

"Don't give me that, lad." Morgan sneered. "Things ain't black an' white no more, are they? The blood lust burns in your eyes–I can see it. Just one small step an' you'll be a rat good an' proper." He rested his head to one side, weary at last of the world and all its torments. "Finish me off, boy," he said plaintively. "Let me cheat Him of my service. Give me that pleasure, let me get one over on Him just once–at the end."

The knife in Piccadilly's paws trembled as the mouse shook all over. He teetered on the brink, and Morgan's words pounded in his head. Was he really like him? He could not be certain. He wanted to push the knife in . . . or did he?

Piccadilly snapped out of his madness—he was no rat! Angry he may have been, but his heart was pure and he never would sink so low. A shuddering sigh swept through him as he realized how foolish he had been about many things, and a joyous laugh rang out in that dreadful place as his noble side won through.

"Never," he said tucking the knife into his belt. "You don't understand and never will—that's what makes you a rat. You see, I trust in the Green Mouse." And as he said it, tears of joy sprang from his eyes. "I honestly do," he cried, overwhelmed at the sudden warmth that brimmed up in his soul. "Now I understand."

But Morgan would not be denied, he snarled and snatched the knife from the belt. "Good fer you, lad," he shouted, "but this rat's no cat's paw anymore."

Before Piccadilly could stop him Morgan raised the knife and plunged it deep into his own heart. There, in the steady snowfall, Jupiter's lieutenant gasped and died.

Piccadilly staggered back, appalled by what he saw. He had seen many deaths, of the innocent and the cruel, yet the suicide of this debauched old sinner affected him deeply.

"Mousey," panted a voice in the storm, "where are you?"

He turned, and out of the dark and the mist came Barker. The sight of him made Piccadilly remember the mission. He ran over to Morgan's body and stooped to take the mousebrass from around his neck. He hesitated as he looked on the dead rat's face. How strange! In the gloom he looked at peace, a smile of restful contentment on his lips. At last he had escaped the chains of his dark master once and for all. Audrey's brass gleamed in Piccadilly's paws as he cut it free of the cord.

"Old Stumpy dead now," tutted Barker, "mousey boy do this?"

"No," the mouse replied quietly, "he released himself." Then, with the mousebrass in his grasp, he strode over to the broken window. "I've got a job to do," he said to the old rat, "stay here and watch out for those phantoms. This shouldn't take long." He ducked through the gap and disappeared into the power station.

With keen, sparkling eyes Barker peered after him and hoped he would succeed. "That's right, boy," he whispered, "everything depends on this now. Get rid of him for us."

The eternal cold flooded through the vast building, filling it with freezing fog and dense cloud. A deathly silence lay over the place, broken only by faint, discordant notes as, high above, the long, slender icicles tinkled like wind chimes. A hush seemed to have settled on the power station, cutting off the noise of the gales outside. Into this enclosed, deserted wilderness stepped Piccadilly, and the sound of his breathing rang around like an alarm.

Bravely he marched through the malignant, misty blackness, ignoring the searing pain of the frostbitten floor and the stinging of his wounds as the cold poured into them. He was as tiny as a flea in that cathedral of despair, but his spirits were high enough to conquer anything. He strained his eyes to pierce the fog which smothered around, yet he could see no sign of Jupiter's infernal spirit.

But in his present mood this did not matter. If the devil wanted to lurk in the dark cloud Piccadilly would make sure he found him. Never had a mouse been more daring as he went bravely on, holding the anti-cat charm high over his head, defying the cloaks of shadow and veils of mist that Jupiter had gathered about himself.

He had gone some distance, and still the unearthly silence prevailed. Piccadilly raised his voice and shouted, "Show yourself!" but only the eerie calm answered him. The air was still, and even the faint tinkling ceased. "Where are you, Jupiter?" he called. "Are you afraid of one little mouse?"

For a moment nothing happened, and then the fog began to disperse, pulling itself away, tearing in ragged shreds and fading into the dark corners. Jupiter was coming.

A deep rumble obliterated the silence and the ground quaked under the mouse's feet. The walls shook and the high windows cracked and splintered. Glass fell shivering to the floor, smashing and crashing into a million glittering shards.

Two pale swirls of blue light formed far above in the velvet gloom between the icicles. They burned with the bitterness of the empty void, and as Piccadilly looked at them they blazed and grew until they were huge, baleful lamps of distilled evil. A great slit opened in the center of each fiery eye, blacker than the deepest chasm, and slowly a horrendously massive head gathered smokily around them. Jupiter's foul face with its rolling jowls appeared, and his monstrous mouth was open. Piccadilly could see his cruel fangs and beyond them his cavernous throat. In a rush of frozen breath Jupiter spoke and the sound of his voice cut through Piccadilly like a thousand knives. "Puny creature, how dare you enter my realm!"

But the city mouse stood his ground and held the brass before his face. "My name is Piccadilly," he shouted proudly, "and by the power of the Green Mouse I banish you forever!"

The terrible eyes narrowed and doubt filled them as they beheld the charm that had once sent his body toppling into a watery grave. A hiss steamed through the building as the lips pulled back over the sharp fangs.

Piccadilly leaned back as he prepared to throw the mousebrass. "Give me the strength," he prayed, and he flung the charm as hard as he could.

Audrey's brass whizzed through the darkness, gleaming as

it spun. Up it soared toward the immense head of Jupiter. Far below, the tiny, gray figure jumped up and down, cheering and punching the air gleefully.

Jupiter snarled as the mousebrass sailed up toward him. Then, with a mighty blast that split the walls and loosened the bricks, he blew hard and furiously.

The mousebrass was left spinning helplessly in midair as the demon's breath hailed violently down. The frost roared out of the unbounded mouth and struck the mousebrass with tremendous force. The yellow metal dripped with rime and turned white. The charm lurched and with a loud *CRACK* became ice. Like a stone it plummeted toward the ground, where it smashed to smithereens.

Piccadilly stared at the fragments that littered the floor. The anti-cat charm was completely destroyed. He swallowed nervously and lifted his gaze. Jupiter laughed at him.

"You think to fling trifling toys at me!" he stormed. "Know now that Jupiter is invincible and you are defeated."

The mouse staggered back, stumbling in his fear. He was defenseless and alone—he had never felt so small in his life.

"Run!" the enormous spirit mocked. "You are too small a morsel for my palate. Escape if you can."

With his eyes fixed on Jupiter's huge, ghostly form floating high above, Piccadilly ran for the broken window as hideous laughter filled his ears.

"Too late," Jupiter whispered, glaring past the fleeing mouse. "Ridiculous insect, your struggles are ended!"

There, pouring in, blocking his exit, was the phantom army. He skidded to a halt and glanced around quickly. Where was Barker? The ghosts of Morgan's rats lifted up their deadly spears and took aim. This was it—Piccadilly closed his eyes. "Help me," he prayed.

The specters opened their hollow jaws and let out a horrible wail. The ice spears left their claws and shot grimly through the air. The power station boomed with Jupiter's laughter.

The small body lay motionless on the ground, the face turned heavenward. Piccadilly's little paw was closed tightly around his own mousebrass kept fastened to his belt–it was the sign of hope, but with his life, that too ended in that dark place.

THE MIDWINTER DEATH

Arthur squirmed through the rusted iron leaves of the Grill. He heaved a weary sigh and turned to pull Thomas out. The midshipmouse ground his teeth when his leg dragged against one of the metal fronds. A shudder of agony rifled up his thigh as the ugly gash wept poisoned, black blood and the skin around it turned blue. The wound was getting worse far quicker than he had expected, no doubt because of some evil enchantment on the ghastly ice spears.

It had been a nightmarishly difficult journey back through the sewers. Trying to negotiate the slippery ledges with someone who could hardly stand was an experience Arthur never wanted to repeat.

"Come on, Mr. Triton," he said encouragingly, "not far now, there's just the cellar steps to get up."

Thomas felt as though he would faint at any moment. A black sickness was creeping over him as the infection took hold. He limped along stiffly, trying not to put any weight on his left leg. The two figures slowly made their way past the dusty bric-a-brac stored in the cellar to the foot of the stone stairs. Arthur looked up and wondered how they would manage; the midshipmouse was swaying dizzily, and he passed a tired paw over his worried, plump face.

"I'll get onto the first step and reach down for you," he said, leaning his ailing companion against the wall while he clambered up.

Thomas nodded but did not reply; his words were stuck in his throat, and the weight of the world seemed to descend on his shoulders. He had never felt so exhausted. Beads of cold sweat pricked his brow and ran icily down his nose.

On the step Arthur lay on his tummy and stretched his arms down. "Here Mr. Triton," he called, "take my paws."

"Where . . . are you?" stammered Thomas thickly. A shadow had fallen across his eyes, and Arthur was just a gray blur that flickered uncertainly before them. Everything was growing dim, and a drowning darkness rose all around. He felt a black gulf yawn under his feet, ready to swallow him whole. "Mouse overboard!" he cried wildly, waving his paws in the air. "He's going under, save him, me boys!"

Arthur jumped down, startled and afraid. The midshipmouse slithered to the floor and lay there gasping as the ice fever seized him altogether. "Mr. Triton," shouted Arthur, "speak to me–please!"

In the sea mists and pathless oceans of his mind Thomas heard his name, but it was carried on a black, silken breeze scented with venomous death and seemed very far away.

Arthur knelt beside him. What was he to do? He looked at the festering wound and shook his head. The flesh of the leg was becoming rigid, freezing before his eyes, shot through with glacial streaks of livid blue. Soon the whole limb would be a solid block of dead ice, and then it would spread until the midshipmouse was a motionless wintry statue.

"Don't worry, Mr. Triton," Arthur said hurriedly, pressing Thomas's paws to comfort him. "I'll not be long, I'm going to fetch help."

Thomas lifted his face in distress and turned it blindly to the young mouse. "Woodget," he murmured hoarsely, "is that you?" Bleak tears rolled and crystalized down his cheeks. "Have you sailed back to me again—after all this time?"

With a last, anxious look at the broken, delirious figure, Arthur scrambled up the stairs. He puffed with the exertion and the breath rattled in his chest as he mounted the topmost step and threw himself against the cellar door.

The Hall was bathed in the orange glow of the fire. All around its lazy, lapping flames the slumbering shapes of blanket-shrouded mice snored and dreamed of harvest feasts. For this short while the sorrows of life were forgotten and they wandered through sunlit daisy gardens, leaf-dappled glades, and golden, corn-filled meadows where the food was abundant. But the sun of their sleep was pale and cold, the fruit they ate was tasteless, and amid the soft snores whimpers were heard and stomachs growled.

Into this troubled peace burst Arthur. He fell stumbling through the cellar door and called at the top of his voice, "Help, help! Wake up!"

At once the sleepers stirred and awoke. Some covered their heads, expecting the roof to fall in, while others shook off the sleep and hurried over to see what was the matter.

"It's Mr. Triton!" Arthur explained quickly. "He's down there, I couldn't bring him up on my own—he's been wounded, please go and help him."

Master Oldnose and Mr. Cockle pushed through the doorway and vanished in the darkness beyond. Gwen came running up to her son, full of concern. "What happened?" she asked. "Is he badly hurt?" Arthur nodded and felt his own legs give way under the strain. He collapsed into her arms.

"Audrey!" called Gwen urgently. "Bring some water, quickly." She pulled Arthur near to the fire and laid him on a blanket with a pillow under his head.

Audrey scurried forward with a bowl of water and dabbed her brother's face. "I'm all right," he told her, "just feel so tired, but poor Mr. Triton . . ."

Gwen looked at the doorway and clenched her paws tightly. Several other mice had gone down to help bring up the midshipmouse and already were carrying him into the Hall. She drew her breath sharply when she saw the terrible wound: his leg was now immovable, transformed absolutely into ice.

They put him next to Arthur, and when the warm firelight fell on his face Thomas opened his eyes. He raised a trembling paw to the flames but the effort was too much and he descended into the black swoon once more.

"What happened, Arthur?" Gwen asked again as she tended to the midshipmouse and tried to make him comfortable.

"We didn't get the mousebrass," Arthur said, shivering at the memory. "Jupiter has an army of ghosts and they threw spears at us. One of them hit Mr. Triton. It was only a flesh wound, but it's gotten steadily worse–there's some evil magic at work in it."

Audrey had grown very pale and silent. Now, with a small voice she asked, "Where's Piccadilly, Arthur? Why isn't he with you?"

Arthur shook his head and sobbed, "I don't know. We were coming back when, all of a sudden, he went mad and charged back to the power station. Barker went to get him, but I don't know what happened to either of them."

The anguish of loss stole in and closed about Audrey's heart. She said nothing but sat back and stared at the fire.

Gwen did not know what to do about Thomas's leg. Splinters of frost were now edging their way up to his waist, his breathing was faint and his face drawn, a shadow of his former robust self.

"It is the winter sickness," barked a cracked voice behind her. Gwen turned and the Starwife staggered into the light. She was haggard and shuffled along feebly; her moist, milky eyes shone orange with the flames that framed and gilded her thin fur. With her arthritic paws locked around the handle of her walking stick she glared goblinlike at the fearful gathering. She waited for the astonished whispers that rustled around on her appearance to die down and lowered her withered head.

"The forces of Hagol have been invoked," she told the frightened mice in a hushed, ominous tone. "Ancient powers long idle have been kindled by the Unbeast, and the spears of Narmoth fly once more." The squirrel stared at Gwen and said darkly, "I fear the sea mouse will die."

"Can't you do anything?" implored Mrs. Brown desperately. "We can't sit here and do nothing while poor Thomas, while he . . ."

"I agree," said the squirrel, shifting her glance, "it is a most painful death. I suggest we finish him off now."

The mice of the Skirtings and Landings gasped in disbelief. How could she suggest such a thing? They were appalled by her callous disregard of the midshipmouse. Gwen said nothing but stared dumbly with shock. She did not understand how anyone could be so cold and unfeeling.

The Starwife tapped her stick on the floor with irritation. "You think me cruel," she snapped at them, "but you do not know what happens to one bitten by a Narmoth spear. You cannot imagine a thousandth of his torture as his body is so totally consumed by frost that it shatters. He will be aware of every crack and every fissure that splinters across his frozen body— until he dies. Is that what you would spare him for?"

For a full five minutes no one uttered a sound, and all eyes were fixed on the prone figure of Thomas. The frost was up to his middle and began creeping down the other leg. Gwen felt helpless and she stroked his chill forehead. "Oh Thomas, Thomas," she wept forlornly.

His two, sunken eyes blinked open and gazed up at her, but he did not know where he was, and the face he saw was a phantom from his youth. "Bess?" he whispered lovingly. "It's Tom. I tried for years to find you again."

Gwen squeezed his paws and nodded. "It's all right, Tom," she said in a voice that struggled to sound bright even though the tears streamed down her cheeks as she pretended to be the lost love of his boyhood, "you've found me now. Bess is here."

Thomas sighed deeply and he spoke in little fits of emotion. "Oh Bess, I never made him come wi' me—honest. Say you forgive me." He gripped her paws fiercely and they shook as he quivered with the pain.

"Of course I do, Thomas," Gwen assured him. "Now you get some rest, my dear."

The midshipmouse threw his head back and screamed piercingly, "I can't rest! I can never rest! Bess, he's gone, Woodget's gone and . . ." his voice became a sob as he fought to control the passion that racked him, "I killed him!"

"Oh Thomas," sobbed Gwen bitterly.

"It is the madness speaking," chimed the Starwife's solemn tones, "and so it will continue till his jaw freezes. Do your best to humor him—he is raving and knows not what he says." She turned away and her eyes closed guiltily, fully aware of the dark secret that the midshipmouse had struggled so hard to forget, of which she alone knew the truth.

Huddled by the fire, Audrey surfaced from her thoughts. The scenes with Thomas had washed over her, and the piteous cries of her mother had rung hollowly in her heart, for she sensed that Piccadilly was dead and all else had faded around her. Now she roused herself and took in the awful plight of those dear to her. Arthur had covered his face, hiding his sorrow from everyone, while Gwen's distraught tears fell fast down her cheeks for all to see as the ice made its way up to Mr. Triton's chest. Audrey looked on all this as though she were observing it through a window. It was a strange sensation, and for a few moments she felt set apart from them and their grief, in a separate, tranquil world.

Then it was over, and the babble of voices clamored around again. She shook herself and the fragments of her heart went out to her mother. If only they could do something. She paused— there it was again, the noise died down and she was viewing her family as though she were cut off from them. Audrey did not know what was happening. She looked around nervously and there was the Starwife, regarding her with keen eyes. The squirrel glowered, but Audrey's spirits lifted. Somehow she had read the other's thoughts!

The real world snapped back, and with a determined, angry expression Audrey rose and strode briskly over to where the Starwife was tapping her stick in agitation.

"Keep away from me, child," said the squirrel tersely, but there was a hint of caution in her voice and she backed away.

"I know!" hissed Audrey vehemently. "I don't know how I do, but that doesn't matter."

"You're demented," muttered the Starwife crossly. "The cold has unhinged you."

She started to move over to her seat by the stairs, but Audrey caught hold of her stick and held it firmly. "You can heal him, can't you?" she declared furiously. "I know you can. I sensed what was running through that nasty, dried-up old brain of yours. You were telling yourself what a waste of time it would be as we're all going to die soon anyway. That's right, isn't it, you mean old hag?"

The squirrel pounded her stick imperiously on the floor. Up till then their conversation had gone unheeded by everyone but now all the mice looked up in surprise. The Starwife apologized for the disturbance. "It is nothing," she told them, "a cramp in my foot, no more," then she resumed the whispered discussion with Audrey.

"What a clever creature you are, girl," she said. "It's true, I may be able to heal the midshipmouse."

"Then why don't you?" asked Audrey incredulously.

"As you said, soon we shall all be destroyed–this I have sensed, child, in much the same way as you. For days I have sought out Jupiter's thoughts to fathom the ways of his mind, and now I know: at sunset tomorrow he will use my Starglass for the last time and the world will be plunged into darkness and despair–a perfect place for a spirit used to the eternal cold of the void. All life will end."

She stood defeated and spent before the mouse. "What would I be saving Triton for?" she asked hopelessly. "His fate may be sweet compared to what awaits us."

"You can give Thomas the chance to live!" answered Audrey, outraged. "How dare you stand there and decide how someone should die when you have the means to save them." Her eyes blazed and were full of contempt for this wizened old creature who idly played with the lives of others.

The Starwife considered the girl's words and she raised her brows. "You may be right," she admitted. "I will restore Triton– but only on one condition."

"I'm sick to death of your conditions," flamed Audrey. "What is it now?"

"Nothing too taxing," said the squirrel with a curious smile. "I merely ask for your help in this, that is all."

"I'll do anything."

"Then go find my bag, the one containing the herbs I used to feed the beacon fire."

*   *   *

The mice were excited and held their breath expectantly as the old squirrel sat beside the midshipmouse and grandly declared her intention.

"There is a way," she told them, holding grimly onto her walking stick. "Just one small chance for this mouse. If I succeed he shall be cured and survive, but if I fail, then death shall come earlier than looked for."

The firelight danced over her face, casting deep shadows over her brows, which gave her a sinister appearance. She looked like an ancient force from forgotten legend that shimmered magically before them. Audrey knelt at her side, the velvet bag clutched in her paws. She watched the Starwife warily, for she did not trust her and sensed that she was up to something; a devious gleam was glittering in those milky eyes.

Gwen put a paw to her mouth as she prayed for Thomas's life. She hoped the squirrel knew what she was doing.

Just then Master Oldnose came into the Hall carrying a large bowl. "I've got it," he puffed, "but my oh my, it's freezing out there." The Starwife had sent him into the yard to fetch some snow, but did not say what she needed it for. The inquisitive mice peered into the fluffy heaped bowl timidly and shot wondrous glances at the proud, mysterious squirrel. What was she going to do?

The Starwife took the bowl from him and examined the ice-covered body beside her. The infection had reached Thomas's shoulders, and frosty lines were creeping relentlessly up his neck. She muttered all the while to herself, nodding or tutting at what she saw, then she placed her crippled fingers on both sides of the wound and shook her head. "There is very little time left to him," she said bluntly, "the dread spells of Jupiter speed through his system. Give me the bag, child." Audrey passed it over and the Starwife foraged inside. With a mumble

221

of approval she brought out a curiously shaped root and deftly bit the end off. A honey-colored sap oozed out and she held it over the gash, allowing three drops to fall into it.

Thomas cried out as each drop touched the dreadful wound. Gwen held his head and stroked his hair soothingly, but his eyes rolled back and only the whites showed.

The Starwife scooped up some of the snow and packed it firmly into the gash, then she tore a strip from a pillowcase and bound it tightly around the frozen leg.

Audrey frowned. She could not see how this would help. Surely what was needed was heat, not more cold. She remembered the squirrel's harsh words concerning Thomas. Perhaps she was merely playing for time until he died.

"The first stage is complete," said the Starwife slowly. "I have applied the poultice, now we must charge it with our prayers so that it may begin its work." She removed the silver acorn from around her neck and dangled it between three fingers over the midshipmouse. With her arm outstretched she sighed and strange words formed on her wrinkled lips. The Hall became tense and a faint breeze stirred, moving her patchy fur and gently swinging the suspended charm.

"Tah!" scolded the Starwife as her arm sagged suddenly and the acorn touched Thomas; she snorted with contempt at her own feeble limbs and rubbed her wasted muscles feverishly. With a grunt of frustration she told everyone, "It is useless, I can do nothing for him, my arms are too weak for this." She raised her eyes to the ceiling and shrugged, "A firmer paw than mine is needed, I fear," and she grumbled scandalous curses at the horrors of age.

The mice all let out a disappointed groan. It seemed that Thomas was doomed after all. Audrey looked at the squirrel sharply. There was something exceedingly odd about what had just happened. It was too like a performance to be true. She had an idea and hurriedly volunteered, "I'll do it." There, she thought, that's put a stop to the old battle-ax's delaying tactics.

The Starwife offered the girl the pendant. She took it and the squirrel smiled, almost from relief. "Excellent," she said. "Now hold it over him steadily, child," she told Audrey, "and do not move or drop it until the process is complete." She gazed around and raised her paw for attention. "Begin now all of you," she instructed the mice. "If you want this mouse to live, you must concentrate with all your might."

Only the sound of the fire was heard as the assembled mice prayed hard and the Starwife closed her eyes and spoke softly under her breath.

Audrey looked suspiciously at the squirrel and wondered what her motives were. She had given in to her request to heal Thomas too easily–there had to be a reason for it. Audrey recalled that it was dangerous to underestimate the Starwife's guile.

The silence lengthened and the whisperings of the squirrel grew more heated as she summoned all her remaining strength. With her left paw she touched Audrey deliberately on the forehead and pressed her nail into the fur, combing a circular shape there. "May this new vessel serve you well," she cried unexpectedly.

Suddenly Audrey became aware of a faint humming sound in her ears, and then a shudder ran down her arms to her paws. She felt a colossal force travel through her and she spluttered with the shock. A cold chill coursed in her veins and passed into her fingers. She gasped in amazement as sparks crackled along the string until it reached the silver amulet, where a white light flickered in small tongues of flame. The acorn was glowing and the humming grew louder until it filled the Hall– a high, piercing note charging the atmosphere and tingling every astonished whisker. The orange flames of the Hall fire shrank down and were overwhelmed by the brilliance flooding from the charm. The mice shielded their eyes from the blinding light and stopped up their ears as the shrill note deafened them.

The Starwife began to cry out the spell she was chanting and she raised her arms ecstatically. The Hall blazed fiercely white, and then, with a thunderous crash and a terrific rush of air, the radiance fled screeching down to Thomas, battering into his frozen body and leaving the house in darkness.

Audrey's eyes and ears were still smarting and ringing as she gazed around. White flames were dripping from the silver acorn hanging from her paws, and they crackled over the midshipmouse's body. Thomas called out in pain, the anguish and agony twisting his face–it was killing him.

So this was the Starwife's plan. She had said it would be better to finish him off, and now she had tricked them into letting her do it. The midshipmouse's head was consumed in cold fire and frost devoured his tortured features.

"Stop it!" shrieked Audrey and she tried to throw the acorn away, but the Starwife reached out and seized hold of her paws, gripping them tightly, bruising the girl's wrists with her iron grasp. "He's dying, you old witch!" protested Audrey as more liquid ice poured from the amulet and totally smothered Thomas.

But the Starwife would not let her go, and the other mice watched them fretfully, not daring to intervene. Only Gwen and Arthur started forward, but the squirrel lashed out with her tail and knocked them backward.

Even as Audrey struggled and wrested her paws free, the white fires died down and disappeared into the floor. She flung the pendant from her but it was too late. Thomas was completely covered, and she gazed only on a statue of ice. A wintry vapor steamed from the grisly figure. It was too horrible to look at, and many turned their stricken faces away.

Before anyone could speak, the Starwife took up her stick and gave the rigid form a sound rap. There was a crack, and two great lines splintered away from the blow.

"What are you doing?" wailed Gwen desolately. The squirrel ignored her and gave it another mighty clout and another until the ice crunched and shattered, flying into the air in sharp little pieces. As one demented she smashed and battered the figure until it was completely destroyed. And there, blinking and gasping for breath, was Thomas, alive and well. He brushed off the icy fragments and sat up grinning as if nothing had ever been the matter with him. "Couldn't half do with a tot o' rum," he said ruefully.

Everyone rubbed their eyes, then cheered, "Hooray for the Starwife!" but she waved them away from her and leaned wearily against the stairs, feeling old beyond measure.

The wound on Thomas's leg was still there and bleeding slightly, but it was clean and free of enchantment–the tissue would heal normally given time. Gwen hugged him and wept and Arthur patted him on the back.

Audrey felt foolish. She looked at the squirrel and hung her head–how wrong she had been for not trusting her. All the time she really was trying to save Mr. Triton. The girl felt her ears burn with shame for her doubts and wondered how she could atone for them. Audrey glanced around for the silver acorn. It had rolled into a dusty corner. She ran over and picked it up. Then, with a sheepish face, she took it to the squirrel.

She looked frail and worn, as if the healing had taken more out of her than was safe. Her body trembled and her long, pointed ears were flat against her skull. She did not hear the girl approach and stared intently into the deep midnight shadows of the kitchen.

Audrey coughed politely to announce herself. "I'm sorry," she stammered, "I didn't understand–I thought . . ."

The Starwife regarded her coolly and a thin smile twitched over her lips. "You nearly killed him, child," she said. "With your nasty suspicions and headstrong impulses you could have murdered him! Luckily I was able to restrain you for long enough. If you had moved the charm away too soon he would have died indeed."

Audrey bit her lip, "I brought this back for you," she said meekly.

The squirrel chuckled and wagged her finger, "Oh ho, and what would I want that for, young lady?"

"It's your acorn," Audrey told her, puzzled, "your symbol of office."

"Ha!" snorted the Starwife. "Not anymore—you took it from me of your own free will and allowed the powers to channel through you—the charm is mine no longer."

"I don't understand . . ." began Audrey, but even as she said it she realized that she had been tricked once again.

The squirrel nodded, reveling in her triumph. "Yes." She laughed softly. "It belongs to you now—my time is over."

"But I don't want it," Audrey protested.

The other dismissed her with a shake of her head. "Too late," she said, melting into the shadows. "You claimed it and it claimed you, Audrey. Both are irrevocably tied together, tethered as one till death." A soft chuckle gurgled in her throat when she spoke the girl's name, and then she heaved a tremendous sigh in which all her cares and responsibilities escaped. Her face wore a serene expression as she gladly told the girl, "It is yours whether you like it or not, there is nought you can do." And with that the Starwife vanished into the darkness.

Audrey looked down at the silver acorn in her palm and tossed her head defiantly. "I'm not your slave." She pouted. "And I'm not having your rotten pendant!" With a furious shout she hurled the charm away and heard it rattle down the cellar steps.

*   *   *

The snow lay deep over the yard. The wind had dropped and the flakes were falling steadily. It was a dark, moonless night, but the snow gave off its own pale glare in which the long icicles that had stretched down from the gutters shone coldly.

An irritated rustling disturbed the grim calm as a cracked voice muttered, "To the devil with all this paper!" With oaths spouting from her lips, the Starwife emerged from the house, tearing up the stuffing that had plugged the exit. "A plague on that idiot Oldnose," she growled, "I never told him to block it again—save me from meddlesome mice!"

The drift of snow that had piled against the hole was kicked and scattered in her temper. Grumbling and swiping the air with her walking stick as though the offending mouse was standing before her the Starwife shuffled slowly to the center of the yard. She lifted her head and stared woefully at the black void of the heavens. "No more the celestial lamps do shine," she crooned sorrowfully, "and the enemy stalks the moonless night."

With a last, regretful glance she lowered her gaze and prepared herself for what had to be done. With her stick the squirrel drew a circle in the snow. When it was complete she looked at it critically and grunted, then, using her feet, tail, and paws, she proceeded to clear everything inside the line. The thick snow was swept up, shoved out, kicked, scraped, and brushed aside until she had made a bare ring in the white garden.

The Starwife mumbled with satisfaction as she leaned on her stick and admired the result of her labor. How tiring it had all been and how cold she was now. Her dry, brittle, old bones creaked mutinously. Memories of the past came unbidden to her, and she remembered a certain night when the stars were like beautiful fiery flowers and their light fell brightly onto her lovely young face. It was the night she had chosen to become the Handmaiden of Orion and had first taken up the silver. Even now she could feel the warm grass under her delicate feet as she raced uphill from the battle to the safety of the throne. War cries echoed around her mind as the image faded and the frost that bit her toes tugged her back to the present.

"They were perilous days," she said quietly, "when treachery and friendship went hand in hand." A grave look crossed her face, "There I learned my harsh lessons, yet what help are they now against the Unbeast?"

The Starwife ambled to the fence and furtively prodded the snow with her stick. "Charts and dreams," she tutted, bending over and foraging in the bare, stony soil, "how jealously we guarded them: all those scrolls and tatters of parchment we believed to be so precious! What use were they in the end?" She held up two good-sized rocks and tossed them into her round clearing. "Never trust a prophecy written on paper," she murmured gruffly to herself as she poked about for more stones, "some clever so-and-so's bound to have fiddled with it and copied the ruddy thing down wrongly, adding twiddly bits of his own that are completely irrelevant." The Starwife picked up four more stones and rolled another one along the ground with her tail. "Oral traditions," she declared, dropping the rocks into the circle and tapping her nose with her forefinger. "Things preserve best from mouth to ear, should've known that."

In the bleak, freezing night the old squirrel carefully placed the seven stones at an equal distance from each other around the ring. Then she stood in the center and touched each one with the handle of her stick and said a blessing over them. "The wheel is made," she sighed when it was done.

The Starwife clutched her back as she bent her knees and tried to sit down. "Waited too long," she chided herself as her spine buckled and she landed unceremoniously on the icy ground. "My time should have ended long ago. What a formidable old boot I have become!" She sucked her bottom lip

thoughtfully and laid the stick across her lap. "Now all there is left for me to do is wait. I pray it comes swiftly."

Between the posts of the fence a dark shape weaved and flitted. It sneaked behind a tin bucket nearby; two eyes glimmered out of the shadows, watching the bowed, hunched figure in the circle. The eyes looked toward the hole in the wall and became wily slits that darted back to the squirrel once more.

"Ha, ha, what have we here?" scoffed a voice from the shade. "What a dainty scene this is!"

The Starwife looked up stiffly, annoyed that someone had disturbed her. If it was that Master Oldnose he would feel the full brunt of her anger, she promised herself. Her clouded eyes stared around, but nobody came from the house. The Starwife glared about the yard and gripped her stick in readiness. "Who's there?" she asked. "Stop hiding and show yourself."

"Aha, hiding indeed!" the voice snorted. "And what pray are you doing, lady?"

"My business is my own," she declared, "and I like to know who I am talking to."

A chuckle sounded, but whoever it was left the shadows and stepped toward her. At first she could only discern the outline; it was difficult to tell what manner of creature was emerging from the gloom, yet there was something about it . . .

The Starwife uttered a little gasp of surprise as into the pale light walked Barker.

She glowered at him. The rat was not waddling and fawning stupidly as before; his back was straight and he strode out with a noble bearing and a haughty sneer on his old face.

He paused and did not attempt to cross into the circle. Putting his claws behind him he began to laugh. "Oh no, petty stargazer! To what end have you brought yourself?" Even his voice was different now; no longer the gibberish he had first spoken, instead it possessed a harsh, ringing authority.

The Starwife studied him, and a look of astonishment and dismay stole over her as she recognized his true identity. "You!" she cried at last. "What are you doing here after all these years? Your time is gone–you should not be walking again." She pounded her stick on the ground and snapped at him. "Artful one," she hissed, "get thee gone, go back to your tomb and sleep till judgment."

Barker smiled indulgently at her. "Away, away!" he mocked. "But see, I am still here–calamity upon calamity. What are you to do?"

The squirrel shivered fearfully. "I shall pray for your destruction, because I count you more dangerous than Jupiter."

At this the rat shook his head. "Oh no," he breathed with a shudder. "He is mightier than I ever imagined. He has a phantom host at his command, and the power of the Green is nothing to him. With these very eyes I saw him destroy the mousebrass. Nothing can defeat him."

It was the Starwife's turn to smile. "So that is why you came," she said with understanding. "Your task was to learn the Unbeast's strength! Thought you could usurp him, did you, and raise the three unholy thrones once more?" She laughed at him contemptuously. "Be gone, unhappy trickster, for He could quash you in an instant and send you shivering into the abyss."

Barker paced around the circle and rubbed his claws together. "At least I have the wit to know when further struggles are futile, Harridan of Orion!" He spat peevishly. "'Night Harpy! I go now only because no other choices are left to me, unlike you who sit and spin your paltry webs. But hear me–Jupiter is too great a fly to be caught in them, and you will find that it is you who are devoured."

There was a silence as each stared into the other's face. "Where is the city mouse?" she said eventually. "What have you done with him?"

The rat put his claws to his brow and spoke forlornly. "Alas," he cried, "he is no more, the nightmare legion returned and it was too late for the lad to run—even Barker was nearly caught."

The Starwife patted her stick thoughtfully. "I guessed as much." She sighed. "You abandoned him! Poor Piccadilly; his folly was in trusting you. That is what I meant when I said you were more dangerous than Jupiter. You can appear fair and good whereas he cannot, and so you ensnare the innocent and unwary."

"You are wrong!" he told her. "The lad was brave and we appreciate such folk, be they rats or no. I was grieved to see the boy die. Many times have I saved him, though he did not know it—he would have perished long ago if I had not been there."

"Rubbish!" retorted the squirrel. "You needed him more than he needed you; the body you chose to hide in was old and weak and could not make the journey here without his help."

Barker shrugged. "What does that matter now? He served his purpose as has this body, but what a fine act it was—Barker the barmy old beggar, one of my greatest performances! But you, wrinkled one, what lies in store for you? Whither are you bound?" He waved his claws over his head and ridiculed her. "To mold you go," he taunted, "and mold you will remain in this darkened world."

"Enough!" she cried, "The time has come for you to depart, shed your flesh and run naked back to your Lord and Lady. Leave me in peace."

A sudden realization flashed into Barker's mind. "Hah!" he squealed hysterically, "Where were my eyes? Your acorn is gone! No longer are you the Drab of the Firmament—your line has ended. Hoo hoo, what a joke you are!" and he capered around her, holding his sides as he laughed. "So, the empire ends at last, the regime is no more—for where are your kin? That proud race, the black squirrels, have long departed, and there is no one left to inherit the silver. All reigns must falter at the last, but what an ignoble finish to your high and mighty monarchy."

The squirrel said nothing but stared bitterly at the ground while he teased and tormented her. "Farewell puny hag, I must leave, but I do so more readily now and rejoice at your downfall."

He strutted away, back into the darkness beneath the fence. "We shall not meet again, Starwife," he called back to her, and then with a riotous hoot he tutted at his mistake. "But of course," he corrected himself, "that title is no longer yours—you have relinquished it. Now let me see, I must call you by your birth name." He hesitated, "What is it, I ask myself?"

"It is a simple name," said the squirrel, weary of his derision and mockery, "but you may use it now, for such secrets are of no avail."

Barker guffawed, "So, you tire of the earth at last, how then shall you be known in this sundering hour?"

She lifted her proud head. "In my raven youth they called me . . . Audrey," she answered plainly. "That was my name."

"Then good-bye, Audrey," Barker called, but his voice was laced with respect, and he slipped away and departed through the night, back whence he came, never again to be seen by mortal eyes.

"Good-bye, Bauchan," whispered the squirrel quietly, as a slow, secret smile formed on her lips.

The snow fell monotonously and her chin dropped to her breast as she succumbed at last to the cruel weather. The night grew old and a stark, gray dawn appeared on the horizon. Through a break in the clouds a slender ray of pale sunlight shone. For a second it touched the squirrel's cheek and all traces of age were smoothed away, but the gap closed and the beam faded. Even as the light left her face the figure in the circle of stones gasped and expired. The midwinter death harvested her.

CHAPTER TWELVE

HUNTED

It was Algy Coltfoot who found the body. For most of the night the mice in the Hall were celebrating Thomas's return to health and listening gravely to his and Arthur's full account of the events around the power station. They were too terrified to think of the ghost army and did not mention it out loud, eventually worrying themselves into jittery sleep. A chill draft seeped through the hole in the kitchen, disturbing the fitful dreams of those closest to it.

Algy had a most uncomfortable night. His blanket kept flapping up with the icy blast, but he was too lazy and tired to do anything about it. It was not until the wind outside began to pick up again, howling around the house and roaring through the kitchen, that he sat up, for all his bedclothes flew up into the air and landed on Master Oldnose, leaving him exposed and shivering.

"This won't do," he grumbled dopily, hauling himself to his feet and rubbing his eyes. He squinted down the step to the kitchen and saw the paper that should have been blocking the hole littering the floor. Muttering drowsily to himself he pattered along and sucked the air through his teeth as his pink little toes touched the freezing linoleum.

"Flippin' Oldnose," Algy said, blaming the one who had last used the exit. He collected the scrunched-up bundles, meaning to stuff them back into the gap, but as he leaned into the narrow space the dismal morning light streamed in and he saw tatters and scraps of torn paper strewn on the snow outside. His curiosity overpowering his tender toes, he passed through the hole, emerging in the yard.

The slim little mouse padded cautiously over to a strange white form. Surely stuffy old Oldnose hadn't been building snowmice. Algy came closer. It was a peculiar shape, whatever it was. He put out a paw and gave the mysterious thing a gentle pat. A clump of snow fell away, and to his horror a patch of silvery fur was revealed.

"Aaarrgghhh!" he screamed, running back to the house. "Help, help!"

Presently the less squeamish of the Skirtings mice were in the yard. Thomas had hobbled there with Arthur's assistance, and he carefully brushed the snow away. Everyone exclaimed in dismay when they recognized the Starwife.

Thomas removed his hat and touched his forehead. "I never had a chance to thank you," he whispered regretfully.

The squirrel's body glistened icily as though she had been coated with sugar, and she was as hard as iron to the touch. Audrey came out, impatient to know what was happening, and looked in astonishment at the old creature's face. "She's smiling," she said hoarsely.

Thomas put his paw on Audrey's shoulder, "Have you still got the Starwife's bag?" he asked. She nodded and he sent her to fetch it. Then the midshipmouse told everyone to find as much fuel as they could. "We cannot leave her like this, we must build a pyre over her," he explained. "I know this is what she would have wanted."

When the mice had gone off in search of wood and he was alone, Thomas gazed at the frozen figure and spoke quietly to it. "So this is why you let me stay and watch your ceremony—you silly old boot. Why did you have to do this?"

"Here's all I could find, Mr. Triton," said Arthur, carrying a few dry twigs. "Everything else is frozen solid."

This was the problem. Nobody found very much useable wood. The cold and damp had seeped into the hawthorn branches and all that was left had already been allocated for the Hall fire. Thomas took what little they gathered and piled it about the Starwife. It was not nearly enough.

"There's only one thing we can do," he told them decisively. "We must use the rest of the wood stored for use inside."

"You cannot do that!" snapped Master Oldnose, outraged. "What are we to do then?"

"We'll freeze like her!" exclaimed Mr. Cockle. Gwen pressed her paw into Thomas's. "He's right," she said. "We need the wood more than the Starwife will, dear."

But he would not be dissuaded. "A pyre I promised her and that's what she'll get," he bellowed. "You don't realize how important she was: this was the Handmaiden of Orion—the Keeper of the Starglass, the Green's regent on Earth. Damn your eyes, she was the closest thing to divinity you're ever likely to see!"

"But she's dead now," put in Arthur, not seeing why their warmth should be sacrificed for a dead squirrel, whoever she was.

Audrey's head swam. That curious feeling was coming over her again. As she stared at the quarrelsome crowd she seemed to drift away from them, and something stirred in her mind.

"Mr. Triton's right!" she shouted suddenly. "We have to do this, otherwise what have we become? Are we rats to leave the dead scattered around? If it were you, would you like your body to be disregarded, left for the crows to peck at? Listen to yourselves, for the Green's sake!"

Her outburst shamed most of them and frightened the rest. Gwen stared in wonder at her daughter, she had never spoken so passionately before. "I'm sorry, Thomas," Mrs. Brown found herself saying. "I was wrong. Of course we must honor the Starwife."

The midshipmouse winked at her and squeezed her paw. "That's my Gwennie," he said.

The other mice agreed and went to bring out the last reserves of wood. The hour rolled by and at the end of it a tall fire had been built. The twigs and branches covered the figure of the squirrel in a cone-shaped frame tied together with string at the top, and any gaps were filled with bits of dry paper. Thomas inspected the work and nodded; it was ready to be lit.

As the pyre was being constructed he had racked his brains to try and remember the exact words the Starwife had used in the ceremony. The mice joined paws and formed a ring while they waited for him to begin.

"Under the stars we are as one," he said, bowing in reverence. "Theirs is the power of countless years. They see our grief and know our pain, yet still they shine." Everyone felt the irony of the speech and shook their heads as Thomas finished by saying, "And their light gives us hope."

He fumbled for the rest of the words, swearing at his forgetfulness. It was something to do with trees and wheels, wasn't it?

"From acorn to oak . . ." began a voice unexpectedly. Thomas turned and saw it was Audrey. She came forward bearing the velvet bag, ". . . but even the mightiest of oaks shall fall," she intoned. "Thus do we recognize the great wheel of life and death and life once more. We surrender our departed soul under the stars and may the Green gather her to him." She lifted her face to the blank, white sky and raised her paws. "Light the pyre," she told Thomas.

He took the tinderbox obediently from the brim of his hat and used it to kindle the paper lodged between the sticks. A pale, wavering flame trembled in the wind, but it caught the wood and cracked hungrily.

Soon the whole thing was ablaze. The fire ravaged through the structure with amazing swiftness. The snow in the yard melted as the heat hammered out from it and the mice thawed themselves. Audrey opened the Starwife's bag. There were only a few dried leaves and herbs left in it but she emptied them out onto her palm and cast them into the flames. "Speed to the Green!" she commanded.

The fire spluttered and for a moment tiny stars of emerald spat and fizzled in its heart. Almost immediately the blackened branches crumbled and collapsed. The flames dwindled and the snow that had melted iced over as the temperature plummeted once again.

"It is done," said Audrey. "It would be better if we went inside now."

Everyone looked at her curiously, not least Thomas, who wondered how she had known the correct words when she had never heard them before. But they admitted it was too cold to remain outside any longer and hurried indoors to escape the wind.

The Hall was not much warmer. Even when they plugged up the hole in the kitchen the extreme chill of winter lingered. Arthur looked at the dying embers on the slate and knew it would not be long before they too froze to death.

Children wailed and turned pinched, hungry faces to their mothers, but there was nothing for them to eat. "What are we to do?" beseeched the distraught parents. "My baby needs food." The Raddle sisters fanned their paws before each other's faces frantically, trying not to faint.

"Oh Oswald," blubbered Mrs. Chitter, "I shan't ever see you again."

Thomas looked on this desperate scene and wished he could do something. "Oh Gwennie." He sighed. "What now?"

"Trust in the Green, Thomas," she replied. "That is all any of us can do."

"Aye," he muttered doubtfully, "but when will . . ."

"Hush!" Gwen interrupted him. "Listen, can you hear?" The midshipmouse wrinkled his brow at her in surprise, but he tilted his head and cocked an ear. There, faint at first, was a curious scraping noise.

"What is it?" Gwen asked. "Where is it coming from?"

"I don't know," whispered Thomas. He called out for quiet, and everyone listened to the sound. It became louder, like sharp nails dragging down a blackboard. The Raddle sisters shuddered and yelped.

"It's coming from out there," cried Arthur, running to the great boarded-up front door. The noise continued to screech, and then suddenly . . .

BANG!

"What was that?" boomed Thomas in alarm as the door shook violently and sent Arthur reeling backward.

BANG!

There it was again and the mice squeaked with fright.

BANG! BANG! BANG!

Whatever was out there was trying to break in. The door quivered as the pounding blows became a battering frenzy. Mrs. Chitter screamed and fled into the Skirtings. The air trembled at the ferocity of the attack and the walls vibrated ominously.

"It's mighty powerful, whatever it is," breathed Thomas.

Audrey felt the back of her neck tingle and a feeling of over-whelming dread rushed down her spine as she sensed waves of pure evil ricochet into the Hall.

"Go away!" Master Oldnose shouted at the unknown thing behind the door, but his voice was thin and fearful. The savage onslaught went on regardless.

"Get out of the way there!" bellowed Thomas, herding the stricken onlookers from the front of the Hall.

"Oh Thomas," said Gwen, "who is it? What does it want?"

But he did not answer, for at that moment the door cracked and splinters sharp as needles flew out. The mice shrieked and cowered as far back as they could.

A chink of light appeared in the towering expanse of frac-turing wood, and sawing and cutting through as though it were paper, a vicious point of ice jabbed its way in. Another glaring hole was punched out and a second stabbing icicle forced the splitting wood inward.

"Ice spears," gasped Arthur, trembling in fear. "He's sent his army to get us."

More of the evil spears smashed into the door, and to every-one's horror, phantom claws reached through the jagged holes they had made, groping and searching for prey.

It was a dreadful sight to watch, as the ghostly legion tore at their only defense with claw and ice. Everyone was too afraid to move, and stared at the nightmare dumbly. The heap of splin-ters and shavings grew thick on the floor as the holes widened and arms thrashed in, reaching greedily out for the unwary.

Thomas shook himself out of his terror. "They'll be through soon," he shouted. "Quick, everyone, into the cellar."

They looked at him in panic. "We're not going down there!" they cried.

"Then where will you go?" roared Thomas. "If you run back to your homes, they will find and kill you, and if you run out-side the winter will get you."

240

"But down *there*," they spluttered, "we'll be running into worse danger."

"Rubbish," thundered the midshipmouse. "Jupiter's not in the sewers anymore! We must get away while there's still time."

"But where will you take them, Thomas?" Gwen asked. "Won't those foul things follow us?"

"Mebbe," he replied, "but what else can we do? There's no use tryin' to fight that motley crew—I've tried. We can only run now, an' that means Greenwich! To my ship we'll go, an' then who knows?"

"Aaaaiiieee!" screamed Algy, pointing at a large hole. There, rising above the floating haze of sawdust, came a hideous, spectral head. The blank, hollow eye sockets peered in and turned malignantly toward the frightened gathering. The black mouth fell open to utter a bloodcurdling moan that was filled with malice and hatred of the living. Shrieking for their lives, the mice surged through the cellar door and poured down the stone steps.

Jacob Chitter ran into the Skirtings and carried out his wailing wife, who protested all the way. "Put me down," she whined, "I'm not going in there."

Audrey was swept along by the panicking crowd. She felt like an autumn leaf plucked up by the ravaging wind and having no control over where it was taken. Her feet hardly touched the ground as the jostling, rushing mice swarmed thickly into the darkness of the cellar.

"Through the Grill, quickly," Arthur called, "or we'll be trapped."

Some of the mice held back. It was, after all, the symbol of the Underworld and had been a place to dread and shun all their lives.

Thomas barked his instructions: "Ladies and children first. Arthur, you go and lead them in."

Nervously they began to scramble through the rusted gap in the ornate ironwork, while from up above there came a sickening crash as the door finally gave way to the phantom horde. At this everyone squealed and pushed harder to escape from those terrible spears. "Careful!" roared Thomas. "You'll crush the little 'uns."

Audrey was shoved and squashed till the breath was squeezed from her body. A hefty mouse from the Landings trod clumsily on her tail, but in the clamor and confusion he did not hear her cry out. Muttering angrily she wrenched it free, but the silver bell on her tail shot off and rolled tinkling out of reach as the crowd moved forward once more, dragging her with it.

"My bell!" she cried unhappily, but it was lost under the heavy tramp of frightened feet.

A rough paw seized her and she was pulled through the throng by Mr. Cockle, who had seen her in difficulties. "There you go, young Audrey," he said when she staggered out of the congestion.

"Hey, it's me next," spat a Landings lady, barging forward. She thrust Audrey out of her way, but Thomas stepped in and gripped the graceless mouse's arm. He brushed her to one side and smiled charmingly. "Manners please, madam," he told her. "Your turn, Mrs. Scuttle," he said, holding the fuming snob back for Audrey.

Thomas allowed Mrs. Brown in next to teach the selfish creature a lesson. "Hurry," cried Gwen, as she followed her daughter and passed through the rusted iron entrance.

"In you go Arabel, don't fret now," said Mr. Chitter as he stuffed his wife through the Grill. "There's nothing at all to be scared of down there." But he kissed his mousebrass nervously before following her.

There were only a dozen or so left to pass through, and Thomas glanced warily up the steps. He could hear the horrible moans of the wraiths dragging their ice spears over the wreckage of the broken door. "Come on," Thomas whispered urgently to himself as Mr. Cockle, the last of the mice, disappeared into the gloom beyond the metal leaves.

The midshipmouse fell to his knees and scrabbled through. Just as he whipped his tail in, an ice spear crashed onto the floor behind.

The sewers rang with small gasps that echoed around the arched tunnels. Only four of them had ever ventured down here, and the other hundred or so gazed fearfully at the dripping walls and slimy ledges. The water below was thick with islands of dirty, black ice, which sluggishly swirled past. It was certainly living up to all their expectations. They could not imagine a worse place, and bleated pathetically.

They had squeezed themselves onto the narrow ledge, and a long, miserable line of them stretched far into the evil-smelling distance. Thomas came limping up from the rear and shouted to the front where he presumed Arthur was.

"You there, matey?" he yelled. The sewers snatched up his voice and it boomed through them like a gong.

"I'm here, Mr. Triton," answered a smaller echo.

"Do you remember the way to Greenwich, lad?" Thomas called.

"I think so," came the reply.

"Then lead on, matey!"

Slowly the great queue shuffled along, and with a last, worried glance backward, Thomas followed.

Audrey was sandwiched between her mother and Mrs. Chitter, who complained incessantly, whining at the state of her muddy toes and constantly blaming her husband for bringing her down here. Audrey would have turned around and told the stupid old biddy to shut up if she hadn't been forced to keep an eye on the treacherous ledge herself. The way was icy and perilous, and more than once somebody cried out as they fell down and everyone behind had to stop and wait till they picked themselves up again before they could continue.

Through the dank darkness they filed, around sharp bends and corners, over fallen brickwork and through narrow arches. As she was gingerly stepping over a pool of frozen slime Audrey recognized the spot where she had first met Madame Akkikuyu. She smiled as she remembered the poor unloved fortune-teller—and then it happened again.

The sewers and the sound of Mrs. Chitter's mewling faded far away and she felt herself drift blissfully from them. "Go back," said a soft voice in her head. "Return to the garden, go back, go back."

"Hurry along there, child," gabbled Mrs. Chitter crossly. "Stop gawking and get out from under my feet, you're slowing everyone down."

Audrey was jolted back to the grim world and stared in confusion at the ranting fusspot. "I can't go with you," she mouthed distractedly. "I must go back."

"Oh my!" exclaimed a surprised Mrs. Chitter as the girl pushed past her.

"Audrey!" called Gwen, turning around. "Where are you going? Stop her, someone!"

"I say," declared Master Oldnose when she approached him. "Just you hang on a minute, young lady. Ooof!" Audrey had dug him in the ribs and nipped smartly by.

Fighting her way through the astonished line of mice, she bustled and squirmed. A fierce determination had seized her, and the urge to return home was overwhelming. She shrugged off the paws that tried to catch her and kicked those who stood stubbornly in her way.

"Now then, lass," barked a stern voice as two strong paws gripped her shoulders. "What's this in aid of?" Thomas asked impatiently.

"Out of my way, Triton!" snapped Audrey furiously. "I have

to get back at once." She glared into his eyes and her temper flared. "Crawl back into your bottle and let me go!" she demanded haughtily.

Thomas flinched as though he had been hit and released her. She sounded exactly like the Starwife! He tugged his hat in respect and stepped aside, "Sorry, ma'am," he said automatically.

Audrey dashed past him. Now that she was free of all those hindering ditherers she hastened through the tunnels, retracing her footsteps. Thomas watched her go with a scared look on his face. The girl was undoubtedly running to her doom. He hobbled after, but with his wounded leg it was useless and he shook his head. "Green save you," he muttered.

The narrow passage that led to the Grill was now lined with frost, and gleaming icicles dripped from the ironwork. Cautiously Audrey crawled between the wintry stalactites and looked out of the grating to the cellar beyond. It was dark, but she could see no sign of the fierce specters. Only a fine layer of twinkling rime covering everything told her that they had been there at all.

Audrey squeezed through the gap, made smaller by the choking ice, and listened carefully. Not a sound came to her. The house had never been so silent. Where had Jupiter's army gotten to? As she made her way over the frozen cellar floor, something caught her eye: it was her silver bell. The tail ornament was glued to the ground by the ice and she had to pull with all her strength to free it. With a sad smile Audrey examined her treasure. The little loop was broken, making it impossible to wear. She closed her fingers around it and looked up at the stone stairway. If only she could manage to get to the garden.

Audrey closed her eyes and readied herself for whatever might happen. Behind the cellar door the entire horde of

Jupiter's phantom warriors could be waiting with their spears raised in readiness. She swallowed hard and began to climb. Up she went, and all the while, ghastly imaginings filled her mind. Maybe they wouldn't kill her straight away! What if they took her directly to Jupiter himself? Audrey's heart was in her mouth and her head was spinning with apprehension and fear as she stood on the topmost stair and put her paw to the door. She gave it a push and it creaked ominously open.

The Hall appeared to be empty, save for the devastation left by the ghosts. A great, gaping, ragged hole glared where the massive front door had stood, and tatters of wood were strewn all over the floor. A biting gale blasted through the house, and snow gusted in. The fire was quenched and its embers had frozen over. The Unbeast's winter had entered the building and nothing could live there now. The cruel cold had cracked the walls from floor to ceiling. The staircase had shrunk away from the banister, which hung precariously from the landing, groaning and threatening to crash down at any moment. The Skirtings had been ripped apart by mindless claws, and the contents of humble homes were scattered heedlessly about. It must have been a crazed, brutal attack to have done so much damage in so little time.

It was a shocking sight, but Audrey was unmoved. Her sole objective was to get to the yard, and nothing, not even this, would stop her. She hesitated for a second to be certain that she was indeed alone, but not a thing stirred, and only the biting wind filled her ears. It whistled forlornly through the rails of the ruined stair rods and swirled the thick snowflakes into a mad ballet about her. Audrey walked slowly down the Hall but her pace quickened. The noise of the creaking banister sounded eerily like footsteps prowling behind her. She ran into the kitchen and tore the stuffing from the hole that led outside and emerged from the exit into the freezing, white world.

The full force of the cold hit her and Audrey lost all sensation in her toes. She had no idea why she had been compelled
to come. There was nothing out of the ordinary—it was exactly
the same as ever before. She shook herself, and the desperate
instinct to return melted away—what was she doing here?
Audrey was suddenly appalled at her stupidity. She thought of
the risks she had taken to get here, and could not believe her
rash actions. She had cut herself off from family and friends
and did not even know why. Her mind was in chaos as she tried
to remember what had made her return. Perhaps she was going
insane: Audrey put a paw to her forehead to steady herself.

In the center of the yard were the remains of the Starwife's
pyre. Nothing was left but a circle of soft, gray ash. Audrey
stared fixedly at it and her eyes grew wide and round. Poking
up out of the cinders was a small, green shoot.

She hurried over, amazed that anything could grow so
quickly in this severe cold. Bewildered at this miracle, Audrey
stretched out her paw, but as she touched it the bulb came away
in her fingers and she lifted it gently from the ashes.

The girl marveled at the tiny green blade in her palm. It
gave her hope. It seemed to show that Jupiter had not destroyed
everything. Somehow nature would always fight through. She
tucked the delicate plant into the waistband of her dress and
decided it was time to leave.

The dismal afternoon light grew even dimmer as the snow
fell more heavily. Audrey hurried to the hole in the wall and ran
into the kitchen once more. Now her only thought was to get
back to her family. She could not understand what had possessed her to run off like that, and could not remember where
the crazy idea had originated from. She walked hastily through
the Hall, shuddering at the creepy noises the banister made,
and only relaxed when the cellar door was behind her.
Gleefully Audrey leaped down the steps, anxious to catch up
with the others. She wondered what Thomas's ship was like

inside and recalled Twit saying something about lots of figure-heads. She hastened past the piles of boxes and bric-a-brac to the Grill.

A misty shape moved in the forbidding darkness beyond, but she did not see it and approached with no thought of danger. Her mind was too full of questions that she could not answer. The figure moved farther into the shadows, allowing the unwary mouse to get within reach. Audrey knelt down before the entrance, and above her head a fine tendril of fog curled as a flicker of starfire shone between the grating.

With a rasping hiss a ghostly claw flashed out and swiped the air. Audrey screamed as more arms flailed out of the Grill, and the chilling wails of the spectral army filled the cellar. Evil talons tore at her. One of them snatched at her ribbon and shredded it in her hair; another sliced a vicious cut across her arm. Spears glinted beyond the ironwork, and grisly cackles issued from dead throats. A face pressed against one of the holes and leered blindly at her.

Audrey whirled around and fled in horror as a cruel, glittering spike jabbed out and sailed through the darkness. It smashed only inches from her head as she clambered up the steps.

"Help me, someone," she sobbed in vain as the ghosts seeped out and pursued her malevolently. She tore up the stairs in a fit of anguish, ripping her nails and bruising her knees with the speed of her flight. The phantoms howled behind her with empty, petrifying voices. They sank their claws deep into the stone and hauled themselves stealthily and relentlessly higher.

As she reached the top step Audrey glanced fearfully down. She was horrified to see how quickly they were moving. A foul head reared over the edge of a stair and stared wickedly at her, the savage jaws wide open and a grisly tongue dangling greedily. The horrendous spirit lunged for her, but Audrey shot through the door and then threw all her weight against it. The immense barrier of wood swung slowly and stiffly but did not close. A ravening claw slashed out through the crack. Audrey heaved her shoulder against the door with all her might and dug her heels in.

It slammed shut and the old latch far above clicked shut. The full force of the wraiths fell upon the door with frightening fury. They hammered and crashed into it, pounding with their fists and shrieking their frustration. Audrey backed away; it would not hold them for long. She looked wildly around the Hall, desperate for a place to hide, but Thomas's words rang in her ears: "If you run back to your homes they will find and kill you." Where, then, could she go?

The door shuddered as the tip of an ice spear crashed through it. Audrey wept in terror as she saw the wood shiver and yield to the battering host. Choking back her cries she raced through the kitchen and into the garden. She had to escape! But Thomas had also told everyone that it was just as dangerous to stay out there, for the winter would claim them as surely as the ghosts.

Audrey struggled through the snow and leaned against the fence panting and breathing with difficulty. She prayed the specters would not follow, for her heart was pounding and her legs quivered with fear. The girl bowed her head and wiped the cold sweat from her face as she fought to control her panic. She had to try and get to Greenwich somehow, and needed all her wits about her.

A thundering uproar signaled the destruction of the cellar door and she heard the yammering phantoms screech into the Hall, but the fiendish voices grew faint as they charged up the stairs to rampage through the Landings.

Audrey's short, erratic gasps eased and she breathed deeply. Gradually her scrambled nerves were settling. She closed her eyes and heaved a sigh of relief. Now she could escape without fear of pursuit. She brushed the hair off her face and was about to pass between the fence posts when she heard a sound that froze her blood.

"Rosieee," hissed a sepulchral voice. "Rosieee." Audrey spun around and stared into the garden in horror. Stalking toward her was a grisly spirit. It was not a rat, yet it was terrible to witness. The phantom carried on its back many bags and bundles, and hung about its neck were straps and chains. But the bags contained grinning skulls and ghostly bundles of bones, and the chains were necklaces of teeth. But even under all those horrible trophies it was still possible to see that the awful specter was that of a mouse. Audrey felt her stomach turn over as she recognized it.

"Kempe!" she cried. Here was the ghost of the peddler who had guided her to Fennywolde last summer.

The phantom's mouth opened as it came closer to the stricken mouse. It reached into one of its bags. "Rosieee . . . Rosieee," it chanted with a flat, jarring murmur—soft as a whisper in a tomb.

From the bag it began to draw out an ice spear. "I'll tell you of poor Rosieee," it sang in dead, mournful tones. "The tragedy that was Rosieee!" On the word "tragedy" it raised the spear and a cruel snarl formed on the bloodless lips.

Audrey stumbled back, too afraid to tear her eyes from the macabre apparition bearing down on her. The spear was aimed at her and the empty sockets burned into her soul. With a last evil laugh Kempe's ghost shrieked, "And why she died so lonely." The spear flew out of his grasp. Audrey ducked and it plunged into a snow drift behind her.

The wraith hissed and ran forward with outstretched fingers. Audrey cried out and started to run but her foot twisted awkwardly and she fell to the ground. At once the cackling spirit pounced and leaped onto the floundering girl. "Why she died!" It laughed harshly. "Died! Died! Died!"

Audrey kicked and fought but Kempe held on grimly. The intense cold that beat out of the starfire in his chest pricked and stabbed into her fur. He brought his face close to hers and she nearly fainted at the stench. She felt his horrible fingers tighten around her throat and he threw back his head to scream with infernal laughter. Audrey could do nothing to save herself, for her paws passed straight through him. Her face turned purple as he squeezed and wrung her neck. She writhed pitifully on the snow and all her strength drained away. Audrey's arms went limp and the fingers of her right paw opened. The little silver bell rolled out and tinkled sweetly.

At the sound of this the phantom lifted its head and gazed down at the trinket, which was rolling in the wind. Kempe took his fingers from the girl's throat and stared after it. The starfire wavered in him as the apparition recalled the manner of its death. It gasped and put a paw to its chest where the white flames crackled and spat. Kempe staggered to his feet and swayed uncontrollably as the memories crowded in and he relived those last moments of agony.

Spluttering for breath, Audrey took her chance and crawled through the fence, leaving the confused specter behind.

Kempe picked up the bell and his paws trembled. "Noooo!" he screamed defiantly, the starfire throbbed and flashed as it tried to regain control. "I won't . . . " but his words were lost as the power flooded through him once more and he turned purposefully back to his victim—but she was gone.

Audrey lurched through the wintry gardens, fleeing blindly. Under hedges she ducked and around frost-glimmering sheds until she reached the end of the terrace. A metal gate clanged in the wind before her. Beyond it stretched the wide, snow-covered road. Audrey pushed herself out and rushed into the bleak landscape.

The glaring white snow dazzled and blinded her eyes while the fatigue from her struggles gnawed at her. It was too cold to move, all she wanted to do was lie down and sleep. Her legs started to wobble as she trudged wearily on, not knowing in which direction she was moving, for the rising blizzard cut her off and whole buildings disappeared behind the lashing storm. All hope of finding her family faded, and her great fear of Jupiter, with his diabolical warriors, vanished as, with a last, forsaken cry, she collapsed into the snow and waited, like the Starwife before her, for the end to come. A curious warmth spread through her body as she felt herself sink into the welcoming arms of deadly slumber. A familiar voice called to her from the depths of her despair as she closed her eyes and surrendered, lost in the freezing waste of Deptford.

BATTLE ON BOARD

The *Cutty Sark* reared high and black above the refugees' heads as they blinked in the light. The masts stretched tall and stark against the leaden sky, like accusing, spindly fingers pointing up to heaven. Thomas grinned fondly at his ship; now that everything was covered in snow she looked like she was sailing on wintry seas and landlocked no longer.

"There's my darlin'," he said, running a loving paw over her timbers. "Are you rememberin' the salty days of your ocean-rollin' girlhood?" He smiled to himself and turned to the crowd. "Follow me," he called out, marching up to the rudder and climbing into the little hole that served as his personal entrance.

The mice stared up in awe at the unfamiliar shape of the magnificent vessel. None had ever seen a ship before, and some of them were frightened. They looked desperately around the deep concrete trough that rose sheer and smooth on all four sides and felt as though they were imprisoned. But the prospect of staying out in the shivering cold was too dreadful, so they swallowed their fears and entered the clipper cautiously.

Thomas led them up a low, dark passage that smelled of tar but which opened out onto an enormous space.

"Aaayyeee!" screeched the Raddle sisters in unison as they pattered into the hold. "Giants!" They flapped their paws at the rows of figureheads and gibbered fitfully. Thomas left others to explain while he ran up to a white figure wearing a gold turban and ducked into a hole around the back.

"Now then," he shouted when he emerged again, brandishing his own sword, "let's make ourselves a plan of action."

"But what can we do?" asked Master Oldnose doubtfully.

"We can post a watch on deck for starters," he said, making practice sweeps with his sword. "I'll not be caught unawares again."

He picked five other mice, including Arthur, and led them to a steep flight of wooden stairs. Up they went, disappearing from sight. Gwen watched them leave. Her spirits were low. She thought miserably of Audrey and prayed she was safe. Mrs. Chitter came and took hold of her paw. A gentle, uncharacteristic understanding shone in the gossip's eyes; she knew what it was like to lose a child. "We must be patient and have faith," she said.

Gwen managed a frail smile of thanks and nodded yes, but she remembered the Starwife's warning about what would happen the next time Jupiter used the Starglass. She covered her face as she realized that that would be this evening.

The wind tore around the deck and snatched at the rigging. Thomas strode out, sword in paw, and waited for the others to follow. Into the gale came Arthur, Mr. Cockle, Algy Coltfoot, Master Oldnose, and Jacob Chitter.

"Right," Thomas shouted above the noise of the wind, "Nosey and Cockle, you go starboard. Algy and Mr. Chitter, portside for you. Arthur, get astern. Keep all your eyes peeled, as soon as you spot Jupiter's scurvy wretches, just holler."

The mice scurried to their designated sentry posts and leaned over the deck rail to stare at the snow-covered ground. Thomas made his way to the prow of the ship and gazed steadily down. Nothing moved over the white expanse. The midshipmouse raised his eyes to the river; it was completely frozen now, a flat, wide sheet of gray, grim ice. A twinge of discomfort bit into his leg—the wound did not like the cold. He looked up at the sky. The sun was hidden behind the thick layers of blizzard-ridden cloud, but Thomas knew the evening was drawing near.

A tremendous rumble shook the world, and the *Cutty Sark* quivered on its struts.

The mice looked around, startled. "What was that?" quavered Master Oldnose.

Thomas did not know, but out of the corner of his eye he saw something glimmer. He turned and looked at the mist-enshrouded power station in the distance. The tiny windows were ablaze with white fire, and he could hear a deep purr echo from it. Jupiter was on the move. A bolt of jagged, blue lightning streaked up from the chimney and sliced through the clouds. Thomas shuddered.

With a thundering roar the towering chimney split and great chunks of it crumbled away. The lightning crackled around it and the fissures widened. With a deafening groan the chimney toppled toward the Thames and crashed onto the ice. It shattered and huge spouts of water gushed up as the massive structure burst through and sank into the depths.

A smoking, ragged shaft was left jutting out of the roof from which an enormous stream of hissing vapor issued. Into the air rose Jupiter. His mountainous bulk soared and gathered, godlike, in the sky. Out of his fortress he stormed, and as he left it the walls shook and swayed perilously. The last of his steaming form billowed from the power station and it collapsed beneath him, smashing and exploding into ruin.

A blizzard of hail and ice rained down from the Unbeast's

mouth as he roared amid the clouds. The lightning flashed about his head like a crown of cold fire and in his savage claws something small shone. It was the Starglass, and he had one final task for it. Tonight the sun would set for the last time.

The mice on the deck of the *Cutty Sark* stared at the petrifying vision and felt the doom of every living creature loom near. Master Oldnose slumped to the deck in fright, and all the color was bleached out of Mr. Cockle's face as he beheld the evil glory of winter's monarch. Jacob Chitter wiped his appalled eyes and his knees became water. He fell with a thump on his tail, and the breath caught in his throat. Arthur bit his lip and shrank against the deck rail in fear. Only two nights had passed since he had first witnessed Jupiter, but in that short length of time the horrendous spirit had grown, bloated now beyond all belief. It did not seem possible that the power station had ever managed to contain him.

Jupiter hung over the land like a great dark cloud. He waited for all the vapor to leave the crumbled wreck of his cathedral of cold and drift up to swell his monstrous size. His raucous, trumpeting laughter traveled around the quaking earth, which would soon be his alone.

With a purr that vibrated through the air and set all teeth on edge he rumbled toward Greenwich, his baleful eyes scalding everything with frost. Thomas ducked behind the rail as the massive, nightmarish shape flew overhead and a dark shadow fell heavily over the ship, plunging it into night. The masts were touched by the outermost tips of Jupiter's trailing, foggy majesty, and immediately a mutilating ice rifled down them, causing the wood to creak in despair. Chunks of hail as large as cannonballs dropped from the hideous cat spirit and mercilessly battered the deck.

Arthur clung to a rope as the *Cutty Sark* rocked violently and the steel struts tore vicious rents in her listing hull. He was flung against the rail and took a sharp blow to his skull. With a cry of pain Arthur held his head and averted his eyes from Jupiter. The blackness of the enormous shadow stole across the cratered deck as the purring Unbeast veered around and made for the observatory.

Arthur hung over the rail and stared woefully down. "Green spare us!" he exclaimed.

Following beneath their evil master marched the spectral army. The phantoms flourished their ice spears and yammered eagerly for blood.

Arthur sprang back and shouted, "They're here! They're here!"

The others came rushing to him and looked over the edge. "Curse them," swore Thomas. "They're surrounding the ship." Sure enough, the ghosts were spreading out and creeping all around the concrete trench that held the trapped clipper. They lifted their ghastly faces and let out shrieks of hate.

"Cockle," shouted Thomas urgently, "go warn everyone. Tell 'em we're beseiged and they'll have to brace themselves."

Mr. Cockle and Algy darted down the steps to the hold and Thomas gripped his sword with determination. "I'll not go down without a fight," he told himself.

The cackling wraiths licked their lips and moved in. With slow menace they crept to the edge of the trough and with frenzied hoots flung themselves onto the long metal poles that impaled the vessel. "They're climbing up," wailed Arthur.

"Aye," bawled Thomas, "keeping us busy while Jupiter flies unhindered to yonder hill."

The specters crept along the struts, their wicked claws scratching the metal in their dreadful advance and the spears under their arms glinted, impatient for murder.

The steel poles that skewered the ship ended two-thirds of the way up her hull; above that the timbers were smooth and looked impossible to climb. Arthur hoped this would be the case as the specters reached the end of their creeping journey.

He leaned out to peer down, but ghostly faces leered up at him and they reached out, moaning for his blood.

"I think they're stuck, Mr. Triton," he said, greatly relieved, "they can't clamber up any farther."

"Don't be so sure, mate," Thomas answered gravely as he pointed down to where the foul soldiers were hammering their spears into the seasoned timbers, one after another like a ladder of icicles. Up they snaked, smelling the mice that awaited them in the ship.

"Can't we do something?" wailed Master Oldnose, gazing hopelessly at them.

Thomas tossed his head back and whisked his sword through the air. "We can die bravely," he bellowed heartily.

The ship shivered as the spears were driven into her sides. The fiendish army swarmed up furiously. A cruel claw appeared over the rim and gouged deeply into the varnished rail.

Thomas sprang forward with an angry cry and brought his sword crashing down. The blade sank into the splintering wood, passing clean through the phantom claw, which slithered along and hauled its owner up. A snarling ogre of a spirit leaped over the side and landed with an empty chuckle on the deck beside the midshipmouse. It was the largest of all the infernal warriors and needed no ice spear, for its claws were long and could rake the wind to ribbons.

Thomas tugged and pulled wildly at his sword, which was still firmly wedged in the wooden rail. "Watch out!" shouted Arthur in warning.

The sword would not budge. Panic-stricken, Thomas uttered a sailor's oath and the slavering phantom pounced at him.

*   *   *

Up in the gray sky a dark mass swept toward Deptford. It stretched into the veiled distance, and the rumor of its coming was electrifying. Thousands upon thousands of shrill, high-pitched voices filled the fading evening. The bats had arrived at last.

Oswald clung to Orfeo and Eldritch's feet as they bore him unerringly through the snowstorm. The albino's face was set and grim. The last few days had taken their toll; he had not slept or eaten and dark circles ringed his pink eyes.

It had taken a tremendous effort to drag the Book of Hrethel up through the foundation of the grand council building, and with Eldritch's help he had taken it to the Elders, who beat their wings angrily at their ancestor's low cunning. What use was a blank book to anyone? They had cast it down from a great height with contempt, and as it fell the spine tore. A plume of fluttering, aged pages soared out in the plummeting book's wake. The bindings exploded into brown dust as they struck the floor, and the hazy image of a wrinkled bat appeared for a brief moment in the blossoming cloud, sneering with derision and triumph.

Cries of doom and despair had reverberated around the dome as the bats consumed the bitterness dished out to them from centuries long gone. They hid their faces behind their wings in defeat and wept desolately.

But Oswald was not so sure. All along he had felt the wary presence of Hrethel's carefully planned revenge, and a certain aspect of it did not seem right. The medieval tyrant had over-looked something–if only he could pinpoint exactly what it was.

He had asked Eldritch to fly him down to examine the remains of the book, and then he knew. As he fingered the tingling parchments he realized in a flash of brilliance that magic is a force that cannot easily be erased. The Great Book had contained many powerful spells and countless magical signs and formulae for hundreds of years before Hrethel had wiped it clean. But he should have destroyed it utterly, for the nature of the writings and the strength of the incantations had soaked into the fibres like water into a sponge. Those blank pages had become charged with tremendous energy. The spells were still there but hidden in the very fabric of the book, a source of living, invisible power.

Oswald whooped with delight at his discovery and quickly told the council. They stared at him, amazed. But how could this help them? The spells may indeed be there, but how would they read them? It was a problem that troubled their hearts for days, but the solution had stirred in Oswald's heart, and he knew what had to be done.

Now the snow beat severely against his face, stinging and numbing it. In the shadow of the two bats' wings the albino looked down at his fluttering coat and smiled solemnly. This was the answer he had found, and it was a truly hazardous venture. The only way to vanquish Jupiter was to use the power of the book against him, yet without being able to read the spells this was their only option–they were taking the Great Book to him.

Remembering the costume worn by Master Oldnose at the midsummer celebrations, Oswald had made a tatting suit from the pages. He had ripped the magic parchment into shreds and sewn them into a loose tunic for himself.

"You realize what you are doing?" Ashmere had asked him fearfully.

"Of course I do," Oswald had cried as he was surrounded by the countless, cheering bats in the dome. He had felt very brave and added, "Down with Jupiter!" But now he felt afraid, for the object of his errand drew near. He had volunteered to fly with Orfeo and Eldritch, while wearing the magical tatting suit, into the very heart of the Unbeast's unbounded spirit. None of them expected to come out alive.

The great multitude of bats flew with them at their head.

Even the elders had flown out to witness the final assault. They sang uplifting songs of daring and courage so that the three heroes should not be dismayed and feel dread steal over them. Squadrons of respectful moon riders wheeled past them, saluting and calling their names proudly.

Oswald readied himself for the terrible time ahead. He could already see lightning flare in the fog on the observatory hill. He hoped they were in time. The tower blocks and estates rolled below them as they swept over Deptford.

"Master Pink Eyes," Orfeo called down to him, "see there, something lies in the snow."

The albino peered at the distant ground but could see nothing, the bat sight having left him days ago. "What is it?" he asked, puzzled that his friend should think it so important.

Audrey was close to death, the cold had entered the very marrow of her bones and a mantle of snow had formed over her. Her faltering thought wandered through twilight as one in a dream, but there would be no waking. Deeper into the shadowy realm she sank, until the black chasm of the midwinter death opened beneath her.

The light failed around her body as a gloom descended. From out of the snow-filled sky a bat flew. With outstretched wings the creature landed beside the near-frozen mouse. He had been sent by Orfeo, who high above had recognized Audrey. Quickly the bat put his ear to her breast. There was a faint murmuring beat.

"Aha, young maiden," the creature declared, "life still runs in your veins, or Hathkin is no judge." He brushed the snow from her with his wings and shook her shoulders. "Awake!" he cried. "Snow is not for slumber, awake little one."

Audrey's eyes opened blearily and she looked on the bat's eager face drowsily. "Let me be," she whined.

"Oh no, mistress," he chuckled, taking to the air and flitting above her head, "a job I have been sent to do and accomplish it I shall. Hathkin may not win the renown of Orfeo or Eldritch this day, but he will do as he is bid." The bat hovered over her and gently took hold of her paws. With a swift flap of his wings he soared up, taking Audrey with him.

The high, gusting winds grasped and tore at the dangling mouse. Audrey flapped beneath Hathkin as wildly as a strip of cloth. Spluttering protests, she came to her senses; her mind left the blackness of the eternal gulf and returned with a jolt to her body.

Audrey looked down at the snow-covered rooftops that rapidly dropped away beneath her. She glanced up at the bat and gasped in surprise. "What are you doing?" she demanded, "put me down at once!"

Hathkin laughed but shook his head, "Sorry mistress, but we must rejoin the others. Observe the host of our brotherhood."

She turned her head so that she could see, and through the dense curtain of the storm Audrey saw the tremendous phalanx of bats.

Hathkin drew level with them and beat his wide wings faster so that they hurtled along. Audrey tightened her paws around his feet and he threw back his head, shaking with laughter. "On we must go," he shouted, "no one outraces Hathkin, his speed is his pride—hold on, mistress." With the wind streaming in her ears Audrey felt herself accelerate and shoot by the other bats, until the vanguard of the dark thousands came into sight.

Audrey frowned. What was that thin, white figure there at the front? "Oswald!" she cried incredulously.

*   *   *

Thomas leaped aside as the specter lunged for him. It ran into the hilt of his sword and impaled itself. The flowing rags of the phantom's transparent hide knitted together once more as it dived off and growled. Thomas ran around and with a mighty yank freed his trusty blade.

Terrible claws slashed through the air toward him and streams of ruby blood spurted from the midshipmouse's shoulder.

Arthur could do nothing to help for other wraiths had clambered on board. They jumped gleefully onto the deck, raising their spears and stalking their prey. Three came after Arthur, two went for Master Oldnose, and five charged at Mr. Chitter. More of the gruesome spirits crawled aboard and smacked their insatiable lips.

Arthur pelted along the deck as fast as he could. He hurdled the pile of thick ropes in his way and jackknifed round a corner, but he could not outrun them forever. He could already hear the horrible gurgling of their breath. Soon they too would turn the corner and strike him with their spears.

"Sssssaaahh," came the sound of the hissing specters as they clattered their claws on the sides of the forward deckhouse. Arthur gazed around fearfully and an ice spear whistled over his head.

The phantoms rushed at him, but he was too quick. With a bound he crossed to the rigging and jumped for the rope. Using the skills he had learned in Fennywolde, Arthur swarmed quickly up the mainstay, leaving the enemy clutching the empty space where he had been.

Up and up he scrambled, not daring to stop until he had reached the mainmast and stood on a little platform there. Arthur gazed down. Thomas was fighting vainly with the brutish spirit on the deck far below, and he could hear the anguished cries of Master Oldnose and Mr. Cockle as their attackers cornered them together. He felt helpless, and could not bear to watch as they closed in on the hapless mice. Arthur turned away and realized his own danger–the ropes were shaking violently as his pursuers began climbing after him.

"Fenny!" he shouted in distress as the slithering bodies surged up the mainstay. Arthur raised his eyes to the sky and opened his mouth in despair, but no sound came out, for he saw a dark, boiling mass sweep down from Deptford, and his anguish turned to joy as he recognized the bats flying toward him.

"Orfeo!" he called, "Eldritch!" He waved frantically and then gaped in amazement when he saw Oswald hanging under them in his rippling suit of torn paper.

The bats swooped down. "Hello Arthur," called out Oswald. They spiraled around the masts of the ship, watching the ghostly army riot on the deck. Oswald saw a pack of them leap toward his father. They raised their ice spears and aimed them at his heart. With an angry yell the albino ordered his friends to fly lower. They dived, and as they did so Oswald let go of Eldritch's foot and tore a pawful of parchment from his suit.

The great host of bats descended about the ship, beating their wings in the faces of the spectral warriors. Spears flashed cruelly and a bat cried out as it toppled to the deck, impaled. Hathkin hovered over the figurehead, eager to join the battle, but with Audrey in his care he could not. The girl was appalled by the savage slaughter going on around her. The bats, despite their number, were outmatched and could not defend themselves against the hail of spears. Their broken bodies began to drop like stones and their death cries chilled the soul.

Audrey shivered as a glittering spear raced toward her. Hathkin lurched backward and it missed them by a hair's breadth.

Jacob Chitter and Master Oldnose closed their eyes, waiting

for the tortuous death to plunge into them. Suddenly, out of nowhere, came Oswald and Orfeo, skimming the ears of the wraiths. The albino scrunched the pages in his fingers and hurled them at the ghosts that menaced his father. The magical missiles whizzed through the air, and one hit a phantom in the chest. It did not pass through the evil apparition but cannoned into it, knocking the astonished specter sideways. It stumbled against the sail locker and let out a shriek of surprise and pain. The bundle of paper that had struck it burst into flames, and as the dreadful spirit recovered from the blow and raised its vicious claws vengefully, they crackled and disappeared. The wraith let out a screech of dismay as the magic devoured it. The strong arms of dead sinew melted up to the shoulders; the grisly head howled as the body spluttered and vanished beneath it, and then that too dissolved in midair.

"Ho ho," chortled Oswald as the bats spun around and came in for a second attack. He ripped off another pawful and threw it at a gibbering group. They too screamed and faded.

Oswald hoorayed and Mr. Chitter, trapped no longer, gave a little dance of pride as his son flew by. "Yippee!" Master Oldnose clapped thankfully.

Thomas was still locked in deadly combat with his own huge assailant. The specter sprang forward and tore another bloody gash down his front.

"Swine!" bellowed the midshipmouse, thrashing his sword through the specter's head.

With a mocking sneer it lunged again and traced a scarlet ditch across Thomas's sword arm. He staggered back, the blood staining his fur. The evil monster darted from side to side, baiting him cruelly, then it leaped at the midshipmouse. Thomas fell under the force of the attack, the phantom grabbed his neck and opened his jaws. The dripping fangs bore down on Thomas's throat and sank into the flesh.

"Oi!" shouted a stern voice. Oswald sped up with a fistful of

parchment. He shoved it into the ghost's gaping mouth and then took off again.

"Aaarrhhh!" The brute choked, clawing at its own throat.

Thomas rolled from under it and snatched up one of the papers that had fallen from the albino's tunic. "Right!" he roared wildly. "Now it's your turn, mate!" He fixed the parchment onto the tip of his sword and brought it slicing through the specter's body.

It screeched and was cleaved in two. The pieces writhed and with a fierce crackle disappeared. A dangerous light was in the midshipmouse's eyes as he brandished his sword and charged into the phantom regiments.

Arthur pressed himself against the mast as his two pursuers scrabbled up to him. The points of their spears shone wickedly and they began to push them into his belly.

Suddenly a whirl of flapping whiteness shot by, and small, screwed-up pellets fired out. The wraiths squawked in alarm, and as the spells sizzled through them, they tottered on the brink, then lost their balance and plunged toward the deck; but they had vanished before they reached it.

"Master Pink Eyes," Orfeo called down to Oswald, "enough. It is now time to deal with the true foe of the world. The sun is setting."

But Oswald was enjoying this. He sprinkled the precious tatters carelessly and put his paw to his suit for more. In a panic he saw that there was very little left. "Oh my," he squeaked. "Quick Orfeo, take me up."

They soared high over the *Cutty Sark*, and Eldritch joined them, Oswald gripping his foot once more as they raced to the observatory.

On the deck Thomas Triton valiantly cut through the fearsome ghosts. His sword swung in arcs of silver light and razored a path through Jupiter's foul army. They fell back before him, wailing at the glowing parchment on the keen blade, and turned their malevolent attention to the winged creatures that swooped over their heads.

The dark multitude of bats continued to dive-bomb the ship, but their number was less than before, and without Oswald the carnage spread. The deck was soon strewn with their speared corpses. Hathkin tore around the hull still bearing Audrey; he was looking for a safe place to put her so that he could enter the fray.

"Don't you dare put me down!" Audrey stormed furiously.

"I must, mistress," Hathkin called to her. "It shall not be said that I hid from the battle in this desperate hour. Would you shame and disgrace me so?"

"I'm not asking you to run away," she said crossly, "I want you to take me to the observatory, quickly."

Hathkin stared down at her, astonished. "You wish to go to Him!" He laughed, dismissing the idea. "You do not understand, child."

In a rush of temper Audrey raged, "Do as you're told! The Starwife commands it! By the power of my ancestors I order you to take me!"

The bat nearly dropped her in surprise, her voice had changed, and the force behind it stung him.

"Very well," he cried, beating his wings hard. "To the hill we go." They became a blur that shot swiftly through the snow.

The dome of the observatory distorted and buckled as the massive, hulking frame of Jupiter descended from the swirling cloud of mist. The building could barely support him, but his iron claws closed over the puny onion-shape and sank deeply into the bricks beneath. He towered over London and snarled at the dim gray sprawl of the city on the horizon. In his blighted youth he had lived a miserable existence there. With his own yellow eyes he had witnessed the Great Fire ravage through the narrow, filthy streets and consume the wooden houses; he had felt the spitting flames singe his ginger fur as he escaped from his evil master and fled to the river. No, Jupiter had no love for the world, and he hissed at the tall glass towers that had risen above the skyline: soon all life would end forever.

His enormous mouth yawned open and a stream of blue fire belched out—he was the master now, and everything must suffer. The Starglass glimmered in his claws, a tiny thing that sparkled in his mighty fist. Jupiter twirled it like a toy and tossed it in the air; the silver light that shone from its depths wove a halo about his gargantuan head.

"Now my pretty," he roared, "the time has come for the fulfillment of my desire." He held the Starglass out in front of him and summoned its power. With hurricane breath Jupiter called, "Clouds scatter, reveal unto me the jewel of day."

The sky rippled and slashes tore through the blanketing clouds. With thunder booming to the western horizon, a ragged fracture split the lightning-blasted heavens asunder. The pale fingers of mist scudded apart, and there in the breach was the glaring pale disc of the sun. It had not yet dipped behind the distant cityscape and looked down on the observatory like an eye filled with fear.

Jupiter laughed at it. "See, magnificent Daystar!" he bellowed. "Behold the bringer of your doom!" The Starglass flashed and the cat spirit ordered it to obey him. "By the charm of the ancient times I invoke thee!" he thundered. "Put forth your strength once more."

The Starglass trembled in his grasp, the light blazed from it, and with a tremendous shudder a bolt of silver fire exploded from its heart. The brilliant beam shot out over Greenwich and hurtled toward the sun. "Now I shall quench thy golden splendor," rumbled Jupiter as the magic of the glass pierced the atmosphere and traveled through the void faster than light.

"Extinguish the heats of Rizul," echoed his triumphant voice. "Plunge all into darkness everlasting."

The shimmering ball of the sun turned a deep, wrathful red, darker than blood, and the whole world was bathed in the gory glow.

Jupiter laughed and the hill shook under the observatory. Snow-laden trees splintered and fell crashing down, chasms burst open in the rupturing ground, and tons of earth were flung up with the tumult.

Out of the chaos soared Oswald, his thin face set hard as flint as the mountain that was Jupiter swept into view amid the blizzard. The albino was no longer afraid. This was his destiny and he accepted it courageously.

The cat god did not notice them at first, too intent was he on his diabolical scheme. "Perish Rizul," he cackled. "By the blade of Tormen I scythe you down. In my mighty name I slay thee, abase yourself at the feet of Jupiter!"

Orfeo and Eldritch flapped their wings strenuously and climbed higher and higher. Up to the horrible head they flew. Jupiter spied them at last and his evil words faltered. They were like gnats to him, but he looked uncertainly at the mysterious scraps of parchment that fluttered on Oswald's tunic, and his searing glance stabbed agonizingly through the mouse.

"What is this?" blasted Jupiter, outraged that any should dare to come against him. "Begone, you flies! Flee while you can!" His ulcerous jowls puffed out a tornado of frost-fire, and the three heroes tumbled helplessly in the air.

The bats struggled through the torrents of ice that were directed at them, and Oswald screwed his face up as the hoary blast smote his body. With a terrible effort Orfeo and Eldritch wrenched themselves from the typhoon and circled the crackling crown of lightning about the Unbeast's head.

"Are you ready, Master Pink Eyes?" Orfeo cried.

Oswald nodded resolutely. "Yes!" he replied with a ferocious shout.

"Then a curse on the abomination!" screamed Eldritch as they veered down.

Jupiter twisted his corpulent bulk around to see what the annoying, tiny insects were up to. He held his breath in surprise and apprehension when he saw them come charging at him. The papers of the tatting suit began to glow as they raced toward the devilish monster, and he growled suspiciously.

The remains of the Book of Hrethel burst into golden flames around Oswald. Their radiance cut through the dense fog Jupiter wrapped about himself and scorched his wintry eyes. Down plummeted the bats and Oswald was transformed into a figure of divine majesty as the spells took him over. "Die, carrion of the void!" he commanded forcefully. Like a flaming dart the bats sped toward the great enemy, and a path of gleaming sparks trailed from them. Into Jupiter's heart they plunged.

The huge spirit screeched as they speared into him. Golden lightning bristled from his chest and he rocked precariously on the misshapen dome.

"I cannot die!" he screamed, "I am Jupiter—Lord of death!"

The crackling yellow bolts wrapped around his body, tormenting him with their heat. At once the battle on the *Cutty Sark* ceased as the ghosts dropped their weapons and the starfire spluttered in their breasts. Thomas stared at the storm-beleaguered hill breathlessly—the fate of the world depended on the outcome of what was happening there. Suddenly the starfire welled up inside the specters once more, and all hope died in the midshipmouse.

Jupiter raked his claws through his spectral fur and the flames died. He drew himself up to his full height and laughed harshly. The Book of Hrethel had not been strong enough.

From out of his vastness two brittle-winged shapes flew.

Orfeo and Eldritch were covered in scales of frost. Jerkily they careered through the air, gliding fitfully on frozen wings. But they were not carrying Oswald. The albino was lost, swallowed by the abyss of the eternal void. The Unbeast's might had proved too strong a force, and the valiant mouse's sacrifice had been in vain–the attack had failed and Oswald was no more.

Jupiter watched the bats fleeing aimlessly and chuckled to himself, secure in the sweet knowledge that nothing could hurt him now. A deadly silence fell. He turned back to the crimson sun and lifted his claw. The Starglass blazed and the horrendous spell continued. The sky became livid as the sun turned a sickly purple. Jupiter had won.

CHAPTER FOURTEEN

THE FINAL RECKONING

Hathkin labored through patches of freezing fog, his foxlike head pulled into his strong shoulders as he flew blindly against the storm. Audrey held on grimly as the wind tossed and battered them.

Suddenly Orfeo and Eldritch burst out of the mist, their bodies withered by ice. With stiff, creaking wings, the brothers lurched through the gale, spinning uncontrollably with the snow. Their eyes were huge and stared madly; terror was graven in their petrified faces and they whined piteously.

"Orfeo," cried Hathkin fearfully. "Eldritch, what has happened?"

The horror-stricken bats circled clumsily around and shrieked desperately, "*He* has won," wailed Eldritch. "The Unbeast has triumphed over the power of Hrethel."

"We are all doomed." Orfeo wept despondently.

"What about Oswald?" demanded Audrey. "Where is he?"

They shook their heads and Orfeo howled, "Pink Eyes is

gone. The gateway to the void opened and the white one was sucked from our grasp."

Eldritch sobbed with anguish. "He has crossed over," he said, "departed from this world forever."

Pangs of sorrow blistered through Audrey's heart. "Poor Oswald," she whispered.

"But whither are you going?" asked Orfeo urgently. "Surely you are not flying to Him!"

Eldritch fluttered his frostbitten wings in dismay. "You must not go that way," he warned. "We must escape before the darkness comes."

"We go on," Audrey said coldly. "There is no way back for me—my fate is tied to Jupiter."

"Then may the Lady bless you, child," stammered Orfeo nervously, "for never would I face that again."

"Nor I." His brother trembled.

Hathkin listened to them gravely and gulped. "Mistress," he began doubtfully: "I fear they might be right, should we not abandon . . ."

"If you want to go back, then you can," snapped Audrey, "but to what? Soon it will be too cold to live. Run if you like, but put me down first, because I won't. I must see Jupiter before the end."

Hathkin blushed. "You shame me, mistress," he said. "I shall not desert you now, come." He beat his wings and with a last look back called, "Farewell, my brethren." Both he and Audrey soared into the fog and disappeared. Eldritch and Orfeo wheeled shakily away and prayed for them.

The observatory rose like a blurred, gray castle out of the mist, but it was surmounted by the towering cliff of Jupiter. The silence was deafening—only the sound of his cackling voice marred the unearthly quiet.

He was intoning the spell of ruin—the sky was now black

and the sun was dim and ghastly. The world shuddered as darkness started to fall. It was a solid thing that seeped over the land and consumed all light. Jupiter crowed with satisfaction.

Hathkin and Audrey sped up the hill, over the fallen trees and gaping fissures, over the tangle of railings that had tumbled down the devastated path, and over the fallen statue that Arthur and Thomas had once hidden beneath. The bat gazed on the strength of Jupiter in awe; the colossal spirit was the most terrible thing he could ever imagine. Audrey looked at the Unbeast but was not daunted–she had been through too much to give in now.

"Take me up to his head," she instructed Hathkin.

The bat shot high over the dome. They flashed by Jupiter's enormous, thrashing tail and ascended quickly.

A glint of blue shone from the mist above them. Before Hathkin knew what was happening, an ice spear ripped savagely through one of his wings.

"Aaarrgghh!" he cried as the leathery shreds flapped uselessly in the gale. He thrashed them feverishly, but it was no good, and they began to lose height. The wind screamed brutally in their ears as both mouse and bat plunged, somersaulting in the air. Audrey's stomach churned over and she saw the white ground rush up to meet them. A fountain of snow sprayed out as the tumbling figures crashed down.

Audrey groaned. The impact had been cushioned by the deep, drifting snow but she ached all over. "Hathkin?" she murmured hoarsely, "Where are you?"

A frightened whimper answered her. She picked herself up stiffly and crawled over the snow to where the bat lay. His body had struck the bough of a tree and had hit the ground awkwardly. He was twisted at an impossible angle–Audrey realized that Hathkin had broken his back.

A sad smile twitched over his tortured face–he too knew the extent of his injuries. "I fear I am no longer the swiftest," he said feebly. "I cannot move either my wings or my feet." He shivered suddenly, and when he next turned his eyes to Audrey they were filled with tears. "You must forgive me, for now I have to leave you, mistress," he said in a croaking whisper. "In the Green hereafter may we meet again . . . " And with that his eyes closed and he was at peace.

Audrey knelt beside him. "Brave moon rider," she breathed softly, "you have won renown indeed."

High above her, she heard the voice of Jupiter revel in the destruction he was causing. The desperate urge to confront him flared up again and she leaped to her feet. With a final, sad look at Hathkin she ran swiftly to the base of the observatory and searched for a way up.

*   *   *

Arthur had climbed down the rope and slowly made his way around the fierce battle that was still raging. The bats were being defeated; heaps of their bodies were piled on the deck as the phantoms struck out with spear and claw. Arthur clambered onto the rail, and from there he could see the blue, woolen hat of Mr. Triton surrounded by the ghoulish, clamoring specters. Thomas was in the thick of the battle. His sword strokes sent many wraiths back to the grave, but the enchanted parchment on the tip of his blade was getting smaller with every swipe. The ghosts knew this and they taunted the midshipmouse so that he wasted his blows; they punched him in the back and leaped out of the way when he swung around. The paper glowed fiercely, gradually consuming itself, and they waited eagerly to drink his blood.

A scream tore Arthur's attention from the vile butchery. The cry had come from the hold, and he leaned over the rail and exclaimed in fear: the apparitions had broken through the side of the ship, and even as he looked were crawling through the jagged holes they had made. Another scream rang out—it was Mrs. Chitter's voice.

"Mr. Triton!" shouted Arthur at the top of his voice. In the circle of specters that drew closer with every failing flicker of the parchment, Thomas heard his name and looked up. "They've broken into the hold," Arthur called to him.

Thomas's face fell. "Gwennie!" he cried in anguish. The midshipmouse spun around and charged through the gibbering wraiths, slicing one of them in half as he ran. He fought his way out of the battle and sped to the hatch. Arthur met him there, and with a quick, backward glance at the slaughter continuing on deck they descended into the gloom.

"Mr. Chitter and Master Oldnose have already gone down," Arthur told him hurriedly.

"If those things harm a hair on her head . . ." hissed Thomas, leaping down the steps and flexing his sword, the tiny piece of parchment bobbing before them like a firefly.

"I hope that stuff lasts," Arthur said nervously.

Gwen Brown stared fixedly ahead. A ragged slash had been torn in the hull, and greedy phantoms were pouring through it. The hundred or so mice backed away, but they were cornered. Mr. Cockle and the other husbands shielded their wives with their bodies as the troops advanced wickedly and waved their claws before them. Mrs. Chitter had stopped screaming; she whimpered against Gwen's shoulder and trembled. The Raddle sisters held on to each other, their faces lifted in prayer. On came the specters, stalking nearer and sniggering with voices of death as they drew out their gleaming ice spears.

Suddenly two shouts issued from behind the unholy warriors, as down the steps jumped Mr. Chitter and Master Oldnose.

"Jacob," gasped Mrs. Chitter, "oh save us."

The spirits turned as the two, frightened mice halted in their tracks and gazed desperately on the evil scene before them.

"Quick," wailed Master Oldnose, grabbing Jacob Chitter's paw and dragging him around the edge of the seething legion. They ran as fast as they could, dodging the claws that snatched at them until they joined the others. Mrs. Chitter wrapped her arms around her husband and kissed him. "We'll die together," she wept.

The ghosts flicked their tongues in and out as they prepared to move in for the kill. With a hideous yell one pounced on Mr. Cockle and threw him to the floor. That was it—the phantoms all screeched and charged. Paws and claws thrashed and struggled as the wraiths swamped the defenseless mice. Algy Coltfoot was the first victim, caught between two apparitions that splayed their claws and gored into his belly. The terrified mice screamed and struck out bravely with whatever weapons they had, but the specters laughed at their pathetic attempts. Master Oldnose struggled boldly through the battle to protect the beleaguered Raddle sisters, but one of the specters brought out a spear and callously rammed it straight through the poor mouse's chest. Master Oldnose crashed to the floor, dead, and the fiends trampled over his body.

"Maggot fodder!" bellowed a voice in the uproar. "We'll beat you yet!" Into the hold rushed Thomas and Arthur, shrieking terrible war cries as they plowed into the center of the ghosts. The sword sliced through them neatly and the spirits howled in alarm as they crackled and disappeared. The midshipmouse lunged and countered, thrust and chopped at the grisly horde and the fragment of paper shone. He barbed, he spiked, he stabbed, he pierced, and the wraiths recoiled from his formidable onslaught, groaning and whining. Thomas's face was terrible to behold, such was the fury that blazed in his heart. He dealt his blows savagely, cutting a swathe through the unhappy enemy till he and Arthur reached the trapped and injured mice on the far side.

Arthur ran to his mother, and Thomas's blade dispatched

the specter that was hovering over her with spear raised eager for the kill. Gwen sighed, relieved to see her son and the midshipmouse still alive. She did not complain about the wounds that gaped in her side, but wept for Algy and Master Oldnose when she saw their bodies.

Thomas launched himself at the specters that were still menacing the rest of the mice; his arm swooped down on them and they vanished. Like one possessed, the midshipmouse battled on, and then it happened. With a final spark of power the glowing parchment dissolved and the sword passed harmlessly through the ghosts.

"Hell's bells," muttered Thomas, as the spirits laughed at him and closed ranks once more.

*   *   *

The sun spluttered in the black sky and Greenwich was steeped in a blind, paralyzing darkness. Audrey reached up and her fingers scrabbled for something to hold on to as she looked down the walls of the observatory stretched below her. Her paws bled from the frost and from the sharp edges of broken bricks, but the balcony that ran around the base of the dome was just a short way off now. Straining and gritting her teeth, she wrenched herself over the edge and rolled onto her back, panting wearily.

Her eyes stared into the pitch-black heavens, and the vastness of Jupiter towered over her. His voluminous bulk reared massively into space, clouds of mist wreathed his distant shoulders like a kingly robe, and the lightning that burned on his brow shone out like the light of a phantom lighthouse perched on a stupendous mountain. The mouse felt giddy just looking at this vast Leviathan of Night.

The Unbeast was facing west where the dying sun choked and waned. So intense was his concentration that he did not see the miniscule figure gasping for breath beneath his feet. His claws clung grimly around the dome, larger than whale bones and sharper than his servants' spears. Great fissures had been gouged in the building, and the dome was battered beyond all recognition. It was just as well, for if it had remained intact Audrey would have found it impossible to climb its smooth, curved sides.

She staggered to her feet and took steadying breaths. This was the end of everything for her—she knew she had to face the cat god and was prepared to die doing so. She had to see Jupiter for one last time and curse him with all her strength. The splintered balcony creaked beneath her feet as she walked around.

"Sssssaaaahhhh!" hissed a guttural voice from the darkness.

Audrey hesitated, as around the corner came a pallid radiance. It was the light from a flame of starfire—one of Jupiter's ghosts was up there with her! The light grew as the unseen spirit closed on her, and Audrey cried out in horror as the glow lit the ghastly specter's face—it was Piccadilly.

The ghost of the city mouse was terrifying. His hair was matted down with clots of black blood and in his freckled face the sockets of his eyes gaped hollowly; his lips were drawn back over his teeth, which were now sharp and fanglike, and in his paws he carried an ice spear. He prowled across the balcony and crept nearer to Audrey, who was too sickened and petrified to move.

"Ssssss," the wraith spat at her.

"Piccadilly," she managed to utter, "it's me, Audrey."

He did not hear her and sucked the dribbling saliva through his fangs as the spear was raised.

"Piccadilly!" she cried. "Stop, please."

But the phantom came on and the spear left its paws. Audrey dived down but its bitter spike caught and tangled in her hair, mercilessly pinning her to the balcony rail. Audrey twisted and squirmed to free herself but the pinnacle of ice was embedded deep into the stout balustrade.

The ghost of Piccadilly snarled and flung itself on her. Audrey wept and struggled but cold paws found her throat. She looked into the black, empty spaces where the city mouse's eyes had been and sobbed, "Please Piccadilly, stop." The chill fingers slowly began to strangle her and a harsh laugh echoed from the phantom's mouth.

"Please," she implored, "please don't." The ghost squeezed and dug its nails in deeply. Audrey choked and battled for breath. The specter brought its face close to hers, and from out of the blank sockets tears started to fall and splashed on the girl's cheek. "Fight it, Piccadilly," she pleaded.

The wraith suddenly let go of her and swayed as though hit by an invisible blow. Piccadilly's ghost staggered back and threw its paws over its anguished face. Audrey watched it strive against the controlling starfire that flashed and crackled angrily, then she tugged and pulled her hair free of the spear.

"You can do it, Piccadilly!" she shouted. "Remember who you were, remember Holeborn, remember Oswald."

The starfire dwindled and as the phantom took its paws from its face, two bright, twinkling eyes gleamed there. "Audrey?" whispered Piccadilly's ghost.

The girl nodded and smiled through her tears. "Oh Piccadilly," she sobbed.

He looked sadly at her and she hung her head. "I'm so sorry," she cried wretchedly, "I . . . I loved you so much. If only I'd told you."

He did not answer, for at that moment a voice familiar to both of them called softly from the other side. "Dilly-O, Dilly-O."

Audrey looked up and shook her head. "Father," she stammered forlornly.

A point of light appeared over the balcony, then it grew larger and a beautiful glow flooded from it. A flickering, blue outline glimmered amidst the shining splendor and the smiling face of Albert Brown beamed out. "It's time you joined me, Dilly-O," his voice said kindly. "Come, I'll lead you once more, and you shall find peace. Take my paw."

Audrey's heart reached out to the spirit of her dead father. "Don't go," she called out, "please, Daddy, I miss you."

Albert turned to his daughter and the warmth of his love surged through her tired limbs. "My darling Audrey," he said gently, "I am so proud of you, my little, lovely child." The light that framed him began to fade. "Tell your mother I understand and wish her joy, and kiss Arthur for me. I have to go now, baby, but we'll meet again one day—I promise."

Audrey could not bear it; the salty tears streamed down her face and her head ached with the grief that welled up inside.

"Audrey," came Albert's failing voice, "remember the festival of spring." And he floated back into the fading glow.

Piccadilly turned to the sobbing girl. "Good-bye," he said. She lifted her face and the blessed light of the other side sparkled in her raw eyes. Audrey could not speak for the emotion gagged her; she nodded to him lamely.

The spirit shot a quick glance at the dwindling gateway and with a typical, irreverent grin he darted over to her. "Audrey," he said earnestly, "I loved you too." He pressed his phantom lips against hers, and with that kiss he told her more than words ever could. They parted, and looking into each other's eyes, he merged with the light and melted away. She touched her lips, which still felt the tender, whispering kiss, and fell to her knees.

The balcony was dark and empty, the wind howled in, and Audrey was alone, one small mouse at the foot of doom.

The sun spluttered its last and with a shattering blast was vanquished. Far, far above, Jupiter tossed his head victoriously and bellowed. The world shook and mountains toppled, seas thrashed the darkened land and rivers broke their banks. Chaos engulfed the earth, and the ravaging cold of the abyss screamed down.

Audrey felt the balcony splinter and snap beneath her as the Unbeast roared exultantly and his lightning laurels streaked triumphantly through the everlasting night. The platform creaked and broke away from the wall. Audrey looked up–there was still one thing left unfinished. The giant abhorrence that rejoiced amid the clouds had destroyed any chance of happiness she had ever had, and the sense of yearning loss that overwhelmed her turned to ice-cold fury and hatred.

The balcony dropped suddenly and swung out from the observatory. Audrey rose and quickly ran along the lurching platform. With a great leap she jumped off just as it crashed to the ground. Audrey clung to the battered dome and raised her head; the gale plucked and tore at her, but she held on grimly and struggled to her feet.

Jupiter was shaking with vicious laughter as the void devoured the world; he raised his claws and the Starglass shone out bleakly.

"Turn and face me!" Audrey shouted with all the strength she could muster, her hair streaming wildly about her face as she glared up. Her voice reverberated around the empty sky like thunder and rang in Jupiter's ears.

He ceased his black mirth and peered down at the insignificant creature below. The terrible eyes narrowed as he recognized her, the slayer of his body. An evil smile split his face as he lowered it, white fire ripped from his nostrils and withered the ground about the observatory. "Why have you come?" he mocked her cruelly, and the hail of his breath struck her violently.

But Audrey was undaunted. The tears had dried in her bloodshot eyes and she stared boldly back at the calamitous nightmare that descended and sneered at her. With a brave,

stern face she confronted her demon and the voice she raised to it was daring and defiant, "I come to call down my destiny—and it is tall and dangerous!"

Jupiter cackled at her ridiculous figure. "Verily shall I deliver unto you thy doom—meek and futile though ye be."

Audrey stood her ground and shouted, "Let it be as the Green Mouse wills it!"

The Unbeast guffawed, "Ha! Listen to how she squeaks of the Green Mouse! Where is your mighty champion now, foolish insect? Why does he not roll back the sun if his strength is greater than Jupiter?" He had had enough and decided to end the mouse's life.

She leaned into the storm as his gaping maw swept toward her and with a swift movement took something from her waistband. The little green shoot she had found in the ashes of the Starwife's pyre fluttered in the blizzard as she thrust it before her and into the vicious face that plunged down. The tiny plant unfurled in her paw and a delicate white flower opened its petals; it was a snowdrop—the herald of spring and symbol of death, but no more than a speck of dust against his vast satanic glory. Audrey pulled her arm back and hurled the fragile bloom into the dark throat that threatened to swallow her.

A blaze of emerald fire ignited and burst from the minute flower as it spun down Jupiter's cavernous gullet. The full, unstoppable might of spring was in those flames, and they radiated out gladly as down into the depths of the Unbeast's stomach the bright kindling fire tumbled.

Jupiter screamed, and his cataclysmic cries convulsed creation. He fell back, stabs of blinding green slicing through his hellish fur. "Witch!" he screeched at Audrey, "What have you done?"

"I curse you with all the force of life!" answered Audrey gravely.

His crown of lightning disappeared as jets of flame steamed

out of his ears, and he gasped typhoons of emerald smoke and shooting sparks. The great, rolling tail smoldered, and the ghastly hackles rose as they turned greener than new grass. Jupiter stared at it in horror and brought it lashing down to beat out the enchanted fires that frazzled his fur. The lumbering tail smashed against the fallen trees; at once the snow melted from their branches and they exploded into blossom.

"It cannot be!" he roared with agony, as the flames danced around him and scalding lava poured from his nose, "I am Jupiter, mightier than death."

"I did not condemn you to death," Audrey scorned him, "but with the doom of life!"

The summit of the observatory erupted with flame as the mountainous spirit tottered on the dome and a furnace of new, purifying growth scourged him. The Starglass fell from his iron claws and spiraled down. "Nooo!" yelled Jupiter, but it was too late. With a resounding smash it hit the floor and shattered into a million fragments.

An enormous rumble shook the world as the power of the imprisoned stars escaped. In a gush of piercing, white light the celestial lamps soared through the night, filling the empty void and electrifying the heavens once more.

Jupiter shrieked as the enveloping flames scorched him; his ghostly hide turned a livid, writhing green and golden flowers stabbed out of his wintry skin. He wailed and tore at his sparkling fur. "I shall escape it!" he screamed. "I shall!"

Audrey watched him solemnly. "You cannot escape it," she tormented him, "for you have proved you cannot die. Torture everlasting is your deserved fate, Jupiter."

The infernal spirit realized then that this was the end–the mouse had conquered him. He was doomed to be incinerated by the spring till the end of time, but never to be consumed by it. He burst into a terrific, blistering rush of flames and became a towering effigy of fire, then he rocketed, howling, into the air.

Higher and higher he soared into the freezing reaches of space, screeching his suffering and fury. Like a green comet he shot up, chased by the forces of life through the universe until he was only a faint blur between the stars. Consigned to the vacuum of the void, he would suffer in the agony of spring throughout eternity.

Audrey dropped with fatigue, her energy spent. A rosy light glimmered on the horizon as a fresh, new day dawned. The golden rays of the reborn sun shone over the dissipating clouds and stretched over the land, ushering in a beautiful morning.

The world was awakening fast. The snow dissolved rapidly, and patches of snowdrop-freckled grass appeared. The burgeoning greenery flooded over the park, the frost-locked trees thawed, and glowing blossoms burst out in vibrant colors. A glorious chorus of grateful birds took flight and soared into the pale blue sky. All the seasons met as summer roses popped open and gave their perfume to the breeze. Fruit swelled on blossom-burdened boughs, and leaves of autumn gold shone in the sweet air.

It was a heady sight, and Audrey absorbed it breathlessly. The earth was thanking her and putting forth all its blissful delights in homage. She bowed her head and wept.

*   *   *

On the *Cutty Sark*, the mice had felt Jupiter roar with anguish. The ship pitched frighteningly, and the specters gibbered, and when the Starglass had shattered, the starfire was ripped out of their chests and shot upward. The phantoms, bereft of will, wavered for a second, then with a yowl each one of the hideous fiends crackled and disappeared.

Thomas gaped in amazement. Above them, on the deck, he heard the surviving bats cheer rejoicingly. The mice hugged themselves and cried with relief. Arthur held on to his mother and she kissed him. The light of the new day streamed into the hold through the ragged gaps, and they all bent their heads and said a humble prayer of thanks.

The injured were carefully tended to. The bodies of Master Oldnose, Algy Coltfoot, and the others who died were carried respectfully out in the warm spring sunshine, and the mice joined the bats in lamenting their fallen. But the nature of the joyous day was such that no one could contain their happiness at Jupiter's defeat. Orfeo and Eldritch felt the sun's rays diminish the horror in their minds, and slowly they recovered.

Ashmere, his bearded face beaten and bruised, sent two of his brethren to the observatory to fetch Audrey and bring her back in honor. "For the new Handmaiden of Orion is the greatest since history began," he said.

Suddenly the Raddle sisters interrupted the celebrations that were taking place on deck; they had remained in the hold and they galloped up the steps in a state of great agitation and excitement, "Come down, come down," they squeaked, simultaneously flapping their paws at them all.

Confused but amused, the mice went down the steps once more, the bats flitting behind them.

"Oh Thomas," gasped Gwen incredulously, "is it true?"

"Aye lass," the midshipmouse replied, bewildered.

A marvelous sight greeted their staring eyes: the hold was filled with luscious greenery, and honey-scented flowers opened and shone like the sun. Sparkling lights shimmered over the lustrous, twining leaves that wrapped and clustered around the figureheads, and golden stretches of grain spilled over the floor. The hold was a forest of burnished gold and twinkling emerald, and there, in the center, was the Green Mouse.

Everyone covered their mouths in awe when they saw him.

He wore a crown of leaves and wheat and his eyes were filled with the light of sun-dappled glades. The Green Mouse smiled and his flowing, leafy coat rustled as he welcomed them. "Enter," said his rich, deep voice. "Come in, all of you."

With astounded faces the mice shuffled forward and bowed. The hallowed spirit of spring and summer beamed and the hold was flooded with warmth. The bats flapped down the steps, and he said to them, "The Lady shall visit you tonight no doubt, worthy night wings."

Orfeo and Eldritch limped forward and bowed. The Green Mouse swept their fears away with his splendor and then he asked gently, "Where are the parents of the albino?"

Mr. and Mrs. Chitter looked sadly up; they knew what had happened to Oswald. The Green Mouse gazed at them, and magic flashed from his eyes. "Do not grieve overlong," he told them, and from his coat he produced a burning flower that cooled in his palm—it was a mousebrass. "Take this now in remembrance of your son, who would have come of age this year."

Jacob Chitter stepped forward and received the precious gift, the sign of courage and bravery. Oswald had indeed earned it.

"He was a valiant, noble boy," said the Green Mouse. "Remember him with the greatest pride." Mr. and Mrs. Chitter nodded and stole into a corner, where they mourned the loss of Oswald together.

The Green Mouse turned and looked through the tear in the hull. The sky was a blazing sapphire blue, and flying high and swiftly toward the ship were three dots. With a flap and flutter of leathery wings Audrey arrived with two bats.

"Praise to the moon riders," the Green Mouse said to the bats who flew in. "And now I must pay tribute to you," he said to Audrey as she alighted and crept through the hole. He bowed his head in reverence and his green mane cascaded over his shoulders. Audrey was speechless, and stole a glance at her family. Gwen swelled with pride and Arthur winked.

"Very great you have grown, my little one," said the Green

Mouse, "and wise beyond measure. I humble myself before you, for you alone are responsible for this glad day and my release." He held out his paw, and Audrey walked over to him. He inclined his head once more and kissed her.

Audrey pressed her paw into her chest with surprise and shook her head. "It wasn't me," she piped up. "It was the Starwife, really. I think she sacrificed herself to create the snowdrop."

Those deep, fathomless eyes she remembered so well twinkled at her. "You, her, she," he chuckled, "all are one now, so I thank you." The girl looked at him, puzzled for a moment, and then she smiled. "Yes," she said.

Audrey then looked at her mother and Thomas and grinned. "I know what is in your heart," she said. "Father knows too and he wishes you both happiness. You belong together now."

Gwen glanced at Thomas, then Audrey, and gasped, "How did you know what I . . . ?" but she blushed and looked at her feet.

The Green Mouse laughed. "Come Mrs. Brown," he chortled, "I give you my blessing." He turned to Thomas and told him, "You are a lucky mouse, seafarer."

Thomas blinked, and then he blushed too. "I reckon so," he mumbled sheepishly.

And so the Green Mouse married them, and the glorious spring sunshine filled the hold and lived in their hearts till the end of their days.

THE CALL OF THE SILVER

The bounteous time lasted for many months and in those splendid days the mice remained on the *Cutty Sark* and made comfortable homes for themselves there. Master Oldnose and Algy Coltfoot and the other mice who fell were buried in the park beneath a hawthorn tree, and the grass that grew over them was dotted with flowers all year round.

The bats had taken their dead away for their own private ceremony, but they raised a little monument to Hathkin on the observatory hill in the form of a crescent moon crafted in silver that shone on dark winter nights to give hope to the weary traveler. The friendship between the mice of the ship and the bats of the air was strong ever after and neither side forgot the part the other played in Jupiter's downfall.

After some weeks had passed, several mice, led by Arthur, returned to the empty house in Deptford. But the damage Jupiter's army had inflicted could not be repaired, and they had to load all the useful items they could find into sacks and take them back to the ship.

Audrey traveled with them, and while Arthur and the others were inspecting the wreckage and tutting at the devastation she slipped into the cellar and hunted till she found what she sought.

On a moonless, May night, when the stars blazed in the heavens, she took leave of her family and made her way up the hill to the overgrown chambers of the old squirrel colony. With the starlight burning on her brow she took a small pendant from the pocket of her dress and held it up to the celestial lamps. Their white fire flickered over the silver acorn in her paw. Audrey tied it around her neck, and her beauty was that of another world. With a sad smile on her lips she became the new Starwife, Handmaiden of Orion.

AFTERWORD

Power-hungry rats, nature-loving mice, mystical bats . . . In *The Dark Portal*, Robin Jarvis delights readers with not just one, but three unforgettable animal societies. By creating characters with human motivations and personalities flavored by their essentially animal natures, he offers a strikingly original, totally absorbing fantasy world.

Of course, tales about animals who act like people have been told as long as people have gathered to listen to stories; Aesop's fables, some of the oldest stories in western culture, are filled with such animals, as are many tales from African, Asian, Inuit, American Indian, and Aboriginal cultures.

In the nineteenth century, when literature for young people blossomed in Great Britain, many books included animal characters who could talk—such as those in *Alice's Adventures in Wonderland*—but none featured animals subsisting in their very own societies. Then, with the dawning of the twentieth century, came the debut of the Peter Rabbit books by Beatrix

Potter. Although without distinct societies or customs, the animals in these stories wore clothes and misbehaved like adventurous children (and suffered the consequences!). Soon after, Kenneth Grahame's *The Wind in the Willows* was published, and the animal fantasy novel truly came into its own; for in this story, Rat, Mole, and their friends lived quite apart from human society (although people resided nearby).

After the publication of *The Wind in the Willows*, animal fantasy books became more popular. In the early 1920s, Hugh Lofting introduced the Doctor Doolittle books, while A. A. Milne created the Winnie-the-Pooh stories, and Felix Salten wrote *Bambi*. The following decades saw the publication of such classics as Walter Brooks's Freddy the Pig books, George Selden's *The Cricket in Times Square* and its many sequels, the Newbery Medal–winning *Mrs. Frisby and the Rats of NIMH*, and James and Deborah Howe's *Bunnicula*. And, of course, there was the phenomenal success of Richard Adams's *Watership Down*.

In *Watership Down*, Adams re-ignited interest in what Kenneth Grahame had created nearly seventy years earlier—a fantasy story in which animal communities had their own distinct rules, customs, and lore based on their animal nature, yet tinged with human qualities. In the wake of this surprise best-seller, many authors wrote animal fantasies aimed at the adult market, but few met with much success.

Then in 1986, a novel by British radio performer and writer Brian Jacques was published, in both Great Britain and America. Almost overnight, on both sides of the Atlantic, readers young and old were caught up in the saga of *Redwall*. Its heroic animal characters gave fresh life to what had been thought a dead literary form—the swashbuckler—and its success helped revive American publishers' enthusiasm for animal fantasy. In the past, more attention had been given to humorous tales like *The Cricket in Times Square* and *Bunnicula*, but *Redwall* had shown readers' appetites for serious adventure stories featuring animal protagonists.

In 1989, Robin Jarvis's *The Dark Portal*, an animal fantasy unlike any other, was published in Great Britain. With its sinister characters of Jupiter and the rats who scurry to serve him (as well as their evil plotting against one another), the novel has a tinge of the occult darkness found in the writing of such masters as Edgar Allen Poe, H. P. Lovecraft, and M. R. James. But countering this blackness are the farseeing bats, who possess mystical visions of the future, and the loving mouse communities, who cherish their mousebrasses and their belief in the living spirit of spring, the Green Mouse. This careful blend of good and evil, combined with compelling mythology and powerful rituals, made *The Dark Portal* and its two sequels—*The Crystal Prison* and *The Final Reckoning*—best-sellers in Great Britain.

The summer it was first published, I was lucky enough to come upon *The Dark Portal* during a trip to London. Over the following years, every so often I would run into another person who had read and admired this series. When S. E. Hinton (the award-winning author of *The Outsiders, Tex, Rumble Fish*, and *That Was Then, This Is Now*) asked me if I had ever heard of the Deptford Mice books, I told her how much I had enjoyed them, then asked her how she came to know about them. She replied that her son had discovered the books when they were in Britain and that they had quickly become his favorites at the time. And she, like all who knew them, couldn't understand why they weren't available in the United States.

Well, finally, they are. At the dawn of this new century, the Deptford Mice books are here for us to share and enjoy. Thank the Green!

Peter Glassman is the owner of Books of Wonder, the New York City bookstore and publisher specializing in both new and old imaginative books for children.

ROBIN JARVIS was born in Liverpool, England, and studied graphic design in college. He worked in television and advertising before becoming a full-time author and illustrator. It was while working at a company that made characters for TV programs and advertising that he began making sketches of mice. From these drawings, the idea for the Deptford Mice was born. *The Dark Portal*, short-listed for the 1989 Smarties Book Prize in England, was followed by two more titles in the series: *The Crystal Prison* and *The Final Reckoning*. Mr. Jarvis currently lives in Greenwich, London.

LOOK FOR THE OTHER BOOKS IN

THE DEPTFORD MICE TRILOGY

BOOK ONE
THE DARK PORTAL

In the sewers of Deptford, there lurks a dark presence that fills the tunnels with fear. The rats worship it in the blackness and name it "Jupiter, Lord of All." Into this twilight realm wanders a small and frightened mouse–the unwitting trigger of a chain of events that hurtles the Deptford Mice into a world of heroic adventure and terror.

BOOK TWO
THE CRYSTAL PRISON

An innocent young mouse lies slain in a moonlit cornfield as the screech of an owl echoes overhead. Newly arrived in the countryside from the horrors of Jupiter's lair, the Deptford Mice soon find themselves embroiled in a series of horrible murders. At first the simple country mice suspect Audrey–but the truth is far more sinister. . . .